SHE FELL IN *Love* WITH A NEW YORK *Hitta*

A NOVEL BY

INFINITY

PROLOGUE

Leilani stared down at the syringe, contemplating her next move. Months had passed since she had had her last hit. Despite her attempts at living a clean life, the deadly formula that floated in the syringe had its hold on her. Once I get this hit, then everything will be alright, she convinced herself. At the prime age of 12 years old, Leilani had shot up more dope than the average dope fiend. Her once innocent glow had deteriorated into an eggshell of a lost soul. The ambition she once possessed mutated into hatred for the world that surrounded her. There was nothing more to live for, since everyone's time on Earth would expire anyway. The influential thought of death being inevitable motivated her to speed up the process. Light thumps rained down on her uterus as her unborn child protested the consumption of the addictive formula that awaited.

"You're up?" Leilani replied to her slightly swollen abdomen. "Don't worry baby, I'll be better than my mother. I won't harm you like she has done me."

The needle entered her skin, releasing pain signals to her brain. Her grimy fingers applied pressure to the plunger, allowing the enslaving prescription to penetrate her vein. Heroin was the only thing that could fill the void in her life. The tears that had once cascaded down her face had begun to dry, leaving streaks of depression. Pure satisfaction was etched onto her dull face as she lay on the dingy mattress surrounded by darkness. Minutes turned into hours, as the sun's orange hues disappeared, leaving the streets grey. The hoods' well-known zombies roamed the streets of Brooklyn in search for their next hit.

Leilani basked in her glory as her hit replaced the pain she lived. The high was indescribable as there wasn't anything on Earth that compared to it. She glided over clouds as the numbing sensation took over her limbs. The annoying sound of the mice creeping against the wooden floor no longer agitated her. A loud knock echoed throughout the vacant apartment, but Leilani failed to acknowledge it as she sunk deeper into the pits of her dope fiend nod.

"La, you better be in that fucking room," a voice shrieked; the harmony of anger and annoyance seeped through the cracks of the door. Her mother stood impatiently waiting for a response from her junkie daughter. Silence oozed from the opposite side, causing her anger to escalate.

"Leilani, open the door," she heavily breathed. Her words fell on deaf ears as Leilani laid on the mattress embedded into her drug-induced nirvana. Annoyed, Rose grew angrier as she began placing all her weight on the bedroom door. It wasn't long before the lock grew weak, granting Rose access into the gloomy room. The stale smell of blood assaulted her nostrils as she stood in the middle of the room. Her presence demanded attention, but Leilani kept her eyes shut as she imagined life without pain.

"We were moved into a better home for you to still be stuck on this shit," Rose yelled, mostly speaking to herself as her words were ignored.

To the naked eye, it seemed as if Leilani were dead, but the slight chest movement informed Rose that she was still alive. Leilani never budged at the sound of her mother's ranting; everything in her remained numb. She no longer felt the wounds that adorned her malnourished body, nor the fetus that grew within her womb. The once light thuds she felt, transitioned into rapid kicks as her baby tried fighting the drugs from entering its system.

"You're high as a fucking kite."

The sight of Leilani would have made a mother cry, praying to their God for the safety of their child. But Roselyn wasn't like other mothers; instead, she prayed every night for relief from being a parent. Being a poor Colombian immigrant, Roselyn Vasquez had dealt with the worst the world had to offer. Escaping Colombia with her sister was the greatest accomplishment she had ever achieved. Unfortunately, she was never warned about the abuse she would endure by the hands of her freedom land America. The brutal attacks she placed on Leilani were the result of Roselyn's past taunting her.

"Do you not hear me talking to you?" her voice bellowed, vibrating off the thin walls. Leilani's battered body remained a permanent fixture on the shabby mattress. Rose walked over to Leilani and proceeded to poke her with the heel of her designer shoe.

"Wake ya' ass up," Rose badgered.

"What is it that you want?" Leilani replied, agitated at not being able to enjoy her high.

"Rocky is on his way to take you to the doctor, so you need to get your ass up."

The mere mention of his name made her skin crawl. ***That slimy mutherfucker****, she thought as a smile crept onto her face. The torture she had witnessed was all because of Rocky; he was the reason her mother hated her so much. Everything was fine before her mother's boyfriend came into the picture.*

"Bitch, did you not hear what the fuck I said?" Rose screeched.

"Yes, I fucking heard you. I am high, not fucking deaf," Leilani replied, as she struggled to stand to her feet.

Rose's eyes burned a hole into the back of Leilani's head, as she watched her twelve-year-old daughter fade into her own thoughts that were laced with the finest heroin in Brooklyn. Rose's eyes focused to La's swollen abdomen that carried her boyfriend's child inside. For most of Leilani's pregnancy, Rose tried not to acknowledge the growing child inside of her daughter. But as the days came and went, she could not help but feel a form of resentment towards Leilani. The growing fetus was a reminder that no matter what she did, Rose could never win.

"That piece of shit that you are carrying should die."

"And the cracks in the streets should spread open so you can fall into the pits of hell," Leilani retorted.

"Listen here your thirsty ass bitch, I am still your mother," Rose declared, as she placed her fingers in Leilani's face. "Just because you fucked my man, don't give you any power for you to talk to me any way. Remember, I will still beat your ass, baby or no baby."

"Your whoring ass could never be my mother," Leilani spat.

The harsh words hit Rose unexpectedly. She was surprised by the reply she received from Leilani, as she never received any back talking from the child. Out of anger, Rose's nose broadened. The vile words that escaped the little girl's mouth could not go unnoticed. Rose lunged towards Leilani, dropping the pregnant, fragile girl onto the ground. Mother and daughter tussled on the floor, neither willing to let go of the other. The anger each of the women had was released through their fists. They both fought until Roselyn released Leilani's hair from her grasp, wrapping her cold hands around Leilani's throat. She squeezed with all her might until the fighting in Leilani had ceased. There wasn't an ounce of remorse in Rose's heart, as the frail body beneath her tried prying her hands away from her neck.

"Don't be a fucking pussy; you had so much to say before," Roselyn replied, as she stood up with her hands still wrapped around Leilani's throat. There was a lot of anger Rose kept contained, as she accepted what the world shoved her way. Years of pent up animosity flowed through her hands, as she refused the release of her daughter. Leilani's pale face began to turn blue, indicating the possibility of death.

"None of this shit would have happened if he would have kept his dick in his pants," she yelled, finally releasing Leilani. The sound of Leilani's body dropping to the floor echoed throughout the room. Coughing filled the air as Leilani tried regulating her breathing. She choked, coughing up spit as she tried to catch her breath.

"You just had to get fucking pregnant."

"It's not my fault that your boyfriend is sick," Leilani replied after she finally caught her breath. She gripped her stomach as she was now concerned about her baby. There was a calm within her that placed fear in Leilani's heart. Little thumps of her child kicking ceased, sending its

mother into a panic.

"What did you do?" Leilani questioned.

"What should have been done from the beginning."

Leilani's uterus began to contract, sending waves of pain throughout her lower back. The feeling was unbearable as Leilani doubled over in pain. She could feel the life within her slipping away slowly. Blood flowed consistently from between her legs.

"The baby," she cried.

"Yes, the baby; that is all everyone ever cares about," Rose replied as she began to leave.

"Mommy, please don't leave me here; get some help."

"If you pray hard enough, then God will send an angel to end the pain," she replied, as she left Leilani alone in the room.

The feeling of death was near as she lay on the floor, bleeding profusely. She was alone in the room forced to face the death within her. Tears flowed freely down her face; shocks of pain invaded her body causing her to yelp. No one was around to save her as she could feel herself slowly slipping away from losing too much blood.

"I am sorry baby; you're safe now," Leilani spoke softly, caressing her stomach. She knew the pain she was suffering from was not normal. Despite being a junkie, Leilani truly did care about the child that grew within her. Unlike most junkies who got high for their own selfish needs, Leilani injected her veins regularly to deal with the beatings she received from her mother. She indulged herself into drugs to mask the reality of the rape sessions she endured daily. Heroin was the answer to her prayers

in keeping her child away from the pain. As she lay on the floor, slowly slipping unconscious, she hoped like hell that God was finally calling her home. She had lived long enough to tell the angels a tale of her nightmare. But unbeknownst to her, God had plans for her that would leave a legacy people would fear. Society would walk the vile streets of New York narrating the ***Tale of a Dope Fiend****.*

CHAPTER 1

Twelve Years Later

The music bounced off the club walls, engulfing him into the pits of tranquility. His hands rubbed on the voluptuous figure before him as the concept of having a threesome invaded his thoughts. The women that stood in his presence were the most beautiful women money could buy. Usually he didn't pay attention to any of the females that gravitated to him because they were only interested in one thing, *his money.* Tonight, was different, as he could not resist fucking with the Thelma and Louise duo. Essence and Candy could not keep his hands off them as they could tell the drinks they supplied him with were beginning to work.

"I really want to fuck the both of you right now," he spoke.

"Then baby let's have a quickie in the bathroom," Candy replied. Her chocolate brown eyes burned with lust as she couldn't wait to have him bleeding on the bathroom floor. The taste of his rancid breath was beginning to upset her stomach. They needed to hurry up and finish the job before she threw up her guts all over the floor.

"Nah, I have something special planned for you ladies tonight," he said as he continued to palm their round bottoms.

Tonight, Joseph Castra planned to relish in his success as he accomplished taking over New York City. Stepping on some toes along the way to the top, he didn't care about the number of people he betrayed, because he was now the man with the A1 supply pushing throughout every borough in the city. A lot of blood was shed for him to be in the position he currently was in. Living in middle-class during his childhood, Joseph saw his mother struggle every day to provide for him. To make life easier, he decided to put school on the back burner and focus solely on being the top dog in the drug world. Tonight, he was on the top enjoying the company of the two freaks on his arm.

"Please Daddy, I need you right now," Essence spoke into his ear as she licked on his sweaty neck. She stared into his eyes, convincing him that there was much more entertainment if they went back to his place. For a moment, he thought about his options. I could stay in the club rubbing on their asses, or I can take them back to my house, he thought.

"Alright, let's go. I need to get in between them cheeks," he confessed as he grabbed both of their wrists. The club was packed with dozens of partygoers, who were attempting to have a good night. Half of the club was intoxicated, moving freely from their liquid courage, while the rest of the club was high off Castra's supply. No one noticed as the trio disappeared through the back doors of the club. Quickly, they entered the backseats of the Cadillac Escalade that awaited Castra's arrival.

"Louis, drive us to the loft in Manhattan," he commanded.

"Yes sir," the driver replied, pulling off into the New York night. Radiant lights flashed through the tinted windows as Castra could not keep his hands off the beautifully built women. Candy, whose milk chocolate skin complexion was rich in melanin, glistened with perspiration. Castra had to thank her mother for creating the Nubian goddess whose nipples rested in his mouth. Candy reminded him of a younger version of Kelly Rowland, with her flawless yet innocent look. Essence on the other hand reminded him of Lauren London with much more body. Essence had to thank her mother's Latino roots and her father's black roots for giving her the mixed beauty she possessed today. Castra never really took a liking to black women, but the two females before him had changed his whole perception on race. Castra was used to dating 100% full-blooded Latino women, as he himself was Latino. His theory was that Latino women were the only beautiful creatures in the world. He never took an interest with the other race, as he assumed based off racial stereotypes black women were lazy and uneducated women. The first time his eyes fell upon the duo, everything he ever believed in was no longer in existence as his manhood stood at full attention.

The car came to a stop as they sat parked in front of Castra's loft. Without much hesitation, Candy opened the car door, yanking on Castra's wrist. Hot off foreplay, Castra mistook this gesture as Candy dying for him to be inside of her. But Candy just wanted to get the encounter over with as she had plans to get dicked down by her man.

"Come on Daddy, I want you now," she spoke as they entered the building. Once they were all in the elevator they went at each other. His fingers snaked their way inside their pants and glided against their clits. The gesture sent ripples of pleasure through their bodies. The elevator doors glided open, and the trio walked over to Castra's door, waiting impatiently as he fiddled with the keys. His mind was wrapped around being plunged in their wetness. After five minutes of fidgeting with the lock, he finally opened the door.

"I want you two in that bed butt naked by the time I finish taking a leak," he said as he dashed into the bathroom to relieve his bladder. Quickly, he peed and then found his way back into the room where the girls sat on his bed, naked as the day they were born. The natural beauty of the two impressed him. There was not an ounce of alteration on their body, besides their freshly manicured nails and feet and waxed eyebrows.

"Come here Daddy and eat this pussy," Candy purred as she opened her legs for him to see her perfectly waxed vagina. Castra didn't hesitate to get down on his knees, crawling his way between Candy's legs. He inhaled deeply, savoring the sweet smell of her nectar. His tongue flickered softly against her clit, causing a moan to escape Candy's thick lips. Shocked, Candy could not believe she had moaned without faking it. The feeling of his soft and wet tongue sent her eyes rolling back, something that nobody had ever made her do.

"Oh Daddy," she cried. Essence was taken aback as she noticed that Candy was really into the oral session. The two had done several of these missions; Essence had heard Candy moan a thousand times before, but this one was different. Her usual unemotional moan vibrated with satisfaction. Eager, Essence too wanted her vagina licked in the same manner.

"I'm next Daddy," Essence said, letting it be known that she wanted to get off too. Castra never replied to her command as he focused on the sweet taste of Candy. It wasn't long before Candy was creaming all over his face, screaming to the top of her lungs.

"Come here Essence, let me show you how to sing Opera," Castra boasted as he yanked her in front of him. Like how he had pleased Candy, he did the same for Essence. His tongue flicked softly against her clit. The feeling was euphoric for Essence as this was her first time ever being pleased orally. Her legs shook slightly, as she closed her eyes, enjoying the oral pleasure. Castra's tongue licked and slurped all of Essence; it was the best feeling Essence had felt in her entire life. *So this is what I've been missing out on,* she thought.

POW!

A loud bang rang throughout the air as Essence felt the weight of Castra on top of her. Blood poured from the hole that was permanently embedded into his skull. His brain matter was warm as it covered her stomach. Anger filled her face as she shot her eyes open. Just as she expected, she met the vision of the trigger puller. Essence was fuming; she couldn't believe her sexual pleasure conference had ended abruptly.

"What the fuck man," Essence yelled. "You couldn't wait until I fucking came before you killed the mutherfucker?" she beefed. The innocent beauty before her held an emotionless facial expression as she stared back at an infuriated Essence. Her long, jet-black hair blew to the light, brisk air that entered from the cracked window. Her perfectly arched eyebrows were scrunched in amusement as she peered at Essence. Her facial features closely resembled singer Amerie, but her mixed roots towered over the singer's Asian features.

"Bitch, get your ass up and help me with these duffle bags," Leilani replied, tucking the glock into the small of her back. "While you were getting your pussy slurped, I emptied his safe. We don't have long before the cops get here."

On her command, the girls rushed to get their items, in hopes of leaving the crime scene before the police arrived. While Essence and Candy got their belongings, Leilani wiped the place down of any possible evidence that would lead back to them. The level of expertise Leilani possessed took years in perfecting. Leilani's exceptional talent could have the crime scene investigators angry with their lack of evidence. The faint smell of the cleaning agent replaced the reeking scent of sex. After spending a couple of minutes on retracing their footsteps, the women grabbed the duffle bags filled with money and found their way into their getaway car.

"Damn man, I was dead ass enjoying that head," Essence confessed.

"Oh, shut up already. You couldn't fall in love with him; he was a contracted hit, and you have a man already," Leilani replied as she pulled off into the night traffic.

"But you know Casper doesn't do that whole tongue action."

"Girl, you are missing out, because when my man does it, he keeps my toes curled," Candy confessed.

Listening to the two women go back and forth, Leilani remained silent, keeping her eyes on traffic. The smooth sound of the engine purred as the Dodge Charger glided in between cars.

"La, what are you about to do after?"

"Work."

"You can't take a break?" Essence asked.

"Nah, I can't. I have to finish up some loose ends with our latest contract," she replied, not wanting to get into a discussion about her latest activities. Looking through the mirror she stared at her girls in search of any discomfort with the fable she told. Both Essence and Candy stared down at their phones, uninterested with Leilani's excuse. For the past couple of months, the trio couldn't hang out like they usually did because Leilani was always busy with work. Despite her excuse being true, the nature of her reasoning hadn't been fully disclosed. Leilani was given a position within a drug organization as head of execution. It was a huge step for Leilani financially, but the problem was she would have to stop her private hit woman for hire organization. Ending her private three employee company would have placed Essence and Candy out of commission. Leilani didn't know how she was going to inform the women about the change in events. The car remained silent as the women sat indulging in their own private thoughts. Essence was very much bitter about her oral escapade being brief, while Candy was lost within her sexual thoughts. Pulling the car up alongside the girls' parked cars, Leilani unlocked the doors allowing the girls out.

"Aight ladies, get the hell out of my car," Leilani said.

"Well fuck you too," Candy replied.

"I'll have to pass on your offer," Leilani smiled, blowing a kiss towards the two ladies.

"Essence, fix that face of yours before it gets stuck like that," she sat in her car laughing, in hopes of lightening the mood so the girls would forget about Leilani's decline to chill with them. Waiting patiently, Leilani sat in her car until her girls got into their cars and safely pulled off into traffic. Turning in the opposite direction, Leilani busted a U-turn heading towards her destination.

The radio blared the hottest hip-hop tracks that were popular amongst the black community. Irritated by the sound of Young Thug's voice, Leilani changed the playlist on her phone. She became engulfed into the pit of silence as she skillfully maneuvered through tracks while searching for a song suitable for her mood. Clicking play, her state of the art speakers thumped to the raw sound of Lil' Kim.

"Now this is fucking hip-hop," Leilani said to herself as she turned the radio up higher. Bobbing her head to the beat, she began to rap right along with her favorite female rapper. *"Bitch with that platinum grammar I am a diamond cluster hustler Queen bitch, supreme bitch, kill a nigga for my nigga by any means bitch, murder scene bitch."*

The popular 90's song had become Leilani's favorite since it was released in 1996. The explicit lyrics that Lil" Kim rapped explained to her listeners as to why she was the "Queen Bitch" of her time. Despite being pint-sized, her lyrics were just as raw as the other guys. She proved she could be more provocative like the other men in the industry, also showing that she could gang bang just like them. In some way, Leilani could relate to Lil" Kim. Growing up in the mean streets of Brooklyn, Leilani had experienced things that no child should ever be exposed to. Her childhood was no walk in the park nor was it some fairytale that could be altered to portray an important message. Her childhood had been corrupted by an addiction that only a dope fiend would be able to understand. It was a blessing that Leilani could escape her tormenting family. After years of abuse, Leilani would escape, but she only left one hell hole to enter another. Her first night in a homeless shelter, she witnessed the aspiration the caged souls had for freedom. Every individual she encountered was confined to the struggle of survival. Leilani was a dope fiend looking for a clean break. She wanted to be drug free and make something of herself. She struggled everyday with trying not to be a statistic. It was already bad enough that at the time she was only 13 years old with a monkey addiction. One day she met a volunteer worker at the homeless shelter, who seemed to take a liking to her because she closely resembled his deceased sister. The two grew very close where Leilani opened up about her heart-wrenching childhood. Feeling the need to save her, he took her in and began to train her on protecting herself, which ultimately led into her training of becoming a hit woman. While other girls were focused on getting the attention of the most popular boys in school, Leilani spent countless hours in the gym with her guardian Isaiah, learning different methods of defensive moves. During her high school years, while other teens were preparing for prom and graduation, Leilani had made great academic progress allowing her to graduate early and focus solely on her training to become a hit woman. Leilani was taught all she needed to know about shooting and killing people, and by the age of 19 years old, she mastered everything there was to know about the industry.

Easily, she mastered the one trade to survival, making her one of the deadliest women in the world.

Slowly, Leilani pulled the car up in front of Isaiah's club. The roaring engine died as she got ready to make her way over to the club entrance. There were dozens of people waiting to get inside the club, anxious to experience the hype that was associated with the popular nightclub. Four guards stood by the entrance doors, only allowing a handful of people into the club at a time. Leilani walked over to the velvet ropes, skipping the long line. Females who stood in the line began sucking their teeth, furious with her going ahead of them. The males who watched her walk past them could not help but to feel hypnotized by the way Leilani's hips swayed in her black Versace skinny jeans.

"Hey La," Bullethead greeted once he realized who the female was.

"Hey Bullethead, how's it looking in there?" she asked.

"Well your brother's club is doing the usual; its packed inside."

"Is Isaiah in?"

"Yeah, should be in his office."

Leilani thanked him, while walking past the velvet ropes. The loud bass that pumped throughout the club drowned her thoughts. It was only Tuesday night and already the club was alive. Women decorated the floor as their half-naked bodies gyrated on one another. The V.I.P. section was all sold to the biggest ballers in New York as they popped bottles, throwing money around the club. Leilani paid no attention to any of the bullshit around her as she made her way to Isaiah's office. Once she made it to the door, she did her usual routine of entering without knocking.

The rhythmic sound of flesh banging on wood filled the large office space, almost competing with the bass thumping from the club. The weird odor of rubber and cologne assaulted her nose. Frozen, she stood in the entrance of the door, entangled within the escapade before her. She was fixated on the physique of the dark god that rested on top of the moaning woman. His muscles flexed as he stroked the insides of his victim into the higher heavens of an orgasm. Her moans morphed into incoherent words, signaling that she was getting closer to her climax. Watching the two engage in their sexual escapade ignited a flame that Leilani didn't think still worked. Her mind wondered on to the thought of her being that woman underneath the dark god. *Would he be able to pleasure me like that?* she thought.

A sweet floral smell tickled his nose, interrupting his thinking process. It was light and powdery intertwined with the light scent of roses and honey. He'd smelt that unique scent before but couldn't place a face to it. Feeling the glare of his onlooker, he decided that he should give a show. *Nosey ass; I'mma give you a fucking show.* Picking up his pace, he motioned his pelvis forward, hitting all angles of her insides. His quick and long strokes caused the girl underneath him to cry out.

"Shit," she cried, as she felt his long member assaulting her insides.

Not saying a single word, he continued his powerful strokes. Finally looking up, his eyes met the grey hues of his spectator. Licking his lips, he gave her body the once over. *Princess' body is stacked in all the right places,* he thought. Her hourglass frame was enticing as it filled into the expensive fabrics that adorned her body. She wore a simple outfit: black jeans, tank top, leather jacket, and her black timbs. Despite her plain look, he found her to be extra attractive. Her long, jet-black hair rested against her heart-shaped face, defining the dark look that she was going for. What popped the most was her grey, piercing eyes. They were bright, almost imitating the luminosity of a light. Her eyes were promising and inviting.

"What the fuck?" the girl underneath him yelled.

Both Leilani and the guy had been entangled within their thoughts, forgetting about the third person in the room. Quickly pulling out from within the girl, he began to cover himself, almost embarrassed at the chain of events. Snapping out of her gaze, Leilani focused her attention onto the girl, who moments ago was being fucked on top of the desk.

"Get the fuck out of here."

"Excuse me?"

"You fucking heard me bitch; get the fuck out of here."

"Bitch?"

Staring into the eyes of the embarrassed woman, Leilani couldn't help but to burst out into laughter. *I am not even going to waste my anger on this stupid bitch*, she thought, as she turned around exiting the office space. The smell of her intoxicating perfume lingered around behind her.

"Who the fuck was that?"

"What?" he asked.

"Who the fuck was that, that just stood there fucking watching me?"

Standing between the legs of the woman he had only met an hour ago, he finally took a good look at her in the light. The beauty that he took her for turned out to be an illusion that the alcohol had created. *Shit I need to stop fucking drinking.*

"Get your stuff and let's go," he replied, not interested in answering her question.

"What? Come on, let's finish."

"No."

"Why not? I thought you were feeling me."

"Yea, and then I sobered up."

***

Leilani walked over to the bar and waited for the bartender to come over to her. She didn't plan on staying out all night. Since her schedule was empty for tomorrow, she planned on catching up on some much-needed sleep. For the past couple of months, things had been hectic as she was getting accustomed to the new alterations in her life. Once she got the bartender's attention, she ordered herself a Coca-Cola with ice.

"I didn't know you started drinking," a voice behind her said. She turned around to face the person that was minding her business. Instantly, she smiled as their eyes made contact.

"Isaiah where the hell have you been?" she asked as she placed her arms around him.

If there was one person Leilani could depend on for anything, it was surely to be her best guy friend/ legal guardian, Isaiah. He was the only person in the world who understood her besides her best friend Essence. Isaiah never judged Leilani about her past, as he was one of the main support systems that helped her focus on bettering herself. He was like the big brother she never had. They both confided in each other, speaking about things that they would never say out loud. Isaiah's reputation in the streets had people defecating their pants. His whole motto was to shoot if your gut tells you to shoot. Underneath the entire rough gangster mentality was a boy that was forced to grow up fast. The Brooklyn streets were not nice to him as they took his mother away from him at the age of 11 years old. The catastrophic event forced Isaiah onto the streets for money to support his older sister, who was eventually killed by a drug lord. After the death of his sister, Isaiah became cold-hearted, willing to take anyone's life with a switch of the finger.

"I caught some guy having sex in your office, and I swear to you I was this close to having his ass toe tagged," she said as she used her fingers to demonstrate what she was talking about.

"You need to calm down more La," he chuckled as he found his little sister to be so amusing.

"Oh, shut the hell up," she replied as she took a sip from her cup of Coca-Cola. Leilani refused to drink any form of alcohol or indulge any form of drugs. After she rid her body of the harsh drugs, she refused the consumption of anything that intoxicated her or gave her a high.

"There is someone I want you to meet," Isaiah replied as he took her hand and guided her towards their destination. They cut through the crowded dance floor, making their way towards a private section that was cut off from the party happening outside.

"Who am I coming to meet?"

"Well since you will be carrying out a lot of our hits, I want you to meet another one of the partners," he spoke.

Entering the secluded section, her eyes met his dark-brown eyes. His furry eyebrows scrunched into pure confusion as he stared back at her, confused about her presence.

"Leilani, I would like for you to meet Sincere. Sincere, this is my little sister I have been telling you guys about."

"This was the piece of shit that I told you about," Leilani replied harshly.

"Well had your nosey ass knocked instead of barging in, then maybe you wouldn't have seen my porno," Sincere chuckled, revealing his pearly white teeth.

"Negro please," Leilani asserted.

"The two of y'all need to stop," Isaiah said ending their disagreement. "Sincere, Leilani will be handling all of our hits from now on," Isaiah declared proudly.

"You think she can handle that much pressure?" Sincere questioned.

"Why would I not be able to?"

"I am just saying, you're a female, and females are only good for two things."

The words poured smoothly from his thick lips. Instantly, any form of attraction Leilani had for the dark god went right out of the door. His doubt in her ability to do her job highly irritated her. Never being one to express her emotions, she contained an outburst, as she believed that the best thing for her to do was to leave before she really chin checked the asshole.

"It was nice meeting you for the second time in a row, Sincere," Leilani said as she cut their meeting short. "Isaiah, I will text you once I reach home," she said as she hugged Isaiah goodnight.

"Princess, you ain't got to leav—" he began to say.

"No, it's ok. You expressed your opinion, and I accept that," she replied as she began to walk out of the room.

"Ok La, get home safe," Isaiah chuckled. He knew that Leilani was going to prove Sincere wrong. In due time, Sincere was going to find out why he trusted Leilani with his life.

CHAPTER 2

Leilani closed her eyes, inhaling the poetic blend of cotton and linen. The scent of the mixture caused her taste buds to water. It was only six in the morning and Leilani was busy counting the money that she was going to put into her savings. *Ninety-five, ninety-six, ninety-seven, ninety-eight, ninety-nine, one hundred*, she counted in her head as she moved the dollar bills from left to right. The only sound that could be heard was the low tone of the news anchor on channel eleven. Despite being highly focused on not miscalculating the count, her ears were listening to the news.

"Breaking news, this just in. Police have discovered the body of businessman Joseph Castra with a bullet wound to the head. Police believe that Castra was robbed then shot in the head by intruders. The community is shaken up about the murder."

Leilani's ears perked up to the broadcasting of her latest handiwork. She focused her eyes on the television. One of the neighbors was expressing her fear for her life, as she now believed that her children were no longer safe on the streets. A chuckle escaped Leilani's mouth as she thought about the woman's statement being pure bullshit. *Bitch, do you know where the fuck you live? This is New York fucking City; ain't shit safe about this bitch*, she thought as she wrapped a rubber band around the stack of hundreds. *Not everyone in this fucking world is going to do right by you.* She'd learned first-hand about the wickedness that roamed around New York. Leilani had met the devil himself and his name was not Lucifer, instead his name was Rocco "Rocky" Legrand. He didn't dress up in a cloak that reeked of death nor did he carry around a satchel. Instead, he was a regular hustler that sacrificed his life to the game. The hairs on Leilani's skin began to rise as the thought of her first encounter with Rocky bombarded her mind.

******

August 1997

Loud chatter filled the beauty shop as the women of Brooklyn busied themselves with the latest gossip. The smell of burning hair synchronized with the sound of their voices, only agitating Roselyn as her concentration was being interrupted. Her mind became warped with different theories that would help her in her financial drought. The bills were piling higher and higher. She owed money to almost every drug dealer in Brooklyn. The job that she worked at the beauty salon was barely enough to cover her weekly expenses. Her latest 'Sugar Poppa' had ended their sexual friendship. Ending their sexual friendship resulted in the end of her extra income. She was in a financial hole, and she didn't have a clue as to how she would get out of it.

There were several solutions to Roselyn's new-found problem. She could have simply gotten another job to help her out with her bills. But for a person with her illegal citizen status, her options were very limited. Nowhere in New York would hire an illegal immigrant as a worker. Roselyn could have gotten a job off the books; the pay would have been *decent enough for her to make ends meet, but it would not be able to afford the partying lifestyle she grew addicted to. Roselyn had options, but there was only one option that was the answer for her. That was hustling. Roselyn was a hustler.*

Born in Bogota, Colombia, Roselyn was born into a family that was below the poverty level. Life was rough for her and her family as they struggled to make a living in the beautiful city. Both of her parents were uneducated and employed in a factory that paid them less than three dollars a day. Things were truly rough for them until Roselyn's father was offered a job working in the jungles to create Colombia's top drug, cocaine. Life seemed to have gotten better from that point on. Her family could move out of their dirt-poor community into an actual home, instead of a scrap metal fort. Everything was looking up for the family until her father was caught being greedy, taking some of the product for himself. His boss, Pablo Escobar, wanted him and his family buried six feet under. Hearing about the hit placed on his head, Roselyn, her mother, and sister fled from the country with the little saved money they had. Piss poor with nothing to their names, Roselyn and her mother used what they had to secure their new life. Selling their bodies for the American dream, they adapted to the hustle.

"Rose, you ok sugar?"

Snapping out of her daze, Roselyn's eyes followed to where the voice had come from. It was her good friend Cheryl. Glaring into the huge Christian Dior sunglasses that hid her eyes, Roselyn became intrigued by what her good friend was attempting to hide. ***I wonder if that nigger of hers gave her another black eye? Maybe that's why she's wearing them***

big ass fucking shades in this dark ass store. *Instead of digging deeper into the mystery behind her shades, Roselyn decided to leave the subject for another time.*

"Yea I'm good girl; you good?" she asked.

"I'm great. You know I'm having a party for Essence, so you should come through with La. It's gonna be this Saturday."

Ugh, why the fuck this bitch telling me about this shit. I ain't gonna bring that girl no fucking where with me, *Roselyn thought. The mere mention of her 10-year-old daughter caused her to roll her eyes in annoyance. No one knew, but Roselyn held a form of hatred towards her daughter that was uncontrollable. People around the neighborhood took Roselyn's hate for strict parenting, when it was the total opposite. She wouldn't allow her child to do the things that other kids did. Leilani was kept inside almost all day because Roselyn didn't want her outside where people could see her. Roselyn kept the child confined to her bedroom every day after school. Roselyn kept the attention off her weird parenting by going to some events with her daughter by her side, but it was never often.*

"If Leilani finishes her homework early then I'll come out with her."

"Ok, the entertainment will be there for 6."

"Ok Cheryl." Ending their conversation, Roselyn focused her attention on the sound of the wind chime, indicating the shop door had opened. All eyes were focused onto the customer who walked in. The conversation within the shop came to a halt as the 6'1 frame of the dark god became their focus.

"Aye yo, any one of y'all do braids?" he asked, filling the feminine

shop with his masculinity. The women stood around dumbfounded by his beauty. His name had rung throughout the streets, but none of the women had ever seen him in person. Growing agitated with the silenced shop, he asked the women the same question, this time allowing his voice to have more bass. "Do any one of y'all know how to fucking braid?"

"Yea, I can braid for you," Roselyn quickly answered.

"Can you do it now?"

"Sure."

Rocky walked towards Roselyn's chair, ignoring the googly eyes of the female onlookers. Sitting down in the empty chair, he sat back, allowing the beautician to run her hands through his hair. Her hands got caught in the tangles in his hair.

"What do you want me to do to it?" she asked, allowing the sexuality roll from off her tongue.

"Just give me a couple of cornrows."

"Nothing special?"

"No."

"You washed it right?" she questioned once more just to get him to start talking.

"Yes, I washed it yesterday."

"Ok."

Running the tail comb through his mane, Roselyn began to place parts in his hair. Observing his appearance, Roselyn knew she had found her next possible candidate. A thick gold chain rested around his neck almost taunting Roselyn with dollar signs. ***That chain had to cost him a***

pretty penny, *she thought. Analyzing the rest of his outfit, she knew he had spent a lot on his clothing.* ***This nigga must be loaded. I need him in my life.*** *From her mirror, she eyed him. She found him to be very attractive, resembling a famous actor. His skin complexion was the perfect shade, imitating the golden hue of honey. Feeling her stare, Rocky glared up at her, meeting her eyes.*

"Where you from?" he asked, breaking the silence between them.

"Here," she responded.

"Negative. Your English is great, but it damn sure can't hide that accent."

"It's good that you pay attention."

"I have to, especially if it's pertaining to a fine ass woman."

"I am from Colombia."

"Really?"

"Yes, I came to America with my mother when I was 13 years old."

The conversation between the two of them flowed so effortlessly. Entertained by their stories, they were surprised by how fast time flew. Finishing the last braid, Roselyn felt kind of sad that the attention that she was receiving from the hood star would be coming to an end.

"How much do I owe you?" he asked

"Thirty-five dollars," she replied. Grabbing the tall can of Olive Oil sheen spray, she proceeded to spray the sheen all over his neatly braided hair. Swiftly, he dug into his denim pockets, pulling out a huge knot of hundreds. Roselyn's eyes lit up like the Fourth of July staring at the neatly rolled dead presidents. The hypnotic scent of the cotton tickled her nose,

causing her taste buds to water.

"Here shawty," he said, handing her two crisp hundred-dollar bills. "Keep the change."

"Gracias."

"You're welcome. What are you doing tonight?"

"Nothing."

"I'm having a party at the club that's not too far from around here."

"Ok, so what exactly are you asking me?"

"Come out tonight; bring your girls with you if you would like to."

"Sure, I don't mind coming, but I am going to need a ride."

"Don't worry my Colombian Princess, I'll come to pick you up."

"Ok," she replied, as she wrote down her address and number on the beauty salon's business card.

"I'll pick you up around nine."

"That's a good time."

The corners of his mouth went up as a smile formed on his lips. The attraction was evident between the two, but neither of them understood how dangerous their connection could be. ***Hopefully tonight I'll be able to get him home.*** *Quietly, Roselyn watched as her next victim exited the beauty salon. All eyes were focused on him as every female in the shop watched his departure.*

"Yes, bitch you got you a paid nigga," Selena said, breaking the ice that seemed to be casted over them.

"Shut up," Roselyn replied.

"Bitch, you know you hit the jackpot."

Ignoring the comments of her inquisitive customers, Roselyn placed her focus back onto her scheduled appointments. She had only one more customer before she could leave to get ready for the party tonight. Her phone buzzed lightly in efforts to get her attention. Quickly, she picked it up, recognizing the number of her clients.

"Hello," she answered.

"Hey Rose girl, just wanted to let you know that I am around the corner and will be making my way to you now."

"Ok." Hanging up the phone, Rose prepared her station for her next client. She just hoped like hell that Rhonda wouldn't be so complicated like all the other times Roselyn had done her hair. ***I just wanna do this puta hair and be done with it, so I can leave and get ready for tonight.***

****

A knock on the door rang throughout the apartment, alerting everyone that there was a visitor. Focused on the television that was in front of her, Leilani's eyes never left the screen as she immersed herself into the famous Tom and Jerry episode. The legendary cat and mouse duo were yet again battling each other without a real purpose, besides the myth of the cat and mouse beef. Amused by the fighting duo, Leilani had forgotten about the visitor who stood behind the door waiting impatiently for an answer. Quickly, Rocky banged his knuckles a little harder on the metal door, anticipating an answer.

"Mommy, someone is at the door," Leilani finally yelled out.

"So go fucking answer it," her mother yelled out from the bathroom.

Getting off the old couch, Leilani made her way over to the metal door. Too small to reach the peephole, Leilani unlocked the door, cracking it open just enough for her to see who was at the door.

"How can I help you?" she asked innocently.

"What's up shawty?"

"Nothing."

"I'm here for your mother."

"Ok."

Moving to the side, Leilani granted him access into the apartment. The stench of his cologne swarmed in, causing Leilani to close her nose shut. His scent was overbearing for her nose. He stared at her scrunched up face, confused at her gesture. The cologne that he had sprayed on earlier was his every day scent that attracted all the women. He received countless compliments about his unique scent.

"What's the matter?" he questioned, staring into her innocent eyes.

"You stink mister."

A light chuckle escaped his thick lips as he was amused by the little girl before him. Being in the streets for all his life, Rocky had grown accustomed to staring down the meek eyes of a grown man. His reputation went a long way as the people of New York knew that he was not the one to be fucked with. For some reason, he expected fear to ooze out of the little girl before him, but unbeknownst to him, the girl was oblivious to his street reputation. To her, he was just one of her mother's friends that was going to take her out.

"You don't like my cologne?"

"No."

"How come?" he questioned. "All the females love this smell."

"Well they are lying to you," she replied while scrunching her nose up. "The smell is too strong."

"How about this, I will start wearing something lighter just for you."

"That's much better." The twinkle in her eyes mesmerized him; it wasn't like anything he had ever seen before. She was innocent and pure, which were two things that were hard to find in New York. What the hell is going on? He questioned himself as he became lost within the grey hues of her irises. Her grey eyes resembled a thick cloud that prowled the City of New York threatening a thunderstorm. He'd never seen anything more beautiful than the little girl before him. It was weird for him; the feeling that had overcame him was something he was not used to. Butterflies fluttered around in his stomach as his hands grew moist.

"What's your name lil" mama?"

"Leilani; what is yours?"

"Rocky."

"Your name is Rocky?" she asked confused.

"Yes."

"Like a Rock?"

"Something like that."

"Why would your mother name you after a rock?" Her naïve question caused him to release a genuine chuckle. ***Shawty is funny****, he thought.*

"Rocky isn't my real name; it's a name that I chose to use in the streets."

"Ok, so what is your real name?"

"How about I answer that some other time," he responded. For as long as he'd been on the streets, he never revealed his name to no one. Not even the mother of his son knew what his real name was.

"Ok, man named after a rock."

The corners of his mouth curved upside down forming a smile. He expected for her to badger him for an answer. But to his surprise, the girl turned her back to him and proceeded to watch her late-night cartoons on the old couch. Following her, Rocky found a seat right next to her. The two sat next to each other deep in thought. Their silent thoughts were interrupted by the sound of Roselyn making her way into the living room.

"Ok, I am ready papi," she replied, as she stared at both her daughter and Rocky indulging themselves with the childish cartoon.

"Aight, where's the baby sitter?" Rocky asked concerned. "She gonna be late?"

"Baby sitter?" A deep chuckle escaped Roselyn's lips as she became amused with Rocky's concerns for her daughter's well-being. "Honey, that little girl is ten years old; she can take care of herself. Now let's go."

Turning to face the little girl that he just met not too long ago, Rocky felt weird about leaving her all alone in the house by herself. He had the desire to argue with Roselyn about her parenting skills. He found it ridiculous that she would just leave the child alone by herself in the hood. Conjuring up his argument, his battle was disrupted by Leilani.

"I'm a big girl; I'll be ok," she said convincingly.

"You sure?"

"Yea, I'm used to being left alone."

Getting up to leave, Rocky felt the tug of war on his conscious. Leaving the ten-year-old alone by herself was something that he didn't think was a good idea. Roselyn watched on as Rocky began to make his way over to her. It was almost as if he cared for Leilani.

"Don't worry papi; she'll be fine."

******

The sound of her cell phone ringing snapped her back into reality as she picked up her vibrating device, glaring at the caller ID.

"Hello," she answered.

"You're up really early."

"I am a businesswoman. I don't sleep; you of all people should know this by now."

"I taught you well," Isaiah boosted, smiling on the other side of the phone.

"What do you want?"

"Well, tonight I need you to go to this dinner as it requires your expertise with our new potential partners."

"What time should I be ready?"

"Let's say around 8:30. I'll honk the horn when I am outside."

"Ok, see you later."

A chuckle escaped Leilani's lips as she knew Isaiah was a piece of work. Being a hired hit woman, Leilani was used to getting job calls, but being hired by Isaiah and his crew full-time was more work then she had anticipated. Before, Isaiah had no problem with calling Leilani about hanging out, but lately he only called her for work. Don't get it twisted, Leilani was about her paper. She'd never turn down a job, and Isaiah knew this as he made sure to keep his promise about always making sure she was put on. Working for him and his partners was a great idea he had produced, as he knew Leilani was the only person that he could rely on to get the job done correctly.

Isaiah was involved in a drug organization well-known amongst the streets as the *Supremes.* The organization was not like any other conjured up drug empire. When the people of New York indulged themselves into narcotics, it was the *Supremes* who supplied their dream drug. Every gram and ounce of drugs that moved through the state of New York was supplied by the *Supremes (well, now that Joseph Castra was out of the equation, the Supremes had full control over New York's pipeline)*. Money was no problem; anything they desired was at the reach of their fingertips. The trio: Don, Sincere, and Isaiah were trying to take their organization to the next level, wanting to leave behind a legacy that could not be matched by any other drug dealers.

"Fifty, fifty-one, fifty-two," Leilani whispered as she concentrated with counting the rest of the money. The dull glow from the sunrise peaked through the cracks of her curtains. It was only the beginning of September and already Leilani was glad that the summer heat had died down a little. She loved the cool breeze that crept through her opened window. Two hours later, her hands began cramping as she finished wrapping up the final stack of bills.

"Not bad," Leilani spoke, placing the wrapped up money back

into the duffle bag.

8:46 p.m.

Leilani sat on her couch waiting for the sound of a car horn. She could feel herself beginning to get heated. Isaiah knew she was a very punctual person. She liked being earlier than the expected time because it gave her the chance to scope out a new environment. Pulling out her iPhone, she began to dial Isaiah's number. Again, she was sent straight to voicemail. She waited patiently until the automated server finished its message before she replied.

"Isaiah, you have until 8:50 to bring your high yellow ass to the front of my building. I swear if you're not here I will find you and light your ass up," she spoke as her words dripped with anger.

Her eyes focused onto the clock, preparing to bring the fire to Isaiah's ass. Leilani found her way into the kitchen in search for a bottle of water to drink. She needed to calm her nerves before she found herself acting a fool outside. The cool liquid entered her system, cooling off all the burning anger within her. Suddenly, the loud sound of a car horn caught her attention. Leilani wasted no time as she made her way to the front of her building in search of Isaiah's all-black Mercedes.

"Where the fuck are you?" she spoke, eyeing the streets. The beaming flashing lights of an Aston Martin caught her attention. Hesitantly, Leilani made her way to the fire red luxurious vehicle with only one thing on her mind: *as soon as I see this motherfucker I am going to curse his ass the fuck out,* she thought. Opening the car door, she was greeted by the drivers Versace cologne. The scent was out of the ordinary as she expected Isaiah's usual musky scent.

"Hello," the dark figure spoke.

"What the hell are you doing here?" she asked

"Well, you're going to dinner with me."

"Excuse me?"

"The dinner consists of you being my date for the night."

"That was not a part of the agreement."

"Princess, get into the damn car. I'll explain everything on our way to the restaurant," he spoke with authority in his voice. Despite being highly annoyed with his tardiness, Leilani sat in the passenger seat. She was seething with anger from the lack of information that she received pertaining to this dinner date. *Just fucking wait, I am gonna tear this nigga a new fucking asshole*, she discussed in her head.

Sincere couldn't help but to divert his eyes on the beauty in his passenger seat. Her scent was fresh yet hypnotizing, and her all-black attire drew him in. The form fitting Gucci dress hugged her frame while her freshly manicured toes sat pretty in the Saint Laurent ankle strapped heels. He had to admit her ethereal features attracted him, as well as her impassive attitude. The car remained silent as he drove to the restaurant. Irritated by the silence of the vehicle, he decided to start a conversation.

"So how long have you known Isaiah?"

"Quite some time now," she replied nonchalantly as she stared out the window. "After tonight, I will have to reevaluate our eleven-year friendship."

"He's cool."

"Like a cucumber," she replied sarcastically. If there was one thing about Leilani, it was that she was a very big asshole. She often made slick comments that would offend a person who didn't know her well.

"Well tonight we will be meeting some potential business partners, and I need you to act like my girl, so I need you to be 100% supportive," he said as he stared at her.

"Ok."

"I'll try to keep tonight PG-13 as I do not want to have your boyfriend pissed off about some new nigga pushing up on his girl," he purposely said to drag information out of Leilani.

"If you wanted to know if I had a man, then you should have simply asked."

"Well, do you?"

Leilani turned her body towards him as she decided to give him her undivided attention. She brought her face closer towards his while he focused on the road. She waited for the car to come to a red light before she began to proceed with setting Sincere straight.

"My personal life and business life are two totally separate things, so keep it that way." Her words came out fluently, not wanting to deliver the wrong message. Her matte red lipstick defined her plump lips, as Sincere could not help but to think about those same red lips around his shaft.

"It's whatever you want in this world Princess," he chuckled.

"Stop fucking calling me that shit; that isn't my name."

"I know what your name is, but I'd prefer to address you as Princess."

"Why?"

"Don't worry about it."

This cocky son of a bitch, Leilani thought. There was much tension between the two, as both desired to speak but there wasn't much to say. The duo was attracted to each other, but Leilani refused to act out on her emotions. She wasn't aware of how to go about the dating life. Sincere on the other hand wanted her in every position that the human body would allow. She was very attractive, but her attitude was what made him yearn her. He knew she was going to be a challenge, but he was very willing to win her over. Slowing down the luxurious vehicle, Sincere approached the front of the restaurant. Placing the car into park, he got out of the car smoothly, running his hands along any creases in his suit. Walking over to passenger side of the car, he opened the car door for Leilani, allowing her to exit the vehicle.

"Here's the key to my car; do not mess it up," he said to the valet as he placed Leilani's hands into his. The feeling of her soft touch was new for him.

"Oh, you're quite the gentleman," Leilani spoke, rolling her eyes.

"And I could be a lot more," he replied as he planted his hand directly on the small of her back. Leilani didn't budge, finding it surprising that the position of his hand felt normal. They walked together to the hostess who stood smiling behind her podium.

"Welcome, table for two?" she asked politely.

"Actually, we have reservations for four guests," Sincere spoke up

"Last name sir?" she asked as she began typing into her computer.

"Anthony."

After a little bit of time, she found his name and led the couple to their seat. Leilani was impressed with the choice of restaurant, as she could tell she would be spending a pretty penny tonight. The upscale French dining seemed as if it would be Leilani's favorite. Once they reached their tables, Sincere pulled out Leilani's chair before sitting in his.

"May I start you two off with drinks?" the hostess asked innocently.

"Sure, I'll take a bottle of the best champagne you guys offer," Sincere spoke.

"And I will have a glass of water," Leilani replied.

Once the hostess disappeared Leilani looked around at her surroundings. Their table was positioned in the back of the restaurant where the two could monitor all activity. Despite being in an upscale part of New York, Leilani felt as if it was still considered the streets as she could be attacked at any time and any place.

"You picked a great table," Leilani said, breaking the ice.

"It's necessary with the line of business we are in."

"You are correct."

The two held a conversation discussing whom they were meeting. Leilani wanted as much information as possible since she was taking the time out of her day to have a dinner date. Their conversation came to a halt when their guest arrived. Leilani expected it to be a couple, but instead they were greeted by two men.

"Hey, what up man," the first guy spoke towards Sincere, as they both dapped each other's hand.

"Nothing much; hey guys this is my girl Princess. Princess, this is Ralph and this is David."

The guys shook Leilani's hand, and then took their seat. Right on time the waitress walked over handing over the menus, giving the group a chance to look over their options. The guys engaged in conversation as Leilani kept her eyes on the menu, but her ears were fixated on the dialogue.

"Like we said before, the offer still stands. We want to buy the product," Ralph chatted.

"Yes, especially since your snowflakes are the only thing causing a blizzard in the streets," David mentioned.

The conversation continued between the guys as they spoke about how Sincere's operation worked. An uneasy feeling washed over Leilani, as her gut experienced a tingling sensation. The tense sensation resulted in her second guessing the two men. Dozens of people have admitted to trusting their gut as a warning sign. But for Leilani, her gut had saved her life several times. She nudged Sincere, and immediately he looked up concerned.

"Princess, are you ok?" he asked.

"I'm fine. I just don't feel too good; my stomach is a little off," she said convincingly.

"Ok," he replied, as he focused his attention on the guys before him. "Fellas, my lady is not feeling too good, so how about we cut dinner short and continue business at my home. Bring the money, and

I will have your product bagged and ready to depart."

Sincere hailed down the waitress informing her about their early departure. Once everything was settled, Sincere placed his hand on the small of Leilani's back, guiding her towards the exit alongside Ralph and David.

"So, guys give us twenty minutes and we will be by your house," Ralph informed them before he departed.

"You ok Princess?" Sincere asked.

"Yea, it's just that these mutherfuckers are very fucking fishy; they got my gut tingling," she replied as she got into the Aston Martin.

"You sure it's not your bubble guts?"

"Boy, if you don't drive this mutherfucking car."

A smile crept onto Sincere's face as he found Leilani's attitude comical. The way Leilani acted didn't steer him away from her. He found Leilani to be the perfect challenge.

"Do you know you're a very beautiful woman?"

"Negro please, you're just saying that to get in my pants," Leilani said waving him off.

Despite his compliment being every form of sincerity, Leilani could not truly accept his kindness. Years of abuse had finally taken authority over Leilani's mind. Time and time again she was forced into believing that she could never be beautiful. Her mother had beaten this belief into Leilani, ultimately lowering her self-esteem.

"I know I can be an asshole, but one thing I don't do is lie to females," he spoke as he pulled his Aston Martin into his driveway.

"Oh really?"

"Yea, I am a gentleman," he said while staring at Leilani. Sincere had met dozens of pretty females in his life, but Leilani had taken the cake. He waited for Leilani's cheeks to turn red from his compliments, but her olive skin tone remained unflawed. *Shit I'mma need to come much harder.*

"Well let's hurry up and get it over with these lames ass niggas," Leilani spoke as they pulled up in front of his home. Once the car was parked, Sincere and Leilani made their way to the front of his house door. Sincere unlocked the door, leading Leilani through his tastefully decorated home and into his office.

"Do you honestly think them niggas fishy?" he asked as he took a seat in his chair.

"I'm positive. Listen, I always listen to my gut; that's why I am still breathing today."

"Ok."

"Let's get some things straight. Did you give them your address for your home?" Leilani asked.

"Umm, I doubt it."

"Have you ever invited them to your home or anything of that nature?"

"Nah, I am not that stupid."

"Have you ever conducted business out of this house?"

"Nah, Princess."

"Ok; if they show up without a text asking for directions, I am killing them."

Leilani took a seat on the desk as she watched Sincere stand up. She didn't bother to continue their conversation as her mind was already made up. As she fiddled with her nails, patiently waiting for the arrival of the guys, Sincere sat there watching Leilani and her every move. *I need a drink,* he thought. Sincere grabbed the whiskey glass bottle along with his cup and proceeded to pour the aged liquor.

"Are you strapped?" Sincere asked looking up from his glass.

"Is that really a question you should ask me?"

"What?"

"How do I know you're not the feds?"

"Really?"

"Hey, Rico killed Mitch, so their ain't no loyalty between lovers, workers, and family."

"You know, you are something else," Sincere replied as he let out a hearty chuckle. His teeth gleamed a perfect shade of white, resembling little tic tacs. "Show me where's it at."

"For what."

"I want to make sure you will be able to reach it in time."

"Well then sir, you're just going to have to come here then," she replied, motioning him between her legs. Leilani knew she was doing something out of the usual, but she wanted to play with Sincere's head. There was no denying the attraction between the two, so Leilani decided to go along with it.

"Right here?" Sincere asked once he was positioned in between her thick thighs. Her skin was warm as his hands were placed on her inner thighs. The sensation of her soft skin caused his manhood to stand at attention. Her soft, velvety skin disappeared as he felt the cold steel of her chrome.

"That's a very safe place for it," he spoke.

"Second safest place in the world."

"Where's the first?" he asked as he felt himself getting lost within her grey eyes. His heart pace picked up as Leilani continued to glide his hands towards her snatch. The warmth between her legs increased. One by one his fingers felt the soft fabric of her lace underwear. Without any warning, Leilani took a handful of his penis, applying pressure to her grip. Immediately, Sincere buckled from her strong grip. She placed her mouth near his ear lightly kissing it. Their moment was interrupted by the sound of the maid's voice greeting their guests.

"We have company," she spoke softly, releasing his manhood.

The door to the office opened slowly as their expected guest walked in. Ralph's face lit up with excitement as he eyed the duffle bag that contained what they wanted.

"Welcome gentlemen, do you guys have the money?"

"We sure do; do you have the dope?" David replied.

"Just like you asked."

Sincere walked over to the duffle bags as he unzipped one to display his product. Leilani kept her seat on the office desk, anticipating the worst. She allowed Sincere to do all the talking while she remained silent. Her eyes remained fixated on the duo with their every move being analyzed. Leilani offered the duo a seat, but like she guessed they would, they declined. When Sincere went over for the cash, both Ralph and David began to act strange. The perspiration on their skin glistened under the intense lighting in Sincere's office.

"What's good with your nigga?" Sincere asked.

"What you mean?"

"Y'all acting all fidgety and shit."

"Nah bro, we good."

"I don't believe that shit. Put y'all hands up and let me search y'all real quick," Sincere spoke as he began to get angry with their suspicious antics. The duo looked at each other, confused on their next move. Tugging on his glock, David was prepared for war while his partner in crime was hesitant. Both men made eye contact in hopes of coming to an agreement on what they thought should occur next. The pressure was on them both, as Sincere proceeded over to David preparing to search him. Annoyed with the way things were going, David pulled out his weapon pointing the barrel at Leilani's temple.

"Listen bruh, we really don't want any problems," David spoke. "All we want is the money and the drugs."

"Y'all niggas got a lot of balls, trying to pull some shit like this," Sincere's voice was calm, but Leilani knew he was minutes away from acting irrational.

"Nigga, you are one of the biggest ballers in New York," David ranted. "You must be hella dumb if you actually think we came here to do some buddy buddy shit." The look of greed bore from their eyes. Both David and Ralph were stickup kids, who grew up with nothing.

They had made something out of themselves by robbing drug dealers. Tonight wasn't any different, as they expected to leave the establishment with whatever Sincere had in his possession.

"So, like we said, we are taking the money and the fucking drugs," Ralph declared as he grabbed Leilani, holding her hostage. "Now, if there is a problem with our request, then I would have no problems with blowing this pretty bitch's brains all over your expensive carpet." Ralph's voice intensified with anger. This robbery was supposed to only last five minutes and already they were running out of time for their clean escape.

"Do you know you're making a huge mistake?" Sincere replied.

"Nigga I don't think you understand; if this is indeed a mistake then it's worth taking," Ralph answered. His eyes resembled ones of a delusional person. "We ain't got time for this sh—" His words were cut short as Leilani's elbow connected with his throat, knocking all the oxygen from his lungs. Ralph doubled over allowing Leilani to twist his arm back, forcing him to release his gun into her possession. Quickly, Leilani released a coughing Ralph as she wrapped her arm around David's neck, snapping it before he had time to protest. The sound of his body dropping to the ground bounced off the thick walls, startling Ralph.

"Now, back to you," Leilani replied as she stood before Ralph. "I am going to give you some pointers on how to do the perfect stick."

Ralph couldn't look her in her face as the pain from the blow caused him to choke on air. Sharp pains rang throughout his chest; death seemed to be closing in on him the longer he struggled to regulate his breathing.

"Rule number one, you do your fucking research on the fucking people you plan to rob," she spoke calmly, but on the inside, Leilani was livid. She could feel her body getting hotter with every waiting moment. "Rule number fucking two, if you plan to pull out a gun, use that shit; don't waste time basking in fucking glory," she said as she leveled the gun in between his eyes. Her finger tapped the trigger once, releasing a bullet into his forehead. Ralph's brain matter splattered against the white walls of Sincere's office. The smell of burning flesh seeped throughout the office. Sincere's face was priceless; it was right then and there that Sincere realized that Leilani was not what he expected. She wasn't the type of female that panicked during arduous situations. She handled the robbers effortlessly, killing both men without a second thought. Leilani was far from the average plain Jane; she didn't dress in colorful clothing that barely covered her assets. She found solace in the absence of color. Leilani didn't seek attention like other females did; she'd rather go unnoticed in the world. She was different, and Sincere took a liking to her divergent characteristics.

Wiping off the brain matter from her face, Leilani turned to Sincere with a calm expression written on her face. She was highly annoyed with the way her night went. Before she received the phone call from Isaiah, Leilani had her night planned. She was supposed to enjoy her night off by indulging in a couple of movies, eating take out, and then finishing her night with a warm bubble bath while listening to some classic R&B. Instead of having a relaxing night, Leilani stood in the middle of Sincere's office with a smoking gun and brain matter all over her face and hair.

"Mr. Anthony, I hope you enjoy the remainder of your night."

"Princess, you can get cleaned up here if you want."

"No, it is fine," she responded walking away from him. "I'll send some guys over to dispose of the trash."

Slowly, she walked over the dead bodies, not wanting to fall on her ass. Sincere watched on, hypnotized by the way her hips swayed in the form fitting Gucci dress. The blood from his body all went to one area, causing his friend to swell within his jeans. *Oh lord, I must have her, he thought. Matter fact, I am going to get her.*

CHAPTER 3

"Maybe he won't change," Candy stated.

"What do you mean?"

"Essence, you and Casper been together for years now and he still pulling the same shit from high school," Candy spoke. "Like dead ass, the nigga does what he wants and expects you to remain faithful. It's time to seriously let his ass go."

Leilani stared at her two best friends, listening to the two discuss Essence's problematic relationship. She sat completely silent, not wanting to speak on the topic of the dysfunctional relationship, while Candy on the other hand continued to negatively speak on it. Despite the truth in Candy's theory, Essence still had hope that her significant other loved her enough to change.

"La, am I not right?" Candy asked. To someone considering the friendship it may have seemed like Candy was being harsh, but in her head, Candy believed that she was speaking the truth. Leilani sat silent as she knew that all the talking in the world would not change Essence's opinion on the man that she had a child for.

"You are somewhat right, but you cannot keep badgering Essence on her decision to love that man," Leilani spoke calmly. "He's a piece of shit, but Essence is in love with him. You have to let her open her eyes and deal with this on her own. You can't force her to see what you see, because the both of y'all have different lens prescription. You see the nigga for what he is and Essence sees him for what he could possibly could be. We care about you Essence, and I want the best for you, so I completely understand how hard it is for you to let go."

"Thank you, La," Essence replied as she took a sip of her Long Island Iced Tea. Leilani's words placed a band-aid on Essence's bruised ego. Essence knew the truth about her fiancé being a piece of shit, but he wasn't always like this. When they first met back in high school he'd done everything right. He was perfect, giving her any and everything she needed. Her fiancé was stuck to her like glue. Time progressed and he became comfortable, knowing that she had a love that would never die. In her eyes, he could never do any wrong, so he used her undying love for him against her. He cheated on her constantly, not caring about the consequences, as he knew she would always come back to him.

"Don't think I forgot about the main reason for you dragging us all the way out here to some posh nail salon," Leilani stated, breaking the weird tension between Essence and Candy. Leilani sat back in the pedicure chair as she allowed the pedicurist to scrub the heel of her foot.

"Well, you guys can't freak out when I tell you," Candy spoke nervously.

"Bitch, hurry up and spit it out."

Candy stared into the two female's eyes as they sat anticipating the news. She knew her girls would flip out about what she was going to confess to.

"Well, this morning I had went to the doctor and they confirmed that I am 12 weeks pregnant," she beamed.

"Oh, my gosh!" Essence squealed at the thought of a baby being amongst the group of women. "We need to start shopping for cribs, clothes, and of course me and La will plan the baby shower. I'm thinking of a diapers and diamonds theme, all-white, don't reveal the gender until cutting the cake," Essene spoke excitedly, her ranting filled the air as a million ideas ran through her head.

The trio were a very close group of women. When they were younger they would have never believed that they would have survived the jungle of Marcy projects. Living in the hellhole was what made their bond strong. Leilani was close with the two girls, but her connection with Essence was stronger than anything in the world. Leilani and Essence knew each other, since for years as Leilani's mother worked in Essence's mother's shop. Being with each other constantly caused the two to form an unbreakable bond.

"How does G feel about you being pregnant?" Essence asked.

"Well he doesn't know yet. I want to keep it a surprise."

"Yea, that shit a surprise alright, to both him and his wife," Leilani interjected, not approving of Candy's decision to mess with a married man. Leilani had a feeling that the mysterious G knew that the situation he had with Candy was very fucked up, which was the reason as to why he didn't want to be around both her and Essence.

"I know; we will figure something out," Candy responded, sipping on her glass of water. "He already told me that he was going to leave her for me."

Leilani stared at Candy as if she had grown two horns on the top of head. Earlier, Candy was bashing Essence about being with her baby father, but here Candy sat discussing the topic of her boyfriend, who was already married to someone else. All Leilani could do was shake her head, disapproving of the whole situation. Never being the one to give her opinion unless asked, she remained silent. Catching on to the head nod, Candy instantly took offense with the head gesture.

"Oh, since you want to be so judgmental about my situation La, where your nigga at?" Candy asked annoyed.

"I don't have one."

"Exactly, always butting into other people's relationships, but you not in one your damn self."

A nerve has been hit, Leilani thought. Candy was very sensitive when it came down to being judged by her best friends. Instead of acknowledging her sensitivity, Leilani let out a chuckle.

"Oh, what will I do with your simple ass Candy?"

"What?"

"The situation is fucked up Candy."

"How?" she questioned. "Everything is good; at least I have a man."

"What you fail to realize is that being a man's secret is the ultimate no-no. You are fucking and sucking him and giving him a relationship title, while his ass doesn't even have you saved in his phone. But you know what, I would rather remain single than be a nigga's secret." Leilani wanted to continue lecturing Candy, but the sound of her phone ringing took her out of her concentration. She looked at the screen to see Isaiah's name plastered on the screen.

"Hello."

"Where are you?"

"Nail salon, why?"

"We need to go shopping for this event at Don's club."

"We?"

"Yes we."

"Ok, well come and pick me up. I didn't drive." Leilani rattled off the address to the salon. She waited patiently until he confirmed how to get there. Hanging up the phone, Leilani focused back on the girls. Their chitter chatter filled the crisp air with the topic of Candy's pregnancy being discussed. Essence could sense an argument approaching, and she knew baby talk would silence the thick tension. Despite their disapproval of Candy's side chick status, both females were excited about the new addition to the family. Leilani wanted to go shopping for some baby clothes as she already had some cute outfits in her head.

"Look here La, you will not have my child dressed in this all-black clothing that you wear."

"What's wrong with all black?"

"Girl, that shit is depressing."

"No, it is not; it is me embracing my inner blackness," Leilani admitted.

"Girl, you're freaking Spanish."

"No hunnie, see that is the problem with you young thangs nowadays. I did that stupid ass ancestry shit and found out I have African roots in my family."

"But still, you Spanish though," Candy spoke proving a point.

"Ok, and I am also black. I embrace it; ain't nothing wrong with claiming my Hispanic side and my black roots." In Leilani's eyes, she was both Black and Hispanic, as she didn't feel the need to deny her Black roots. She wore all black for three reasons: she felt comfortable in black, she loved embracing her black roots, and black was a bomb ass color to wear.

The sound of the opening door caught everyone's attention as they were focused on seeing who had entered the establishment. Isaiah walked in smoothly, allowing his arrogance to replace the faint scent of the acrylic. Every female eyed him as he walked over to the trio.

"Hey big heads," he spoke, flashing his perfectly aligned teeth. He walked over to Leilani and planted a kiss on her cheek, and then acknowledged Candy and Essence.

"Shut up," Leilani replied, still annoyed with the events that occurred the night prior.

"Why are you so angry?"

"Nothing."

"Just like a damn woman, so complicated," he chuckled. "Ladies, I know it's a girl's day but I just came to snatch my sister."

"It's cool, she was getting on our nerves anyway," Essence replied.

"Oh, shut your asses up; you know y'all enjoyed my company."

Leilani placed her pedicured feet into her Birkenstock sandals. Isaiah examined her nails and feet, noticing that they looked perfect. The fire red polish complimented her skin tone.

"Why are you staring at my nails?"

"I wanted to make sure they did them shits good before I pay," he replied as he handed the pedicurist his card to pay for their nails.

"Oh La, tonight we are having dinner at Candy's spot, come through," Essence said.

"I will. I'll call you guys to see when you're ready," Leilani replied as she gave her girls a hug goodbye. Leaving the nail salon, Leilani followed Isaiah to his car.

"So, I heard you did a good job with handling the dinner," Isaiah said.

"Yeah, thank you for fucking informing me about you not going to the dinner."

"What?"

"Don't fucking play with me you shit faced asshole."

A chuckle escaped Isaiah mouth as he gripped his stomach in laughter. He knew Leilani was pissed off about him not being present during the dinner. But he knew she would eventually get over it. The conversation picked up as they pulled off into traffic. Leilani had been so embedded into her work that she didn't have any spare time to enjoy company. Spending time with Isaiah was well needed.

"Nah, I don't see myself settling down for some clown."

"I know, but not all niggas out are clowns," Isaiah tried convincing her.

"Name one."

"Sincere."

Leilani was confused on why Isaiah was mentioning his name. It shocked Leilani on how he vouched for Sincere. For the ten years that the two knew each other, Isaiah never vouched for any guy when it came down to Leilani. He knew how she was and how she would react to certain situations, so he respected her decision to stay away from guys. But Sincere was different. Isaiah had witnessed the glow in his eyes any time Leilani was brought into a conversation, or if she was in his presence. Since the two had met each other, every time they were together they would bicker like an old couple. Which only proved to Isaiah that the two had feelings for one another.

"That fool."

"Well La, that fool has something for you."

"What you mean?"

"He likes you; so give the nigga a chance."

"Chance?" Leilani questioned. "That nigga probably just wants to get into my pants."

"If he does, then let the nigga in so you could finally get some dick," he suggested as they pulled into Roosevelt Field Mall.

"First let's hit up Nordstrom," Isaiah suggested.

"I don't mind."

The two left the car, making their way into the mall. The sweet smell of cinnamon permeated the air.

"Mister big shot, you ready to run them pockets?"

"Of course, for my baby sister I could allow my pockets to do a couple of marathons in the mall."

"That sounds good to me."

Leilani took in the ambiance of the wealthy mall, grateful at how far she had come. Twelve years prior, Leilani wasn't as hip to the fashion game as she was today. Her mother would decorate her body in expensive fabrics, while Leilani on the other hand wore clothes that barely fit her growing frame.

******

The faint aroma of sizzling meat roamed throughout the two-bedroom apartment, saturating the air with the hypnotizing scent of home cooked food. Life for Roselyn had picked up within the past couple of months as her relationship with Rocky became serious. Glaring into the living room, she observed her man while he sat on the couch watching his favorite comedy show ***Martin*** *on her television. The sound of his laughter filled the air as he found the behavior of the main character Martin Payne to be comical.*

"This nigga so crazy," he chuckled. Bringing the glass of beer up to his mouth, he took a swig of his favorite pale lager.

"How is he crazy?" Leilani questioned. Turning to face the little girl, Rocky had completely forgotten that the ten-year-old was still in his presence.

"He just is."

"That is not an accurate answer," she challenged.

For the past couple of months Rocky found himself spending more time with the mother and daughter duo. His long nights in the strip club and all day sleeping had come to an abrupt halt as he enjoyed the company of both Roselyn and Leilani. Never in a million years would he have thought that he would be focusing his attention on only one female, especially her kid.

"Fine lil" mama, Martin is crazy because he just does crazy shit. He does things dramatically which makes him funny." Staring down at the little girl he waited patiently for her answer.

"Ok, you're right," she replied, as she focused her attention back onto the television. Releasing a chuckle, Rocky stared down at her. Taking in her appearance, it was then that he noticed her clothing. The clothes she wore were old and dingy. He could tell that the grimy clothes were passed down for some years. Seeing the pretty little girl dressed in rags only agitated Rocky.

"Lil" mama, do you have any other type of clothing?"

"No," she answered with her eyes still focused on the television.

"So, your mother doesn't buy you any form of nice clothing?"

"This is what I have."

"And nothing better?"

"I have school uniform."

Looking up at him, Leilani was confused on his line of questioning. *Why does he care so much about my clothes?* The question rang throughout her head. In her eyes, the clothing she wore was fine. Despite having a couple of holes and several stains that she couldn't get out. Her clothing was just fine for her.

"Don't worry lil" mama, I will get your gear up there," he said as he sat his hand on her small thigh. Not thinking much of the gesture, Leilani placed her eyes back onto the screen to focus back on the all-black scene of Martin. The hilarious character walked around the table with a stuffed Rottweiler as he questioned his close friends about his recently missing cd player. Leilani's laugh filled the living room as Martin jumped on the table with his stuffed dog in efforts to intimidate his suspects. Peering on, Rocky found comfort within her laughter. The happiness within the spontaneous sound that escaped her mouth was filled with lively amusement. He never heard anything like it before. Her laugh was carefree. It was genuine. It was innocent. Pure, not mixed nor adulterated by the sins of life. It was refreshing for him to be in her presence. It was what he needed.

******

"Get whatever you are getting. Maybe we can get matching suits?"

"I love you Sai, but not that much nigga." They both laughed, finding amusement in Leilani's quick response. Despite not being blood related, the two shared a bond that neither had ever had before. Isaiah had taken Leilani in when she was just a teenager. When he first laid eyes on her, his heart skipped a beat. She resembled his deceased younger sister, who he couldn't save. Since the first day he met Leilani, he promised her that he would never let her down. It was the same promise he had made to his sister, but this time he had planned on being true to his words.

8:53 p.m.

Click Clack

Click Clack

Click Clack

The sound of Leilani's Giuseppe heels clicked against the pavement while she walked with Isaiah. Together, they walked hand in hand as they made their way to the back entrance of the club.

"How many people are going to be here again?" Leilani asked

"Honestly, I can't give you an answer," Isaiah replied as he held the door open for her. The smell of smoke hovered around the exit as two male figures stood, smoking their joints. The loud bass that erupted throughout the club drowned their words out. Isaiah kept his hand on the small of Leilani's back while guiding her to their designated V.I.P. booth. Once she sat down, Leilani's eyes scanned the club. They darted left to right as they analyzed every piece of the establishment.

"Is the place good?" Isaiah asked noticing her surveying the club.

"Yea, should be. I don't see anything out of the ordinary."

"Good, so let me hail down the waitress," he replied as he waved over their waitress.

The woman walked over seductively once she realized who needed her attention. Her vision was set on Isaiah, not once caring for the woman that sat next to him.

"Yes baby?" she asked

"Yea, let me get a bottle of Ace and a side cup of water with lemon and mint."

She stared at him confused with the order. Knowing better than to question Isaiah, she walked away to get his desired drinks.

"How many females in here are on your dick?" Leilani asked

"Hopefully more than I think," he chuckled as he bobbed his head to the bass. Tonight, Isaiah had planned on enjoying the company of fine women along with the finest alcohol the club had to offer. He was already feeling the effects of the Kush he had smoked prior to the club. Usually, he wouldn't get carried away in public, as he knew he was an easy target for a nigga to come up. But tonight, he was with Leilani so he knew he could get lifted and Leilani would ensure nothing would happen to him.

"Do you know that I love you?" Isaiah admitted.

"Wait, you haven't even started drinking yet; are you ok?"

"Yea, I am fine. I just wanted you to know," he replied as he eyed the waitress heading over to their booth with his Ace and Leilani's cup of water.

"Here you go Isaiah." The waitress bent over in front of Isaiah, giving him a clear view up her mini skirt. Instantly, Leilani snickered at the young woman's desperate attempts on Isaiah.

"These thirsty ass females I swear," Leilani replied as she placed a straw in her cup of water. She knew how women overreacted when it came down to Isaiah. Their behavior was comical to her, as she knew what his real motives were. Isaiah was ready to settle down but not with any of the females that spent their lives in the clubs. She knew that Isaiah was waiting for the perfect person to dedicate his life to. It was no secret that Isaiah and Essence had a connection that was undeniable. Any stranger viewing the two would be able to admit that the connection was evident. But both Isaiah and Essence were afraid to speak on that connection. Their love was forbidden as Essence remained in a committed relationship with her boyfriend of eight years.

"Hey, if these females wanna be thirsty then I got just what they are looking for."

"Oh, really what is that exactly?"

"A bi—"

"Never mind I do not need to know anymore," she replied, hoping to rid her mind of the concept of Isaiah in a sexual manner.

"Fine, but I know who might spark your interest."

"Who?"

Leilani considered his eyes as his finger pointed in the direction of his referral. An eccentric sensation overcame her as she felt the glare of someone burning a whole into her back. She looked up, meeting Sincere's warm eyes peering back at her. Time ceased before them, as they became the only two in the club. So many things were exchanged between the two without any words escaping their lips. Her body became warm with his eyes fixated on her. She didn't know why, but her feelings for Sincere were beginning to flourish. The sound of bickering brought them back to reality.

"Excuse me, I know you not eye-fucking some bitch while I am standing right here," Sincere's date rambled.

Sincere opted with not addressing her as he greeted Isaiah. He gave his business partner a dab and then focused his eyes back on Leilani. He gave her a head nod, acknowledging her presence. *Later I will address that connection we shared,* he told himself. Her face remained straight as she returned the gesture. Neither of them spoke to each other as Sincere found his spot on the couch along with his date, Rena. Unbothered, Leilani sat next to Sincere sipping her water.

"What you are drinking?" he asked.

"Water."

"Why?"

"Because I do not drink," she admitted.

She placed her drink down on the table as she gyrated on the couch. The club was packed to capacity with all types of New Yorkers. People were hyped up, ready for what the night had to offer. It was only a Friday night and Leilani was surprised at how packed the establishment was with working people. Their bodies gyrated to the vibrant beat of Drake, not concerned about what tomorrow brings. Leilani sat on the couch, chuckling on the behavior of the partygoers. She had no choice but to respect their moves as they were enjoying themselves the best way they could.

"La, come on, Don wants to see you in his office," Isaiah whispered in her ear, interrupting her.

"For what?"

"Business," he replied as he took her hand into his, leading her through the packed club. The smell of sweat penetrated her nostrils as she maneuvered her way through the throng of intoxicated people.

Isaiah led her to the back of the club, where Don's office was located. Before they entered Isaiah knocked five times, signaling his presence. They entered once their knock was approved. Thick clouds hoovered in the air as an older Spanish man sat behind his desk, puffing on his Cuban cigar. The smell of the finest tobacco was intoxicating as Leilani could feel herself becoming light-headed.

"You must be the woman who has taken care of all of our problems," he replied as he stood up. His older features resembled those of a character from a gangster movie. Don's full black hair remained slicked back with not a single grey strand adorning his scalp. His fingers were laced with the finest gold mankind had to offer while the fabric that cradled his skin had designer names imprinted on the tags. There was no denying, the man was rich.

"You must be Leilani," he spoke as he took her hand into his, planting a light kiss against her flesh.

"You are?" she questioned.

"Please forgive me, I am Don; I am your brother's business partner," she'd heard the man's name several times but never actually had the chance to meet him with both of their schedules always conflicting. *Finally, I can put a name to a face*, she thought.

A smile crept onto Don's face. The woman before him didn't only possess beauty but she was also smart as hell. There were several times when he was in need for a person to take care of his problems. Isaiah had vouched for Leilani, explaining that she was the perfect person for the job. Believing in Isaiah, Don took a chance which he till that day never regretted. In his eyes, Leilani was perfect and just what they needed to fulfill their team. Don had spent years in the game, gaining the expertise and wisdom of a pro. His soul bled a formula that was completely different from blood. His arteries pumped a liquid that only the streets could create. Don was classified as an OG, not because of all the savagery the game put into him, but because of all the savagery he put into the game.

"When Isaiah told me that his sister would be able to handle the weight, I have to admit I did have my doubts. But you, young lady, have proved me wrong every time."

"Well I was taught by the best," Leilani replied.

"Yes, you were," Don replied. "Now that the Castra problem has been handled, we can proceed with making our money."

"How was Castra even stopping the money train?" Leilani asked.

"Well, the fucker held control of New York's pipeline. Since we want the Supremes to be the biggest organization ever, we need full control over our territories."

"He was dealt with."

"And I appreciate what you've done for your team," he replied, pulling Leilani into a tight embrace.

"Well you put me in charge for a reason, right?"

"Yes, I did make the right decision," he responded, displaying his perfectly white teeth. "Now I have three million for you. When you leave tonight, my guy Tim will escort the money to your car."

"Ok."

"I hope you enjoy being a part of the winning team. But I must warn you, some of the older heads who have been working with me for donkey years may have a problem with your position within the organization, and they will test you."

"That's ok Don, just as long as you are aware that I have no control over how I will deal with the matter. You may end up with a couple of dead bodies on your hand."

Staring into her grey eyes, Don was happy with the way she handled things. For some reason, he had a feeling that working with her wouldn't be as difficult as he thought it would have been. *Placing her in charge was a good idea.*

CHAPTER 4

The sun gleamed down on her golden skin as she sat before both Essence and Candy awaiting the arrival of their food. It was part of their usual routine to get together and enjoy brunch. Despite being coworkers, the trio were great friends.

"Candy, how's the pregnancy going so far?" Leilani asked as she sipped her water.

"Morning sickness is a bitch."

"Tell me about it. When I was pregnant with Emery that little girl gave me the worst morning sickness ever," Essence replied.

"I remember, but this little bugger is really kicking my ass."

"Well, just remember to stay away from all that caffeine. I know how your butt loves some soda," Leilani stated.

The girls conversed amongst themselves, catching up on any missed details since their last encounter at the nail salon. It had been three weeks since they had last spoken to one another, which was odd for the group of women.

"So, La, that night we had the dinner what happened?" Candy asked.

"What are you talking about?"

"Well I was hosting a dinner and I told you about it the day we did our nails. You never came nor did you call to tell us something came up."

"I'm sorry, things just have been a little crazy that's all."

"Really?"

"Yes."

Candy stared at Leilani, silently judging her decision to lie. She knew her good friend was not being truthful with them, and she wanted to get to the bottom of the situation. Picking up her glass of cold water, Candy placed her lips around the straw, pulling the liquid into her mouth. While she drank the water her eyes never left her friend's emotionless face.

"So, La, I'mma ask you one more time," Candy said. "What happened that night we had dinner?"

"And like I told you Candy, something came up."

"That's interesting because Keisha told me that she saw you at some club with some guys."

"Ok, and?"

"And my fucking point is, you have the audacity to go out to the club instead of having dinner with your girls," Candy yelled. "Wait, let me correct that, with your fucking family?"

The commotion gathered the attention of the other guests that sat in the restaurant. It was obvious that the tension between the two women was thick. The other customers glared on, anticipating an altercation.

"First off, lower your fucking voice before you have one of these motherfuckers kick us out of this god damn restaurant. Second, I wasn't out clubbing, I was actually in a meeting with someone discussing business."

"At a fucking club?"

"Yes nigga, at a fucking club," Leilani replied calmly. Her nerves were messing with her as she itched to punch Candy in her mouth. She desperately wanted to but thought against it. *She's with child; I can't do that, especially because she's my friend. If I explain the reasoning behind the meeting then maybe this would calm down the whole situation.* "The meeting I had last night was with the leader Don of the Supreme. He wanted to talk to me about joining his operation as the head of the cleaning department."

"You turned it down, right?" Candy asked.

"No, why the hell would I do such a thing?"

"Wait, hold the fuck up, so you basically said fuck us and decided to do your own thing?"

"What the fuck are you talking about?" Essence asked, clearly confused. "If you would shut the fuck up and stop assuming shit, then La could finish telling us her good news."

"There isn't any fucking good news; were you not listening? Leilani said fuck us and decided to do her own thing."

"Candy what the fuck are you talking about?" Leilani asked, annoyed with Candy's behavior.

"I am talking about you being fake, basically taking the position without coming to see if me and Essence were cool with it. This is fucking bullshit, I swear; all I ever do is work for your ass. This shit ain't no fucking teamwork. It's clear who the fucking boss is, and it ain't me or Essence," Candy replied. She grabbed her belongings and stormed out of the restaurant. Highly irritated with the exchange of events, she got into her car, slamming the door shut.

"Bitch reaping all of the benefits of my hard-fucking work, not once did she ever come to me about my opinion on what business we do," Candy said to herself. Seething with anger, she placed the key into the ignition, turning the car on. The roaring sound of the engine filled the parking lot as the lean machine became alive. Not caring about warming the car up, Candy placed the vehicle into drive speeding into traffic.

"How the fuck you just gonna pull some shit like that?"

Feeling the anger within her threatening to boil over, Candy needed to calm herself down as she was driving. She couldn't afford to be in an accident risking the life of her and her unborn child. *I will not risk my life for that female,* she thought, focusing her mind on the road. It wasn't long before Candy arrived at her house, pulling her hundred-thousand-dollar car into the driveway. Shutting the car off, she took a deep breath, inhaling the fresh air that entered through the cracked window.

"Relax, everything will work out," she persuaded herself. "Yes, it will."

Grabbing her purse from the passenger seat, Candy exited her car allowing her Gucci sandal heels to hit the concrete floor. Sliding out of the car seat, Candy could feel a light pressure on her uterus. The whole pregnancy thing she was getting accustomed to as she placed her hand on the lower part of her abdomen.

"Goodness, I really hope this baby don't blow me out of shape."

Slowly she walked up her brick stairs until she came to her gated front door. Unlocking the locks, and entering her home, she finally felt at ease. The tension she felt earlier came off as she unbuckled her heels, releasing her foot from the restraints of the designer shoes. *Thank god, I am home,* she thought as she turned to lock her front door. Her eyes were caught by the sight of her welcome home mat. A black smudge rested in her white furry welcome home mat. She knew for sure that her designer heels didn't leave such a mark. Immediately paranoid, she dug into her purse pulling out her Sig Sauer P938 - 9mm. *Today is the perfect day for someone to get their head blown,* she thought as she silently maneuvered through her home, peeking for an intruder. *Come on you fucker, where are you?* The cold wooden floor felt weird against her foot as the adrenaline rushed through her body. She didn't know what it was, but for some reason she was nervous about having an intruder. Her thoughts were interrupted by the sound of crunching. Instantly her ears peaked at the sound. *The sound is coming from the kitchen.* Using her thoughts to guide her, she slowly walked into the kitchen expecting the unexpected. Aiming her pistol in front of her face, she creeped into the kitchen surprised to see what was before her.

"Babe?" she said, surprised with his appearance.

"Girl, what the fuck?" His eyes bulged at the sight of her 9mm.

"Listen, I thought you were an intruder," she replied, placing the 9mm in the small of her back.

"Really, you were going to shoot me?"

"Hey, just be glad I am not a trigger-happy person."

He stared at her with his mouth a gape. He was aware of her choice of profession but still, it took him a while to grow accustomed to being with a hit woman. Her gun toting behavior wasn't what he was used to seeing in a female. Growing up, he learned about the role a woman was supposed to play in a man's life. His mother installed into his brain the behaviors of a woman, and Candy was everything that his mother told him to avoid. Despite his mother's warnings, Ghost still found himself in bliss with the spawn of Satan. Glaring at her, Ghost knew exactly why he was so wrapped up in Candy. *She is one bad ass woman.* Her chocolate skin complexion glistened with perspiration as her adrenaline began to die down. Licking his lips, he loved the sight before him.

"Why the hell you are staring at me like that?" she questioned.

"Nothing," he replied as he walked over to her with his hands out. "I just really missed you."

Wrapping her in his arms, he placed light kisses on her neck. The smell of her sweat mixed in with her perfume tickled his nose. He loved the natural scent as he could feel his friend swelling at attention. He needed to get in her or else he would lose his mind.

"Bend over that counter," he told her.

"What?"

"You heard me; bend over that counter," he replied with more bass in his voice. Doing as he asked, Candy walked over to the white counter, bending over. Forcefully, Ghost ripped her skirt down, not caring about his roughness. The feeling of her silky skin against his palm was different. Placing light kisses on her thigh he allowed them to trail until he reached her mound. *This is going to get interesting,* he thought to himself.

"Be ready baby."

******

"La, don't worry about that heffa; her hormones are probably raging," Essence said as she took a sip of her drink.

"She's lucky I care for her because if she was some regular bitch, I think I would have had her ass buried by now," Leilani replied, trying to calm her nerves. It was the first time anyone had ever gotten away with talking out their neck, and Leilani was confused on how to react. Her first instinct was to jump over the table, choking the shit out of Candy. The amount of years Leilani had known Candy, she'd never experienced this form of anger. *All this bitch's decisions are immature, she never cares about anyone but her fucking self,* Leilani reasoned.

"I wanna choke that bitch so bad."

"Whatever you do La, just know I am down till the last piece of dirt settles."

"And you know I will ride with you till death do us part."

"Got that shit right," Essence boosted, proud of the connection that the two established throughout the years. It was hard to find a female friend that would remain loyal throughout the years of a friendship. "What you going to do after this?"

"Well, after this it's a meeting with the guys about business; would you like to join me?"

"I don't know La, you're the one they wanted."

"Ok and you're the one I want to be my right hand. Why shouldn't you be there?"

"Because I don't think I should."

"You are a fucking fronter. The only reason why you don't want to go is because you know Isaiah is going to be there," Leilani replied as she watched her best friend blush at the name of her secret crush.

"Alright fine. I don't want to go because I feel as if I do go then it's just like putting gas into an open flame."

"In a damn meeting?"

"That nigga is fine as shit," Essence replied. "Wherever, whenever, that fine piece of wine can get it."

Leilani doubled over in laughter, finding Essence's rachetness to be amusing. The relationship that Essence and Isaiah had was weird, but Leilani knew deep down in her heart that the two would be together creating something so great. They had the ability to be the next Beyoncé and Jay-Z, minus the lemonade drama. Believing in their true love, Leilani had plans to make their relationship work, getting rid of their unnecessary baggage.

"Don't worry Essie, I will get y'all together because I need to see you happy."

"I am happy."

"Bitch don't fucking lie to me. I know you being with that piece of shit is putting a toll on you."

"I am fine La."

"Listen Essie, I love you very much; I really do. You are one of the few people that I trust with my life. So, believe me when I say this: whatever decision you make, whether it is to be with Isaiah or stay with Nick, I fully support it. If you want to remain single for the rest of your life, girl I will support it. Shit, if you decide that you're into females too, I fully support you on whatever you decide. Just if you're happy. I don't care.

"I appreciate you La."

"I know you do." Leilani smiled. "Now, let's go because I am gonna be late for this meeting."

"Wait, quick question La."

"Wassup?" Leilani asked as she looked up from her purse.

"What's up with you and that guy Sincere?"

"Ain't shit going on between us."

"You need to stop fucking around and put your paw print on that man."

"Really?" Leilani stared at Essence confused on her analogy. "Really, my paw print?"

"Duh girl, like the lion and shit," she replied, imitating a lion roar.

"Essence, I will definitely be praying for your crazy ass," Leilani replied, as she began to take out her credit card to pay for their food.

"Girl put away that damn card; I got brunch."

"You sure?"

"I got this shawty," Essence replied, as she waved her hand in effort of getting the attention of the waitress. Once she could pay for everything, both girls prepared to go their separate ways.

"I will call you later," Leilani replied, as she got into her Dodge Charger.

"Alright La."

Sitting in her car, she waited patiently until Essence pulled out of the parking lot before she left. The Brooklyn weather had cooled down a lot, and Leilani was thankful for the October weather. A cool breeze blew through her window as she drove to her next destination. August Alsina's smooth voice snaked through the speakers, causing goose bumps to elevate on her forearm. The way he sang was intense yet enticing, blending well with Jeremih.

"I'll hold you down," she sang.

The song blared from the speakers as she pulled up in front of the Italian restaurant that she was instructed to come to. She parked her car, getting out with her Givenchy sunglasses blocking the bright sun from penetrating her eyes. Despite the weather cooling down, the sun still illuminated, blurring her vision. "Hi ma'am, reservation for one?" the waitress asked with a faint smile. "Last name please."

"Don," Leilani replied as she was instructed to do.

"Ok, I will direct you to your table."

The waitress sat the menu's down and began the journey to where the meeting was being held. Leilani followed right behind the thin woman as she led her to the back of the restaurant. It seemed as if the duo were going through a maze, as they were making several turns until they finally entered an office. The waitress turned around, facing Leilani. A bright smile was plastered on the woman's caramel face. Her smile was bright and cheerful as the chaos called life had not decapitated her soul yet. The freckles that were sprinkled against her face caught Leilani's attention as they smiled back at her. They were small and almost unnoticeable, but Leilani found beauty in the waitress' insecurity. It was odd, to see someone in such a merry mood when the world was corrupted. *You look like a Madison*, Leilani thought, *a carefree, young, vibrant girl. Only a Madison would be this cheery when there are people on Utica Ave dying with a needle attached to their arm.* It was then that Leilani finally stared at her name tag. *Stacy?* she thought, *you don't even look like a Stacy. Stacy is more of a seductive mistress, maybe.*

"I'm sorry about this, but before you enter the lift it is required that I must search you."

"Sure, but I do have a glock on me," Leilani admitted.

"Ok, please remove all bullets and take the bullet out of the chamber."

Leilani did as the waitress had asked, pulling out her glock from the small of her back. The joyous smile that was once on her face perished at the sight of the cold steel. Her eyes remained fixated on the glock as she wondered how many lives had ended with the tool before her. Stacy, the once carefree waitress, was hit with reality of how harsh the world could be. Leilani observed the depleted look as she continued the process of removing the bullets.

"First time?"

"Huh?"

"Is this your first time seeing a gun up close?"

"Being honest, yes."

"If you plan on working this route then you need to get used to seeing this."

"I'm trying; this is all too new to me," the waitress stated as she began the body search, running her hands through the fine fabric that adorned Leilani's body. Diverting her attention from being searched, Leilani's eyes analyzed the office. The gloomy feeling of work lingered throughout the space. Papers lay scattered on the mahogany desk. The desk name plate sat upright, gleaming the name of the owner, *Don*. Leilani looked around the space in search of any pictures that would confirm the name plate but nothing came up. *Shit, maybe it's a decoy.* The body search ceased as Stacy verified that Leilani was clean.

"Mrs.?"

"Ms. Leilani Vasquez," Leilani responded.

"I am sorry Ms. Vasquez, just follow me and I'll take you to the meeting," Stacy informed as she smiled. The smile seemed tainted with reality, Leilani observed. The freckles that sat on her face no longer danced to her joyful smile. Fear replaced the joy as she now knew who the woman was before her. Leilani Vasquez put fear into her heart as she replayed the conversation she eavesdropped into. Stacy had overheard Don and Isaiah discussing the details of a hitman's contract.

The brutality that the woman had used scared the normality out of Stacy's heart. Heart palpitations began, causing her palms to sweat. *Leilani Vasquez*, the name rang throughout her head, spinning the wheels. *This woman has killed people with her bare hands.*

"Don't worry, I am not that dangerous," Leilani responded as she saw the scared look in her eye.

"I am sorry."

"Stop apologizing Stacy. I am a regular person just like you." The waitress took in the sincerity as she proceeded on their journey. Their destination resided in the basement of the establishment. The only access that lead to the basement was the hidden lift that was behind the book casing. Following the strict instructions that were given to her by Don, Stacy pushed open the book casing revealing the private lift. Leilani watched on in pure confusion.

"The meeting is being held in the basement," the waitress replied, acknowledging her confusion. Leilani followed Stacy's lead as they both got onto the lift. The sound of the creaking metal descending echoed, leaving an aching sensation in the duo's ears. Once it came to a stop, they got off, entering the dimly lit alley. The nauseating smell of a foul odor assaulted their nostrils causing Stacy to almost gag. Leilani recognized the familiar scent as she had been in the business for a long time. A body was beginning to decompose within the vicinity; it wasn't harsh, so she knew the body was fresh.

"This is our stop," Stacy said as they both stopped in front of a metal door. Using her key, Stacy opened the door granting Leilani access into the meeting room. Dozens of eyes stared back at her as

Leilani stood by the door like an outcast. Silence washed over the once chatty group of men as they tried to figure out how the women gained access into this part.

"Leilani, I am so happy you could join us. Don said, breaking the awful silence. Leilani looked around the room noticing that she was the only female in attendance. Their menacing glares burned a hole into her forehead. They wanted to read her in hopes of learning the reason as to why she was present.

"Please Leilani, take a seat next to me," Don said as he guided her towards the available seat next to him. "Let me give a quick introduction: the men around the table are the street bosses, they run the day-to-day operations of the organization." Quickly he went around the room, introducing the men to Leilani.

"Now let's get back to business. What we were discussing again?" Don questioned.

"We were discussing the new drop off days and pay day," Sincere replied.

"Right, the new dates for drop offs will now be on Fridays instead of Sundays. Pay date has also changed to Friday. Now I will only say this once: now that we are growing in numbers I will be accommodating our growing family with new shops throughout the five boroughs. There will be no need for us to fight over territory as everyone will have a position within the organization." Don paused as he took a sip of his water, clearing his throat. "Great things will be happening within our team, and I want all of us to work together to accomplish a goal. I want to conquer the whole drug trade throughout America. I want my hand in any and everything that pertains to the

drug world. To accomplish this goal, I've decided to split the Supremes into three separate categories. There are three major components to running a drug organization, which consist of drugs, money, and murder. I will be dividing the crew into these three components. The drugs enterprise will be run by me and Isaiah. The money component will be run by Sincere, and finally the murder component will be run by the newest member of the team, Leilani."

Everyone's attention became directed on Leilani as they were all confused on what was going on. An awkward silence fell upon the meeting room as everyone tried their best to digest the news of a female running a part of their organization.

"Whose idea was it to have this girl running the team?" a thick Italian accent broke through the silence. Leilani focused her attention onto the voice that spoke. The first thing that caught her eye was his Hulk Hogan horseshoe shaped mustache. She found it creepy to see this grown ass man with a horseshoe of hair barricading his lips. The style reminded her of a pervert who lived during the 70s.

"Well Toro, if you must know, Leilani has been handling all of our hits privately with her crew. Time and time again she has proved to us that she was worthy of the role. So, it was only right that we make her a partner."

"There are components in this game which include selling the drugs, murder, and legitimate business. We have decided that it would be best to break up these components, giving each board member their own individual section. Don, along with myself, will take over selling the product and Sincere will take the position of the legitimate business. Leilani will be the muscle of our team as she will do all of our hits and take care of anything that requires violence," Isaiah spoke, explaining their plan.

"So, you guys think this little girl is best to run a murder team besides one of us?" Toro complained. His brow furrowed in anger as the concept of Leilani being at a higher ranking didn't settle well with him. Toro had been a part of the Supremes before it became known as the Supremes. He joined the populated organization when it only consisted of full-blooded Italians that abided by the strict mob rules. Toro had supported Don in every decision he had made, including the time Don and the mob had a huge issue. He was always there for Don, but today something clicked in his head. He felt betrayed by his own friend, as he felt that his loyalty should be rewarded with some form of reign over the organization.

"Well, Toro, actually she's perfect for the role," Sincere vouched.

"You shut the fuck up," Toro yelled as he pointed his chunky finger directly in Sincere's direction. "I allowed Don to hire you despite your being a negro, but hiring a bitch is something I cannot go for. For her to have control, or have some power, is considered disrespectful within our Italian tradition."

The room began to get warm as Leilani could feel her blood simmering underneath her skin. Being called out of her name was one of her biggest pet peeves. She hated being degraded by anyone, especially someone who had no idea who she was. Isaiah stared at her, noticing the red hue that glowed through her skin. She was getting aggravated, and Isaiah knew that soon she would paint the walls red.

"I will let you slide with your disrespect, but it will not happen again. The next time you utter the word bitch regarding me, I will have the morgue toe tagging your ass as another John Doe," Leilani's words dripped with a form of silent violence that scared the guys. Her voice was calm, never once rising. The room remained quiet, leaving an eerie feeling amongst the group. Leilani didn't want to ruin the atmosphere, but Toro had tested her. She knew that she would have to use her actions instead of words as Toro stared back at her with resentment. *Don't worry, I got something for you that will fix that cock eye you have,* Leilani thought.

"Now that you guys have met Leilani, it is time to talk about our plans," Isaiah replied. "We plan on extending our territory all over the world. Over the next couple of months, we will sit with various drug kingpins throughout the United States. We want the Supremes to be involved in every drug ring. It doesn't matter how we are involved, we just want a percentage out of every city," Isaiah spoke while eyeing the room.

Taking over various territories throughout the United States was just the beginning of the Supremes' plans. They had plans on conquering the whole world, including politically and judicially. The concept of controlling the world may have seemed delusional, but they were willing to try and succeed with this mission. Throughout the meeting, the leaders, Sincere, Don, Isaiah, and Leilani discussed with their workers what needed to be done. By the time the meeting ended, Leilani was tired and hungry.

"Princess, what would you like for dinner?" Sincere asked as they eyed the waitress standing before them ready to take their order.

"I'll take the chicken Marsala with pasta," she replied. The guys placed their order and resumed their talking. It was only the four of them in the meeting room now, as their conversation filled the air.

"So, our first family trip will take place in Georgia and after we will be making our way to Miami to visit Drug Kingpin Harley, who runs the Trey Pound," Isaiah said as he scanned through the file before him.

"So, we are going to Georgia?" Leilani asked.

"Yes, we are."

"When?"

"It will be either the end of this week or next week; which one is better for you La?" Isaiah asked.

"I am down for whenever."

"Good, we will go this Saturday," Don clarified.

The four discussed their options on approaching the drug kingpins that ran Georgia and Miami. Leilani was handed his file and she read it as if it were her bible. She took her time reading each sentence word for word. She had a tendency of wanting to know the whole background on her targets. Harley wasn't any different. Despite never meeting him, Leilani wanted to be able to recite all his likings and dislikes. Once she was finished reading his file, she analyzed his photo that was attached to the file. He was attractive, as he resembled the singer Trey Songz, but in a much more thuggish version.

“Do they need to be killed?” Leilani asked.

“No, I don’t think we need to. The plan is to basically allow him to continue running his spot, but we want a 25% cut from his profits. If he declines, then we offer to supply him with our product as I am the connect. If he denies both options, then we kill him,” Don answered.

“I don’t think that’s really much of a good idea. Who cares?” she stated as she stared at all three men. “If a nigga came to you talking about wanting a percentage, Isaiah what would be your reaction?” she asked.

“Kill him for stepping to me.”

“Exactly, so instead of doing that, why not hit them where it hurts? We attack their money supply first. We start with the petals of the flower, which is his home. Then it’s the stem; we start killing his soldiers in a bulk. When we meet with him, that’s when we give the proposition. We can either continue down the flower until we get to the root, which is his connect, or he gives us a 25% cut from his profit.” The guys stared at her as she took a sip from her wine glass that contained water. Her plan was pure genius. Despite it having more work than their original plan, her idea made much more sense. “The only thing is, this isn’t a plan that can be executed in a day. We need to send some men out there to be a menace to their organization. So, about a week before we leave, we need to have our men out there to fuck with them. It’s a lot of work, but it will get the job done.”

“You smart, you loyal,” Sincere began as he imitated Dj Khaled in the music video “Hold you down.” Leilani let out a chuckle, realizing that Sincere was such a jerk at times.

"So, do you guys think it's a good idea?" she asked.

"It's the perfect idea," Don replied. "Thank God we chose you and not Toro."

"Best decision you guys have ever made," Leilani replied. Their conversation continued over dinner. Leilani enjoyed the company of the guys, as they didn't treat her differently because of her gender. The guys embraced her presence, never making her feel out of the loop.

CHAPTER 5

February 1998

The sweet sound of Next played throughout the hair salon. Love was the main topic of discussion as women throughout the shop couldn't help but to be enticed with the romantic holiday. Roselyn sat perfectly in her chair as she conversed with a couple of females who sat waiting to get their hair done. It had been a couple of months since Roselyn had quit her job working as a beautician at Cheryl's shop. She had returned to the salon so she could gloat about her new relationship to a hood star. Lost within her conversation with one of her old customers, she barely felt the light taps on her forearm until she was notified by the person she was talking to.

"What Lei?" she asked as she turned to face her daughter.

"Mommy, can I please get a bag of chips?" her ten-year-old daughter asked.

"No, I am almost finished with my hair. Once I am done, then I will get you something to eat," she replied, glaring at her blossoming little girl. Her grey eyes gleamed with innocence that was pure. Roselyn had spent years searching for a love that was pure and real in men that saw nothing in her but a quick fuck. The little girl that stood before her loved

her unconditionally. Leilani saw her mother as a queen that was captured within the grasp of the ghetto. Roselyn was Leilani's ghetto queen. The two stared within each other's eyes for a moment, both carrying different gazes. Leilani's gaze was nothing but adoration while Roselyn glared back with a sense of hate. Just as she was about to say something, the shop doors swung open as every female directed their attention to the male figure that walked in. Instantly, panties began to get soaked as the male attraction made his way over to Roselyn.

"What's up baby?" he said as he placed a light peck on her cheek.

"Nothing babe, just waiting for Cheryl to blow my hair out."

"Tryna look good for your nigga?" he replied as he began to finger his chin hair. All eyes were on them but mostly on Rocky, as the females in the shop yearned for his attention. Rocky stood 6'2 without an ounce of fat on his body. Every cut on his body had been worked on in the gym for countless hours. He easily resembled the actor Laz Alonso, as he displayed his Afro-Cuban descent.

"Yes papi, only for you."

A hint of lust glistened in his eyes as he stared into the face of his girlfriend. There was something about her that really held his attention, as he was used to sleeping with females and discarding them. It was safe to say that he was slowly falling for Roselyn. He'd changed his everyday routine to accommodate the duo.

"Lei, why didn't you get your hair done?" Rocky asked.

"Mommy said I didn't need to have it done," she replied as she fiddled with her thumb.

He stared at the curly hair that rested on top of her head in a sloppy ponytail. He never judged anyone's kids based off their looks, as he feared karma retaliating on his own kids. But the little girl before him was going to grow up breaking the hearts of anyone she encountered.

"Rose, why you ain't let my shawty get her hair done?"

"Because it would be a waste of money; her hair would not last."

"That's quite fine, I will pay for it," Rocky replied as he dug into his pocket, pulling out a thick wad of hundreds. "Marisol, come hook my shawty up," he yelled, calling Cheryl by the wrong name.

"But papi, my hair is almost done. Who is gonna stay here and wait for her to finish her hair?" Roselyn questioned. "I have things to do."

"Then go get your shit done. I'll stay here with her since you got better things to do."

Just like that, Rocky sat down in the black leather chair as he waited for Leilani. When Roselyn had finished getting her hair blown out, she stood before Rocky, anticipating him to leave with her. But like he had said earlier, he was going to stay with Leilani, and that's exactly what he did.

"Nah, I already told you that I'mma stay with baby girl."

Annoyed with his response, Roselyn stomped her way out of the shop as the females chuckled at her childish behavior. Unconcerned, Rocky sat in his chair patiently waiting for Cheryl to finish with Leilani's hair. He didn't care for the time that he spent waiting if the result placed a smile on Leilani's face. An hour and a half later, Leilani's hair was blown out and wrapped neatly. Handing over two large bills to Cheryl, Rocky thanked her for working on Leilani and then left the shop.

"Thank you so much Rocky. I love my hair," Leilani said as she

wrapped her thin arms around his waist. He hugged her back, staring into her beaming face. A burning sensation entered his chest. He didn't understand what was going on with his body, as he wasn't under any stress. He was happy about being in the presence of the little girl. Not thinking much on it, he walked over to his BMW 3 series, opening the passenger side for her. Once she was secured in, he walked over to the driver side getting in.

"How's school?" he asked to make conversation.

"Oh, it's good," she replied. Leilani began to talk about all the new things she had learned in class. For the first time in his life, Rocky listened attentively as the bright young girl reasoned as to why she would no longer be celebrating Thanksgiving.

"So, what you mean to tell me is this Thanksgiving you won't be eating any turkey?"

"No sir."

"Do you honestly think you will be able to resist your mom's good cooking?"

"Yea, I'll be fine. She doesn't cook."

The more he spoke to the young girl the more he became intrigued with her. Once he pulled the car up in front of her building, he honestly didn't want to stop talking with her. He parked the car, shutting off the purring engine. He then faced Leilani as he placed his massive hands on her thin thighs. Softly, he rubbed his hand up and down her thigh. The feeling of the soft fabric against his skin gave him goosebumps.

"Rocky, you're making me uncomfortable."

"Oh, my fault lil" mama. Go upstairs and tell your mother to be ready by 8," he replied, as he snatched his hands away from her thigh. Nervously, Leilani exited the car, making her way into her apartment building. The stench of urine violated her nostrils, almost blinding her on her journey into her apartment building. Don't breathe, she thought as her feet quickly jogged up to the third floor. Once she entered the hallway of her floor, she exhaled, releasing the air that was held restrained in her lungs. She walked to the front door of her apartment, using her keys to unlock the door. A weary feeling washed over her as the heavy door slammed shut.

"Leilani, bring your stupid ass into my room now," her mother yelled.

Immediately Leilani found her way into her mother's room. The thick cigarette smoke clouded the room, making it hard to see. Despite being blinded, Leilani could see her mother clear as day. She stood by the entrance of the door mesmerized by the beauty of the woman who birthed her. Her mother held a very close resemblance to the Hispanic actress Jessica Pimentel. The two carried the same rich skin complexion that was adorned by voluminous thick hair. There was no denying that Roselyn was a beautiful woman on the outside, but on the inside, she was colder than Hitler himself.

"What happened when I left the hair salon?" she asked as she pulled in all the nicotine from the cancer stick.

"Nothing Mommy. Marisol blow dried my hair an—"

"I am not talking about no fucking Marisol stupid; I meant with Rocky," she interrupted. "What the fuck was he doing there while you

were getting your hair done?"

"Nothing Mommy. He sat there and just waited until I was done with my hair," Leilani replied.

Silently, she puffed on the cigarette as her mind began running with a whole bunch of scenarios. ***Why did he wanna stay with her?*** *Rose questioned in her head. The more she thought about it, the angrier she became, as the thought of another female taking her time away was etched into her head.*

"So, you want to steal my man?" Rose questioned.

"What?" Leilani asked surprised.

"That's the only thing that makes sense; you want my fucking man," she replied, as she inched closer to Leilani with the cigarette light burning a hue of orange.

"No."

"Yes, you fucking do. Then why else would he be willing to pay for your hair?" she yelled as she grabbed Leilani by her arm, bringing her closer to her. It was as if a light was switched on, as Rose's mind became bombarded with the thought of her daughter trying to steal her man. Raging with anger, Rose smashed the lit cigarette on Leilani's arm, burning her flesh. A gut-wrenching scream left Leilani's lips as the sensation of the burning stick melted a circle into her skin.

"This should fucking warn you to keep your fucking legs closed," Rose yelled as she tossed a crying Leilani onto the cold, wooden floor. "Stop them fucking tears or else I will give you something to really cry about."

Rose stared down at her tearful daughter without an ounce of regret for her actions. ***If I don't do it now, then some other bitch will do it later in the future,*** *Rose explained in her head.*

"Maybe that will teach your fast ass to stay away from him," she yelled as she walked out of the room in pursuit of getting ready for her date with Rocky.

******

"Ms. Vasquez, Mr. Moretti would like to see you now," the secretary said, snapping Leilani out of her thoughts. *The thoughts are starting up again,* she thought. For the past decade, Leilani had done her best to force those thoughts of her troubled past deep within a portion of her brain that she wouldn't be able to access. Lately, the truth of her past was beginning to resurface, which petrified her.

Leilani followed right behind the petite secretary, with her eyes focused on the screen of her iPhone. A notification alerted her that she had an unread message. Sliding her finger across the screen, her eyes quickly read Isaiah's text message. *What the fuck does this nigga want?* she thought. It wasn't even the afternoon and Leilani could feel herself becoming agitated. Her schedule for the day was jam packed with tons of stuff.

Busy? he texted.

What could he possible want? Her fingers tapped lightly against the smartphone's screen as she typed her reply.

"Mr. Moretti, Ms. Vasquez," the secretary said, making the client's presence known.

The young lawyer looked up, making eye contact with his

favorite client. His eyes were the color of deep sienna, reassuring but filled with mischief. He reminded Leilani of the Brooklyn actor Jerry Ferrara. Both of their Italian genes were strong, almost making the two identical. She told him about the resemblance every chance she had.

"Leilani, it's nice seeing you two times in a row," he said as he pulled out a chair for her to sit in.

"I know. It's good if we are both busy."

"Yes, it is," he responded, taking a seat behind his desk. "I was contacted by the record label's lawyers; they have written up the contract. I have gone over it and everything is in order. All I need for you to do is sign it."

He handed her the contract, allowing her to go over what her potential partner was offering her. Her lips spread into a smile as her eyes danced along the Times New Roman font. Once she approved of the contract, her lawyer handed her a pen.

"Do you really think this is a good decision?" she asked him. She valued his opinion, knowing that he would be completely honest with her. The two had a relationship that wasn't unusual for a lawyer and his client. John Moretti knew all about Leilani's illegal activities, including her new business decision to join the Supremes. He was aware, making sure that every decision she made, she was well protected legally.

"Well La, the company is facing bankruptcy so it could either be two things: either you make tons of money off the deal, or you could lose everything trying to revive this music label. I think you should take the chance."

"Oh, what the hell. Scared money doesn't make no money," she replied as she inked her signature onto the paper. "If they screw me over, I'll just kill them."

They both laughed at Leilani's statement, knowing that she was serious about killing her new business partner. She had invested five million into the company, which was mostly everything in her savings account. She was playing Russian roulette with her money, which caused her to break a light sweat. *Everything will work out,* she persuaded herself. *You made the right choice.*

******

The bright sun glared above the neighborhood, shedding light on the perfectly cemented sidewalk. This neighborhood was different from the poverty riddled community Leilani grew up in. Souls filled with ambition walked in the community as they had an agenda ahead of them. Leilani grew up in an environment where drugs fueled their waking moment. The neighborhood allowed Leilani to picture what life could have been like had she experienced a different life. Sitting in front of the flawless sculpted homes had become a routine over the years for Leilani.

The door to the house opened as the woman in all black walked out with a taller, handsome young man following right behind her. The woman's voice was stern as she spoke to the teenager about something that occurred earlier.

"I already told you no, and you still went ahead and did it," Elena said, highly annoyed with her adopted son Juelz.

"Ma, I told you I was sorry."

Elena turned, staring into her son's innocent face; immediately she became filled with regret as she felt like she had overreacted. Juelz was turning thirteen years old; at this point in his adolescent years he would want to explore. His sexual hormones were experiencing a significant increase as he was becoming obsessed with the opposite sex. Elena didn't want her son to grow up so fast, but there was no way she was able to stop his growth. Those same grey eyes she watched age over the years stared back at her so sincere.

"I know you're sorry, but you will definitely do it again, because you're turning into a man now," she spoke with much sadness in her voice. "I understand you are going to have some interest in life and I just have to get used to this."

A small smile crept onto Juelz' face as he became overwhelmed with joy. Wrapping his long arms around his mother, Juelz inhaled her scent. Her comforting fragrance placed his mind at ease. This women that he held in his grasp was all he had ever known. He'd been in her custody since he was one week old. Growing up, he believed that Elena was his biological mother until she set the story right for him. She explained to Juelz that his biological mother was a thirteen-year-old drug addict, who wasn't fit to raise the little boy. Elena didn't want Juelz to grow old believing in a tale that she conceived to cover up his truth. Throughout the years, Elena had prayed for the young mother to get her life together. It seemed as if God had answered her prayers as every year on Juelz's birthday, Elena would find a package with money in it. The money was great as it went towards things that Juelz needed, but Elena hoped that one day Juelz's mother would find her way to their front door, ready to meet her son.

"I love you son," Elena said bringing him into her embrace.

"The feeling is mutual," he replied.

"You ain't too grown for an ass whipping boy."

"I am joking, relax. I love you too," he said.

Leilani sat in her car eyeing the small family. Over the years, she watched the young man grow. She was amazed at how fast time flies. It felt like just the other week she had found the family and the little boy was just learning how to walk. The sound of her ringing phone brought her out of her thoughts. Picking up the phone, she eyed her screen, recognizing the unsaved number.

"Yes."

"Come to the restaurant and bring the girls," Isaiah said.

"Ok."

She placed the car into drive, pulling off into traffic. The sound of the engine purred lightly into the New York air. A warm gust of wind blew into her car, caressing her golden skin. Life for Leilani had changed drastically over the years. At one point of her life, her body depended on a drug to keep her moving. She was different now. She changed into the very thing that the world feared: a strong woman. Her life held more value now more than ever. Everything she did today had a purpose. A future she had to consider. Her mind flooded with several thoughts as she pulled up in front of Isaiah's restaurant. She cut off the purring engine, getting out of the car. The sweet sound of the birds chirping echoed throughout the air as she focused her attention on texting both Essence and Candy in their group chat. *I won't even be surprised if Candy's ass don't show up.*

She made her way into the restaurant that was under major construction. The smell of new wood entered her nostrils as she walked inside with all eyes on her. Her grey converses tapped against the floor lightly as her hips swayed to the tune of her own beat. The construction workers couldn't help but to stare at her hourglass frame. On que, Isaiah walked out from his office from the sound of silence that echoed throughout the establishment.

"Um, I ain't paying you motherfuckers to be watching my baby sister," he shouted. "Get back to fucking work."

"Relax big head, there is too much testosterone in here," Leilani chuckled as she walked over to give him a hug. "They can't resist an hourglass shape."

"Shut up La and get your ass into my office," he said.

Chuckling, Leilani walked into Isaiah's office, taken aback by the appearance of his private space. She knew the restaurant was still under construction, but she didn't expect him to move into the office space so soon if his office wasn't ready. Isaiah walked inside the office space with his mind set on one thing. Grabbing a glass cup, he poured himself a shot of Hennessey.

"So, what the fuck is going on with your office?" she asked as she looked around eyeing the unfinished office.

"These niggas are fucking with me," he responded as he prepared to take another shot. "These motherfuckers told me that my office space will be done within a month. Believing that lying nigga, I hired an interior designer and had all my shit delivered for last week since last week was the deadline. I come here expecting my office to be up and running, but the bitch ass foreman gonna tell me some shit about they won't have my shit done for another two weeks."

"Relax, everything is going to be alright."

"I can't fucking relax. I'm dishing out fucking money, but I ain't seeing no fucking results," he said, downing the shot.

"Shit will be handled. Remember we are going away for the next two weeks, so relax."

"You're right."

"Yes, so when we come back your office will be officially done."

"You're smart. Thank God I decided to keep you around," he said, releasing a chuckle.

"Whatever motherfucker. Is that all you needed me for?"

"No, actually I wanted you here so you could sample some of my food."

"Sure, no problem. Let's just wait for Essence to come. I doubt Candy will show up."

"What's up with you two?"

"I don't know, but lately she's been out of her fucking mind."

"What do you mean?"

"The other day we went out for brunch, and she began to question me about my whereabouts."

"She's your nigga now?" Isaiah interrupted.

"Shut up and let me finish. So long story short, I told her about the new position with you and she bugged out calling me fake and shit."

"Wait, what?"

"Yup, she called me fake because I didn't turn the job down."

"What the fuck?"

"Same thing I sai—"

The sound of the door opening caught both of their attention, as they diverted their eyes to the door. Essence stood before them with her daughter in her arms and a smile on her face.

"Sorry I am late."

"I totally forgot that you were coming," Leilani said, jokingly.

"Sounds just like you."

Walking over to the two, Essence placed her daughter on the floor, allowing her to walk on her own. She walked up to Leilani, placing a kiss on her cheek and then sat down in the chair closest to Isaiah.

"So, I couldn't get a kiss or a hug?" Isaiah questioned.

"For what?"

"What the hell? That's the most respectful thing to do when you walk into someone's office interrupting their conversation."

"Really Isaiah?"

"Yes, nigga."

"Well I am sitting down. I don't wanna get up."

"And that's still cool," he responded as he took a hold of her hand, pulling her into his embrace. Locking his arms around her frame, he inhaled her intoxicating scent, losing himself within the illusion of them together. He secretly wanted her, and not just physically. He wanted her mentally and spiritually. Knowing about her current situation, Isaiah refused to pursue anything considering that she was still involved with someone. Instead, Isaiah opted on waiting for her patiently. *She will be mine, soon.*

Leilani stared on, observing the embrace of the two. Desperately wanting the two to be together, Leilani knew not to push them as it would result in them growing apart. She knew they would happen eventually, and she too was waiting patiently.

"Well umm, so like let's try this food out," Leilani said interrupting them.

"Right, that was supposed to be done," Isaiah replied releasing Essence. Quickly, he disappeared out of his office, leaving both Leilani and Essence alone.

"Shut up," Essence said, noticing the look Leilani gave her.

"What the hell?"

"I know what you're thinking."

"Really?"

"Yes, and I don't wanna hear you."

"What the hell? I wasn't going to say anything," Leilani replied as she placed her hands up defensively. "You already know how I feel. There isn't a need for me to keep saying it."

"Ok."

"Whatever you decide to do that is fine; just want you to know that Isaiah is a better pick tho."

"La."

"What, I am just saying." Leilani chuckled. "He can make you happy, and that's all I want for you."

CHAPTER 6

Her stomach felt nimble as she glared out into the clouds. It was only six in the morning and Leilani did not feel tired at all. Everyone else on the G5 private jet was knocked out. Just a couple of hours ago, they were in Atlanta terrorizing the streets, seeking ownership of the streets. Expecting the task to be difficult, Leilani was surprised when the man who ran the drug trade in the ATL gladly gave up his throne without much of a fight. Not caring, Leilani was just grateful that she didn't have to get too crazy. Staring out of the small aircraft window, she became captivated by the orange hues of the sky that left a warm sensation within her. It was breathtaking for her as she had never once left New York. This was new for her.

"You seem very excited to be going to Miami," Sincere said.

"Yes, you're supposed to be asleep."

"And so are you."

"No, it's six in the morning. I never sleep past 5:30," she focused her eyes back out into the clouds. *Once I get all the business over with, I will be enjoying my time out here in Miami. I may even make these assholes leave so I can stay by myself,* Leilani thought. Over the little time that she had known the guys, Leilani found them to be very cool, as all three men didn't judge Leilani because she was a woman. But instead they saw her as their equal.

"What's on your mind Princess?"

"Nothing really."

"Is everything going according to plan?" he questioned.

"Yes, I just received a text from one of our soldiers. We have confirmed that we are right on task."

The two indulged into a conversation amongst themselves, making the plane ride even shorter. Once the plane landed on the Miami air strip, they all got out, embracing the humid air. The clouds that floated above them were white and fluffier then any cloud she had ever seen. The sky was even bluer then in New York. The air even smelled fresher, rather than the stale air she was used to. Miami just seemed to be ideal for the fast life. Soon, the same bright, clear day that she admired would be destroyed, as Leilani planned on ruining the streets of Miami.

"Y'all ready to turn this shit upside down?" Isaiah asked.

"Fuck that, I'm ready to make these streets bleed," Leilani chuckled.

Leilani had her mind focused on conquering their new territory. She had no idea how the niggas in Miami were, but she honestly didn't care, as she knew she would bring the heat. Whether it was new territory or old territory, either way, it was going to be theirs.

******

Neon lights gleamed from the ceiling, illuminating the illusion that was being sold. Tonight, the stage was covered in hundreds of singles as Lexie started the night with her sexual choreography. Baby oil glistened from her perfectly man-made curves, with dozens of eyes glaring on in awe.

"These bitches are hot tonight," Wallace spoke.

"Mph," Harley responded, not fully paying attention to what was being discussed. Every male in the building had their eyes focused on Lexie. Harley on the other hand had fully invested his attention into the female that sat in the booth across from him. He had been watching her since she had first made her way into the club. Being a King of Diamond regular, Harley had known the strippers on a personal level, as there was not one female he did not sleep with in the establishment. Seeing this fresh face was like fresh air colliding against his face on a hot summer day.

"Yo man, Harley what's up?" Wallace asked concerned. "You seem out of it."

"Nothing man, you see shawty over there?" he said while pointing towards the female.

"Yea, she bad as fuck."

"I know, I never seen her out here before. Have the waitress send her over a bottle," Harley responded. This was his attempt at trying to impress the fresh face. *What better way to impress a pretty woman? Only way is to spend money on her and the illusion that you're after her love*, Harley reasoned. She was beautiful, just as every other female in the place, but he wasn't just attracted to her physically. The thought of the challenge turned him on. He had never seen her a day in his life, so he knew already she was from out of town. She hadn't been poisoned by the regular Miami niggas, which placed a conniving smile on his face.

"Aight, ain't she with them niggas?"

"Who cares about them simple ass niggas?" He took a notice to the three guys who were around her. Being in the presence of other guys didn't faze Harley, as this only made the challenge even harder. He watched on from his sectional as the waitress handed his interest the expensive bottle of champagne. He watched as the waitress pointed over towards him, finally connecting their eyes. The anticipation of her response ignited him. He knew she wouldn't have a problem fucking with a nigga of his stature. The waitress and his interest spoke for a little before the waitress was sent back over to his sectional.

"Sir?" she asked.

"Yeah," he replied while eyeing her. She stood before him in nothing but her latex bodysuit that left little to no imagination as to what was underneath the fabric. He found it hard to stare into her eyes with her breast bursting out of the seam.

"She has declined your bottle."

"Well that's a shame, because I don't take no for an answer."

"Yea, well to compensate for her decline, she has sent over a bottle for you," the waitress replied as she pointed to a girl behind her with a bottle.

"Well she's gonna have to do better than that if she wants to impress a nigga," Harley interrupted. He chuckled, finding it amusing that she tried to outdo him at a game that he knew so well.

"No sir, this one is for you," the waitress said while placing his bottle of champagne on the table in front of him. "Those are for the people in your crew," she replied while pointing towards the dozens of bottle girls that came walking towards them. Each female held a bottle of the club's finest alcohol for every individual that was in Harley's crew.

"I guess someone finally outdid you," the waitress spoke, leaving Harley alone to sulk in his embarrassment.

Harley's eyes scanned the club in search of the woman who had outshined him. *Maybe shawty spending that niggas money*, he tried reasoning. His eyes focused, searching for the mesmerizing grey hues. He searched high and low, finally landing his sight on the beauty. It was the second time that their eyes had connected for the whole night.

"You gonna talk to shawty or not?" Wallace questioned.

"It's that noticeable?"

"Hell yeah, you've been eye-fucking the girl all night."

"Aight, I will, but don't you see them niggas she's around?"

"So?" Wallace asked. "What them niggas supposed to mean to hustlers like us? You the fucking nigga of Miami; you run this bitch." Wallace's words were supposed to be words of encouragement. Harley had a tight hold on Miami; everyone that resided in the beautiful city was afraid to tamper with his reign. If the thought of deceit boiled amongst his city, Harley didn't give a fuck if he had to paint the city red. He would do whatever was necessary to ensure he remained King of Miami. The two men walked over to his interest's sectional with a stride that only a man with power could possess. Their designer sneakers cleared their paths. *These bitches chase me; what the fuck am*

I doing? He stood in front of the grey eyed woman, glaring at her. Her face remained emotionless as she took a sip from her cup.

"Can I help you?" she spoke. Her plump lips caught his attention. They were full and looked soft enough to kiss.

"I see you like playing games."

"Nah, I don't like playing fuck boy games."

Her words rolled off her tongue smoothly but still held a form of harshness. He knew she was from out of town; her New York accent was thick with street. It was proper but twined with a little bit of hood.

"I like you. Let me take you out for dinner or something of that nature."

"You mean you wanna fuck?" She chuckled.

"What?"

"Nothing, I'm cool. I'm not here in Miami for fun, strictly business."

"No fun?"

"Strictly business."

"Can I at least get your name and number?"

"Don't worry sweetheart, in due time you will get all of that information," she spoke as her lips spread into a smile. She turned her back away from him, focusing her attention back onto the shapely stripper that danced on stage. Embarrassed, Harley could feel the warmth cascading down his face. He was the man of Miami; bitches from all over this area fought to smell his dirty draws. He just couldn't understand as to why she was being stuck up. *Shawty must not know who the fuck I am.*

“I see you haven’t learned the rules of Miami.”

“Doesn’t make sense to.”

“And why not?”

“Because they will be rewritten,” she spoke. Her grey eyes bore a hole into his face. Her glare was all too familiar as he had seen this look dozens of times. It was not built off excitement with being with a baller, instead her hard glare was filled with no emotion as she found Harley to be amusing. They were cold and empty. Like the pits of her heart. The signs were all there; she was not the one to be fucked with. His gut twisted as death stared him right in his eyes. Rather than listening to his gut, Harley took his chance, inching closer to her. His hands found their way around her waist as he slightly pulled her in towards him. The attraction was undeniable on his end. But for her, all she saw was a mission.

“Instead of hanging around these lames you should get with a real nigga,” he whispered into her ear while he stared at the guys in her sectional.

“You should stop thinking with your dick and start trusting that weird feeling in your gut. I ain’t what you want,” she whispered back, removing his arms from around her waist. She moved away from him, joining back with the guys that she was with. Harley stared back at her shapely figure. Determination rested on his chest as his pride would not allow the beauty to walk away from him. She mesmerized him and he wasn’t afraid to admit it. Just like she planned, Harley was right where she needed him to be: wanting her. Everything was going according to the plan as she looked down at her Movado watch that read 12:45. Right on cue, Harley's phone vibrated in his pocket. He took it out, glaring at the unexpected name on the screen.

"Speak."

"Boss, we got a problem."

"Speak?"

"The house has been robbed."

All the air escaped his lungs as his fingers wrapped tightly around his cell phone. He didn't know why, but he could feel his chest beginning to tighten. *What the fuck?* The question rang throughout his mind searching for an answer.

"Boss are you there?" the worker asked, snapping him Harley out of his trance.

"I am on my way," he spoke into the phone. Hanging up the phone, Harley glared at his right-hand man with malice. No words were exchanged between the two as Wallace took notice to the death glare. Both men exited the club, making their way to Harley's parked Dodge Challenger. Once they were both in the car, Harley turned the vehicle on, allowing the muscle machine to come alive. The revving of the engine filled the air, drowning the sound of the thick bass inside of the club.

"You aight my nigga?" Wallace questioned.

"No, my house was hit."

"Do you know who did it?"

"Probably them fucking Haitians," Harley spoke as he pulled

off, wasting no time getting to his trap house. Traffic wasn't heavy like Harley had experienced earlier. Within twenty minutes, Harley pulled up in front of his prized possession. He cut the engine off as he got out the car. Silence oozed from the community, with tension lingering in the air replacing the humidity that once hovered amongst the people like a dark cloud. Staring at his million-dollar home, he was skeptical about entering his once humble abode. He didn't know the extent of the damage done to his home and he didn't think he even wanted to know. The million-dollar home was his baby. With years of hustling in the streets, Harley had sacrificed his life to make it. The home was the only thing he had to show for his hustle.

"It can't be that bad," Wallace said. Unbeknownst to the two, the damage done to the property was more than they could both fathom.

Opening the front door to the home, Harley inhaled deeply, preparing himself for what was behind the door. Pushing the door open, he immersed himself into the chaos that was once his home. His breathing became labored as the aroma of gunpowder watered his taste buds. Both men pinched their noses, in efforts to stop the smell from watering their eyes.

"Shit man, whoever did this has some fucking balls man," Wallace said breaking the awkward silence. There was a dozen of Harley's security that lay dead on the marbled floor. The scent of burning flesh infiltrated the thin walls, upsetting Harley's stomach.

"How the fuck could they have done this?" Harley questioned.

"I don't know; them Haitians man, they something else."

"You sure it's the Haitians?"

"It has to be."

"Yea, but these niggas have bullet holes in them. They were not killed by machetes."

Slowly, both men continued to walk around analyzing the crime scene that was in Harley's home. Clueless as to who had caused the chaos within his home, Harley was just about ready give up when the faint sound of vibration rang through the dank air. Confused, Wallace and Harley stared at each other. They didn't know where the sound originated from as they both searched for the cellular device like squirrels looking for a nut. After twenty seconds of searching, they finally found the phone resting in between the dead bodies. The iPhone screen lit up, revealing the missed call from an unknown number. The black screen came alive with vibration as another phone call came in. Harley motioned for Wallace to answer the phone.

"Hello?" Wallace answered. He listened attentively to the caller before he broke out into a suit of laughter.

"Who is this?" Wallace questioned. The caller on the other end chuckled right along with Wallace, amused at his ignorance. "Nah, you speak to me," Wallace protested.

"Fine nigga, it's your death," the caller stated before hanging up.

Both men stood before each other dumbfounded by the actions that occurred. Harley began to say something to Wallace when his phone came alive with an incoming call. Annoyed, Harley answered without glancing at the caller ID.

"What?"

"Is that any way to talk to someone?" the person asked.

"Who the fuck is this?"

"Is that really any way you should be speaking to a woman that you're trying to impress?"

"How the fuck did you get my number?" he asked confused.

"I am a woman of many talents. You're actually standing in my handy work as we speak right now," she said.

"You did this shit?"

"Yes, I did."

"Bitch, I want my fucking money for the dope you stole."

"Oh honey, that's not how this shit works." The caller chuckled. Her New York accent was smooth, entangled with danger. "I will be arriving at your house tomorrow morning at 10 a.m. to discuss some important business. If you try anything stupid, then you will see what I really am capable of."

"You must really have some fucking balls trying to pull a stunt like this," he spoke, seething with anger.

"Oh baby, only the biggest," she chuckled.

Before Harley could conjure up a reply, the phone went dead as the sound of the dial tone echoed in his ear. *I will show this bitch who she's fucking with*, he thought.

"Get some niggas to clean up this fucking shit," he demanded as he stormed out of his home, highly irritated.

CHAPTER 7

The bright sun glared into the office space. It was only nine in the morning and yet Harley hadn't gotten an ounce of sleep. His mind had been corrupted with vengeance as he had spent the night searching for anything to help preserve his reign. The news of the massacre in his home had spread through the streets like wildfire. He didn't need niggas questioning his authority, so he had to come up with a solution quick and fast. *How the fuck can I deal with this bitch? I can kill her, but first I'mma rape her fine ass before anything. Fucking bitch think she can do some stupid shit like that and get away with it? I got something for her ass.* A light knock echoed through the office space as his maid peeked her head in.

"Señor, your guests are here," she informed him.

"Let them in."

Pushing the door open wider, Maria allowed the guests to enter the disastrous office space. Harley looked up, expecting to see only one person, surprised to see the group of people before him. The four people that stood in his office held emotionless glares as their eyes looked around the office.

"Still no fun?" he asked.

"No honey, this is strictly business," she spoke as they took a seat before him.

"Bae, we could have talked, just me and you. You didn't have to bring these niggas along."

"Well if you must know, I am not a one-man army. When you see me then you will most definitely see my partners," Leilani replied. "Where are my manners? I didn't even introduce myself to you. My name is Leilani, this here is Sincere, Don, and Isaiah."

"Ok babe, now that we all know each other, what do I owe this pleasure of having all y'all niggas in my office?" Harley asked as he laid his body weight back into the reclining desk chair. Despite being pleased to meet the girl from the club last night, Harley was concerned as to why they were all in his presence.

"Well we are here to give you a business proposition," Isaiah stated.

"A business proposition?" Harley questioned. "For what?"

"We understand that you are the man who is running Miami," Isaiah asked.

"Yes."

"With running such a lucrative business, it comes with perks."

"Cut to the fucking chase man. What is it that you fucking want?"

"We would like 25% of your profits or..." The words Isaiah spoke rolled off his tongue smoothly. But instead of being intimidated by the smooth talking pretty boy, Harley found the group amusing as he let out a gut-wrenching laugh.

"Join y'all?" He chuckled. "Who the fuck are y'all?"

"We are the Supremes," Isaiah replied.

"Y'all niggas got some fucking nerves to come into my home with this bullshit," he said as he stood up, towering over his sitting guest. "Some funny niggas," he began ranting, degrading the Supremes. His laughter was now filled with rage. *These mutherfuckers got some nerve coming to me, of all niggas,* he thought.

"Get the fuck out of my house."

"Nigga, sit the fuck down," Leilani replied, now highly agitated.

"Who the fuck you talking to?"

"You the only one standing up being a fucking bitch. Now sit your ass down in that fucking chair," she stated, not once taking her eyes off Harley.

"Excuse me?" he asked surprised.

"I would hate to have to show you how violent I can get."

His eyes penetrated the perfect tones of her iris. He had mistaken the beauty she possessed, as she was not the woman he portrayed her to be. She was different than any female he had ever met. Her feminine voice could be as soft as a rose petal but could exude more poison than a venomous snake.

"Now like my partners stated before, it's either you join us, giving us 25% of your profit, or I will single-handedly dismantle your empire from the petal of the flower down to the very dirt it grew out of," she spoke.

It was then that he began to realize the severity of the company before him. They weren't joking around like he had presumed. The group wanted a piece of the empire that he had grown from the ground up. He had worked hard at getting himself out of the hood and into the mansion that overlooked the ocean.

"Nice try but—" He began to protest their demands, but Leilani cut him off as she silenced him with her finger.

"I do not think you understand how I can get down. If you deny this offer the late-night phone calls will continue to get worse, and I will no longer be killing your soldiers. I will begin to hit closer to home, starting with that snow bunny of a wife of yours."

A chuckle escaped his lips, filling the quiet office. It would take a lot more than a pretty female for him to feel threatened. Harley propped his body up in the chair he sat in; he spoke slowly, holding the sternness in his voice.

"Let me say this one time only: I will not be giving y'all niggas shit." His eyebrows furrowed into pure anger as he banged his hand on his desk. "I spent years building this bitch; ain't no fucking way in hell I will happily sign off on 25% of my profit."

The room flourished in silence. The blank stares he received from the group that sat in his presence confused the hell out of him. They didn't seem upset or happy. Harley waited for a response. He expected their guns to be drawn, but they remained still, staring into his soul. They never said a word as the group stood together preparing to leave.

"It was a pleasure meeting with you," Sincere spoke as he stuck his hand out. ""I am sorry you didn't see comfort in our proposition."

"Well you guys will find someone else as your income source,"

Harley responded as he stared directly into Leilani's eyes. Her innocent face brightened as he shook her hand. The quick change of her attitude had Harley convinced she had to be bipolar.

"Maria will show you the way out," he spoke as he called for her. Within seconds, Maria came rushing into his office. "Show them the way to the door," he spoke.

"Ok."

Once his room was vacant, he sat in his chair replaying the events that had just occurred. He didn't regret his decision, but Leilani's words were reiterated into his head. She had correlated a relationship between a flower and his drug empire. She gave him a warning about depilating his rose and destroying it down to the soil it grew out of. Those words were cold, filled with violence. The more he thought about it, the more he became paranoid. Leilani had planned on destroying his world and it was too late to stop her.

CHAPTER 8

The clocked ticked continuously as night began to approach. The air was still thick from the previous rainfall that captured Miami. Leilani sat in her car staring off into the dark folds of the night. Her eyes remained focused on the trap house that sat on the corner of the block. The streets were infested with dope fiends as they searched for their next hit. Their hollow stares were all too familiar to her; the pain of escaping reality was evident within their empty souls. Leilani was once one of them, searching for happiness within the drugs. Isaiah stared at a dazed Leilani, concerned about her mindset.

"Are you ok?" he asked.

"What?" She looked at him confused.

"Are you ok?"

"Yes, I am fine. Why would I not be?"

"Because we are in a crack infested neighborhood, and I know this is a lot for you, considering your past."

"I'm fine Isaiah. I wasn't on crack; I was a dope fiend," she replied as she focused her attention back onto their target. It had been a long night, with the duo spending hours in the car, scooping out their desired target.

"When do you think it will be best to get in there?" Isaiah asked.

"I think there should be enough people in there now; let's get this over with," she replied as she placed the ski mask on the top of her head.

"Let's do this."

They both exited the car, making their way through the dank Miami air. It was two in the morning, and Leilani knew that the trap house was at its capacity with dope dealers and dope fiends. This was the perfect time for her plan to come to life. Isaiah led the way to the trap house as he knocked on the rigid door.

"You ready?" he asked facing her.

"Nigga, I've been doing this shit for years," she replied as she pulled down the ski mask.

The door swung open as a beastly man stood confused. Without any communication, both Isaiah and Leilani bombarded their way through the door, knocking down the beastly man.

"Say a fucking word and I swear I will blow your fucking brains out," Leilani spoke as she shoved the gun in his mouth. "Now we can do this the easy way or shit can get mighty technical big man. All we want to know is where is the stash?"

She slowly removed the nozzle of the gun from out of his mouth as she anticipated his answer. The guy shook his head, signaling that he didn't know where the money could be. Annoyed, Leilani smashed the gun against the baldness of his head. Blood gushed from the open wound, causing him to become dizzy.

"Now I am going to say this one more fucking time, where the fuck is the money?" she spoke as she bore a hole into his eyes.

"Playboy, I don't think you would want to fuck with her right now; just tell her where the fuck the money at," Isaiah said.

"I-ts lllocated in the bacccck," he stuttered.

"Well done," Leilani replied as she brought the gun down against his temple, knocking him unconscious.

"Let's begin rounding up these assholes," Leilani replied as she led the way. For thirty minutes, both Leilani and Isaiah walked through the whole trap house gathering up every single person that was present. Once they were done, the living room was filled with over thirty people tied up, along with all the money and drugs found in the house.

"Do y'all know who y'all fucking with?" one of the dope dealers yelled. He sat on the floor wiggling his body in hopes of freeing himself from the restraints. "Y'all really think fucking with Harley is going to get you far? Y'all a bunch of pussies; only pussies would wear a ski mask."

"Well sir, that's where you have this whole shit wrong," Isaiah replied as both him and Leilani removed their ski masks, revealing their identities. "I am known as Isaiah, and this here is my sister Leilani."

"Now, we gonna keep the introduction short, because I guarantee you fellas will hear about us soon, but for right now, we would just like for you guys to relay a message to Mr. Harley," Leilani replied as she began pouring gasoline all around the piled money and drugs. "Inform Mr. Harley that I don't like being told no," she replied as she lit the money up into flames. "I am a woman of my word, and he just signed his death certificate."

The scent of burning money and drugs filled the air as the intruders left the scene of the crime. They began making their way to their car when Isaiah began questioning Leilani's tactics.

"I don't mean to question your actions, but La, what was the point of us burning the money and leaving witnesses?"

"Well my brother, if there is one thing I learned, it is that y'all men are very big on y'all pride and your possessions. I didn't take his money because it shows that he can be touched at any given moment. It shows that I can hit three of your spots in less than 24 hours. It shows that he's touchable, and leaving behind those witnesses is exactly what it is; they are witnesses to Harley being touchable."

Leilani started the car, driving away from the crime scene. The night was still young as Leilani anticipated being out all night causing some form of destruction. A million things ran through her head as she thought about what could be done tonight.

"What do you think about burning down some more of his trap houses?" Leilani asked.

"You know I'm down for whatever."

She turned towards her brother, displaying her smile. For as long as she had known Isaiah, he was always down to ride for her no matter what the circumstances were. They rode together in silence as they both prepared their minds for the destruction they were going to cause. The all-black Mercedes glided through the streets of Miami, silent as a mouse. The headlights were off as Leilani crept onto the block of their destination.

Once she was certain they were at the correct location, Leilani shut the car off gathering her glock.

“How are we doing this?” Isaiah asked as he gathered his piece. “Knock knock who’s there type of shit?”

“Yea, we gonna get one of these dope fiends, have them cop, and we barge in.”

“No mask?”

“Fuck it, not this time,” she spoke as she got out of the car, eyeing the first dope fiend that came into sight. She smoothly walked over to him getting his attention.

“You wanna make a quick buck?” she asked.

“What I gotta do?”

“Go over to that building, cop whatever you want, and I’ll pay for it, including the buck.”

“Aight lil’ mama you got it,” he replied as he took the hundred from her hand, leading the way over to the trap house.

Leilani signaled for Isaiah to follow as she walked right behind the fiend. Once they arrived at the door, the fiend knocked in the secret code, notifying that he wanted to cop. The trio stood in silence, anticipating an answer. Chains and deadbolts could be heard unlocking as the door was opened just enough for the exchange to occur. Just as their hands touched, the door was kicked in, knocking over the dealer.

“What the fuck?” Rocco exclaimed as he struggled to get back on his feet. A powerful blow was delivered to his stomach, causing him to land hard back on the ground. His arms were suddenly pinned together, prohibiting any movement.

"How many more people are in here?" Leilani questioned.

"Fuck you," he retorted as he spat into her face. Rocco had sacrificed his soul to the streets. He had seen the look of death in dozens of people. Throughout his years of being on the street, he let it be known that he wasn't afraid of death. But tonight, was a totally different story. The woman before him had a facial expression that was so calm, yet so cold. She wiped his glob of spit from her face as she glared into his eyes. At that very moment, Rocco realized that he fucked up.

"Fuck that no murder bullshit," she spoke. Before her actions could be protested, Leilani raised her gun high and pulled the trigger, allowing the bullet to penetrate Rocco's chest.

"Bitch ass nigga," she said as she walked over him, entering the trap house. Isaiah followed right behind her as they surveyed the rest of the trap house. Once the house was cleared, they discovered that it was only Rocco alone doing the midnight serve.

"What should we do?" Isaiah asked as he stared at the pile of drugs and money.

"Leave it sitting there," she replied.

"So, we not gonna do no dramatic shit?"

"His body is all the dramatics we need," Leilani replied as she found her way out of the house. There was nothing else that she felt they needed to do. Leilani knew that at that moment, Harley was being notified about all the chaos she had caused. If he didn't agree to their terms, then Leilani didn't have any problems with getting closer to home. Just as she entered the car, her phone vibrated violently. An unknown number popped up on her iPhone screen, and her mind began running as she tried figuring out who could be calling her.

"Hello," she answered.

"I'll do it," the person said into the phone.

"You'll do what?" she questioned.

"Meet me at my house now," Harley said, highly annoyed with Leilani.

Without saying another word, Leilani hung up the phone and focused her attention onto Isaiah. She stared into his eyes before displaying her perfect smile.

"What are you smiling for?"

"He finally agreed. We are going to his house now," she replied as she started the car, pulling off into traffic.

"See that's how you get the fucking job done," Isaiah proclaimed as he began to rain kisses all over Leilani's face. "Let me call these niggas and let them know what's up," Isaiah ranted as he began to dial Sincere's number.

The cool Miami air blew through the open window. Traffic was light as the car glided down the street. Something about the scenery caused the goose bumps to protrude through her golden skin. She had made it far in life considering what she experienced in her childhood. From being addicted to drugs at a young age to becoming pregnant twice from her stepfather, no one could tell Leilani that she didn't have a rough upbringing. There were times where she couldn't believe that she had survived the turmoil of her childhood. She had pushed her painful past into the back of her mind, but tonight she decided to remember.

******

"Where the fuck are they?" Roselyn questioned, as she tossed apart the things in her dresser. Turning the same things over for the hundredth time, the item she was searching for didn't appear. Becoming agitated, she pulled out the drawer, allowing the wooden frame to crash onto the floor. Her cluttered clothes lay scattered all over the floor. Running her hands through the clothes, she searched for her missing gold hoops.

Several things ran through her head as she tried to make sense of what could have happened with her favorite pair of earrings. ***Where the fuck could they have gone?*** *she questioned herself.* ***I went out last night, came home, and knocked out. I remember putting them on the dresser after I got undressed.*** *She remembered placing the earrings in their designated jewelry box, but when she went to put them on, they were nowhere to be found. Tearing apart her room in pursuit of finding the lost gold earrings, she could feel herself going crazy as she searched the same area for the hundredth time. Beginning to panic at the thought of losing her earrings, she frantically tossed her shirts into the air to see if she had missed them. No luck; the earrings didn't appear.* ***What the fuck? The only person that could have even stepped foot in my room is that little girl,*** *she concluded. The wheel within her head began to turn slowly, as the concept of her daughter taking her earrings seemed accurate.* ***That bitch took my earrings.***

"Leilani," she yelled. The anger in her voice was noticeable. Trying

to calm herself down was almost impossible, with the concept of her earrings being in her daughter's possession tormenting her. The door to her room slowly creaked open, and Leilani stood there, confused on what was going on.

"Where the hell are my gold earrings?"

"What are you talking about Mommy?" Leilani asked confused.

"Don't play fucking stupid. The gold fucking earrings that I wear when I am going out."

"I don't know."

Leilani stood at the front of the door, watching her mother go crazy for the pair of earrings. Clothing lay scattered all over the wooden floor. Leilani knew how important the earrings were for her mother, but she was clueless as to where her mother could have misplaced them.

"Mommy calm down. I am pretty sure you'll find the earrings."

"Don't fucking tell me to calm down," Roselyn yelled. Staring into her eyes, Leilani noticed the crazed glare that her mother had. She'd never seen it before. It was like Roselyn had lost herself within the concept of Leilani's thievery. The conjured up theory opened the gates to Roselyn's insecurities. "You must have taken them," Roselyn concluded.

"Wait, what?"

"You fucking took them."

"No I did not."

"So, you're fucking calling me a liar?" Roselyn challenged.

"No Mommy."

"You must be."

"No."

"You took my damn earrings just so you could look cute for Rocky." The accusation sounded crazy, as Roselyn was hesitant about making the broad statement. But the more she thought about it, the more accurate it seemed. "You trying to look cute for my man so you can steal him away from me."

"What?" Leilani questioned. "I didn't do anything."

Roselyn's accusation was completely wrong. Realistically, it was far from the truth, but for Roselyn, it was the only answer that made sense to her. Staring at her daughter, Roselyn was envious of her innocent beauty. When Leilani grew older, her mother knew that the little girl would have men falling at her feet, and that's what pissed Roselyn off. No matter how mean she would be to Leilani, the little girl always seemed to never be effected. The concept she had created in her mind evolved from her jealousy. Staring at her beautiful daughter, Roselyn could feel her body beginning to get warm. Slowly she was losing her composure, glaring at her daughter who stood innocently. Her feet walked over to where Leilani stood, the floorboard creaking loudly the closer she got to her daughter.

"Just admit that you took the fucking earrings," Roselyn said, barely over a whisper.

"But Mommy I didn't take them, I swear."

Roselyn knew she was telling the truth. Leilani wasn't bold enough to pull a move like that. ***She wouldn't steal from me; the little girl is afraid of me,*** *Roselyn reasoned. She knew the truth, but Roselyn just could not accept it. Jealousy would not allow her to. Reaching her hand out, Roselyn grabbed a fist full of Leilani's mocha brown hair. Gaining* *full control of her head, Roselyn brought her daughter closer to her.*

"Don't ever fucking touch my things," she said.

"O-k."

I don't think she understands, Roselyn thought, I need to show her how serious I am. *Feeling the need to prove a point, Roselyn raised her hand up, bringing it down against Leilani's face. A gush of air escaped her thin lips as she could feel the anger within her escape. Raising her hand again, she brought it back down, leaving Leilani's face a crimson red.*

"I am warning you. Stay the fuck away from Rocky."

"O—" Leilani could barely let out her response before she was stricken again across her face.

"Don't fucking play with me little girl," Roselyn warned. "I am not the one to be fucked with. Now take your ass into that living room and watch TV."

Releasing Leilani's hair from her grasp, Roselyn watched as her little girl walked out of her room, holding the side of her face. **Let me catch that little fucking puta flirting with my man, I swear to God I will kill her.** *Turning her back to the door, Roselyn faced the mess she had made searching for her missing earrings. Picking up her clothing off the floor, Roselyn busied herself with cleaning up the mess. She needed something to help her get her mind off the recent exchange of events and cleaning was the perfect solution. Lifting her shirts off the floor, she neatly folded them, resting them on her bed. Calming the boiling anger that threatened to spill out, Roselyn became distracted by the sound of knocking.*

"Answer the door," she yelled out.

There wasn't a response from Leilani; only the television could be heard. Picking up the clothing, Roselyn's eyes were caught onto a gold glimmer that peaked from under one of her shirts. **Is that what I think it is?** *Lifting the shirt, Roselyn revealed what her mind had already confirmed.*

"Oh shit, I forgot I had put these shits in my shirt last night," she said to herself. Before she could say anything else, the sound of knocking erupted through the apartment, catching her attention once again.

"Leilani go and answer the fucking door," Roselyn yelled.

Snapping out of her thoughts, Leilani was confused as to what happened so in tune with her thoughts she didn't hear the knocking on the door. Standing up, she walked over to the door, cupping the burning side of her face. She was sure there would be a bruise left behind. Opening the metal door, Leilani was confused seeing Rocky.

"What's up lil' mama?" he asked. Confused on how to greet him, Leilani turned her back towards him, making her way back to the couch. Noticing the change in her behavior, Rocky knew something was up. He had grown accustomed to being greeted by a smiling Leilani who was very talkative. Sitting down on the couch next to her, he waited for her to say something. But sadly, she sat there in her own world.

"So, what's been up?" he asked. Expecting an answer from the little girl, she replied with a head nod. "Are you good?"

"I am fine," she responded, barely over a whisper.

"Are you sure?" he asked concerned. "Everything is ok?"

"Yes."

"Ok, well how was your day?"

"It was ok."

"What did you do?"

"Nothing."

Sitting there staring at the little girl, the awkward silence began to bother him. He wanted to have a conversation with her like he usually did. He wanted to laugh a kind of laugh that she could only create. Her personality was like a breath of fresh air in his life of sin. Talking to her, being in her presence, relieved him of all mental stress that he deals with on the regular.

"Lil' mama, tell me what's going on?" he questioned. "You don't seem the same; you're very quiet."

"I'm just upset," she admitted.

"About what?"

"Mommy beat me for something I did not do."

"Are you sure you're not overreacting?"

"No," she responded, almost yelling. "She smacked me because she thought that I took her stupid earrings. But I did not," she replied, pointing to the part of her face that was turning a bright red.

"Well lil' mama, would you like a special hug?"

"A special hug?"

"Yea I don't give people regular hugs; I give special hugs," hearing about the special form of a hug, Rocky noticed her hesitation. "It'll make you feel better," he reasoned.

"I guess," she responded as she stood up to receive the hug. Standing up, Rocky towered over her, wrapping his thick arms around her small frame. Inhaling her scent, his taste buds began to water. The feeling of her skin reminded him of the touch of a feather. It was so delicate. Slowly his hands went up and down her back. Getting lost within the soft touch of her embrace, he didn't realize that he was holding on for such a long time.

"Um, are we done?" Leilani questioned. "Because I feel better now."

"Oh, I am sorry. I feel better too; it actually worked."

Releasing her from his grasp, Rocky sat back down next to her. The simple hug was a method to make Leilani feel better about the situation that transpired between her and her mother. Unbeknownst to her, the simple hug was the beginning of a chapter in her life that would change her forever.

******

Her past still held a tight grip around her as she was still learning how to cope. Many people who had a troubled past seemed to forget certain details pertaining to traumatic events. But Leilani, on the other hand, remembered every detail, every tear, every hit, every kick. Her mind refused to let her forget anything that had happened.

"Can't front, this nigga living lovely," Isaiah said, snapping Leilani out of her thoughts.

"You're right; you got to give it to him," she replied as she pulled the Mercedes into Harley's driveway. The home resembled a huge castle that was fit for royalty.

"This nigga gonna make me want to move down here and buy some shit like this."

"Really?" Leilani questioned. "I would never want to buy such a huge amount of space with only me in it."

The duo continued their conversation as they exited the car, making their way to the front door. Isaiah rang the bell but still focused on their conversation. The hefty door opened as Harley stood before the two, visibly upset.

"It's so nice to see you again," Leilani spoke as she entered the home with Isaiah following right behind her. Harley never replied to her as he led them back to his office space. Both Leilani and Isaiah found Harley's childish behavior amusing.

"Was it you who made those attacks on my trap houses?" he asked.

"I did not come here to discuss that," Leilani replied as she remained standing. "We came here because you called about our proposition, so it's either you take our offer or else them late-night calls won't end, and the news will just keep on getting worse and worse," she spoke.

Harley remained quiet as he sat in his oversized chair. The stress from the day was beginning to show on his face. Ever since he met Leilani, he noticed that his world had been turned upside down. It aggravated him that a woman was becoming close enough to control his emotions. Out of the many years of being in the streets, there was never a woman close enough to getting Harley this upset. It was new to him, as he caught himself being irrational earlier. But after a couple shots of Hennessey, Harley was seeing clearer now.

"I'll take the offer, but only one catch."

"Ok, what is it?" Isaiah questioned.

"I only want to deal with Leilani when it comes down to the

exchange. If she isn't the one dealing with the money, then the deal is off."

"Deal," Leilani said.

"Sounds like a plan; now was that complicated," Leilani said as she ended their meeting. Harley stared on as he followed Leilani to the front of the door. The way her hips swayed in her tights caused an erection to form in his pants.

"Bruh, keep your eyes up fo' I have to empty a clip into your ass for staring at my lil' sister," Isaiah whispered. His New York accent was strong, unlike anything he had ever heard in his life. Harley took heed of the warning as he opened the door for Leilani, but kept his eyes focused on Isaiah.

"Next time won't be a warning; I'll just straight shoot you," Isaiah replied as he placed his hand on the small of Leilani's back, lightly pushing her towards the car.

Harley stared on, watching as the duo drove off his property. Things in New York were going to get interesting as he planned on rocking the Supremes.

CHAPTER 9

Neon lights gleamed onto the stage as everyone anticipated the performance from King of Diamonds' most popular stripper, Misty. The whole club sat in silence waiting for the choreography to begin.

"You sure this bitch is actually good?" Leilani leaned over asking Don.

"Baby girl, she's supposed to be some really good dancer," he replied.

Usher's sweet voice sighed through the speakers as Misty swayed her hips to the beat. Misty's hands roamed her oily body as it glided against the stripper pole. The sound of the guitar and sweet sounds were completely different from the other sets that the previous strippers performed. Tonight, Misty wanted to grab every man's attention by being sexy with a love making song, instead of using some upbeat ratchet song. Usher sang a tune about making love nice and slow.

Let me take you to a place nice and quiet

There ain't no one there to interrupt, ain't gotta rush

I just wanna take it nice and slow

(Now baby tell me what you wanna do with me)

See I've been waiting for this for so long

We'll be makin' love until the sun comes up

Baby, I just wanna take it nice and slow

Leilani sang along as she too felt herself becoming hot by the sexual performance. Sincere sat right next to Leilani, noticing the change in her demeanor. Her poker face was softer, as she grinded her hips into the couch.

"Princess, you are giving the cold ass couch too much play; come do that on my lap," he said as he patted his thighs.

"You think you fucking slick?" she replied, knowing that he was a little tipsy. The crew had been in the strip club for only an hour and a half, and already Sincere was tipsy. She was the only sober person amongst the crew so she used it to her advantage. "I'll dance on you, but keep your fucking hands to yourself," she said as she got up to sit on his lap.

"Don't worry Princess, I'll keep it PG-13," he responded. None of the other guys paid attention to the two as Leilani began to gyrate her hips to the song. Sincere sat back as he observed Leilani's backside grinding into his crotch. He tried keeping his hands to himself, but the way she was grinding caused him to place his hands on her hips. He pushed his hips upwards in hopes of Leilani feeling the hard on that she was causing.

"Do you feel that?" he questioned.

She felt the thick python, but rather than boost his ego, she simply nodded her head no. He knew she was lying, but rather than address it he knew exactly how to make her talk. He placed his lips on the back of her neck, placing light kisses on it. Instantly he felt her shudder in pure pleasure. His hands began roaming her thighs until they found their way in between them. *Thank God the lights are low and this table is hiding his hand movements*, Leilani thought.

"Let's see how good your poker face is Princess," he said as his finger grazed her clit. The sensation of his masculine hands left Leilani shivering. It was the most pleasurable thing she had ever felt, as it had been a long time since she was touched like this.

"You are such an asshole," she whispered in his ear.

"Well Princess, I only want to be your asshole," he replied. He took the opportunity to enter her golden gates. She was soaking wet just like he expected, but that didn't stop him from grinding on her G-spot. He knew what he was doing, as he saw her trying to hold in her moan. When her head tilted back, he knew there was only one thing to be done, and that was to make her cum. He slowed down his movement as he kept his focus on her G-spot.

"Now Princess, if you were mine I would bring you back home and devour this flower you have between your legs," he said as he dug deeper into her.

"Then what's stopping you?" she replied.

"Let's take this back to our room then," he stood up, taking his hand from out of her skirt. Both Don and Isaiah were so focused on their strippers that they didn't acknowledge Sincere saying bye. Sincere found this to be ok, as he placed his hand on the small of Leilani's back, guiding her towards the parking lot. Once they got into their car, Sincere peeled out of the parking lot and into traffic. There wasn't any time to be wasted, as he needed to be all in Leilani.

"Slow down fool before you crash," she yelled.

"Oh, don't worry Princess, I would never allow that to happen," he responded. Within ten minutes he pulled the car up into the parking lot. The two wasted no time as they got out and into the hotel. Once on the elevator, their hands couldn't be kept off each other. The taste of Leilani's lips was sweet and soft as Sincere sucked on them for dear life. His hands found their way back under her dress as he once again began to play with her.

Her head fell back in pure ecstasy as he caught her neck, placing his lips on them. He sucked on her skin, releasing slurping sounds until he felt her skin swell from the hicky. A light vibration disrupted the two, but they both ignored the alert as they came off the elevator. Sincere grabbed his hotel key card out of his pocket and swiped in, granting access to the spacious suite.

"Princess you don't understand—"

"No talking, just straight fucking," Leilani replied as she replaced his lips with hers.

Sincere took heed of her demand, but he knew that what the two were doing was not just a one-time thing. The way he planned on putting it down on her, he was sure their relationship would escalate into something serious. He kept his mouth shut as he lifted her up, wrapping her legs around him. Their lips never left one another as he placed her body onto the bed. He broke their kiss as he began making a trail down to her vagina. Pulling down her dress, he revealed the cute thong that protected her goods. Without any hesitation, he ripped the thin piece of cloth, causing Leilani to moan.

"That shit was not che—" Leilani tried speaking, but was silenced by the wet sensation of Sincere's tongue. The euphoric feeling caused her to shut her eyes tight as she released light whimpers. A light vibration interrupted them once again, annoying the couple.

"Princess, I think you should get that," Sincere replied as he kept his lips planted between her lips.

"No, this is too good," she answered, while placing her hands on top of his head. She lightly pushed him deeper into her vagina, hoping he got the hint.

"Princess, answer your phone," Sincere said as the vibration continued.

"Ugh, fine," she said as she reached for her iPhone, glaring at the unknown number. She never answered numbers that she didn't know, but she wanted the ringing to stop so she decided to answer.

"Hello."

"Hi, is this Leilani Vasquez?" the caller asked.

"This is she, may I ask who's calling?"

"Hi Ms. Vasquez, this is Detective Underwood. I am calling about an incident that occurred with Essence Banks."

"Is she ok?"

"I am afraid not; she was assaulted in her apartment."

"Wait, what?" she questioned as she pushed Sincere off her. "Where is she?"

"Right now she is being treated at Kings County Hospital."

"I'm on my way," Leilani replied as she hung up the phone. The feeling between her legs dried up as the thought of death attempting to grant access in her home conquered her mind. Sincere stared on, confused on the severity of the situation. He tried grabbing Leilani's attention but she was fixated on gathering her stuff. The soft, sensational look departed as she became evolved into worry.

"Princess, is everything ok?" he asked as he grabbed her arms so she could finally face him. A look of fear was in her eyes as her eyes became glossy. Tears threatened to cascade down her face but she wiped them away quickly.

"No, I have to get back to Brooklyn," she whispered. "It's Essence."

Nothing more needed to be explained, as Sincere gathered his items following Leilani out of the door. Neither of them bothered packing their belongings. Instead he sent a text message to the pilot to have the jet fueled and ready to depart within 30 minutes. Sincere didn't bother to get details out of Leilani as he led her on their journey back home.

CHAPTER 10

Hours Prior

The apartment filled with the delightful aroma of steamed seafood. Essence had spent the past two hours preparing a dinner for her significant other, Casper. Weeks had passed since her last hit and lately she had been neglecting Casper, diverting all her attention into their daughter. Being together for practically a decade, they both had experienced some ups and downs. There were times where the two were inseparable, while other times rumors of Casper's infidelity drove them apart. Instead of being wrapped up in the arms of her boyfriend, Essence had spent many nights alone until her daughter came along. She'd lay at night cradling their offspring while the theory of adultery poisoned her mind. Casper would come home after clocking long hours in the streets with excuses about him trying to support their family.

Her hands turned the steel pot clockwise, stirring the spices in the boiling water. She could smell the strong garlic as the steam elevated into her face. The heat didn't bother her, but the memory of their first encounter began to replay in her head.

******

The shop was packed with females, replacing the scent of burning hair with the loud chatter of gossip. It was the beginning of February and everyone was excited about the special holiday, Valentine's Day. Most of the women in the shop were getting prepared to look their best for some man that they considered was worth the effort. Everyone was excited, including Essence; she was nearing her fifteenth birthday and she was happy about becoming older. Even though she had to spend the weekend at her mother's beauty shop, Essence did not actually mind as her thoughts were now consumed with several ideas for her birthday.

"Marisol, girl I need you to hook up my edges as my man should be doing something for us tonight," Roselyn said, plopping down into the brown leather chair.

"Girl, you know I got you. When have I ever let you down?" Marisol asked as she began to unpin the rollers in her client's hair. "So chica, what's up with your daughter La? Will she be getting anything done today?"

"Oh no, for what?" Roselyn answered quickly.

"Damn, I am just asking. Doesn't hurt to have a mommy and daughter beauty salon date."

The two adults spoke amongst each other as Essence tried her best to eavesdrop on the conversation. She noticed how Roselyn would bring her daughter with her for every hair appointment but never bothered to do her hair. Trying not to be too suspicious, Essence swept up the dirt into the dustpan, deciding to drop the garbage in the can that rested outside. Swiftly she carried the dustpan outside, dumping the remains into the garbage can that awaited. She tried making her way back into the shop when her attention was directed to the light skin boy that came jogging across the street, trying to get her attention.

"Hold up shawty, I just want to talk to you real quick," he replied as he smiled his way over to her.

"What's up?"

"Nothing much, I just wanted to let you know that I've been watching you for a minute now."

"Ok, and?"

"And I just wanted to know if I could take you out to dinner tonight? It's Valentine's Day."

"How do you know that I don't have a boyfriend?"

"Well that nigga must not be doing such a good job, as you're still standing here with a smile on your face."

He was right, but Essence refused to show that he was right. Instead, she agreed to his date, not believing that he would show up. Once she agreed, a smile came across his face as they exchanged numbers, and he agreed to come and pick her up from work. Essence went back into the shop to continue working. When it was time to shut the shop down, the mysterious boy came back like he promised, waiting for Essence. During their date, they instantly hit it off, as the attraction for the two was evident. He showed her a good time, making her feel like she was the only girl in the world.

******

Fast forward ten years later, Casper got down on one knee asking her for her hand in marriage. Being in a relationship with a nigga in the game wasn't as nice as society had portrayed it to be. Movies glorified street dealer's lifestyles, portraying it to be a glamourous life. Essence was the only one donating any time into their relationship. All his time went into making money and sleeping in the streets. The game was his wife and Essence was the jump off. She was simply engaged to a married man. Whenever the streets called he would go running off to her with no questions asked. No matter what he did and how he treated her, Essence always found herself making her way back into the relationship.

Grabbing the expensive porcelain plates from the cabinets, she began to set the dinner table for the two of them. The sound of the apartment door opening and closing shut caught her attention. The sound of Casper's voice echoed as he continued rapping along with the music that pumped through the speakers of his phone.

"Babe I'm in the kitchen," Essence yelled out.

"What are you doing in the kitchen?" he asked as he followed the scent of the food to her presence. He found her standing in front of the sink as she continued to wash out all the pots she had used to make them dinner. It had been months since Essence had cooked Casper a meal where they both sat and ate together. Usually, she was busy with her shop or working with Leilani, and he was doing what he did best.

"Umm, what else do people do when they are in the kitchen?"

"Cook crack," he replied with a chuckle.

"Go wash your hands and get ready for dinner. Tonight we are having a seafood special. I made all of your favorites," she replied as she finished washing the last pot. Without much debate, he walked away from the kitchen to do what she had instructed. The sweet smell of the perfume on him followed right behind him leaving the kitchen. Essence noticed the feminine smell, making a mental note of the familiar scent. *Vanilla musk*, she knew that scent from somewhere, but just couldn't place it with a face.

"Babe, how was your day?" she questioned.

"It was decent, nothing crazy," he yelled back from their bathroom. Casper eyed himself, making sure that he looked presentable. He smoothed down any fly away hairs while quickly checking his body for any scratch marks. Approving his appearance, he washed his hands and walked back into the kitchen. The food was on the table, steaming. He took his seat at the table and began eating the plate of food Essence had prepared. His mouth watered at the delightful infusion of seafood and the spices. *At least shawty can cook,* he thought as he devoured his meal.

"Could have at least waited for me to sit down," she said.

"Sorry, just couldn't resist."

"Is everything ok?"

"Yea everything is fine so far," Casper said proudly.

"That's good my love."

Essence ate her food in silence, anticipating that Casper would at least try to keep the conversation going. But instead, he remained silent on the other end of the table. Lately, this is what life had resorted to between the two; Casper spent most of his time in the streets, leaving Essence and his daughter all alone. Her eyes glared at the Tiffany's engagement ring, admiring the elegant cushion diamond. Casper had done extremely well picking out such a perfect ring for her, as it was big and garish just like she liked it. The ring had been placed on her finger just a little over a year ago. They had been together for almost a decade without a promise of real commitment. Essence had nagged Casper about them making their relationship official, as she felt unsatisfied with only being his girlfriend. She wanted way more than just that. She wanted to carry his last name.

"When are we going to start planning the wedding Casper?"

"Why are you in such a rush to get married?"

"We have been engaged for a little over a year now and we haven't even set a date. You plan on being engaged for another ten years?" she questioned, as she could feel her voice picking up with annoyance.

"You can't wait?"

"No Casper, I can't wait. I've been with you for how long before you fucking decided to propose only after I began to nag you."

"Either way Essie, shit will get done. It ain't like you gonna leave me or anything, so chill the fuck out."

"Really?" she asked.

"Yes, we got fucking time. Either way, you're gonna be my wife regardless. If you want, we can go right downtown and have a quick wedding."

"Casper, I don't want things done like that. I deserve the whole packed church, then huge reception party. Don't you think so?"

"Right about now, you're being fucking ungrateful. You want to get married, and I'm telling you that we could go to City Hall right now, get married, and still be back for the re-runs of Martin," he yelled.

"That's not how I want our wedding to be."

"Well, Essence it's either that or we don't get married at fucking all. Because the way I see it, regardless we are still going to be considered man and wife based upon that common-law shit."

"Are you serious?" she questioned. "That shit is not even effective in New York."

"Yea nigga, I am dead fucking ass."

Dissatisfied with his reply, Essence grabbed what was left of her food and threw it into the garbage can. The loud thud caught Casper's attention as he watched Essence walk into their bedroom. Not bothered, Casper sat at the table as he continued to eat his food. He knew she would calm down, as she often threw tantrums whenever he didn't give her things her way.

"I'll give her ten minutes and her ass will be calm," Casper said, convincing himself. Once he finished his plate, Casper got up from his spot and sat the plate in the sink. Intrigued, he kept silent as he tried his best to hear what was going on in the room. He thought that Essence would be cursing to herself by now, while flinging his expensive merchandise, in hopes of causing damages. But unfortunately, not a peep came out of the room. He finally decided to check on Essence just to see what she was up to. Casper walked into their room and was surprised as to what was before him.

"What are you doing?" he asked confused.

Essence didn't bother replying, as she knew her actions were obvious. She had three suitcases open as she moved between the closets and her suitcases. The couple had been through this a dozen times, but for some reason Essence felt different. She wasn't being blinded by her tears and snot. Instead, her mind was clear while she packed up all her stuff. She was finally fed up with Casper's shit. She had reached her breaking point.

"Woman, I am talking to you. What the fuck are you doing?" his voice boomed.

"Is it not obvious?" she replied. "I am leaving you."

"You say that shit all the time, and then bring your ass right the fuck back home."

Bizarrely, a chuckle escaped her lips, causing Casper to be confused. He was expecting her to yell in anger or throw something his way. But she was calm, folding her clothing up neatly. He had never seen her like this before, which freaked him out. He wanted a reaction from her just to confirm that this wasn't the end.

"You always put on a show, and then go back to them lonely bitches you call your friends, and you share my damn business to them bitches," he said.

"You damn right."

"You not going no fucking where."

Essence finally stopped her movement to stare into his eyes. The sweet smell of vanilla musk and pink lilies invaded her nostrils as Casper continued to rant about her not leaving. She stared at the man before her and could tell something was different about him. Those thick eyebrows she loved so much were neatly shaped to perfection as they arched into pure frustration. His goatee had outgrown, but his barber did a hell of a job taming it. His big brown eyes were lightly red, as the weed he had smoked earlier had finally entered his system. Two things that had the birds flocking to him was his perfectly curly hair and his skin. He always wore his hair in a low Caesar hair cut with sea waves that were out of this world. His medium brown skin complexion was the right mixture, as it helped broadcast his African roots; all the females were putty once they got a good look at him. The tattoos that were carved onto his body told a story of the street life that he lived. Despite never changing his appearance, Casper was not the same guy that had walked into the beauty salon years ago.

"Who is she?" Essence asked.

"Who is who?"

"That bitch that got you acting so fucking stupid."

His eyes met her body as he stared intensely at her curves. Her pretty face was twisted into pure anger, and for some odd reason he found it very attractive. All her daggering words fell on deaf ears as he continued to admire her body. One thing he could never deny was that Essence was one of the most beautiful women he had ever met. At 5'5, his girl was every hood bitch's worst nightmare. Her body was the perfect build as other women around the world paid thousands of dollars for a body like hers. Even with having their daughter Emery, Essence could snap back and adjust to the extra weight. Despite having an amazing body, she was beautiful with piercing brown eyes and blemish free, light skin. Her exotic appearance would make any man stop to stare or even sacrifice whatever it took to be with her.

"Come here baby."

"For what?"

"Let's stop arguing and start on what I told you about the other day," he walked over to her and allowed his hands to roam her body until they found their destination. His fingers felt around her insides in search of her G-spot. A gush of air escaped her thick lips as she was in pure ecstasy. The feeling of his touch caused her to shiver as he laid her down on the ground. He parted her inner folds and began to play with her insides. The sensational feeling caused her to moan out in pleasure. His tongue glided against her smooth skin, leaving a streak of saliva. Slowly, he made his way down to the crease of her vagina, taking his time to go between the folds. The heat from her body sunk into the air as Casper pleasured her into an orgasm. He knew what he was doing and how she had liked it. He used his tongue to carve her pleasure into a masterpiece. Slicing and cutting, using his tongue as a weapon.

"Baby," she cried. The feeling of his warm tongue gliding against her clitoris was immaculate. This was the first time he had ever given her oral sex, and she couldn't help to but to be wrapped up in cloud 9. Her walls got tighter as she could feel herself coming closer to an orgasm. Noticing that she was ready to cum, Casper held her down and began to dig deeper into her. Her heavy panting increased the longer he flapped his tongue back and forth. She cried out in pure ecstasy as she came.

"Baby, I've missed you," he spoke. His words were soft and genuine, nothing compared to the asshole he had been over the past couple of years. Maybe he can change, she thought. She wanted to try and make their problematic relationship work. There was still some fight left within her. She just wanted to see if Casper was willing to fight alongside her. She stared at her name that was forever embedded into his skin. The cursive red lettering was his way of showing her that he was serious about their relationship, only after being caught in another lie. The tattoo was almost perfect until she noticed a red bruise that sat on it. The skin blemish was faint, but there was no denying its existence.

"What the fuck is that?" she asked.

"Is what?"

"You have some fucking nerve, you fucking piece of shit."

She pointed towards the hickey that was red and fresh. Filled with anger, Essence smacked him straight across his face. Out of all the years they had been together, he had never brought home any evidence suggesting he wasn't being faithful. But today, the hickey was beaming, taunting her.

"After all I have fucking done for you, this is how you fucking repay me; you piece of fucking shit," she yelled. Essence became blind with rage as she began swinging, connecting her punches with his face. Pain shot through his jaw as he knew if he took another hit it would come out of its socket.

"Baby relax," he replied.

"No, fuck you bitch; I am leaving. How could you fucking do this to me when all I have ever been to you was faithful you piece of shit," she answered, as she stood up from the ground and continued her packing. The tears refused to descend from her eyes as she was just too angry to cry.

"You're not leaving me Essence."

"Nigga, you should have thought about that when you allowed that fucking bitch to suck on your fucking neck."

"So, you gonna leave me because some irrelevant bitch was sucking on my neck?"

"No nigga, I am leaving you because you do not know how to be fucking loyal," she said as she began zipping up her suitcase. "Have fun, cuz I know Isaiah will be a better father and husband to your family than you would ever be."

"What the fuck you said?" he asked.

"You fucking heard me nigga," she replied as she turned around to face him. "That nigga Isaiah, the one you can't stand. I guarantee you he will be a better boyfriend and father to your daughter. Shit, he may even dick me down better than you. I might even scream his name, calling him papi," she chuckled.

The mere mention of Isaiah angered Casper, as he knew that Isaiah had a thing for his girl. But for him to raise his daughter and do a better job than him, set Casper off. His pride had taken a huge blow. His heart was being ripped out of his chest, as the only girl he ever loved spoke about fucking another nigga. Her words were filled with years of pent up anger. She had been faithful to a cheater for years, only to end up number two to some hoe that didn't even know his government name. Anger seethed through them both as the infidelity between the two had them seeing red. Casper rushed towards Essence, knocking her onto the ground. The two struggled on the ground, neither of them willing to back down. Love was no longer an element within the two, as they both wanted to harm each other. Essence had hated everything she had become. She was submissive to all his demands, not caring about herself. Her only desire was to please the man she had claimed. The lies and deceit had burned out all the love she once had for him. He had given away a part of him that he could not take back, which in her book was untrustworthy. Casper could see the pain within her eyes, as it pained him to see all the hurt he had caused her. He didn't hate Essence; he simply hated the situation he put them into.

"You can't leave me," he said. "I cannot let you go."

Pain saturated his masculine voice. The fantasy of his infidelity had evolved into his nightmare. He no longer had control over what was happening, as the love of his life was going to leave him. Underneath him, she ranted about him being disloyal and dishonest. Her voice erupted throughout his head, interrupting his thinking process. He needed her to shut up so he could explain to her how sorry he was. The more he tried taming her, the more she fought back. For such a little woman, her blows really caused some damage, as he could feel his eye beginning to swell.

"Would you shut the fuck up already so I can explain to you—"

"Nigga, there ain't shit to discuss," Essence belted as she began to attack him some more. The pain of his disloyalty motivated her fists as they drove into his face. He was bigger than her, but she knew exactly what she was doing. Her right fist connected to his jaw while her left fist caught his nose.

"She was a mistake," Casper yelled as he began to fight back. His hands pounded into Essence's flesh, leaving the imprint of his knuckles. With every hit he placed on Essence, she fought back. But then her yelling quieted down as her punches became lighter. It wasn't long before Essence lay underneath him unconscious, near death.

"What have I done?" Casper asked himself as he stared down at Essence's battered body. She no longer resembled the beauty queen that he took pride in. Her battered body was the replica of something from a freak show. Her eyes were swollen with dark purple circles forming around them. Blood decorated her face, replacing the beauty she once possessed. Casper stood staring in disbelief. *What should I do now?* he thought. His mind began running a million times faster in hopes of producing a plan. Home would no longer be the same, as he knew what could be the consequence if he stayed. Leilani would come hunting after him for what he had done to Essence. There was no way he could even stay in Brooklyn. He had to do the only logical thing, *run.*

CHAPTER 11

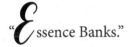

"Essence Banks."

"One moment," the nurse replied as she began to slowly type the name into the computer screen. Nurse Jackie's fingers tapped lightly on the keyboard as she searched the database for the patient. Her eyes quickly scanned the screen, missing the patient's name a dozen times. The twenty-second search began to turn into minutes as Leilani began to get agitated.

"You said Essence Bank?"

"Banks," Leilani corrected. Nurse Jackie continued typing away once again, only to miss it again.

"I am sorry ma'am there isn't a patient in here by that name."

Leilani released a huge gush of air, annoyed by the ignorance of the nurse. Her pressure was increasing at a quick pace, causing Leilani's hands to shake. Receiving the phone call about Essence's assault resulted in Leilani's nerves to go bad. Both Leilani and Sincere didn't waste any time firing up the jet back to New York. She didn't even bother with packing any of her belongings back at the house, as she stood in the hospital lobby wearing her club ensemble. The black Versace knee length dress fit snug around her hourglass shape while her French manicured feet sat perfectly in her Giuseppe Zanotti sandals. The nurse stared into Leilani's eyes, glancing over her appearance. *This little bitch can't be over thirty, and her outfit is more than my fucking paycheck,* Nurse Jackie thought.

"Miss, I don't mean any disrespect. Had you been anyone else I would not even be saying this right now. I understand that you're overworked and probably just pulled a double shift, but let me make this clear: I am not the one to be fucked with. I got a phone call pertaining to my sister Essence Banks. A detective informed me about her being brought in after an assault. Now if you want to piss me off more than you already have, I would like to warn you my fellow sister, I don't think them emergency room doctors will be able to bring you back from this flat line," Leilani replied. Her blood was boiling as she could feel her anxiety beginning to take over.

"Excuse me little girl."

"Ma'am please do not make me repeat myself."

Eyeing the young woman, Nurse Jackie could tell that right now wasn't the time. Annoyed and filled with fear, Jackie began her typing, miraculously pulling up the information pertaining to Essence. She pulled out the nametags, writing Essence's name on it and handed it over to Leilani.

"She's in room 365."

"Thank you," Leilani replied, grabbing the nametags. Proceeding towards security to be cleared, Leilani could feel her heartbeat out of her chest. The smell of cleaning products engulfed her nose. The scent of the bleach left a weary feeling on her heart. Everything was moving in slow motion as both she and Sincere entered the elevator. She pressed the button for the third floor, and waited for the elevator to get onto their designated floor. The duo walked around the hospital floor until they found the room that read 365. Walking into the gloomy room, they anticipated the sweet sound of Essence's voice. Instead they were met by the unconscious shell of Essence's battered body. The body that lay in the bed was a domestic violence victim. The patient was badly disfigured and barely recognizable.

"We are in the wrong room," Leilani replied.

"Are you sure?" Sincere asked. "I'm pretty sure the nurse said room 365."

"Yes, but this can't be Essence. I can't recognize this person." Leilani stared on at the battered body in disbelief. She couldn't wrap her mind around the damage that was done to her best friend. All the tubes that were connected to her body caused Leilani's heart to cry out in pain.

"You must be her sister, Leilani," the nurse asked, interrupting Leilani's thoughts.

"Yes I am. Can anyone tell me what's going on?"

"Well, your sister came in badly beaten," the nurse began, informing Leilani about the brutality of Essence's injuries. The descriptive words left Leilani astonished. Her heart felt heavy with grief as she was not there to save her best friend. If she was present, then there was a chance that she would have been able to do something. The doctor walked into the room and began explaining to Leilani the severity of Essence's condition.

"Well, your sister has flat lined three times within the course of an hour," he spoke. "We took her into surgery to stop the bleeding in her brain. The surgery was a success, but for the next 72 hours we will have to monitor her as these hours will be crucial to her recovery."

"Thank you Doctor, but did the police mention anything about her little girl?"

"There wasn't anyone that came with the patient. The police will be in to ask you some questions later."

"Thank you Doctor," Sincere said as he took a crying Leilani into his chest. The tears saturated his shirt but he didn't care; his girl was in pain. Sincere found the nearest chair, taking a seat and resting Leilani on his lap. She wept in his arms while he gently stroked her hair. They sat like this for hours, with his arms comforting her. Her cries lessened, but the tears still poured through her eyes. Light snores escaped her lips as sleep overcame her.

"Don't worry, Princess; I got you shorty," Sincere whispered as he placed light kisses onto her forehead. Her face was soaked with tears, but that didn't stop him from caressing it.

******

72 hours later

Heavy rain cascaded down on Brooklyn as millions of people ran around searching for cover. The dark-grey clouds hovered over dozens of buildings, threatening a thunderstorm. As Leilani stared out of the hospital window, she couldn't help but to feel angry. Two days had passed since she got the phone call, and it seemed as if there wasn't any progression with Essence's health. On top of that, both Casper and Emery were missing. Not knowing the whereabouts of her goddaughter generated a feeling that Leilani was not accustomed to: fear. Leilani's mind ran wild with thoughts. Having dozens of enemies, anyone could have kidnapped the child and that bothered Leilani.

"Princess, did you eat yet?" The sound of Sincere's deep baritone voice dragged her out of her cold thoughts.

"Nah."

"What would you like to eat babe?"

"I am ok."

"I didn't ask you if you were ok Princess, I asked you what would you like to eat," he replied sternly.

Leilani turned around, finally facing him. His face was scrunched in irritation as he was aggravated by the way Leilani had been taking care of herself. He had stayed in the hospital with Leilani, only leaving her side when he had to shower and check on the streets.

"Like I told you before, I am just fine."

"Leilani, I didn't ask you shit about if you were fine. Now I am gonna go to Five Guys and pick you up a burger with that fucking bubble tea shit," he replied.

"Why you going all the way downtown?"

"Because I have to go handle something in that area, and two of your favorite food places are over there." Gathering all his belongings, he prepared himself to leave. "I'll be back in the next hour and a half; don't go around shooting anyone."

The annoyance could be heard in his voice as he made his exit from the hospital room. Leilani knew why he felt the way he did with her. She was so headstrong, turning him on most of the time, but right at that moment he didn't want to deal with her stubbornness. He wanted to help her during this sensitive time in her life.

"Sincere," she called after him.

"Yes?" he answered, turning to face her. Unexpectedly, Leilani grabbed his arms, wrapping them around her waist. She placed her lips on his, snaking her tongue into his mouth. Time ceased, making it seem as if it were only them in the world. The feeling was foreign to Leilani, but she was learning how to enjoy it. Finding potential in someone was all she had ever desired in life. After what seemed like eternity, Leilani broke the kiss, broadcasting her smile.

"What was that for?" he asked confused.

"A little thank you for being there for me."

"Well Princess, that isn't enough. You could thank me by actually taking that chance on me."

"What chance?"

"Be my girl."

"How about we take this slow and see where this leads us."

"Anything for you Princess."

"Alright boy, now go and get my food."

This was all too surreal for her. Leilani never believed that she would ever get the chance to experience anything like this. Leilani stared at Sincere's back as he walked out of the hospital room. He was a good man and she knew that, she just didn't want to be hurt. She'd heard too many stories about men being players, and she didn't need that.

"I hope he treats me good Essie," Leilani said. "Lord knows I cannot deal with any more crazies in my life," she chuckled.

The door to the hospital room squeaked open as two men walked into the room. Leilani didn't need to ask questions to know who they were. Turning her nostrils up to their scent, Leilani grew defensive, fucking swine.

"Ms. Vasquez?" the taller one asked.

"Detective."

"I'm Detective Underwood. This here is my partner Ramos; we just have a few questions about your friend."

"I just may have some answers for you."

Getting comfortable in her chair, Leilani knew this would take some time. The detectives were going to ask her some unnecessary questions in hopes of finding Essence's attacker. Deep down inside, Leilani knew for a fact that they would never find him because they weren't motivated to close her case. Leilani was motivated, and she vowed that she would bring her best friend's attacker to street justice.

"We have reasons to believe that the possible suspect could be her fiancé named Casper," Detective Ramos began.

Leilani stared up at the detective, becoming lost within her own thoughts. The friendship that she and Essence had was so weird, but Leilani loved the hell out of her best friend. Seeing her like this fucked with Leilani's mind. Leilani remembered the huge fight she had with her mother over coming home late, as she and Essence had gotten lost on their way to Wendy's after school.

******

"Ok students, I want you guys to enjoy your weekend," Mrs. Smith said. Looking into the eyes of the 11 and 12 year olds, she could see

the excitement within them. Summer was starting in a couple of days, which meant it was the end of the school year. For the next two months, thousands of students would enjoy going to sleep whatever time they wanted, waking up late in the afternoon, and the best part of it all: **No Homework.** *"Monday morning be prepared to take home your school work."*

"Ok Mrs. Smith," they all yelled out.

"Alright kids, have a great weekend."

Grabbing their bags, her children ran out of the classroom excited to start their weekend. Big things were going to happen this summer. Hormones were raging within the pre-teens as they each had a crush on the opposite sex. Everyone except for Leilani. Leaving the school building, Leilani dreaded going home. Things between her mother and her hadn't been the same since the whole missing earring incident. Leilani noticed the difference with the way her mother treated her. The way her mother would speak to her was different. Her mother no longer talked to her, instead she spat at her. Roselyn had this annoyed look whenever Leilani would ask a question. Not knowing what she did wrong, Leilani fought her thoughts everyday as she tried to come up with a solution to repair her relationship with her mother.

"Hey La." Turning to face the person who had spoken to her, Leilani was surprised to see Essence. The two friends had not communicated with each other for a while due to Roselyn no longer working at the hair salon.

"Oh, hey Essence."

"Was sup, where are you going?"

"Home."

"Come with me real quick to Wendy's. I don't wanna go alone," she responded. Leilani's face twisted in confusion as she analyzed her decision in her head. Her mother had told her that after school every day she must return home by a certain time. Every day like clockwork, Leilani would walk through her house door no later than 4:15 pm. "I'll even buy you some chicken nuggets," Essence said convincingly.

"Alright, where is it?"

"Right up that road," Essence pointed. Following the direction her finger pointed to, Leilani tried her best to see the Wendy's.

"Ok, let's go. We have to make it quick because I have to make it home by a certain time."

"Don't worry, I got you."

Together the two walked in pursuit of Essence's favorite fast food restaurant. Silence towered over them as neither of them knew what to say to the other. Their minds were corrupted with the same question: why isn't she talking to me? Fed up with the silence, Essence broke the iceberg by surprising Leilani with a statement.

"So, La, I heard that your momma got a new man," Essence said, trying to start a conversation.

"Yea, they been together for a minute. I'm surprised that you're just now hearing about him."

"Well, the females at my mother's shop have been talking about them. So, I've been hearing about them for a while now. I just wanted to see if the gossip was actually true."

"Girl, the gossip is true."

"How do you like him?"

"He's cool I guess. It's just Mommy swears that I am doing something with him."

"Well did you?"

"Hell no," Leilani replied. She couldn't believe that Essence would ever ask such a stupid question.

"What?" Essence asked defensively. "I am just asking."

"I didn't do anything with him."

The two continued their conversation as they made their way to the fast food restaurant. Leilani couldn't help but to laugh; she was happy that she finally had someone to talk to. At home, Leilani didn't have anyone to talk to. Whenever she would try to talk to her mother, Roselyn would behave as if Leilani was annoying her. So, having a conversation with her mother never happened. Rocky on the other hand was cool to talk to about her problems, but her mother was the issue. Her mother believed that she was doing something with the grown man, so what she and Rocky used to have was stopped.

Entering the establishment, a bright smile broadcasted onto Essence's face. The smell of the overused oil filled the air, causing their taste buds to water. Leilani's stomach grumbled underneath her clothing. The little girl had not eaten a single thing at school today because the lunch menu didn't look too appealing. Going the whole day without eating, Leilani didn't even realize her hunger until now. Staring at the menu with the perfectly stacked burger, she couldn't stop her stomach from making sounds. Patiently waiting on line, they ordered their food receiving it within five minutes. Quickly, Essence went through the bag to make sure all her things were there. Once she verified that everything was ok, she handed Leilani her chicken nuggets as they continued their journey back home.

"These nuggets taste so good," Leilani said as she dipped her nugget into the barbeque sauce.

"I know right," Essence replied as she took a bite of her french fries.

Together the duo walked, their laughter filled the streets of Brooklyn with people staring at the pre-teens. Munching on their food, they turned corners and walked down long blocks, so engulfed in their conversation they never noticed the change of scenery. The once highly populated black community transformed into a more Jewish neighborhood. Bodegas were replaced with more apartment buildings. Storefronts looked cleaner compared to the dingy Chinese restaurants that adorned their low middle-class community. Once she noticed that they were no longer in an area that she recognized, Leilani stopped walking.

"Umm."

"What's wrong?"

"Do you know where the hell we are?"

"No," Essence responded while eyeing their surroundings. "Do you know?"

"No."

Looking around, they both took in their new environment. They didn't recognize not one thing about the community. It was clear that they were both lost. Staring at the street signs, Essence tried to see if the street name rang any bells. **Rutland,** *she read. She wasn't familiar with the name of the street.*

"Do you remember which way we came from?" Essence questioned.

"No, you were the one who brought us here."

"I know, but you could have at least paid attention to the route we took to get here." Dumbfounded, Leilani stared at Essence as if she had two heads. Preparing to reply with a smart answer, Leilani second-guessed that decision. Staring at her digital watch, Leilani read the time, **3:45 p.m. How the fuck am I gonna get back home?** *she thought.*

"Listen, I don't have time to figure out whose fault it is. Let's just figure out a way to get me home."

"Cool, let me ask this man the quickest way to get you home."

Empathetic to Leilani's situation, Essence walked up to a stranger and began asking for help. Knowing how weird her mother was, Essence wanted to do anything just to get Leilani home within a reasonable time. Conversing with the man, Essence could gather the information that she needed. Quickly, she turned around to face Leilani with their new travel route.

"He said to basically take the B35 to the B44."

"And that will get me home?"

"Yes, it will."

Together, both girls put their differences to the side as their main goal became getting Leilani home safe and sound. Continuing their journey, they walked the unfamiliar street in silence. Neither of them could develop a conversation, as their thoughts remained corrupted by the consequences of their afternoon detour. Their feet moved as fast as they could dodge in between the many working people of the popular area. Getting onto the B35, Leilani's anxiety began to ease with the possibility of her making it home at a decent hour. Traffic wasn't moving good for a Thursday afternoon, which surprised both girls. Transferring off the B35, she ran off the bus just in time to get onto her second bus. It wasn't long before she got off the bus and began her speed walk to her building. The familiar low-income apartment eased her conscious the closer she got to home.

"We are almost there," Leilani said to Essence as she made a light jog.

"Yes, we are."

Placing her key into the lock, Leilani opened the lobby door to her building. The strong stench of urine smacked both girls in their face, almost blinding them. Quickly, they entered the elevator taking it to the eighth floor. Light thumping echoed in the air, as millions of scenarios ran through Leilani's head. Clueless to how her mother would react, she was hesitant on entering her apartment. Turning to face her best friend, she gave a pleading look for help.

"I can't do anything La, you have to face the heat."

"I know but—"

"But nothing, just go and deal with it, or else you will make things worse."

"Fine."

"Just tell her the truth about you going with me to Wendy's and you got lost."

"You think she's going to believe it?"

"It doesn't matter if she does because it's the truth."

"Fine," Leilani replied as she wrapped her thin arms around Essence, hugging her tightly. Inhaling deeply, Leilani let go as she turned around to face her apartment door. Placing the key into the lock, she unlocked the door, entering the darkness. The smell of cigarette smoke watered her taste buds as she timidly walked into the living room. Her mother sat silently on the couch in the dark with the afternoon sun beaming through the small living room window. Releasing the cancerous puff of nicotine, Roselyn never turned her head to face her pre-teen daughter, instead she brought the cigarette up to her lips, pulling the addictive blend of nicotine into her lungs. Slowly she exhaled the smoke.

"Where have you been?" she asked, finally.

"I went with Essence to—"

"Before you finish that lie, I am going to let you think about your answer first," she interrupted as she took another pull. "I am listening."

"I went with Essence to Wendy's to pick up something to eat."

"And?"

"And when we left we began to walk and got lost."

"Really?"

"Yes, we were lost and had to find our way to Church and Utica."

"Really?"

"Yes, then we took the 35 to the 44."

Standing before her mother, Leilani was a nervous wreck. Her fingers twitched watching her mother silently smoke a cigarette. The anticipation within her began to build as she waited for a response. Sweat slowly slid down her furrowed brows only making her more nervous. Her mother smashed the remainder of the cigarette into her astray and turned, facing her daughter.

"So, you expect me to believe that bullshit?"

"Mommy, it's the truth."

"Really?"

"Yes."

"So, you went to Wendy's with Essence?"

"Yes."

"Leilani I am going to give you five seconds to tell the truth, and if I don't hear it, I swear you won't like what I will do to you."

"Momm—"

"5….4…3…2."

"I am not lying."

Her response was ignored as her mother grabbed a handful of Leilani's hair. Bending her head back her mother glared into Leilani's terrified eyes. In one swift motion, she smashed her bald up fist into Leilani's face. Doubling over, Leilani cupped her face in pain. Unbothered about her daughter's pursuit to protect herself, Roselyn began to kick her daughter.

"Lies, that's all I keep hearing out of your mouth," she yelled as she unleashed a beating onto her daughter. "You were probably out there being a fast little girl. Opening your fucking legs for any and every fucking thing."

Pain erupted throughout her whole body as Leilani remained curled into a ball in hopes of protecting herself from her mother's attack. She didn't understand why she was receiving this form of punishment. ***I told the truth****, she reasoned. Nothing made sense to her as she received the beating of her life. She wanted it all to end; she needed an escape.*

"I do all this shit for you to fucking be a puta. Te doy una vida nueva para que mientas, y seas una puta."

Pushing the feeling of her pain to the side, Leilani quickly thought of a plan to escape. She needed to escape before her mother killed her. Quickly, Leilani dashed to the front door with her mother running right behind her.

"Bring your ass back over here," her mother yelled behind her. Running down the flight of stairs, Leilani had no time to wait for the elevator. Her feet moved hurriedly as her mother's footsteps began to get closer. "Get the fuck back over here."

Finally reaching the lobby, Leilani made a run for it, exiting out of the back door of her building. The sound of her mother's voice became distant as she had outrun her. ***Maybe if you stop smoking cigarettes you'd be able to catch up to me****, Leilani thought as she turned around, searching to see if her mother was near.*

"I need to find a place," Leilani said to herself as she began to walk aimlessly. She had no clue as to where she could go. Thanks to her mother being the bitch she was, Leilani didn't have a special family member that she was able to go to. Leilani's list of friends was very scarce as her mother wasn't highly liked amongst their community. Her only true friend was Essence, but she couldn't go to her because she knew her mother would

go searching there for her.

"Where can I go?" she asked herself. Her feet moved aimlessly without a location in mind. A sharp pain entered her side, making her wince in pain. She'd never felt anything like this before. Unable to walk a long-distance, Leilani needed somewhere to sit down, and fast. ***I should just go into the park,*** *she thought while cupping her side. Deciding that it was a good option, she walked into the park searching for a spot to sit. After some time, she found the perfect spot; it was a bench that was shaded by a long branch. Limping her way over, she took a seat on the wooden bench, relieving her aching body. It almost hurt for her to sit down. A gush of air escaped her lips as the pain from her body seemed to ease. With her pain subsiding, now her mind could focus on her main problem,* ***What the fuck am I going to do about my living arrangement?***

"I don't even think I can go back home. My mother tried to kill me once, she'll probably do it again," she said out loud. Watching the children run around the playground, Leilani couldn't help but to crack a smile. She wished she could go back to that age where she could live carefree. The only thing that would be on her mind would be her mother buying her something from the ice cream truck. She missed when life wasn't complicated.

"What are you doing here all alone?"

Turning to face the person that was talking to her, Leilani was surprised to see Rocky. Immediately, she knew her mother had sent him out after her. Panicking, she tried to stand up to run away, but a shock of pain entered her rib cage that caused her to sit back on the wooden bench.

"Woah, take it easy," he said. "What the hell happened to your face?"

"What's wrong with it?"

"You have a black and blue mark on your face."

"Nothing happened."

"Don't lie to me; tell me what happened." Staring into his eyes, Leilani could see the sincerity in his eyes. Feeling safe, she explained to him the events that had transpired between her and her mother. She watched as his eyes became sincere the more she spoke about her troubles. Once she was done telling her story, they sat there in silence. Leilani wondered what was going through his head as he sat there deep in his thoughts.

"Come with me lil' mama."

"Where?"

"Just come with me," he responded standing up. Leilani tried to stand up, but the pain within her side prevented her from doing it alone. Noticing her struggle, Rocky helped her up, placing her arm around his neck. Together they walked out of the park and towards his car. "Are you hungry?"

"No, I'm good," she replied as she sat down in his car. Closing the BMW door, Rocky walked swiftly over to the driver's side. Getting into the car, he sat behind the wheel and began to dig into his pockets. Pulling out a zip lock bag, he proceeded to roll up his spliff. Sitting next to him, Leilani remained quiet, confused on what was happening. Once he was finished rolling his nice sized blunt, Rocky placed it between his lips as he dug in his pockets searching for his lighter.

"What are you doing?"

"Don't worry about it," he replied as he lit the end of his blunt. An orange hue glowed as Rocky inhaled the smoke. Taking two puffs, he handed the blunt over to Leilani, waiting for her to take it. "It will help with the pain on your side," he said.

"Are you sure?"

"Yes, take it."

Believing him, Leilani took the blunt from his hand. Staring at the perfectly rolled joint, she contemplated on her decision to smoke it. She'd never done drugs before and hadn't planned on doing so. But staring at the joint, she wanted something to take her pain away. Oh, what the hell; why not? she thought. Placing the butt of the joint in between her lips, she inhaled the smoke, allowing it to penetrate her lungs. Releasing, she coughed deeply as her virgin lungs weren't accustomed to the toxic smoke.

"You did good for a first timer lil' mama," Rocky commended her.

"Thank you, that tastes nasty."

"Yea it's always like that the first time around."

The two remained in the car until they finished their blunt. Leilani was higher than she had ever been. She felt stuck in her seat watching the passing cars zip by. Lost within her own world, Leilani never noticed Rocky's hand slid onto her premature thigh. Steadily he rubbed it, asking for her attention, but unbeknownst to him she was too high to even talk. The car pulled into her hood with all eyes on the BMW. People knew exactly who it was as their eyes gawked at the infamous Rocky. Finding the perfect parking spot right in front of her building, Rocky shut the car off.

"Ok, lil' mama let's go inside. Your mother is probably worried sick about you."

Unable to reply Leilani, gathered her things and exited the car. The thick summer air smacked her as she found it hard to breathe. ***Why do I feel like this?*** *she questioned herself. Her feet felt as if they were walking on fluffy clouds. Entering the building, the stench of urine did not irritate her. The journey up to her apartment didn't seem as it usually does. Walking on to her floor, Leilani walked with a smile on her face, careless about the exchange of events that had occurred earlier.*

"As soon as I open this door, I want you to walk straight into your bedroom," Rocky told her.

"Ok."

Unlocking the door to her apartment, Leilani did exactly what he said, walking straight into her room. Her mother called behind for her, but Leilani kept her head straight forward, not once caring for her mother.

******

"Ms. Vasquez?" the detective called, snapping Leilani from her trance.

"Huh?"

"Here's our card," Detective Underwood said with his hand held out with his card.

"Ok, I'll give you a call if I hear anything," she said.

"Thank you."

Both detectives exited the hospital room as they discussed what was next on their shift. Leilani sat back in the chair, eyeing the thin business card. *Must be out of your fucking mind if you think I am going to call you motherfuckers to deal with this situation when I can handle Casper's ass my fucking self,* Leilani thought as she tossed the card into the nearest trashcan.

CHAPTER 12

7:12 p.m.

"Aye yo Casper, where you been hiding at?"

Turning to face where the voice was coming from, Casper grew agitated with the fact that his incognito attire wasn't working like it was supposed to. He had been on the run from the police for the past couple of days for the assault of his fiancé Essence.

"Wrong person," he yelled back as he continued his walk to his destination with his hoodie tightly tied over his head. *I need to get the fuck off these streets,* he thought to himself. He didn't want to risk the chance of being caught slipping as he knew there were people out there that wanted his head on a platter. Arriving at his destination, Casper buzzed the bell waiting impatiently for his aunt.

"Who is it?" she yelled through the intercom.

"Aunty let me in, it's your nephew," he replied.

"Which one? I got a lot of 'em."

"Ugh Aunty, it's me, Casper."

A loud buzz erupted through the intercom as his aunt granted him access onto the property. Entering the building, Casper was immediately greeted by the strong scent of marijuana. *Shit, that shit is strong as hell,* he thought as he made his way to his aunt's apartment. Arriving at the door, Casper rang the bell twice, waiting for his slow ass aunt.

"Who is it?" she yelled from behind the door. Casper's face scrunched up with pure annoyance as he was confused on why his aunt liked being so extra.

"Aunty, open the damn door man."

"Boy I oughta knock your ass silly," she responded, yanking the door open. Towering over his 56-year-old aunt Lira, Casper's face lit up at the sight of his favorite aunt. "Don't fucking touch me," she yelled as he wrapped his arms around her.

"Aunty why you so mad?"

"Nothing, come and get your daughter because I have things to do tonight," she said, closing the heavy metal door behind him.

Walking into the apartment, Casper was instantly greeted by the warm smile of his three-year-old daughter Emery. Out of all the wrong he had ever done in his life the little girl that stared back at him with such love was the only right he'd ever done.

"Come here mama," he said as he squatted to the ground with his hands opened for his daughter. Just like he expected, she ran into his open arms. "I missed you so much," he informed her.

After the assault, Casper had to go into hiding, which resulted in him and his daughter splitting up. He had to leave her with his aunt, which pained him. Now that the coast was clear, he needed to get him and his daughter the hell up out of New York.

"Daddy where is Mommy?" Emery asked.

"Well baby, Mommy decided to go on a trip and leave us."

"She's gone?"

"Yes baby."

"Ok."

"Don't lie to that little girl," his aunt Lira interjected.

"But I am not; she left me for some nigga."

"You just like that son of bitch father of yours."

"What?"

"All that nigga knew how to do was lie."

"But Aunty."

"Don't fucking Aunty me. I know that girl ain't leave you, and especially not her daughter. That's a good girl you had, and I don't know what the hell you did, but I hope you didn't do anything bad to her."

"Alright Aunty if you say so."

Feeling as if a lecture was on the horizon, Casper grabbed his daughter and her belongings and exited the apartment. Quickly he maneuvered through Brooklyn streets with his daughter tightly secured in his arms.

"Daddy I want nuggets."

"Ok I'll get you some McDonald's," he responded.

"With french fries?"

"Yes, baby with french fries."

Silently, he walked with his daughter in his arms. Knowing that his daughter ate already, he decided against stopping at the nearest McDonald's. Instead, he walked straight to his building with the speed of a New Yorker. *What do I need to do once I get in there?* he asked himself. Entering his building, the smell of a cleaning agent watered his taste buds.

"Shit, that nigga gotta be easy with all that bleach," Casper said as he entered the elevator. Pressing the sixth floor, he patiently waited for the steel lift to bring him to his desired floor.

"Daddy, nuggets?" his daughter asked half conscious. Turning to face his sleeping daughter, Casper released a light chuckle, *half asleep and this little girl still worried about them damn nuggets.*

"Yea baby, later."

The metal doors sprang open, granting him access to his floor. The hallway was empty, surprising him. *It's a Friday night; I would expect niggas to be out. Maybe they on the roof,* he concluded. Walking over to his apartment door, he unlocked the metal door entering his unfurnished hideaway home. The living room was empty with a 75-inch flat screen mounted onto the wall. The bedroom was furnished with a blow-up bed along with his daughter's Minnie Mouse toddler bed. The apartment wasn't furnished with much, but Casper didn't care because at least he was safe. Walking into his room, he placed his daughter in her bed, tucking her underneath her covers.

"I should really take off her outside clothes but fuck it; I ain't tryna risk waking her up," he convinced himself.

Leaving her alone to sleep, Casper decided it was the perfect time to catch up on his gaming. Being in hideout for the past three days resulted in him missing time on his game system. He didn't understand the addiction to his video games, as in the past he would find himself fully invested into a video game. Picking up the video game controller off the floor, Casper turned on his PlayStation preparing himself for a night full of video games.

"Prepare to get your ass handed to you," he said.

Buzz!

The sound of the doorbell buzzing caught his attention. Baffled as to who could possibly be at his door, he immediately went for his gun. *Don't nobody know where the hell I am. Who the fuck could that possibly be?* Letting the video game run, he stood up slowly, proceeding to the door. Taking the safety off his 9mm, he was prepared for anything to open. Slowly he unlocked the door, yanking it open with his weapon drawn.

"Nigga, put that shit away," she said noticing the barrel of his gun.

"What the fuck are you doing here?"

"I came to see my man."

"How the fuck did you figure out where I would be?"

"Listen baby, I'll always know where you'll be," she answered and placed a soft kiss on his lips. The scent of her Chanel 5 was intoxicating. He missed her and it was evident as his groin grew. Taking her into his embrace, he rained light kisses on her neck. The sensation caused her to moan lightly into his ear. "I got rid of her."

"You what?"

"I dealt with our common problem so now it's just us," he lied, staring into her eyes.

Granted, assaulting Essence was not a part of the plan; none of this was a part of his plan. He wanted to ride out the affair until he could no longer use his mistress. But with the chain of events, he lost his cool during a heated disagreement resulting in his fiancé being in a coma.

"You did that for me?"

"Yes, baby I did it all for you."

The look she gave him clarified what he already knew, S*he in love with a nigga.* She gazed back at him as if he were the answer to her problems all along. She'd spent years praying to God for a man to love her. Growing up she watched countless people experience the kind of love she yearned for. Finally, to have that kind of love, she was ecstatic.

"I love you," she said, smashing her lips onto his. Closing the door behind her, she lightly pushed him further into the apartment. There wasn't any furniture for her to push him into so she opted with bracing her back against the wall. Ripping her shirt open, she released a gush of air to cool herself down from the heat of both their bodies. Pulling her bra down, he placed her breast in his mouth, teasing her nipple.

"Ah shit," she moaned. Her hands ran down his sides until they found their way to his front zipper. Fumbling with his zipper, she pulled out his stiff manhood. Without wasting much time, she wrapped one leg around his waist guiding his penis into the opening of her vagina. Feeling the tip of his penis push through her insides made her groan in pure pleasure.

"God I've missed this pussy," Casper whispered, allowing his passion filled voice to tickle her earlobe. Flexing his hips back and forth, his stiff dick worked its way in and out of her. Feeling his body clench, his mistress knew exactly what was happening, *he's about to cum*. Lightly pushing him off her, she got down on her knees, placing his member within the depths of her mouth. As she swallowed his whole member, Casper's toes curled at the sensation of his dick bypassing her tonsils.

Staring at the beautiful sight of his "girlfriend" with his whole dick down her throat heightened his sexual appetite. He loved how freaky she was willing to be just for him, which was something he couldn't get out of Essence. He loved his fiancé more than life itself, but for some reason he was intrigued with the woman who kneeled before him with his whole dick in her mouth. Things had gotten out of hand with the attack on Essence. He never wanted anything like that to happen. Arguing and fighting had taken its toll on their relationship. All he yearned for was for their relationship to go back to how it once was.

Those faithful thoughts he aspired to abide by were now dismissed by the sexual act Candy performed. Their secret affair began two years ago, as they remained sexual occasionally. Casper had tried to convince himself that Candy was just something to make time go by. Instead, their affair turned into something more than what it originally was. Candy offered Casper what his mind craved, which was attention. Essence had dedicated herself to work and being a mother often forgetting about Casper. Candy on the other hand, didn't hold as much responsibilities.

"Shit, I am about to cum," he said, grabbing a fistful of her hair, pushing his hips forward, forcing his dick deeper into her throat. "Get up and let me hit it from the back," he said, as he pulled her up towards him.

As he demanded, Candy turned around, allowing him to enter her from behind. She closed her eyes as she held onto her legs for dear life. He stroked her insides in search of her favorite spot. Once he found the familiar spot, he began hitting it with each stroke. The feeling of her tight insides caused him to get lost. Something was different about her tonight. He had noticed her extra weight gain, and she felt warmer than before. Her insides felt like a soft velvet cushion as he continued to increase his strokes. His orgasm was building as his fingers found their way to her clitoris.

"Damn Daddy keep going," Candy cried.

"Whose pussy is this?" Casper asked as he continued pounding away at her insides.

Chh!

Chh!

Confusion replaced their sexual drive as the couple stopped their movement. Facing the entrance, both Candy and Casper stood, their bodies entangled, scared as hell. They knew they were in trouble by the way their trespasser stood at the entrance of the door with her gun pointed. The black leggings gripped onto her thighs, revealing her curvaceous frame. She wore nothing but all black. Candy already had an idea to how the night would end. Holding her position, Leilani's hand twitched from the feeling of the cold steel in her palm. Anyone who didn't know Leilani would have sworn up and down that she was scared about shooting the gun. They would have assumed that it was her first time holding a gun, the way her hand shook uncontrollably. The menacing glare she held placed fear in both of their hearts as they stared back at the Grim Reaper.

Leilani's heart broke; her mind was filled with confusion as she tried to comprehend what the hell was happening. For years, she had witnessed Essence deny the accusations of Casper's infidelity. Rumors had spread like wildfire throughout the hood, and Leilani watched her best friend tackle those rumors the best way she could. The nights where Essence cried herself into an anxiety attack, or the times when Essence refused to care for herself because she was consumed by the rumors, Leilani was there for it all. Still till this day, Essence loved that man unconditionally.

"La, it ain't what it looks like. I was ju—"

"You were just what?" Leilani interrupted.

"Look, I am sorry; none of this was supposed to happen," Candy replied as she tried covering up her naked body. Candy knew this was coming, as she had feared it for weeks. Her hands brushed past her protruding stomach and instantly Leilani focused in on it. The thought of her carrying Casper/Ghost's child sent a chill down her spine.

"Is he Ghost?" Leilani asked, while pointing the gun at her pregnant stomach.

"What?" Casper asked confused.

"Oh, so you never told him?"

"No, La, I never got the chance to tell him."

"You're going to be a father," Leilani replied. "Again."

Casper's eyes beamed with guilt; he didn't know how the hell he was going to get himself out of the mess that he created. Leilani stared on, knowing exactly what Casper was trying to do. He was trying to conjure up a lie to save his ass, *just like a ain't shit nigga.* A cold feeling infiltrated her heart, replacing whatever warmth was once there. Her trigger finger began to itch as she replayed the images of Essence in the hospital bed. The image of her friend's badly bruised face was etched into her memory.

"You slimy piece of shit," Leilani began. Her hands picked up a tremor as the thought of his deceit ran a dozen times through her head. *This fucking piece of shit almost destroyed Essence for this hoe.*

"You almost killed my best fucking friend for some hoe?" she asked calmly. "She could have died, but you don't fucking care because you have your little side fucking piece."

Leilani raised the gun, pointing it right in the middle of his forehead. Casper stared into her eyes, searching for the person that was his daughter's godmother. He searched for forgiveness, as he knew he fucked up. He searched for the little girl that he had heard numerous times from Essence who was addicted to heroin. That person was no longer there; the grey eyes that glared back belonged to a person who had had her heart torn out from her chest. Her best friend lay in a hospital bed, fighting for her life. All he could see was the loyalty Leilani had for Essence.

"It's time that you paid for the shit you've done," she replied. Her finger pulled the trigger, releasing the bullet into his skull. His body dropped to the ground, making a loud thud sound. Those brown eyes stared into nothing, as his last thought expelled his mind. Candy stared on in disbelief; her once warm and inviting best friend stood before her so cold. Leilani's eyes met the frightened glare of Candy's. Searching in Leilani's eyes for a weakness that she could feed on, all she saw was a monster that had been hiding for the past eight years.

"La, I am sorry."

"I am not the one you should be apologizing to, so fuck your sorry. You should be apologizing to the woman whose man fathered your child," Leilani said. "To think that we actually considered you to be our sister, and this is how you do us?"

Dropping to her knees, Candy began to beg for forgiveness. Her words became incoherent as the fear of death fucked with her thinking process. Leilani lifted the gun to Candy's forehead, training the barrel in the middle of it. Her mind ran a million things at once. The feeling of the betrayal was still fresh, burning like salt on an open wound. Agitated, Leilani brought the butt of the gun down, smashing it against Candy's skull.

"Aggh."

Blood poured from the open gash, blinding Candy's vision of her best friend. Leilani's face did not hold an ounce of emotion, as the betrayal left her mind baffled. Leilani's expectations were to kill Casper and get back her goddaughter. She never expected this chain of events. Denial rang through her mind. *I can't kill my family,* Leilani thought.

thought.

"Give us this day our daily bread, and forgive us our trespasses, as we forgive those who trespass against us; and lead us not into temptation." Candy trembled as her life flashed before her eyes. The vivid memories of her childhood came rushing through her mind. Memories of times where she, Leilani, and Essence were thick as thieves. All three women had a connection that was never deniable. But now their bond had been broken for some dick. She was wrong for sleeping with her best friend's fiancé, especially because she knew exactly how Leilani was.

The barrel of the gun was placed in between Candy's eyes. Leilani's fingers were wrapped tightly around the .45, Smith & Wesson. The stainless steel glistened, antagonizing Candy with death. The delay was not in an effort for entertainment, but solely on the concept of Leilani forgetting how to pull the trigger. Leilani's body stood above Candy frozen in a trance that she mentally could not break free from. Her heart weighed heavy, refusing to admit to what rested before her. *No, she would never do this to her best friend,* she thought.

"Nah, not you," Leilani whispered.

"What?"

"You are not fucking stupid enough to fuck your best friend's man," Leilani yelled agitated. "Not you; can't be."

"Honey, if I was able to fuck him then he was never her nigga," Candy responded.

The emotionless facial expression that covered Leilani's face altered as her brow furrowed in anger. Her velvety grey eyes grew darker as she was now enlightened. The once warm stainless steel was now cold, embedded into Leilani's hand. Her manicured nails pressed into her palm, cutting through skin due to the grip she held. Her index finger edged near the trigger; now she remembered. Her mind was no longer vacant; *place my index finger near the trigger and pull,* she thought. Her finger tapped the trigger once, emptying the chamber. Candy's body collapsed on the floor, right on top of Casper. Their blood mingled together dripping onto the wooden floor. Blood splattered in Leilani's face as she scanned the living room.

"Let me go get my baby," she said as she tucked her smoking gun into the small of her back. Walking over the dead bodies, she went into the room, and wrapped her sleeping goddaughter in the Minnie Mouse comforter. Exiting the apartment, Leilani never looked back as she escaped into the night.

CHAPTER 13

Darkness captivated the room, driving out every source of light. The hot scent of sweat lingered in the air, as the harsh sound of bodies smacking infiltrated the thin walls. Leilani lay on the bed bug infested mattress, staring up at the molded ceiling. Her mind was wrapped around the dark veil of her sweet drug heroin. The illusion that was painted by the addictive opioid blinded her from the pain that she was enduring. Rocky's sweaty body humped her small frame. He dug his tool deeper and deeper into her body, nearing his climax. The sensation was euphoric to him as Leilani's high pleasured her pain.

"You feel so good baby," he moaned.

His tongue slithered around her pale skin, leaving streaks of saliva. The body underneath him remained mute. He knew that the drugs had taken their toll on her as he stared into her lifeless pupils. The beauty she possessed was held captivate by the heroin. She had only been on the opiate for three months and already her health was beginning to decrease. He noticed her skin becoming paler. The twinkle of life she once possessed was replaced with the darkened glare of death. She was no longer the Leilani he once knew her to be. Underneath him lay the lost shell of a girl who had seen the worst in the world. Instead of acknowledging her demeanor, Rocky continued pumping in and out of her. Her muscles clenched his tool, forcing him to dig deeper. His toes began to curl as he could feel his balls beginning to tighten. The sensation of her warm insides caused his eyes to roll back as he felt his climax approaching.

"Shiit," he yelled, as he released his bodily fluids deep within her womb. His arousal began to simmer down as he stared at the young body of his lover. She just wasn't a simple fuck like the other hoes he had on the streets. To him, she was the one for him. Despite their great age difference, Rocky's heart now belonged to her. He wanted her more than anything on this Earth. The love he had for Rose was not love at all; it was merely lust. The mother of his son once held his heart, but his heart no longer beat for her. It was something about the grey hues of Leilani's eyes that had him mesmerized. The way she smiled made him believe that everything was going to be alright. He wasn't simply attracted to Leilani, he was in love with her.

"Lei, are you ok?" he asked as he gently caressed her face. She stared back at him with her clouded eyes. There weren't any emotions within her glare.

"You got what you wanted, so leave," she spoke.

"What?"

"Leave."

"Bu—"

"But nothing; get the hell out of here," she yelled as she turned back around. The tears poured out of her eyes. She was coming down from her high, opening the gates to her emotions. The pain had resurfaced. She was no longer on a cloud drinking her favorite soda. Instead, she lay on an infested mattress with her stepfather's semen leaking out of her. Her *insides pounded in pain as the tears profusely poured down her cheeks.*

"Why God?" she questioned. "Why me?"

"Is something wrong?" Rocky asked. "Lei, did I harm you?" he questioned concerned.

"No Rocky, you changed me," she replied.

******

"Princess, wake up; it's ok. I am here," Sincere whispered lightly in her ear. Her body felt clammy as perspiration stuck to the silk sheets. It had been yet another night of her having nightmares where she would wake him up, screaming for help. Sincere was concerned about Leilani's well-being, figuring that there had to be something haunting her. For the past couple of nights, they were sleeping in each other's beds, and her nightmares had picked up significantly.

"I am sorry," she said.

"It's ok Princess; why do you keep having these nightmares?"

"I have been through a lot Sincere, and I have done a lot of vicious acts towards other people. It's probably my mind playing tricks on me."

"Are you sure?"

"Yes baby, I am fine," she replied as she buried her face into his chest. She refused to cry or even think about the nature of the dream. Lately, her mind was beginning to play tricks on her, forcing her to relive the very moments she tried so hard to forget. Instead of dwelling on the complexity of her troubled past, Leilani shut her eyes and began to say a silent prayer. *Please God, put an end to these nightmares. I really don't need Sincere to go questioning my past, Amen.*

It wasn't long before she began to lightly snore, falling back into a deep sleep. Sincere chuckled lightly; Leilani could make a snore sound so good. He planted a light kiss on her forehead, while wrapping his arms around her. They had been together for a couple of months now and Sincere could honestly say that he had found his soul mate. She was everything that he wanted and a bit more. Leilani was perfect for him but he also knew that she had went through some traumatic events. She never clarified how bad the events were, and he didn't want to pry the information out of her unless she was ready to talk about it, and at the time she clearly wasn't ready. Leaning over onto the nightstand, he picked up his cell phone. Unlocking the screen, he began searching for a specific number. Once he found it, he clicked on it, placing the phone to his ear. The phone rang four times before the caller answered.

"It's four in the morning Sincere; why in the fuck are you calling me?" Isaiah asked.

"I need to know what's up with Princess."

"What do you mean?"

"Every night that I am with her she has these fucked up dreams that cause her to sweat."

"Did she tell you what is happening in the dreams?"

"No, she keeps telling me that they are just bad dreams."

"Well maybe it is just that, bad dreams."

"You're right," Sincere huffed. For a minute, the phone went silent as their minds began to reason. "Did anything happen in her childhood?"

"To be honest with you, everything you know I know."

"Aight negro, I will holla at you later at the meeting."

"Aight."

Sincere hung up the phone staring down at a snoring Leilani. *Baby I can help you deal with your demons*, he thought. He had been in and out of relationships, but none of them felt like this. Everything about this relationship was different. It was like a splash of fresh air after spending endless hours in a stuffy room. It was refreshing to have her in his life. The relationship gave him hope for love.

******

"Settle down, I have a few things to discuss with you fellas," Don said calming the group of men.

The massive room was filled with all of Don's workers, from low ranking soldiers to the underbosses. Everyone was in attendance preparing to hear what their boss had to say about the recent rumors that they heard from the grapevine.

"I know there has been a lot of confusion about the news of expansion. I held a prior meeting with the street bosses, and I was under the impression that they would be able to relay the news about expansion to you guys, but I was sadly mistaken. To clear up the confusion, I will confirm that we will be taking over both the East and West coasts."

Light murmurs filled the room as everyone tried to make sense of the new decision. Trying to reign over both the East and West coasts would be considered a suicide mission with the amount of problems it was going to cause. For decades, territory had been an issue amongst the drug world. But the decision Don had put into action would cause a bloodshed that could not be placed into words.

"Don, how will that be done?" one person in the room asked. "That shit is a death wish."

Just like that, their doubt-filled voices filled the air. Their concerns ricocheted off the cemented walls, irritating an already annoyed Leilani.

"That's where our new leader comes in place: Leilani will be the fourth and final boss; she will be the muscle behind the organization, and she'll operate anything that has to deal with the murder game."

"So you're really fucking serious about giving that bitch a man's position," one of Don's trusted workers asked. The anger in his voice would have terrified a regular person who wasn't built for the lifestyle that they lived. Leilani stared on, clearly amused by his irrational behavior.

"I can assure you that I wi—"

"It doesn't fucking matter what you say; you are a bitch. You're supposed to be in the kitchen at home, not in a man's fucking business," Toro said highly annoyed. "Juro perras en América no saben una mierda de mierda. Perras de mierda se supone que debe permanecer en su lugar de mierda en casa dejar las calles para los hombres."

Standing up from his seat, everyone's eyes were directed onto the huge figure. Their anticipation grew as they waited for their new boss to retaliate against the disobedient worker. Toro continued his rant with all eyes on him.

"Tor—"

The words couldn't fully escape Don's mouth as a loud bang erupted through the warehouse. Toro's tall frame crumbled to the ground with everyone's eyes searching for the shooter. Leilani sat in her seat with her smoking gun. Standing up from the table, she slowly made her way over to his body that laid on the ground. Her Christian Louboutin's soaked up his blood as she stood over him, watching him struggling to breathe. Squatting down, Leilani got low so she could get a better look into his eyes. His beady pupils pleaded with her for help, yet she stared back anticipating his last breath. The fear of dying invaded his pupils as he stared down the barrel of her gun. His whole life replayed throughout his mind as he thought about all the things he had done. *Did I live my life to the fullest? What did I do wrong?* he thought. The questions ran throughout his mind, almost torturing him. Leilani glared down at him knowing exactly what was running through his mind.

"Te advertí acerca de llamarme puta," she replied, answering the question that tormented his mental. When she pulled the trigger, Toro's brain cavity exploded all over the ground. The look of fear in his eyes disappeared as Toro lay on the ground, lifeless.

"Now, if any of you think that since I am a woman I cannot carry out the duties that my title requires, let your opinion be known so I can handle it personally," she spoke loud and clear. The message she wanted to deliver was that she was not the one to be fucked with. If the men wanted to try her, they could. But there was no way in hell they would be able to live to tell the tale of disrespecting Leilani.

"Good, now let's continue with the meeting," she replied, as she walked back to her seat with the trail of Toro's blood behind her. The meeting resumed as if nothing had happened. The guys spoke to everyone in the room, telling them how life was going to be for the next couple of months. With Isaiah, Leilani, Sincere, and Don running the whole operation, there was no way that what they had planned wasn't going to happen.

"Whose crew did we contact first?"

"Well our first crew was the Atlanta team; it didn't require much," Leilani replied. "But for Miami, Harley on the other hand he gave a little bit of trouble. It took a lot more, but we got control over Harley's trade; he agreed to giving us a percentage."

Everyone in the room approved of Leilani the more she spoke, explaining her actions. The more they interacted with her, the more they realized how gangster she was. She wasn't naïve or frightened by the lifestyle. The task that was set in front of them was at an all-time high, but Leilani was determined to excel. She knew it would be hard for them to conquer all the West and East coast, but she gave them motivation to conquer their task. While she spoke, Isaiah sat back in his chair, proud of the woman before him.

"Ok gentlemen, are we good?" Sincere asked.

"Yea."

"Ok, the meeting is officially over. Like we mentioned earlier, everything that was spoken in this room will remain in here," he continued as he watched everyone leave, hopping over Toro's deceased body.

"You did a good job Princess," Sincere said smiling.

"I hope everything I do is alright. Sorry about Toro."

"Don't worry about him; he had it coming sweetie," Don spoke.

"Yeah, but the way you killed him was something straight out of *Scarface*. The shit was beautiful," Isaiah joked.

"Do you guys really think I can do this?" Leilani asked with a hint of negativity in her voice. She was nervous about becoming a leader in something she had never done before. All she could think about was the millions of ways she knew she was going to fuck up.

"Princess don't worry, you got this in the bag." Just as he was about to finish his sentence, the doors to the office opened as the servants began to pile in, pushing carts of food.

She sat at the table and listened to the guys talk; she felt comfortable around them. Despite their mean mugs and 'NO BULLSHIT' attitude, she enjoyed being around them.

"La, you will need to clear your schedule on the 28th," Don stated.

"For what?" she asked curiously.

"Because we are flying to Philly. We meet with a Drug King by the name of Neeko."

"Ok, I should be good to do that," she replied, as she pulled out her phone to pencil in the meeting into her calendar. Looking at the time, she instantly remembered that she had to pick up Emery from school. "Oh shit, sorry to cut lunch short guys, but I have to go pick up Emery."

"Oh, I forgot you had Emery. How's Essence doing?" Isaiah questioned.

"She's getting better, still not out of the coma yet, but she's doing good so far," Leilani replied, as she stood up preparing to depart. "I'll keep in touch fellas," she spoke over her shoulders as she left the building.

Once she got outside, the stale smell of the New York street bombarded her nostrils. She inhaled the air deeply, taking in everything. She really needed this. With Essence's health being up in the air, Leilani felt the anxiety attack on the horizon. The stress for the past couple of weeks was beginning to take a toll on her, as the light at the end of the tunnel was getting farther and farther away. Leilani walked over to her car wasting no time to turn on the moving machine. *Please Lord, just let my best friend get better*, she silently prayed. She hoped that her prayer didn't go unnoticed; she needed God now, as she didn't know what she would do if she lost her best friend.

"It's all in your hands now," she said, ending her private conversation with God. Placing the car into drive, she pulled off into traffic with her destination in mind. For the past couple of weeks, Leilani had been caring for her goddaughter while Essence remained in the hospital. Things have been going good since she had Emery. Leilani found herself enjoying the company of the toddler.

Arriving in front of her school, Leilani double-parked the car. Getting out, she walked into the private school greeting the security guard.

"Hello Mrs. Vasquez."

"Hi Leo," she greeted, as she opened the white binder searching for Emery's name. Finding her name, she signed her goddaughter out and proceeded up the stairs to where her classroom was. The bright green paint job annoyed the hell out of Leilani, as it was such an eye sore.

"I don't know how the hell they do this shit with this bright ass green," she spoke as she knocked lightly on the door before entering.

"Hello Mrs. Vasquez. Emery, your godmother is here," the teacher greeted.

"Hi."

Walking over to the cubby, Leilani signed Emery out and began to gather Emery's stuff, as she cleaned the paint off her hands.

"How was she today?" Leilani asked once Emery made her way over to her.

"She was great; only thing is, she did have an accident, but it's expected because we are trying to potty train."

"Ok, I'll send in more clothing," Leilani responded as she placed Emery's jacket on. "We will see you on Monday."

"Have a great weekend."

"Same to you too."

Picking Emery up, Leilani made her way out of the school, so ready for the weekend to begin. She was tired as shit and planned on staying in the house for the remainder of the day.

"Nini, where's Mommy?" Emery questioned. Her words were almost unrecognizable, causing Leilani to strain her ear to understand.

"Oh honey, Mommy is sick; she's at the doctor."

"At the doctor?"

"Yes love, she's at the doctor."

"She come home soon?"

"Yes, soon baby."

I hope, she thought.

CHAPTER 14

1 month later

Tension lingered in the air as all the guys in the warehouse kept their eyes trained on their new boss. Things had been looking up for everyone, but Leilani felt off about something. She wasn't feeling the vibes within the group.

"Like I stated in the meeting, the whole plan is to dominate all regions. We were going to try to negotiate with the other dealers and allow them to join our ring, but fuck that shit," she stated angrily. So far, she had spoken to over a dozen dealers, and they all seemed to laugh in her face about the proposition she offered them. She had given them a chance, but time was running out for her. There were things she had set in place, as the bar was set high for her. "I've tried to be cordial with these fucking dealers. But they have taken me for a fucking joke, so now if they do not accept our proposition, I don't fucking care what you want to do. Let it rain blood; I don't fucking care. Kill their fucking asses," she spoke with no remorse. "I want their fucking territory."

"Princess, you have to set a goal for these niggas so they can have some type of motivation," Sincere spoke.

"You're right. If y'all don't have at least the rest of NY by the end of today, no one will get paid," she replied. "I want the rest of New York fucking City in my fucking possession. There are only two rules to this shit. One, kids are not allowed to be killed. And two, make sure the fucking job is done."

The whole warehouse stood before her quiet, listening to her every word. They had all doubted her strength, refusing to believe that a woman could do any of the things that were required in the drug game. But in a four week span, Leilani proved them wrong. She had taken control over several drug organizations within the short amount of time, gaining the loyalty of her crew forever. Today, Leilani had just received news that the territory that she thought she had control over wasn't hers, as the leaders of the previous organization had went back on their word.

"Get started gentleman, and remember, I will not be feeding anyone unless I have all the boroughs," she stated as she ended the meeting. She walked away with Sincere following right behind her. Sincere had been the support that she needed dearly.

"Princess let me take you out for some lunch; you seem tense," he replied.

"I wish, but I have to go and relieve the baby sitter and take Emery to the hospital to see her mother."

"When will I actually get to spend time with you?"

"I don't know, but soon."

"Damn Princess," he replied as he held the Cadillac door open for her.

"I know babe; shit is crazy."

Sitting back in the car, a million things ran through her mind. Her best friend was in the hospital fighting for her life. Leilani was starting to get a weird aching feeling in the pit of her stomach. Something bad was going to happen, but she was clueless as to what.

"Don't worry Princess, we will get time to spend with each other," Sincere joked, noticing the stressed look on her face.

"Boy, ain't nobody worried about spending time with you."

"Yea whatever girl," he told her placing a peck on her cheek. It was nice to see her smile; he noticed lately that she wasn't herself. Understanding about what was going on, Sincere wanted to keep things breathable within their budding relationship. He didn't want to push her too far to the point where she didn't want to continue their relationship. "But seriously Princess, everything will be ok."

"I hope so."

The rest of the ride to Leilani's house was quiet with Leilani staring out the window. New York's scenery seemed to calm her temper down. The thirty-minute ride went by faster than Leilani expected, as the driver pulled up in front of Leilani's building.

"Let me walk you to your apartment door," Sincere said.

"Ok," she replied, as she exited the car with Sincere following behind her.

Hand in hand, the couple walked into her building. Gaining access into the building from the security guard, they both entered the elevator taking it up to the fourth floor. Walking to her apartment door, they stood there for a moment, staring at each other.

"Call me, Princess," he said, breaking the silence.

"Alright," she answered, giving him a quick kiss on his lips.

Loving the sensation of her soft lips, Sincere pulled her back into his embrace, placing his lips onto hers. He placed his hands on her backside as he loved the feeling of her soft butt. *I can get used to this,* he thought.

"Go before you start something you can't finish," she said, breaking free from his embrace.

"Ok Princess."

Entering her apartment, Leilani instantly knew something wasn't right.

"Evelina?" she called out. The sound of the quiet apartment freaked Leilani out as she anticipated the light pitter patter of Emery running throughout the apartment. The apartment remained still, only confirming the worse. Leilani wasn't stupid, already knowing what the silence meant. Pulling out her favorite piece of steel, Leilani made her way over to Emery's room. The wooden door was closed, heightening her senses. Slowly pushing the door open, she revealed the pink décor Emery had personally picked for her new room. Nearing a panic attack, Leilani eased her glock at the sight of her sleeping goddaughter.

"Where the fuck is this bitch I hired?" Leilani questioned. Needing answers, she exited her Emery's room on the hunt for the baby sitter. Hearing light giggles coming from her room, Leilani instantly grew annoyed. *What the fuck is she doing in my room?* Not caring for the reason, she swung her door open to find the twenty-three-year-old giggling on the phone. Scared shitless, the woman hung up the phone at the sight of her boss.

"Boss, I ugh—" she stuttered.

"I don't even want to hear it. Get your shit and get the fuck out of my house; you're fired," Leilani said without even raising her voice. Tucking her gun into the small of her back, she went into Emery's room to get her niece ready for the hospital visit. Walking over to the sleeping child, Leilani lightly shook her awake.

"Wake up Emery."

"Tía?"

"Yes baby."

"I tired."

"I know sweet cakes, but we have to go visit Mommy," Leilani said, lifting the three-year-old up. Quickly, she pulled out an outfit for her and got her dressed. Emery remained asleep as Leilani carried her.

"Ms. Vasquez, I just wann—"

"Evelina, get out; I don't wanna hear shit. Your pay for the day is on the counter. Take it and get the fuck out of my house," Leilani responded as she left her apartment. Anyone would have called Leilani crazy for leaving her apartment with her ex-worker still there, but Leilani knew that Evelina wouldn't try anything. If she did even attempt to do anything, Leilani knew exactly where she rested her head. *I don't got a problem with lighting that bitch ass on fire,* she thought as she placed her goddaughter into her car seat. She buckled Emery into the car seat while listening to Emery mumble.

"I'm going to see Mommy?"

"Yes baby, you're going to see Mommy," Leilani replied as she placed light pecks onto Emery's toffee complexion.

Leilani slowly closed the door then proceeded towards the driver's side, getting into her car seat. Once she was buckled in, she pulled out her cell phone to call Isaiah. One the first ring he answered, out of breath.

"Yea?"

"I'mma kill you."

"Why?"

"That fucking bitch you told me to hire?"

"La, what bitch?"

"Evelina."

"Oh that bitch," he chuckled. "What she do?"

"Found her ass in my room on the phone, giggling like a fucking school girl."

"Ok where was Emery?"

"In bed sleeping."

"Ok and the problem is?"

"The problem is the bitch was in my room, on the fucking phone."

"I think you're overreacting."

"I'm fucking overreacting? God forbid something happened to Emery, how would the bitch know?"

"La, it ain't that serious."

"Nigga please, it's very fucking serious."

"Ok La, if you say so, but I still don't see where the problem is."

Agitated with where the conversation was going, Leilani hung up the phone tossing it into the passenger seat. *Only reason why this nigga backing her up is because he want her pussy; ole' nasty ass.* Pulling off into traffic, Leilani wasted no time with getting to the hospital. When she arrived, she took out a sleeping Emery and made her way into the building. She was greeted by the smiling nurse who sat behind the reception counter. Leilani rattled off the necessary information before she was given her nametag and given Essence's room number. Despite knowing where Essence was located, Leilani allowed the older woman to give her directions.

"Thank you," Leilani replied as she carried her sleeping niece into the elevator. Once they got onto the third floor Leilani got out, making her way over to the room. She entered the room hearing the sweet laughter of her best friend.

"You fucking bitch," Leilani said as she walked over to Essence. Her face looked joyful as she inhaled the fresh hospital air instead of being forced to breath with a tube down her throat. The swelling had gone down on her face, causing her to look much better than when she first arrived in the hospital. Leilani placed a sleeping Emery between her and her best friend. Hugging her best friend, Leilani inhaled the hospital scent, grateful that she didn't smell like death.

"I swear to fucking God this shit will never fucking happen again," Leilani said. "I almost lost your dumb ass."

"Well at least I ain't dead," Essence said as she placed a dozen kisses on her little girl's forehead. It felt good to be able to do that. After being in a coma for weeks, Essence was grateful to be alive.

"Where is Candy?" Essence questioned.

"I never lied to you and I won't start now," Leilani said fearing the worse. "I caught her and Casper having sex."

"You what?"

"Yes, I caught the two having sex."

"That conniving bitch and that no good piece of shit," Essence said as their betrayal burned her soul. She knew he wasn't shit, but for him to sleep with one of her good friends sent a dagger through her heart. She thought they were better than that. "Please tell me you put those two six feet under the fucking soil."

"Really bitch, you gonna ask me some stupid shit like that?" Leilani asked surprised. "I fucking buried they ass, don't worry. I got your back."

CHAPTER 15

The luminous sun beamed through the window as Sincere lay in bed watching a sleeping Leilani. Peacefully, she slept in his arms while his fingers moved smoothly against her caramel skin. Loving the soft feeling of her skin, his mind began to replay the chain of events that occurred hours prior.

******

10 hours prior

"So, I called down to the kitchen and had them make us dinner."

"Ok, have them bring up some ice cream too. I have a craving for some chocolate," Leilani said as she entered the elevator with a sleeping Emery in her arms.

"I can cure those cravings," he replied, wrapping his arms around her. The smell of her perfume tickled his nose as he tried his best to bury his face into her neck. He wanted to have her in the worse way but decided that he would have to wait until she was ready to give him her all. "I don't think you understand how bad I want you right now," he whispered into her ear, placing light kisses onto her shoulder. She pushed him off her, breaking their embrace. Her eyes gazed into his as she spread her lips into a smile.

"Boy, if you don't get ya hot ass breath off of me," she joked.

Sincere couldn't help but to laugh, as he wasn't expecting that to happen. They kissed each other like today was their last day together. It was passionate, filled with love and lust. They hadn't been together for long, but Sincere knew that he was falling deep in love with her. Whatever she wanted, he was willing to give it to her on a silver platter. The elevator came to a stop as the silver doors opened revealing their floor.

"Come on Princess, before these white people think we're trying to make some weird ass porno," he said. "Do you want me to take baby girl?"

"Nah, I'm good; we are almost to your apartment."

"Ok."

Leading them to his apartment door, he unlocked the door granting them access into his bachelor pad. The lights were turned down low, leaving the candles to be the only source of light. Instantly, Leilani's eyes were attracted to the dining table that was set up for a dinner for two.

"You did this for me?" she asked.

"Yes. I noticed how stressed you have been lately so I wanted to do something special for you," he said. "I had one of the guest rooms set up for Emery; it's the first room to the right, nearest to my bedroom. On the bed is her favorite Minnie Mouse pajamas, and I had some milk bottles set up just in case she gets cranky."

Staring at him, Leilani was shocked at how considerate he was. ***He pays attention,*** *she thought. They'd spoken several times on the phone, and Leilani would explain how it was taking care of Emery, but she didn't think that Sincere was paying attention.*

"Thank you, I appreciate what you did," she said, as she took his directions going into the room that he designated for Emery. Like he mentioned, a pink nightgown rested on the bed for her goddaughter. Dressing the toddler, Leilani tucked her into bed, placing a kiss onto her forehead. "He's doing good so far baby girl."

Walking back into the living room, Leilani was greeted by a smiling Sincere. Taking in the whole scenery, Leilani could tell he paid a pretty penny for the whole dinner; from the expensive bottle of Armand de Brignac Midas Champagne *to the lobsters, she knew it wasn't cheap. She was truly impressed at how well he had put together something for her. Pulling out her chair as he motioned her to sit, she discovered he had manners.*

"Now Princess, I don't want you stressing about anything; just relax for the rest of the night. I got you," he replied as he poured them both a glass of champagne.

"Let's make a toast," he suggested

"To?"

"New beginnings."

"Ok, toast to new beginnings," she said as they raised their glasses. Taking a sip from the champagne flute, she eyed the delicious food in front of her. Picking up the lobster tail, she cracked the shell and began to devour it. One thing Leilani loved the most was seafood. She could honestly eat it every day, if she were given the option. Looking up from her plate, she caught Sincere staring at her. His stare was vivid, burning a hole through her.

"Sincere, stop staring at me," she said, afraid of the truth that his

eyes held. Leilani saw in his eyes what he was willing to give her, which was love. Sincere was willing to give her everything and anything to make her happy. All he wanted to do was give her a love that was pure and happiness that he planned to make unlimited.

Standing up from his chair, he proceeded over to Leilani's side of the table. Without any motivation, he grabbed her out of her seat, pulling her into his arms. Their lips became one as Sincere's lips sucked on hers. Leilani's arms wrapped around his neck, letting him know not to stop. The feeling of his hands rubbing over her butt cheeks caused her to leak onto the panties she had on. Feeling her body temperature rise, Leilani began to remove her clothing, revealing her lace bra and thong. Nothing entered her mind as all she wanted Sincere to do was enter her guts. His thick lips explored her body, leaving a trail of fresh love marks as he made his way between her legs. A warm sensation crept through Leilani's spine, causing her to moan out in pure ecstasy. Sincere's tongue found its way to her clitoris, and each stroke of his tongue sent a jolt of pleasure waves, making Leilani's moan escalate. She began to tighten her muscles as she could feel herself nearing an orgasm.

"Sincere I am going to cum," she cried. Those words were like music to his ears, as his tongue slowed down its strokes, focusing on a specific spot where he knew she was sensitive. Within minutes, her creamy orgasm milked his face. He licked up all her juices, savoring her sweet taste.

"Come on Princess, I ain't finished yet," he said as he got on top of her. Sincere took off the remaining clothes, releasing his manhood from the threads of cotton. Leilani caught a glimpse of his member and instantly fell in love with the curved head. She was pleased with his

package, anticipating how he would feel in her.

"Now Princess I must warn you, once I give you this dope dick, there ain't no leaving this," he replied as he stared into her eyes. "Once I mark you, you're mine forever," he replied.

"Then go ahead and mark your territory baby."

His lips spread into a smile as he placed them on top of hers. He placed himself at her opening, gently pushing himself in her. A slight whimper escaped her lips, as his mushroom-sized head dug its way through her. Once all of him was in, he stopped to bask in the grip of her love muscle. She was super tight, suffocating his penis. He moved slowly in and out as her juices leaked on him.

"You're mine, right?" he asked as he slowly pumped in her. Stubbornly, Leilani refused to answer him. "Don't worry Princess, after I make love to this pussy, I am going to tear this shit up," he said, meaning every word.

The mushroom-sized head grazed against her G-spot, making her groan in pure pleasure. It had been years since she had groaned like this. It was pure pleasure, not a rushed sex session where Sincere only thought about himself. He made love to her body, never leaving an inch of her untouched. It wasn't long before he felt her tightening around him again as she prepared herself for another orgasm. She moaned out loud, filling the air with pleasure.

"Good, milk on Daddy's dick," Sincere said while nibbling on her nipples. When she finally released her grip, Sincere turned her around doggy style as he entered her from the back. She arched her back perfectly so he would get a perfect view of her plump ass. Sincere began to pump in

and out of her, hitting corners of her pussy that had never been touched. Her ass jiggled with every stroke he made.

"Is this mine?" he asked as he took a fist full of her hair, pounding deep inside of her. Leilani never said a word as her eyes rolled to the back of her head in pure pleasure. His paced picked up as he dug deep into her G-spot. The sight of her perfectly round backside put him into overdrive. He could feel his balls beginning to tighten, signaling that he was on the verge of an orgasm.

"Whose pussy is this?" he asked

"Oh, it's yours," she yelled back as she came again and Sincere followed right behind her. Exhausted, they both collapsed on the dinner table. They both had never had sex like that before, leaving them both mind fucked. After a couple of minutes, Sincere picked up Leilani's body and carried her into the bathroom where he ran her a bath. Sincere had to admit, he was quickly falling in love with Leilani, as he showed her more affection than any other women he had ever been with. During their bath, he washed her up and she had done the same for him. Once they were done, they went to lie in bed together wrapped up in each other's arms.

******

His fingers glided against her soft skin, encountering a rough patch of skin. It was then that he noticed the scars on her arms. The scars were very faint. *What the fuck is this?* he questioned. He made a mental note to ask her about the scars, as at that moment he didn't want to beef about anything. He just wanted to be in bliss after their long night of lovemaking. The love they had made last night was something he had never done with any other woman before. He never knew he was capable of being so gentle with her, but a little rough. One thing he had to admit about her was that she really was competition. The way she fucked him back had his manhood rising just from the thought of it. A light vibration echoed throughout the air, interrupting his sexual thoughts. Sincere looked over, noticing that it was his phone that was going off. He stared at the screen surprised to see the name displayed.

"How can I help you?" he answered, not in the mood to deal with any of the bullshit early in the morning.

"Well good morning to you too," she replied with an attitude.

"What do you want now?"

"Well, I have things to do today so I need you to come and pick up your son."

Sincere held his breath in hopes of keeping his anger at bay. Being a laid-back person, Sincere knew how to keep his cool. But the only person that controlled his anger was the mother of his son, Amiya. She knew exactly how to push his buttons to get him to react how she wanted him to. He couldn't stand her, which surprised a lot of people because there was a time when Sincere had loved the very ground she walked on. She was his ride or die, willing to do anything for him, proving her loyalty time and time again. Shortly after the birth of their son Cason, she turned into what he had despised. She became needy, always wanting Sincere for money, finding ways to qualify herself as an ordinary hood rat. Their son was Amiya's meal ticket to success, as she used him to get Sincere to do anything that she wanted.

"When do you plan on going out?" he asked.

"Soon, so I need you to come pick him up like right now."

He didn't reply to a word she said as he hung up. In a rush, he began to prepare himself to go get his son. Being a man in the game, Sincere wanted what was best for his son. He had promised himself that once he got his money right, he would take custody of Cason. Sincere had money, but he wanted his son to live comfortably, dining with only the best in the world. Just like how he planned, he got his money right but only sacrificing the one thing he truly cared the most about, his son. Drug dealing was his occupation, which only meant countless hours in meetings and several nights in the streets. Once he was ready, he wrote a note to Leilani letting her know that he was going to pick up his son and he would be back.

The echo from the door closing shut woke Leilani from her sleep. She stared at the clock, trying to figure out how long she had been asleep. *Only four hours*, she thought. She looked at the empty spot next to her, noticing the note Sincere had wrote:

Good Morning Princess, I must pick up my son. Don't worry, I will be back in the next hour. Don't go anywhere because I want to spend the rest of my day with you.

"At least he had the courtesy of writing a note," she said to herself. Her lips spread into a smile as the thoughts about how considerate he was played in her head. Slowly, snippets of the night before invaded her mind. Sincere had possessed her mind with his lovemaking. One thing she had to affirm, Sincere was hands down the best she ever had. The one night they had spent together was one of the best nights of her life. In an elated mood, she decided to make breakfast for everyone.

Getting out of bed, she brushed her teeth and threw on his shirt and shorts. Walking into the kitchen, she began pulling out pots and pans preparing herself to cook. The fridge was well stocked so she planned on making as much as she could. *This mofo better like this shit too,* she thought as she began to fry the turkey bacon. Less than 45 minutes later, she had finished cooking, and Emery was up watching cartoons waiting on her plate of food. The front door to the condo opened and closed as footsteps echoed throughout the condo. Sincere's voice could be heard as he scolded his son.

"Cason, I do not care if your friend was doing it; this is you, you are my son, you came out of my balls," Sincere said as they walked into the kitchen.

"I'm glad you guys were able to make it back," Leilani said planting a kiss on Sincere's lips.

"Princess, I want you to meet my mini-me, Cason; son, this is my girlfriend Leilani."

Leilani gazed at the little boy, embracing the offspring that was the spitting image of his father, from the tamed thick eyebrows to their dark-brown eyes. Their skin complexion was the color of a rich, dark roast coffee. Sincere's genes were strong; Leilani didn't think the little boy had any features of his mother's.

"Hello, nice to meet you." Cason said as he took Leilani's hand into his, planting a light kiss on it. The respectful gesture caused Leilani to blush; she knew Sincere was in the process of raising a lady's man.

"It's so nice to meet you too sweetheart. Have you eaten yet?"

"No."

"Good, because this morning I made a big breakfast, and I don't think me and your father would be able to eat it all," she said as she began making plates of food for them.

"Did you use any peanuts or nuts?" Sincere questioned.

"Nope, why?"

"Cason is allergic."

"Mental note," she said handing them their plate of food. She made Emery a small plate and walked into the kitchen, handing the toddler the cut-up pieces of pancakes. "Eat all your pancakes baby girl and tía will take you to the zoo."

"Ok," she responded with her eyes glued to the television.

Going back into the kitchen, Leilani began to clean up the mess she had made. The sound of Sincere moaning caught her attention.

"Princess hands down this the best breakfast I ever had," he spoke while eyeing his son enjoy the meal.

"Even better then grandma's," Cason agreed. "Pops, after breakfast can we play *Call of Duty?*" Cason asked as he stuffed his mouth with more pancakes. "Do you have any homework that needs to be done?"

"No, I finished it."

Sincere approved his son for playing the Xbox, as he continued eating. The sight of Leilani's plump backside caused his friend to stiffen. *Damn my Princess got it going on,* he thought as he watched her butt cheeks swallow his boxers that she had on.

"Princess, what do you have planned for the rest of the day?"

"Oh, nothing really; why what's up?"

“Spend the rest of the day with us?” Sincere said smiling, showing off his white teeth.

“Wow, I got you wanting to spend time with me?”

“Of course, Princess,” he replied as he motioned for her to come to him. She wiped her hands on a dry rag as she walked over to his open arms. He wrapped his muscles around her as he planted a big kiss on her lips. The feeling of his soft lips sent a chill down her spine. Their tongues danced together along to the sound of affection. Cason took this as his cue to leave the area, as he could feel something inappropriate was going to happen. Once they broke from their embrace, Leilani stared into his loving eyes and couldn’t help but feel grateful for what God had given her.

All her life, she had felt as if she was given the shit end of a steel pole. Nothing good had ever happened for Leilani. Between the dope and abuse, she never thought she had a chance at life, besides ending up six feet embedded into the Earth’s core. But after many trials and tribulations, Leilani stood in the embrace of a man who was truly in love with her for who she was.

“I’ll finish cleaning up Princess; go relax,” Sincere said as he gently pushed her out of the kitchen.

“Oh, really Sincere?”

“Yes, baby go relax. You’ve had a very hard week; just go and be normal for once,” he joked as he smacked her round backside.

“Sir, don’t start nothing you can not finish.”

Sincere let out a light chuckle, as he couldn’t help but agree with Leilani. He was drained from their session last night and honestly just wanted to relax. He got up from the chair and began to clean up the kitchen. The light sound of gunshots rang through the air as his son began to enjoy playing *Call of Duty*. Leilani looked on, watching him shoot at the zombies that were on a mission to attack him.

"Do you want to play Leilani?" Cason asked.

"Sure, you just have to refresh my memory on what the buttons are for," she replied as she took the controller into her hands. He explained to her what each button was for as she carried out her mission on killing the zombies before they attacked her. She was an okay player; she remembered some of the game when she used to watch Isaiah play. She went up to the fifth level before she was killed by one of the zombies.

"Here, let me see how far you can get," Leilani replied as she handed him the controller to play. She watched him as his fingers jabbed vigorously against the game controller buttons. Cason was adamant on beating Leilani, as he was very competitive, just like his father. Leilani's eyes remained focused on the television screen as Sincere walked out of the kitchen and sat on the couch, wrapping his arm around her neck.

The couple sat in each other's arms while they watched Cason play his video games and Emery sat playing with her Leap Frog device. Loud shots rang out from the surround sound system, imitating the actual tone of real gunfire. Cason's furrowed eyebrows arched in pure annoyance as he died in the game. Leilani could not help but to release a light chuckle as the sight of Cason angry was amusing for her. The video game was something non-life threatening, but Cason was furious about dying to another one of his teammates.

"Son, it is just a game," Sincere said in effort to try to ease his anger.

"No Dad, it's all his fault; if my teammate had been doing what he was supposed to be doing, then I would have never been killed."

"Well son, make this a lesson as you should never count on people and put your life in their hands."

Leilani listened on to the conversation between father and son. The moment was breathtaking as Sincere gave his son key notes on life. The juncture left Leilani with an awful pain as her heart longed for these types of moments with her own offspring. The connection she wanted with her son, was vacant. She had never held a real conversation with him, and it was killing her slowly.

"Princess, are you ok?" Sincere asked as he noticed the emptiness in her facial expression. For the short amount of time that they had been together, Sincere took it upon himself to learn everything there was to know about his girlfriend. He studied her facial expression and the one she had on now was nothing he had ever seen. It was a look of confusion, infused with regret and pain. Something was bothering her, and he wanted to know what it was.

"I am fine," she responded as she considered his eyes. The glare from her grey eyes no longer carried life in them. The hint of joy he once saw in those grey eyes vanished as he stared into her. Before him sat an impaired beast that was not wounded physically, but mentally. Leilani was what the game identified as a beast. She was unstoppable with the amount of knowledge she possessed and her beauty was the downfall of many men. But the beast that was created in the heart of chaos, had no control over her mind as the past often haunted her. Her childhood had a hold on her mentally as vivid images of her pain flashed before her eyes.

"Are you sure Princess?"

"Yes, I am fine," she replied, annoyed as she got up from the couch. She headed into the kitchen where she stood gripping the kitchen counter. The memory of her past came rushing towards her like a sea wave. Her image went blank as her pain flashed before her eyes.

******

December 25, 2002

9:45 a.m.

Light taps on the window caught her attention as she turned to see the culprit for the sound. Pushing back the curtains, Leilani stood in her window amazed by the sight before her. Snow descended from the grey sky, covering all the broken needles, condoms, and pipes that lay scattered on the ground. Little kids of color filled the streets as they had nowhere to go. Their screams filled the cold air, waking up every living soul in Marcy projects. Staring down at the little kids, Leilani wished that she could be down there enjoying the snow with her adrenaline pumping. The sound of the door opening and closing caught her attention as she faced the door. Rocky struggled to come in with bags hanging from both arms.

"Hey lil' mama, where's your mother?" Rocky asked.

"She's in her room."

"Rose, get in here," Rocky yelled out loud. Placing the bags on the ground, he stood there staring at Leilani. Her mother's door opened and shut as Roselyn came waltzing out with her satin robe on.

"Where's the Christmas tree?" Rocky asked her.

"At the store."

"So it's Christmas and you didn't even bother to do something nice for Leilani?"

"Well, I forgot."

"Really?" Rocky asked staring at her.

"Yes, I've been busy."

Rocky knew where their discussion would have ended if he kept on questioning her. Rather than continue, he just kept his mouth shut as he needed his plan to work perfectly.

"Ok, well here. I got you some things for Christmas," he replied as he dug his hand into one of the bags. Pulling out two pairs of keys, he handed both to Roselyn. She glared at him, confused as to what the keys were for. "The first pair of keys is to your new apartment, and the second one is for your new ride."

"What?" she asked surprised. "You got me a new apartment and car?"

"Yup." Squealing for joy, Roselyn jumped up and down like a nine-year-old kid getting what she wanted for Christmas. Thanking her man, Roselyn quickly threw on her shoes as she wanted to check out her new ride.

"The apartment is already set up."

"Where is it?" Once he rattled off the address to her, Roselyn wasted no time running out the door in pursuit of her new ride and home. Alone with Rocky, Leilani remained seated on the radiator, looking out the

window.

"Lil' mama, I ain't forget about you," Rocky said as he began to pull out her gifts that were in the bag. Handing her the perfectly wrapped gifts, he couldn't contain himself as he anticipated the smile on her face. She stared at him, confused on his excitement.

"Why are you cheesing so hard?"

"Lil' mama, just open the damn present."

Complying with his demand, Leilani peeled off the gift-wrapping paper revealing the box of her present. ***A game cube?*** *Not much of a gamer, she was still happy for receiving a gift. She never received anything from anyone, not even family members. Due to her mother's irrational behavior, they were on bad terms with other family members. Never getting the chance to meet her father, Leilani spent all her time with her mother. All she knew was her mother. Nothing else.*

"Open the rest of the bags," Rocky said.

She did as he said, opening the rest of the bags to find brand new, expensive clothes inside. This was the first time in years since she had a genuine smile on her face. She finally could dress like the other kids in her school without being made fun of for her either too small or too big clothes.

"Lil' mama, do you like your Christmas gifts?"

"I love them; thank you Rocky," Leilani said as she ran over to him throwing her arms around him. Holding on to her, he inhaled her intoxicating scent. As she prepared to release her hold on him, Rocky's hold got tighter.

"It's one of our special hugs," he said.

Staring into his eyes, she noticed the weird glare that he was giving her lately. She didn't know what it meant, but soon she'd grow to hate that glare. **What is that poking me?** *she questioned. Wiggling her small form to get away from Rocky, he only tightened his grip on her.*

"Rocky, please let go of me," she begged.

Tuning her out, his hands glided up and down her back until they arrived on her small buttocks. Feeling uncomfortable, Leilani tried breaking free from him, but it was pointless. Rocky was going to have her that night no matter what it took.

"I was hoping you wouldn't fight this," he replied.

"Fight what?" Quickly, he used much of his force taking her to the ground. Maneuvering on top of her, he restrained her to the ground.

"If you move you're going to make me hurt you, so I suggest you stay very fucking still," he warned. The menacing glare terrified her. Heeding his warning, Leilani remained still on the floor as Rocky rolled up her sleeves revealing her pale arm. She felt him wrap something around her wrist as he kept her movement limited. Wrapping a belt around her arm, Rocky waited until he saw what he wanted, a nice, plump green vein. "Now all you're going to feel is a pinch: do not move."

The needle broke through her skin as Rocky pushed down on the syringe, releasing the mysterious liquid into her bloodstream. The addictive poison pushed through her veins, traveling all throughout her body. Her face felt warm as her mouth became dry. The liquid inside the needle felt so good as she could feel every organ in her body pulse. She could feel her heart hitting her rib cage as it tried to pump blood faster *throughout her body. Noticing the change within her body, Rocky began raining light kisses over Leilani's neck.*

"How do you feel?" he asked.

No words escaped her lips; her body felt light, as if she were floating on a cloud. Leilani's mind ran black as she became drowsy. Picking up her limp body, Rocky carried the girl into her mother's room. As he lay her body onto the rough mattress, Leilani felt as if the clouds got softer. Everything around her seemed distant and out of reach. Her hand stretched forward trying to touch the nightstand, but instead she felt nothing but thin air. Her surroundings seemed so unreal.

Unconcerned about her state of mind, Rocky ran his calloused fingers into her pajama pants. She wanted to fight and protest, but the drugs in her veins caused her limbs to be numb. His fingers entered her, scraping against her virgin walls, allowing blood to pour from the opened wound. The friction from her dry insides caused unwanted pain, but soon ended as her high took over again. No sound escaped her mouth as she lay on the bed motionless. He unzipped his pants, allowing his manhood to hang. The whole event went unnoticed as the drugs masked the pain of her innocence being taken away. She closed her eyes, nodding off into a world that was better than the one she currently was in. Life seemed so dead, as she no longer cared about anything that consisted of life.

CHAPTER 16

The white wall stared back at her, influencing her suicidal thoughts. ***I should just kill myself and end this,*** *she thought. Her emotions were all over the place as she couldn't contain herself. Things hadn't been the same since Christmas. Her mother had moved her out of their apartment and into the condo that Rocky had purchased for them. It was a major change for them as all Leilani had known was the projects. Being moved to the posh neighborhood was something different for her. Every morning when she leaves her apartment building, she anticipates being smacked with the stench of urine, or while walking down the staircase she could only use one half because the other half was occupied by a sleeping bum.*

"What do I want?" she questioned herself. Her mind was filled with millions of ideas to deal with her situation. Since the night of Christmas, things had not been the same for her. Her memory was hazy as she couldn't remember what had happened. Leilani only remembered waking up the next morning with an aching feeling down there. ***What could have possibly happened?*** *she questioned herself. The possibilities were endless and it drove Leilani crazy. Tears fell freely down her cheeks, retracing the tears that had dried on her face.* ***Try to remember,*** *she coaxed herself.* ***I remember Rocky bringing the gifts and me being happy. I gave him a hug and everything from there is blurry.*** *Staring at the wall, Leilani racked her* brain to find

the truth. A light knock on her door brought her out of her trance. Quickly, she wiped her tears, covering up any trace of her mental breakdown. The door silently opened as her guest walked in. The smell of his Burberry cologne filled the room, replacing the scent of fresh paint.

"What's up lil' mama?" he asked.

"Nothing," she mumbled.

"You alright?"

Unable to answer his question, Leilani shook her head yes, fighting back the tears that threatened to descend. Her built up emotions held within for too long came exploding out as she erupted into tears. She'd never experienced these set of emotions before. Concerned, Rocky rushed to her side, prepared to console her.

"What is the matter?" he asked. Instead of answering, the young girl turned her head into his chest, crying harder. She was broken apart. Not used to seeing the little girl this emotional, Rocky was lost on how to help her. "What could I do to make you feel better?"

"I just don't want to feel this pain," she answered.

Looking down at her, he was confused on what to do. The only thing he knew that could help her would only mask the pain and not help her along the long road. Battling with his decision, Rocky thought about what he should do. He could let her cry into his shoulder and caress her or he can dope her up, helping her forget about her pain. There was only one answer to his question that could get the job done.

"I have something for you that will help you forget everything."

"What is it?" she questioned.

"Just believe me; it will get the job done."

"Ok."

Pulling out the needle, Rocky prepared everything she would need for her hit. In less than ten minutes, he was prepared to inject her.

"Is it going to hurt?"

"No, it will feel like a small pinch, so don't worry."

"You sure?"

"I promise lil' mama."

Placing the needle at her forearm, he slowly pushed the needle in, allowing it to break her skin. Pushing down on the syringe, he injected the toxic drug into her. Her tense body relaxed within his embrace as the heroin entered her body.

******

"Hi, I am John Carter; you must be Leilani."

"Yes, I am Leilani Vasquez. It's nice to finally meet you," Leilani replied as she shook the hand of her business partner. "So, let's discuss your music business. What was your goal with the company?"

Leilani took a seat in the comfortable leather chair anticipating the background story of the company she now owned 50% of. She glared into John's eyes as he spoke on the vision he once had for the company. He first started the company with high expectations of making a name for himself. Years of blood, sweat, and tears had been used to build his company, but poor money management resulted in the downfall of his empire.

"Do you think we could rebuild Carter's Dynasty?" he asked with much hope and aspiration.

"Of course, we can. I've already fronted my end of the money, which should help get this empire running. All we need is good, talented artists."

"I have a couple of artists, but they are all attempting to leave for other labels."

"And that is fine John, clean up house," Leilani stated. "Get rid of those ungrateful ones and build the empire back up again because I can guarantee you, we will have this baby back up and running in the big leagues."

"I believe in you Ms. Vasquez."

"And you should got dammit, the amount of money I forked over for this shit," she joked.

Their meeting continued with the two discussing their approach on what was good for their company. John was an easy-going guy that could charm his way into anything. Closely resembling the handsome actor Idris Elba, he was a female's weakness. The way his dark skin complexion gleamed with rich melanin would soak any girl's panties. Leilani sat across from the dark god not fazed by his good looks. She was more focused on what was being discussed.

"I know this rapper by the name of Ricky Bobby; he's really good. I mean his rapping skills will guarantee us many gold plaques."

"Do you have any of his music on hand?"

"No, the way the internet is, just go on sound cloud, type in Ricky

Bobby 'Trap Love.'"

"Oh god, another one of those rappers?"

"Believe me, that rapper is talented; just listen to his album." She was going to continue vouching for the young rapper, but she was interrupted by the light vibration of her cell phone. She took a glance at the smartphone noticing Isaiah's name beaming in bold white letters on the screen.

"Yea Sai."

"We have a problem."

"What's up?"

"Harley's transporter has been robbed," he said with much annoyance in his voice.

"What do you mean he was robbed?"

"I mean as in, he can't give us the agreed upon percentage."

"I'll handle it," she replied as she got up, preparing to depart from the meeting she currently was in.

"Aight do you need assistance?"

"Nah, I got this," she replied hanging up.

"So, I take it our meeting is over?"

"Yes John, I am so sorry about this," she spoke. "Listen to Ricky Bobby and tell me what you think about him."

"I'll give you a call once I have."

The new partners said their goodbyes, relieving Leilani back into the streets. She exited the building highly peeved with the bullshit.

October was coming to an end and this was the third time something had happened with Harley's cut. His transporter was either robbed or the money would be short. Leilani had given him two warnings already about fucking up, but he did not heed her warning. Giving Harley a third warning was not an option now; Leilani was fed up with his antics. Since Harley didn't think she was a woman of her word, then she would have to prove herself. She pulled out her iPhone and began dialing the number to her head honcho.

"Hello," he answered.

"I need you to round up the fellas; we are going to Miami."

"Ok." Hanging up the phone, she continued to make phone calls preparing for her unexpected trip to Miami. Picking up her phone, she dialed the number to the baby sitter she hired.

"Hi Ms. Vasquez."

"Hi Emma, I need you to do me a favor and pack a bag for Emery. She has a Minnie Mouse suitcase that you can use. Also, I need you to go into my room. Go into my walk-in closet, there is a suitcase already packed, and I need you to bring that along with Emery to an address I will text to you."

"Ok, anything else?" the chirpy young girl asked.

"How do you feel about spending a couple of days in Miami?" Leilani asked. "Don't worry about paying for anything; I will handle it. Also, don't worry about clothes; I will supply you with clothes."

"Sure, I have no problem with that."

"Ok good. You will be watching Emery for the night while I

handle some things, then for the remainder of the trip you can do whatever you want."

"Ok send me the address."

"Alright, pack something cute for Emery because once I am finished with my business I'll be taking her to Disney world."

"Ok Ms. Vasquez."

Hanging up the phone, Leilani quickly texted the girl the address to the private airstrip. Once everything was set for her trip, she got into her car, pulling off with her destination in mind. She was highly annoyed with the shit Harley was pulling, but that was ok because she had something in store for him. Since he wanted to play like his balls were bigger than hers, then she had no problem with showing how much bigger hers were. She drove her car until she arrived at her destination.

"Let the games begin, bitch," she said eyeing the private jet awaiting her arrival.

******

Glaring around the room, Harley loved all the attention he gained from his workers. All eyes were focused on him as everyone anticipated what he had to say. Dressed from head to toe in Gucci, Harley was feeling himself.

"I am sure you guys have heard the recent news about the Supremes coming to me negotiating a percentage off our earnings. I know you guys have concerns about the new deal, but I come to you as a friend informing you guys that you must not worry, as I am currently working on a plan to break up the deal," Harley said. "For the past month, I was expected to deliver the percentage over to the team, and I have found every excuse on why I didn't have the money."

"What does that mean for us?" Red asked.

"Well Red, it means you need not worry about a damn thing cuz I ain't giving them a penny of our hard-earned money," Harley smiled brightly. His short afro was tamed and curled, complimenting his thuggish appearance. Gold jewelry adorned his chiseled chest, amplifying the power he possessed. The jewelry was a reminder for him about him still having power within his hometown. *I run this bitch; no one else, just me,* he thought.

"You sure?" Red asked.

"I am positive. Now remember everything remains the same; keep y'all nose clean," he said. "Now y'all can get the fuck out my house. I have shit to do," he chuckled.

Laughter rang throughout the dining room as each of his workers knew that his joke was him being serious. Harley wanted them out of his house. Complying with his demands, they all left his home without an ounce of fight.

"Thank God, now I can go back to making love to my woman," he said out loud, making his way to his office. There was some paperwork he needed to sign before he could end the night in between the arms of his girl. The slight thought of her velvety, vanilla skin motivated him more with handling his paperwork, as he put a little more pep in his step. Pushing the wooden door open, Harley entered his office space.

"Now where the hell did I put that paperwork," he thought. Inhaling the air, Harley noticed a peculiar scent that saturated the air.

The floral scent tickled his nose; it was light and powdery, harmonizing with the faint scent of roses and honey. His leather desk chair swiveled revealing, the presence of a person he hadn't expected.

"Fix your face dear Harley, looks like you were caught doing something wrong."

"What the hell are you doing in my office?" he asked.

"I warned you," she said.

"About what?"

"Fucking with my money." Her long jet-black hair was sleeked back into a low ponytail away from her face. Standing up, she revealed her shapely figure that filled the designer threads. Instantly, Harley's member stood erect at the sight of Leilani. No matter how hard he tried he couldn't help himself; she was beautiful. "And see, that's where you fucked up. You believe that because I am a woman you could just play me. You actually thought you could cry wolf and I would sympathize with you?"

"I didn—" His words trailed as the sound of gunfire erupted through the air. Instantly, Harley's mind began to think of the worst. He was clueless as to what may have happened so he looked at Leilani for answers.

"Harley, there ain't shit you can say," she replied. "You wanted to cry wolf, so now I'll give you a wolf."

The doors to the office space swung open as her goons walked in with their guns drawn. Harley was completely alone, with no one available to help him in his time of need. Budda grabbed Harley by his collar, forcing him to get down on his knees.

"So, Harley, amuse me," Leilani said as she took a seat on top of the wooden desk. "Where's the money that you owe the Supremes."

"We were robbed."

"Really?"

"Yes."

"Why do I fucking get the feeling that you're lying to me?"

The warm look she had on her face radiated with anger as she could feel herself getting agitated. He was trying to play her for a fool with the deception of a robbery occurring, but Leilani was a product of the streets; she was already hip to the game.

"I ain't lying to you," he responded.

"Really?" she replied, as she began removing the gold rings that adorned her fingers. She handed the jewelry over to Budda, who stood anticipating the next chain of events. No one had ever seen Leilani do any dirty work. So, the scene that was beginning to unfold before them had their full attention.

"I am going to ask you one more time, if you lie to me again, so help me God what I am going to do won't be so fucking holy," she spoke. "Where the fuck is the agreed upon percentage?"

"I told you already, we were robbed."

Just as the fabrication poured out of his mouth, Leilani balled up her fist, connecting it to his jaw. The impact of her clenched hand pounding into his face echoed through the thick air. Sweat formulated at the tip of his mustache as Harley spat out a wad of blood.

"Now again, where is my fucking money?"

"I do not have it, my runne—"

BLOW! The words couldn't leave his busted lips as Leilani sent another blow to his jaw. Pain shot through his jaw causing him to double over in pain.

"I've concluded that you were never robbed. A man of your stature would never allow the rumor of you being robbed to even be speculated. That would fuck up your reputation so you would never allow that to happen. You were never going to give us that percentage, were you?"

"What are you talking about?"

" See that's why you're in the predicament you are in now. You wanted to fucking play me and that has costed you the lives of your workers and the life of your girl," she yelled, as she gave him another left hook to the jaw and right hook to the stomach. Her MMA background did come in handy when she didn't have a gun to protect her from an enemy.

The thought of his deceit motivated her to deliver an ass whooping that he had never received in his whole entire life. Blow after blow, he could feel his jaw loosening. The pain was unbearable, but there was nowhere for him to run as he was restrained. The marble floors turned a shade of dark red as his blood decorated it.

"Fucking piece of shit," Leilani yelled. Her voice was filled with pure anger as she rained punches on his face. Her mind went into a frenzy as her attack became more violent. The punishment was no longer based off his deceit, as her mind portrayed him as every person who had done wrong in her life. The world had taken advantage of her while she held her tongue. Her stepfather stole her innocence while the drugs concealed the pain. Her imagination took authority of her mind while her mother abused her.

"That's enough boss, he's dead," Budda replied as he pulled Leilani off Harley's body. Harley's life seeped out onto the marble floor. He wasn't dead, but he was barely alive. Leilani stared at his battered face, satisfied with the work she had done.

"Budda, I want your men to take over his traps. There is a safe behind the painting. Break into it and whatever you find you can keep; distribute it amongst you and your men," she spoke as she pulled out her glock turning off the safety. She raised the gun, leveling it to Harley's chest. She pulled the trigger, allowing the bullet to rip through his chest. "Now he's dead."

CHAPTER 17

Knock

knock

knock

"Nini, the door," Emery yelled out.

"Hold on, I am coming," Leilani yelled out as she sat the pot of boiling macaroni down. She placed the oven mitts on the counter as she ran to answer the door. She focused her eyes in the peephole to see who was on the other side of the door. Expecting to see the unexpected guest, Leilani was surprised that the person had covered the peephole. *Really, think you gonna catch me fucking slipping*, she thought as she pulled her gun from the small of her back. Yanking the door open she aimed her gun at the person who stood outside her door.

"Really bitch? Put the gun down," Essence said.

"What the fuck are you doing home from the hospital so early?" Leilani asked as she wrapped her arms around her best friend.

"Doctors cleared me," Essence replied before pushing her best friend off her. "Get off me; where the hell is my daughter?"

Right on cue, Emery came bolting to the door at the sound of her mother's voice. Screaming at the top of her lungs, Emery's voice filled the hallway as the child was happy to see her mother.

"Oh, I missed you too pumpkin," Essence said as she picked her three-year-old off the ground.

"Wait, how the hell did you get here?"

"Isaiah dropped me," Essence replied as Isaiah finally made it to the door.

Instantly meeting the gaze of Isaiah, Emery released a loud scream, squirming to get out of her mother's arms. Quickly, Isaiah chased after her with his best T-Rex impression. Leilani couldn't help but to let out a small chuckle at the sight before her. The way Isaiah bonded with Emery, it was evident that he loved the little girl.

"Care to explain what's going on?" Leilani asked as she pointed between the two.

"Why you are being so nosey, big head?"

"Oh nothing."

Leilani stepped to the side granting the two access into her apartment. Essence immediately walked into the living room and took a seat on the leather sectional, getting comfortable in the expensive furnace.

"You two are something else, I swear," Leilani said, as she proceeded back into the kitchen to finish making dinner. "Well people, I am cooking and on tonight's menu I am making chicken parmesan with garlic bread."

"I'll set the table," Isaiah offered.

"Thanks."

In less than thirty minutes, Leilani could expand her meal to accommodate the extra people. Once the table was set, Leilani placed their plates on the table.

"I hope this food is good," Isaiah stated as he stared into the neatly stacked plate of food.

"Negro, eat the damn food and stop complaining," Leilani ordered as she took her seat at the table.

"I am older than you so remember that," he said while he took a bite out of the crispy chicken. It had been a while since he had a decent home cooked meal, as work had taken over his life. Being such a dedicated solider in the street, Isaiah often went nights eating fast food or nothing at all. Enjoying his meal, he could not help but glance over at Essence. She sat across from him exhibiting her perfect teeth. He could tell she was in high spirits, although just not long ago she was fighting for her life.

"So, when do you think you'll allow me to get a cut of that piece of cake?" Essence inquired.

"I was honestly waiting for you to give me the green light."

"Girl, I need to get back to work. I am tired of being trapped in the damn house all day."

"Well you've been spending time with Emery."

"I know, but I am not that type of stay at home broad that does nothing all damn day. I love my buttercup but I am sorry, I need to make my money so I continue to support my family," Essence confessed.

"Understandable."

"Speaking of kids, Leilani what is going on with Juelz, how's he doing?" Isaiah interrupted.

"Juelz?" The name of her son sounded foreign. She hadn't said that name out loud in years since getting over losing custody of Juelz was troublesome. She had gotten pregnant with Juelz not too long after suffering a miscarriage with her first pregnancy. Her mind went back in time as she remembered finding out she was pregnant with her first child.

******

Tick tock

Tick tock

Tick tock

The clock ticked its way through the hours as Leilani sat in her chair waiting for her name to be called. It was only twelve in the afternoon, yet it felt as if she'd spent eternity in the doctor's office. Her patience was running thin the longer she sat waiting. Anxiously, she chewed on what was left of her nails. Loud grumbles erupted from her stomach, catching the attention of her mother. She hadn't eaten all morning, which now was beginning to take its toll on her.

"Why the fuck is your stomach making that sound?" Rose questioned.

"I don't know."

Despite knowing the cause of her talking stomach, Leilani decided against replying. It had been a tough morning as she had spent it searching for her high. She hadn't had a hit since last night, and she knew that if she didn't get it soon then the body aches would come back. Her new lifestyle was different compared to the one she once lived before. She spent her days indulging in a high that only drugs could create. She no longer cared about school or anything else for that matter.

"Leilani Vasquez," the nurse announced out loud.

Leilani got up along with her mother as they followed the nurse into the back of the office. Despite being in the office only a couple of days prior, the environment held a different vibe for Leilani. Something about the cream walls made her sick with blandness. Her taste buds watered, leaving a weird after taste in her mouth.

"Right in here," the nurse instructed. Both Roselyn and Leilani entered the office, greeting the doctor. His bald head glistened with sweat as his eyes met Rose's. Fear penetrated his pupils as he stood up to shut the office door.

"I don't know what the fuck you two are up to, but if you think I will be losing my practice license for you, then you are out of your cotton-picking mind," he spoke. His lips quivered in anger as his chunky finger pointed in the direction of Rose.

"Doc, what are you talking about?" Roselyn asked confused.

"Don't play fucking stupid with me."

"I do not know what the fuck you're talking about, so get your stink fucking finger out of my fucking face."

"You don't know what the fuck I am talking about?" The doctor's eyes grew wild with rage. "The fucking girl has heroin in her fucking system," he said almost in a whisper-like tone, just so people outside his

office would not be able to hear the news.

"That has to be a mistake."

"Oh, so the positive pregnancy test must also be a fucking mistake too?"

"What?" Rose asked perplexed. Maybe she was suffering from selective hearing as she felt her hearing diminish at the doctor's revelation.

"Your daughter tested positive for heroin, and her pregnancy test came back positive. I should be reporting this shit to the police for child abuse. You're fucking lucky that man of yours is giving me a hefty pay, or else I swear," he exclaimed. Learning about the condition of his patient placed his whole life in jeopardy. Dr. Selby's conscious told him to report the messy situation to the police, but he knew that he would disappear into thin air. Being on Rocky's payroll came with perks, but he didn't consider this when he decided to accept the hefty pay.

"Are you sure she's pregnant?"

"I've ran the test ten times and did a blood test," he responded. "She's definitely pregnant."

The theory of Leilani's drug dependence didn't burden her mother. Instead, Rose was surprised at the pregnancy news. Rose always had her suspicions that Leilani would turn into a sexual little girl once puberty hit. If they were back in Colombia, Rose would have sold her daughter into the sex trafficking business so she could make money off the pre-teen. ***That's a good idea. I know that El Jefe needs some girls for his business; he would spend a pretty penny for a pregnant teen,*** *Rose thought.*

"Doc, don't worry, I will take care of this."

"What will you do about this?"

"Don't worry," she replied as she grabbed Leilani's hand, escorting her out of the doctor's office. Her initial plan was to put her hands on the girl, but now Rose decided against it as the concept of money motivated her. Silently, Leilani followed right behind her mother lost as to what had just occurred. She had completely zoned out once the doctor began to discuss her health and the big news. In all honesty, Leilani didn't even care about what the doctor had to say, as she knew that the thought of her death nearing controlled her mentality. Becoming addicted to drugs enlightened her to the truth about life. **You're only living to die.** *The simple five-worded sentence had become her motto. She lived as if she were to die at any given moment. Getting into the back seat of her mother's car, Leilani stared out the window, anticipating the scenery she would indulge during the car ride. She expected her mother to pull off once the car warmed up, but was surprised when her mother pulled out her cell phone and began to dial a number.*

"Come home now," Roselyn said and hung up. Placing her foot on the gas, Roselyn reversed out of the parking spot and then drove off into traffic. It wasn't long before Roselyn pulled into her designated parking space in front of their apartment.

"Let's go," she said once she cut the car off and got out. Rose was eager to get back into the apartment so she could pack up Leilani's things. She finally found a reason to get rid of Leilani and she didn't plan on wasting any time. They entered the building quietly, taking the flight of stairs instead of the elevator. The whole concept of Leilani being pregnant did not register in her brain, as all she could think about was getting her next high. She had

heard the doctor talk about the positive test, but by then she had blanked out into her own world. Entering their apartment, Roselyn kicked off her shoes as she briskly danced to the music in her head.

"Go pack your bags," Rose demanded.

"For what?" Leilani asked confused. "Where am I going?"

"Just go and do what the fuck I asked you to do," Rose yelled. Leilani ran into her room, doing as she was told. A chuckle escaped Rose's lips. "Dumb bitch," she exclaimed as she lit her cigarette. She inhaled the potent blend of rat poisoning and tobacco, allowing the cancer mixture to soothe her. "I can have her ass on the next plane home by the end of the night. I just need Rocky to fund it."

The noise of the front door opening and shutting echoed throughout the apartment. Just as she expected, Rocky walked in with a look of disgust on his face. He hated the fact that Rose smoked the cancer sticks, knowing the effect that they had on someone's health.

"Put that shit out," he greeted.

"Why?"

"Because you know I hate the smell of them shits."

"Well I am fucking sorry," she replied as she did as he asked.

"Anyways, what did you call me here for?"

"I need money," she answered smoothly.

"For what?"

"I am sending Lei back home to Colombia."

"For what?"

"Let her answer," she answered as she yelled out for Leilani to come into the kitchen. Leilani walked into the kitchen confused on why she had been called.

"Yes?"

"Tell Rocky what happened at the doctor's office."

"Umm, I don't know," Leilani replied truthfully. "I wasn't paying attention."

"What?" Annoyed, Roselyn stared at her daughter, ready to throw something at her face. "Her pee came back dirty with heroin," she spoke as she took out another cigarette, lighting it. She inhaled deeply, not caring about Rocky's distaste for the tobacco scent. "That fucking girl I swear, and then she has the nerve to turn around and be pregnant."

"What?"

Shocked with the news, Leilani felt as if her knees were going to give out on her. She had no clue about her condition, with this being the first time that she heard the news.

"The doctor confirmed it today that her test came back positive, so I am going to send that puta back home to be one of El Jefe's call girls."

"What the fuck?" Rocky replied. The words that she was saying didn't register right in his head. **What the fuck is she talking about?** *he thought as he began to pace around the kitchen. His mind began running a million miles a minute as the concept of Leilani being pregnant taunted him. "I used protection," he whispered to himself in efforts of trying to convince himself.*

"You what?"

"I used protection."

"What the fuck you mean you used protection?" Roselyn asked confused. "You fucked my kid?"

"I wouldn't want to start lying to you now."

Her heart ached as her worst fear had now become her reality. Rose couldn't believe what she was hearing. Despite Rocky admitting to taking advantage of her daughter, Rose still stuck up for him, blaming Leilani for her boyfriend's infidelity. **That fucking bitch; she just couldn't keep her fucking legs closed,** *she debated in her head. She tuned out Rocky's voice as she began battling with her thoughts.*

"Things just happened," Rocky reasoned. "I'm just going to have to be a man about it and own up to my responsibilities."

Snapping out of her trance, Roselyn's eyes zeroed in on her daughter, who stood staring at her boyfriend. The boiling rage that she had within got harder for her to contain. She could feel herself slowly losing her sanity watching the exchange between the two.

"You fucking bitch," Rose spat. "This is what you wanted the whole fucking time." Lunging forward, Roselyn was in pursuit to attack her enemy. Landing on top of her daughter, Roselyn began to viciously attack her teenage child.

"Are you fucking crazy?" Rocky's deep voice boomed throughout the room as he was taken aback by Rose's actions. He began to break up the scuffle between the mother and daughter duo.

"What the fuck are you sticking up for that girl for?"

"Bitch, are you fucking stupid?" Rocky growled. The fire glowed in

his eyes, scaring the shit out of Roselyn. "She's carrying my fucking kid."

"No baby, it's not yours."

"What?" he asked confused. He didn't understand how she could stick up for him even after learning about his sick infidelity. "Shut the fuck up man. You're in denial, but that girl is having my fucking kid so get the fuck over it."

Completely concerned about the well-being of Leilani and the fetus growing within her uterus, Rocky helped her up off the floor.

"Are you ok?" he asked.

"No."

"What's wrong?"

"I need a hit," Leilani admitted, as she began to scratch the irritation on her skin. The recent events hadn't phased her as she only cared for another hit. She knew her life would be coming to an end soon, and she knew her life would be taken by the hands of her mother. ***My mother is going to fucking kill me. I might as well do it myself,*** *she thought.* ***Let me have a death by the hands of my favorite thing, rather than the person who hates me.***

"Fucking junkie."

"Rose watch your fucking mouth," Rocky yelled. "From now on, things will be different around here. Rose, you can't be putting your hands on this girl anymore. She's carrying a part of me and I need my child protected, by any means necessary," he spoke as he stared a hole into her face. It was crazy that he was sticking up for his young lover, but there was nothing else to do as he was the cause of all the chaos. It was his fault

as to why the pre-teen may never have a chance at living a normal life. But there was nothing he could do about it.

******

Six months after finding out that she was pregnant, her mother had beat her until Leilani fell unconscious. That very same day, she lost the fetus that she'd grown to love. A single tear freed itself from the entrapment of her eyes as the thoughts of losing her first child tormented her. It was warm compared to the cold achy feeling she sensed in her heart. All her strength was placed in not breaking down in front of her best friends. Several people have stared down the same glossy eyes as they feared their fate. Putting fear into their hearts was what Leilani had done for a living. She had spent many years rebuilding her once tarnished reputation. Despite, being compared to the Grim Reaper, Leilani was still a human being that had emotions. It had been a while since her emotions had resurfaced, but her heart ached with a familiar feeling.

"To be honest with you Isaiah, I've gone to sit by the house a couple of times, but I haven't actually gone in or anything," Leilani finally replied as she wiped the lonesome tear.

"Well La, he's getting older. I don't know if his adopted mother has told him about you, but you should get in contact with her to see what is best for your kid."

"I know, but what if it's best that Juelz doesn't know that his mother was a thirteen-year-old dope shooter when she gave birth to him?"

"Maybe he doesn't need to know all of that," Essence reasoned.

"You're right, but he's going to want to know why La didn't keep him. I mean, she doesn't have to get fully in depth about her past, but she could give him a brief outline," Isaiah countered.

"I don't know. His birthday is coming up, and since he's turning thirteen years old, I've decided that I will give him the package that will have all the papers to all of the companies he will own, and I'll include my number for them to call."

After giving up her son, Leilani decided that she would get her life together. Kicking the drug problem was her first task, and then she solely focused on grinding. She had saved up to a million dollars, placing the money in a savings account in Juelz's name. She had invested in a bunch of stocks that Juelz was entitled to. When she had decided to grind, Juelz was her motivation. The night she had given birth to him, he stared into her eyes with unconditional love. He didn't judge her like the dozens of people in her life, and he didn't want to hurt her. That glare of pure love was all she needed to get everything together.

"When is his birthday?" Essence asked.

"November 5th."

"Ok, tomorrow."

"Yea."

"Do you think you're ready for this?" Isaiah questioned.

"I think I am," she confessed. "Can you do me one favor?"

"Sure."

"Can you drop off the package for me?"

"Hell no, you can do that shit yourself," Isaiah yelled.

"Please Sai, can you do me this one favor?"

"Why can't you do it?"

"Sai, please just do me this one solid favor."

"Fine, I'll do it," he replied.

CHAPTER 18

Blank bombs detonated within Leilani's brain cavity as she stared into an empty crate. Today's shipment was supposed to contain New York's finest uncut drugs, valuing at three million dollars. Heart palpations captured the hearts of every worker that stood within the vicinity of the warehouse. No one knew how such a large shipment could simply disappear in thin air with so many workers around. Leilani was expecting someone to dabble in the shipment, but to take the whole thing was downright gutsy.

"So, what do you think?" Don asked. His eyes were relaxed, staring into the empty crate. Despite appearing calm, his blood was boiling within him. If the value of the shipment had been lesser, then he wouldn't be as upset. Replacing the three-million-dollar shipment would take months, as the workers back in Colombia, Bolivia, and Peru would have to scrap for crumbs.

"Well Don, what I can tell you is that I am not a damn detective."

"I know that, but what do you think?"

"Who oversaw the shipment?"

"Roberto, but he called out last minute so there wasn't anyone sitting with the shipment."

"Ok, so it was just the pilot on the plane?"

"Yes."

"I need to question him; how badly do you need this shipment?"

"How badly?" his voice cracked. "La, that was over three million dollars' worth of uncut, raw, pure drugs. This shipment was being prepared for months. The workers back home may not have enough time to get me this big of a shipment by the end of the week."

"Relax Don, just breathe," Leilani instructed. "How much do you have left pumping throughout the streets? Just call your connect and have him send something over not as big."

"Leilani, what you don't understand is that I am the connect."

"Ok Don, I understand. Just have another shipment come in, but not as big. Our territory isn't as big as we want it to be right about now, so we should be fine. Give me two weeks. I will have your shipment back to you."

"Are you sure?"

"There is a reason why you gave me my position Don; I will get your shipment," she spoke. He stared into her eyes becoming mesmerized with hope. Over the short amount of time they knew each other, Don and Leilani grew a bond. Don viewed Leilani as the daughter he always desired.

"Ok La, I trust you to fix this."

The sound of yelling rang throughout the spacious warehouse. Leilani looked around, seeking the source of the loud vocals. Her eyes fell upon a short Italian man. His arms swung loosely along the side of his body as his voice boomed off the metal walls.

"How could you fucking lose such a big fucking shipment, you fucking cocksucker," he bellowed.

"Cheadle, watch your fucking mouth ok. Just because we are half-brothers does not mean I won't smack the fuck out of your double chin," Don replied.

"You can't put your fucking hands on me, as you can't even fucking control your own organization."

"Ok fellas, that's enough of the bashing. We need to chi—"

"And who the fuck are you?" Cheadle asked, visibly annoyed with the presence of Leilani.

"I am Leilani."

"Oh, so you're the bitch they put in charge."

"Cheadle, watch it."

"I don't fucking care. This fucking girl has no right speaking to a man of my stature."

The two brothers continued to bicker, filling the warehouse with their masculinity. Neither of them gave up on their argument. Obscene threats were exchanged, causing a scene. Leilani stood before the two men, watching their heated argument.

"Hey, how about the both of you guys shut the fuck up," she yelled over them. "I will handle the situation, so shut the fuck up."

"Excuse me?" Cheadle questioned.

"You fucking heard me," she replied. "The both of you guys are standing here bickering like some old women. I said I would handle the situation, and that is fucking final."

Leilani walked away from both men, annoyed with their behavior. *Over three million fucking dollars is missing and these assholes wanna fucking bitch about some fucking nonsense,* she thought as she walked over to Essence, who stood reviewing the surveillance cameras.

"Essie, did you find anything?" Leilani asked.

"The only person who was on the plane was the pilot, but he was never seen engaging with the crate. The route was never intercepted and no one else is seen on the cameras but the pilot."

"Once the crate was lifted in the forklift, it was immediately opened and there wasn't anything inside."

"Which can only mean?" Essence questioned confused.

"It could only mean that the drugs were never on the plane." Leilani glared at the monitor, analyzing the face of the pilot. She noticed the tattoo that was engraved into the inside of his palm. Making it out was hard, so she magnified the screen by 75% to get a better look.

"Is that a bull's head?"

"Yes, the hell it is. I think we just solved this shit," Leilani stated.

"Yes, you did; it was the Mexican cartel."

"Yup, now let's go retaliate."

7:30 p.m.

Don focused his vision into the grey hues of Leilani's irises. Relief washed over him now that there was a solution to his problem. All morning, Don had been on the phone with Bolivia hoping to get a new shipment out before the week ended. But like he suspected, their crop wasn't ready to birth another set for his empire. After hearing the depressing news of not getting his product out and losing a significant amount in merchandise, Don felt like it was time to drown his problems in his favorite brown liquid. Unexpectedly, Leilani came into his office bearing exceptional news. She had located his merchandise and was in the process of getting it back. The sound of the good news brought back hope into his life as he sat there looking at the angel who saved his empire. There had been so many speculations about Leilani coming into power. Being a woman in this industry was unheard of. Despite the world evolving into their undivided sexual roles, the underworld was still left in the early 30's, where women didn't have any rights. There was nothing Don could do, but to prove these inconsiderate assholes wrong about Leilani. So far, she was doing an exceptional job at shitting on niggas. Feeling generous, Don stood up quickly, turning around to face the painting that he adored so much. The painting glared back at him intensely, remaining mysterious to the world around him. No one understood the significance of the painting. Many people thought that the mural was simply a painting of a beautiful woman. But the painting was much deeper than that.

"Do you know who this is in the painting?" he questioned Leilani.

"No."

"This painting is of my daughter," he confessed.

"You have a kid?" she replied flabbergasted. Leilani had been in his office dozens of times but she had never thought anything of the painting. She stared up, glaring into the eyes of his once mysterious woman. The grey and white painting sculpted this beautiful woman. Her curvaceous body glowed perfectly in the dress she wore. Mystery loomed over the only visible portion of her face. The fire red Chinese hand fan hid what was necessary to identify the young seductress. Despite the conspicuous fire red hand fan, what drew people in was her facial features. She was almost sculpted into pure perfection. Her eyebrows were polished perfectly, arching with pure power. Her eyes bore the look of determination. Leilani could feel the fire burning through the painting's eyes.

"When I was younger, I met this woman and fell in love with her. She was like the apple to my pie. She was everything," he began to explain. "Granted we had our ups and downs, our fair share of groupies and other things. But I loved that woman to the core of my soul. When she got pregnant, it was like there wasn't anything anyone could tell me. I was finally happy," he said, filling the air with his emotions as he stared into the eyes of the portrait. "When my daughter was born, it was like I was staring into a mirror. She was my everything, and for a while after she was born, everything was perfect. I had no stress, I had no worries, and I was happy with my fiancé and daughter. Ya know, it was like I was finally free from the grasp of my past. At the time, I looked around and realized I had made it. I was no longer the little boy who didn't have a pot to piss in. I was no longer the boy without a family. I spent so many nights praying to God for happiness that

I almost lost hope. But considering the eyes of the child that I had created with the woman I'd loved, it felt like he had finally answered my prayers. He answered Leilani. My daughter restored my faith in God. I was a believer. I believed in him. One night me and Ala decided to go out as we both had spent months in our home caring for our daughter. We hired a baby sitter and went to enjoy our night as new parents. The night we spent was incredible as we ate, laughed, watched a movie, and went to the Promenade. It was amazing. It was simply too good to be true. When we ended our night, we came back home to no house and no daughter. Our home had been burned down to the ground with our six-month-old daughter inside."

Leilani sat in her chair with the weight of his truth heavy on her heart. She couldn't imagine bearing the news of her son suffering such a horrible death. A tear slid down her cheek as her emotions took over her. No one ever said life would be easy but they both had survived.

"I am so sorry about your loss," Leilani replied, wiping her tear away.

"It was a sad thing La, but there isn't anything that anyone could do to prevent it from happening."

"I know, I just feel so bad."

"Here let me pour you a drink," he said.

"I don't drink Don."

"I am sorry; I forgot," he replied placing the glass container down. "I am so confused, why don't you drink?"

"I am just afraid of becoming dependent on a substance that alters my perception."

"You were once an addict?"

"Yes, but not for the Devil's piss; I was a needle pusher," she admitted. Don looked her over, waiting for her to crack a smile. But her stone-cold face didn't flinch. She never budged, revealing that her tale was simply just that, a tale. Instead, she gleamed into his eyes confirming the truth. "I ugh, I didn't have a normal childhood where my mother cared about my well-being. My father was nowhere in sight as he was just another deadbeat. Despite my mom's behavior towards me, I never stopped loving her nor did I badmouth her. It wasn't until he came along when everything changed. He took everything from me and replaced it with a monkey addiction and my mother just allowed him to do it. She stood there while her boyfriend injected me with heroin and raped me like I wasn't even human," Leilani revealed. The story of her childhood was like a shock to his heart. He had never heard anything like it. The pain in her voice was infused into her words. "I understand your pain when you say you lost your daughter. I got pregnant with my first son at 12 years old. But I lost that baby, and not too long later I ended up pregnant again with a boy," she reminisced.

"Where is he?"

"I had to give him up. I didn't want him around the environment I was in. I was only 13 years old with dope running through my veins; there was no way I was fit to raise that little boy," she replied. Her background story was raw and gritty. She couldn't bring herself to consider Don's eyes as she felt ashamed of her past.

"Have you had the chance to see your son?"

"No, I haven't built up the courage to meet him. But for every holiday and birthday I drop off packages of money for him. I promised myself that once I got clean I would work to ensure his future is set."

"And you're doing a damn good job at it," he replied as he took down the portrait of his daughter, revealing his hidden safe. Turning the dial to the correct combination, he waited until he heard a click before he pulled the lever opening the safe.

"I am going to give this to you for your son," Don stated.

"Don, that won't be necessary."

"La, you are family now, which means your son is my blood," he replied as he began to stack the bills in front of her. He knew she would try to deny him his offer, but Don wasn't going to take no for an answer. For such a short amount of time he grew fond of Leilani. He felt very overprotective over her as he wondered how his daughter would be if she were alive.

"Just remember I am always here for you," he stated as he took out a duffle bag placing all the money inside. The hypnotic blend of the crisp hundreds watered her taste buds. It was good to finally have people that cared for you. She wasn't used to it, but she was happy to have some sort of family amongst her.

CHAPTER 19

Loud roars filled the air as dozens of children ran throughout the Flatbush Garden playground. It was only the second week in November, and the crisp air didn't seem to bother the children as they found delight in the playground. The scenery was picture-perfect for a safe community, despite the drug transaction that occurred not too far away from the jumbo slide. Leilani entered the gates of the playground in search of her target. Skimming through the dozens of diverse faces, she found her target located amongst the group of drug dealing thugs.

"There you go," she said, making her way over to him. Her timberland boots thudded against the ground as she tuned out the catcalls that were addressed to her.

"Hey lil' mama, what you wanna cop?" a short guy asked her.

"I am good. I actually wanted to speak to Ricky Bobby and Chaos," she said pointing the two guys out of the group.

"And you are?" the short guy asked.

"Not here for you. Ricky and Chaos, can you two come with me," she asked turning her back away from the nosey guy. Confused, both men followed behind her, anticipating her reason for needing them. They walked behind her as she led them into a corner away from the group of guys they were with before. Once they were out of earshot, she turned around facing the two, analyzing their features. Chaos stared at her waiting for her to tell them what she wanted. There was money to make and she was interrupting that. At the mere age of 20 years old, all Chaos knew was the streets. He'd called a whorehouse his home for the first fourteen years of his life, before selling his soul to the streets. Calling a prostitute his mother and her pimp his father, he was a product of the streets. He ate, slept, and breathed the cold streets of New York City. It was easy to get caught up in his handsome features, neglecting his malicious intent. He resembled Detroit rapper Big Sean, charming the boots off anyone. But he carried a mouth piece on him that had caused many problems in his life. From his music, it was evident that he was intelligent, proving the stereotype that Black people were dumb, wrong. He was the type of rapper that had a good flow while spitting knowledge about the injustice in the world. Chaos was a great rapper and Leilani knew he would make it big in the music industry. Ricky Bobby on the other hand was the total opposite of Chaos. While he was raised in a middle-class home, with both parents, he always found an interest in the rap industry. He had a desire to be like his rap idols Snoop Dog, Lil' Wayne, and Future. Leilani knew they were gifted with the skill of rap.

"Hello fellas, you may not know me, but I am very close with both of your fathers," she began.

"What's your name?" Ricky Bobby asked.

"My name is Leilani, but you guys can call me La. I know you guys are rappers. I've heard your music and think you guys are good.

So, I would like to sign you guys to Carter's Dynasty."

"Wait, *the* Carter's Dynasty?" Chaos asked.

"Yes sir."

"The same Carter's Dynasty that went bankrupt, losing almost all of their artists?"

"Listen, I do not want to get into that stupid bullshit about the money issues within the company. I am part owner now, so we are rebirthing the company. I can only assure you that the money issue has been handled, and right about now, all I need you two to do is agree to sign under the label."

"What makes you think that we would wanna sign under your record label?" he asked.

"Well, for the simple fact that you have a record Ricky, almost twenty arrests in a month and you're facing some serious charges. Many record labels would not take a liking to an artist that has such a lengthy criminal background, but I am willing to work with you. All you must do is meet with my partner John Carter, discuss the contracts, sign the contracts, and then start making music. Simple and easy."

"How much are we talking?" Ricky asked concerned.

"If you are able to succeed, we are talking about a $20 million contract, no strings attached. Sell out concerts and sell albums; that is all that is being asked of you. Just make sure you find yourself at John Carter's office bright and early tomorrow morning."

"We will see about that."

"Don't let $20 million walk out of your life; this is a chance of a lifetime," she replied as she walked away. The hefty check wasn't what they expected to receive as they weren't top selling artists. But Leilani had faith in their work. The two were going to rebirth the record label; they didn't understand just how important they were.

5:45 p.m.

"So, do you think they will sign?" John asked.

"With that hefty paycheck, they have to sign; ain't no other record label offering them that much money."

John sat before Leilani's desk, nervous. Their whole company relied on these two rappers, as they were the only artists on the roster. The dynasty had suffered a huge lost when their money began to dry up. Noticing the huge cutbacks, all their artists left without hesitating.

"I know you're nervous John, but don't worry; I got this all under control," Leilani responded, noticing his worried expression.

"Our company is riding on you La, please get it back up and running," John begged. His voice was filled with much desperation. If her ideas didn't pull through, then John would have to file for bankruptcy, giving up everything he owned. He'd worked too hard for all his hard earnings to be auctioned off for less than their worth.

"Like I told you John, I got you partner."

Leilani stood up to overlook her new office space. Just like she had requested, John had given her, her own office. But what she wasn't expecting was for the office to be so huge. As his token of appreciation, John had combined several rooms to create a luxury office. His contractors had done a phenomenal job at achieving the look he was going for. What really set off the office space was the spectacular view that overlooked the Hudson River.

"You did a great job at reconstituting my office space."

"Well I had to show you that everything you are doing is well appreciated."

"Don't thank me yet; thank me when we get this company to that number one spot," she smiled.

"I definitely will," he replied, standing up preparing to leave. Leilani stood in her office looking at her beautiful scenery. In all her life, she'd never imagined she would ever be in the position she was today. Overlooking the Hudson River was a great accomplishment compared to overlooking crack pipes.

"This is a picture-perfect view ain't it?"

She turned around surprised to face the masculine voice. Sincere stood in the doorframe looking better than she had ever seen him. It had been a couple of weeks since they had last seen each other. Life had taken over, controlling what she had devoted her time to. With helping her best friend Essence raise her daughter, along with controlling an empire and rebuilding a record label, Leilani didn't have any time to spare. With everything life had thrown her way, she had disregarded Sincere. She had declined every offer he had made to spend time together, but today he refused to accept her response.

"Yea, it's an amazing view."

"Yes Princess, you look amazing."

"Thank you Sincere, but to what do I owe the pleasure of your presence?"

"Well, every offer I have made to spend time with you, you have declined. So, I decided to stop by randomly because now you cannot deny me for lunch."

"And what makes you think I won't deny you?"

"Because Princess, I am paying, so let's go."

"It's oh— "

"Woman, I didn't ask you for your opinion. We are going to lunch, so let's go," he demanded, displaying his perfect smile.

"Fine, let's go," she responded.

She grabbed his hand, leaving the sanctuary of her own office space. Sometimes Sincere could be so demanding, but she knew he had her best interest at heart. The couple made their way through the building until they ended up in front of Sincere's parked car.

"Princess, what do you have a taste for?" he asked.

"I don't care; you're dragging me out of my office so you better fucking figure it the fuck out."

"Ok, I may know of a perfect restaurant."

Leilani sat back in the car seat viewing the scenery before her. New York was so different with diversity. Every corner they stopped at it was a different race. The melanin within the people was like how the urban culture stated, *Popping.*

"How has life been?" Sincere questioned.

"Well it's been hectic. I am helping Essence with Emery, I'm rebuilding the record label, and I'm being the Queen Bee of the murder game."

"Well besides the fact that you're basically dividing yourself amongst three different things, I must say you are doing a very good job at it."

"Thank you very much."

Silence fell upon the couple as they drifted into the depth of their thoughts. So many things had occurred during their brief separation, but neither of them wanted to discuss those topics. Leilani was comfortable being in his presence.

"So, what restaurant have you decided upon?" she asked.

"It's a diner I partially own."

"Is the food good? And don't you dare lie to me."

"Yea, it's pretty good."

"Ok, I'll take your word for it."

Sincere pulled the car up in front of an old-fashioned diner parking lot. Leilani had heard about the location several times but never took the time to try their food. Once he cut the car off, they both got out and proceeded into his establishment. She could tell their goal was to resemble a modernized old-fashioned diner. She found the navy blue and white color scheme to be appealing. The smell of the home cooked food watered her taste buds as she stared around, taking in her surroundings.

"Hey boss," the hostess greeted Sincere with her broad, coffee stained smile.

"Hey Tina, I will be having dinner in my usual booth," he directed.

"Ok sir," she spoke, leading the two to the back of the diner where Sincere's favorite booth was. Once they were seated, the waitress handed over the menu anticipating their response for what they would like to eat.

"I will start off with a cup of Pepsi, and for Princess, she'll have a cup of water with a lemon," Sincere began.

"Right away sir, I will be back with your drinks and to take your order," the young waitress replied. Turning his attention back to Leilani, he smiled while gazing at her. Over their little break, he found himself missing her terribly.

"Have I told you that I've missed you so much?"

"No, but it would be good to hear you actually say it."

"Princess, I miss you baby."

"Such an emotional thug," Leilani joked.

"Well Princess, I am your emotional thug baby," he spoke as he combined her fingers with his. The feeling of her velvety hands sent a sensational shock through his body. He'd been with dozens of women, but to him, Leilani was different. She wasn't with him for his money, or for reputational purposes. The emotions that ran through the two was pure. Their love could grow into something unstoppable. That thought scared Leilani as she knew how destructible it could be. They could grow loving each other or grow bitter hating one another.

"So, tell me how work has been for you my emotional thug."

"Same ole bullshit basically; had to compromise with some of our business partners."

"What happened?"

"Nothing really, they didn't like the new contract we had put out so we compromised with what they wanted. Which wasn't really much of a problem."

"That doesn't sound as bad as I thought."

"What about you Princess, how's your end of business?"

"Surprisingly, it's not as bad as I thought it would have been. I mean granted there are some niggas testing my patience but ain't nothing I haven't dealt with before."

"So, you basically going around shooting niggas," he joked.

"Well it is my job title."

"You're right, Princess."

Their conversation continued with light laughter. It felt good to laugh genuinely after the weeks they've been having. They sat together enjoying their food, discussing the topics of the world. Their conversation was getting deep as they noticed a pretty, petite woman make her way over to them.

"Sincere, I hope you know this girl that's coming over to us, because if not, she's gonna be one sorry ass bitch," Leilani stated as she observed the body language of the woman. It was evident that she was pissed off making her way over to them. Sincere looked up, meeting the glare of the woman he once loved. *Amiya.*

"If it ain't my no good baby daddy," she said smiling.

"Amiya don't start with the bullshit."

"Nigga, you came to my restaurant, and on top of that you bring one of your bitches here of all places," she ranted.

"A restaurant that I own too."

Their voices filled with anger as they continued going back and forth. Leilani sat back in the booth observing the whole encounter. She didn't want to say anything as this argument was between him and his baby mother. Amiya noticed that every insult she said didn't aggravate Leilani like how she wanted. Leilani didn't even acknowledge their argument as she placed her attention on her food.

"Is your bitch deaf or some shit?" Amiya asked. "I'm talking shit about her and she's sitting there like I ain't talking shit."

"And that's all you are doing, talking shit," Leilani replied staring into the pits of her child-like eyes. "I am ignoring your ignorant ass, because if I reply I know I will hurt your little girl feelings."

"You nee—"

"No honey, you need to find your damn lane and get into it. Because right about now, you're dredging into a dangerous territory that could take your life."

The authority in Leilani's voice didn't faze Amiya as she continued ranting. Without saying anything else, Leilani began gathering her items, preparing to leave. She knew what kind of female Amiya was and knowing her own temper, Leilani was not trying to get physical in public. Instead of listening to their argument, she got up to leave.

"Princess, where are you going?" he asked.

"Don't worry Sincere, you two need to straighten this shit out. I have other things to do," Leilani responded, leaving them alone.

CHAPTER 20

Focus La, you got to stay focused!

Dozens of eyes remained fixated on her moves as she blocked the hits from her attacker. Tensions were high as their pride was on the line; neither competitor was willing to lose. Despite gaining the approval of some of her workers, she still had the urge to impress them. While Isaiah on the other hand refused to be beaten by a girl, who he had trained. He held no remorse; his hands moved quick, leaving an impact on Leilani's skin. Black and blue bruises formed on her golden skin, displaying the harsh competition between the two fighters.

"Remember I am the one who taught you everything you know. There ain't no way you beating me," he boasted. He delivered a kick to her leg, causing her to buckle from the blow.

"You're right, but I also took time researching the body. Learning all of the body's weakest points," she spoke softly as she regained her composure. Quickly, she caught his jaw with her right hook then delivered a blow to his bladder. Instantly, Isaiah buckled over in pain. The blow caught him off guard. It felt as if all the air had been knocked out of his lungs.

"You piece of shit," he called out.

"I am a smart piece of shit that you trained." Leilani chuckled as she helped him off the mat. Their competitive wrestling match had developed a crowd. Everyone had taken their sides as the winning team cheered on, watching Isaiah throw his mouthpiece on the ground.

"Aight you assholes, get back to fucking work," Isaiah responded. The match between the two siblings was supposed to be a demonstration for the workers in the gym on some techniques to use in the work field. Isaiah, being an opinionated person, disagreed with everything that Leilani tried teaching the guys. So, to settle whose ideas was better, the siblings decided to battle it out in a quick match. Forgetting the purpose of their demonstration, both Leilani and Isaiah found a competition within the friendly match.

"Don't be such a sour pus, just admit it, you lost to your baby sister, that's all. Ain't shit to be ashamed of."

"Shut up, you freaking cheated."

"You are such a sore loser."

Leilani walked over to the bench to sit down and catch her breath. Sweat dripped from her body, leaving her with a sticky and uneasy feeling. Isaiah followed suit as he took a seat right next to her.

"I meant to ask you, how's the whole record label thing going?" Isaiah questioned.

"Oh, it's going fine so far. I was able to talk to Ricky Bobby and he signed the contract. Right now, he should be in the studio working on some single."

"Are you nervous?"

"About?"

"The success of the company?"

"To be honest with you, I haven't even thought about that. My mind has been so focused on other things that I haven't even dwelled on that yet."

"Well don't, because knowing you, you'll begin to overthink everything."

"Shut up. You ready to go?" she asked him.

"Yea, I am hungry."

The duo walked together towards their gym bags. Isaiah grabbed both of their bags but kept the sour look on his face. Leilani chuckled a little bit, only to be greeted by Isaiah's straight face. She knew he was very much a sore loser, which only made the situation even funnier.

"Don't worry Isaiah, maybe next time," she joked.

Isaiah attempted to reply to her comment but was interrupted by the sound of a ringing phone. Recognizing the ringtone, Leilani realized that it was her phone.

"My phone is in the front pocket," she said to Isaiah. Once he found it he handed it over to her, and she stared at the unknown number. She had no clue as to who it was, which caused her to second guess answering the phone. *I don't know anyone by this number*, she thought, sending the number straight to voicemail. *Now if they call back, maybe I'll answer.*

"Who was it?" Isaiah asked.

"I don't know the number. But if they call back I might just answer it," she said. Holding the phone up, she glared at it, waiting for the phone to ring once more. The duo walked towards Isaiah's car anticipating the phone ringing. The six-inch screen vibrated once more displaying the same number on the screen.

"You gonna answer?"

"Yeah, I'll answer this time," she responded, pressing the green button. "Hello," she answered.

"Is this my—ugh Leilani?" the caller huffed. Leilani could hear the panic in his voice.

"Yes, who's this?" she questioned.

"This is Juelz and I need your help."

The realization of who it was stopped her breathing. It felt like time ceased for her as she stood in her spot, frozen in time.

"Hello?" he questioned.

"Yea I am here."

"Ok, I was told to call this number in case of an emergency. Right now, there are some masked men in the house."

"Where are you now?"

"Hiding in the closet."

"Ok, first thing the guys are going to do is look in that closet, so I need for you to escape through the window and hide in the shed in your backyard. Give me five minutes and I will be there," she said.

"Alright."

"Juelz do not hang up the phone; stay on the line with me,"

she spoke. Quickly she got into Isaiah's car and directed him to their destination. "Do you see anyone?" she asked.

"No, I think they are all in the house."

"Good, if they are any good there should be a getaway car. Do you see it?"

"Yea, but only one guy."

"Ok tell me his nationality."

"He looks Mexican."

"You're doing a good job Juelz; now make your way to the shed."

She remained on the phone listening to his movement. Her heartbeat was uncontrollable as hundreds of scenarios ran through her head. *What the fuck?* Arriving at their destination, Leilani looked out the window noticing the black Escalade parked out front of Juelz's home.

"Juelz, are you in the shed yet?"

"Yes."

"Ok, stay in there and I will come get you out," she said, hanging up the phone. She wasted no time pulling out her silenced glock. Isaiah followed suit, clueless as to what he was getting himself into.

"I think Sanchez is retaliating; that slimy mutherfucker," Leilani revealed.

"So, it's shoot to kill?"

"Yes sir," she replied, getting out of the car. Sneaking quietly to the awaiting vehicle, Leilani thought of all the other alternatives Sanchez could have taken. *He could have robbed my house, he could have come after me, he could have done anything else besides come after my son. If it's war he wants, then a bloodshed he shall receive.* She walked closer to the driver side of the car with her weapon drawn. Gripping the driver by his greasy hair, she yanked his head back. Focusing the tip of the silencer at his temple, she tapped the trigger, allowing his brain matter to explode all over the place. Once the lookout was taken down, she signaled for Isaiah to exit the car.

"Do you know how many guys are inside?"

"No."

"So, should we grab your son and leave?"

"No, we can't. I have to find his adopted mother first."

"Ok, so the plan is to get his adopted mother and him out of this place."

"Basically."

With their plan orchestrated, they creeped their way into the house, neither one caring about their surroundings. The smell of gasoline infiltrated their nostrils as they entered the quiet home. Leilani's eyes analyzed the surroundings, noticing the dozens of pictures of Juelz and his adopted mother. Happiness rested on their faces, causing jealousy to seep into La's heart. Thirteen years' worth of memories were plastered on the wall, only reminding Leilani that she hadn't been there for any of them. She'd missed thirteen birthdays, and twelve years' worth of holidays. The pain ached her heart in the worst way possible.

"I hear voices coming from the kitchen," Isaiah whispered, leading the way into the kitchen. Leilani followed right behind him entering the kitchen space. The sound of the intruder's thick voice bounced off the walls. Leilani listened on to the conversation being held in front of Juelz's tied up mother. The men discussed in Spanish what their boss wanted them to do. Confusion rested upon the hired hitmen as they began to disagree on what they were demanded to do. Juelz's adopted mother remained bound in the middle of the kitchen, restrained to a wooden chair, unconscious. Leilani's blood boiled at the sight of the innocent woman. She was innocent, but due to Leilani's involvement with a feud, that woman's life was placed in danger. Coming from behind the wall, she revealed her identity, aiming her silencer at the intruders.

"Well gentlemen, relay the message back to Sanchez for me: you let him know that Leilani said Checkmate bitch," she yelled as she released bullets into the skulls of the robbers. Instantly, they dropped dead onto the cold tile floor.

"Do you think she's alive?" Isaiah asked, while walking over to the unconscious, restrained woman.

"I hope she is. We need to get her to a hospital and fast."

"I'll put her in the car; go and get your son."

Not needing much motivation, Leilani followed Isaiah's orders, running out of the kitchen and into the yard. The frigid November air snuck up her gym attire, but she ignored the cold as she ran towards the shed. She yanked the door open, finding her teenage son crouched down on the ground.

"Juelz?" she asked.

His big, grey eyes stared back at her with relief. He had imagined meeting his birth mother a dozen times. Every time he imagined their reunion, he conjured up the scene with him graduating high school being Valedictorian. He knew exactly what he wanted to say as his speech centered around the idea of him being worthy of his mother's time. Learning about his adoption at the age of ten years old, Juelz tormented himself with the question, *why wasn't he enough?* He expected to meet his mom with the look of satisfaction on his face. He wanted her to be proud of him, instead as he glared into the eyes of the woman who birthed him, all he could see was regret. The pain within her spoke volumes. Leilani crouched down onto the ground as she wrapped her arms around her son. Over the years, she had watched him grow up into the young man he was today.

"I am so sorry," she said rocking him back and forth. "I am so sorry for everything I have ever done. In this life of sin, you are the only good thing that has come out of anything."

He had expected his mother to be some cold-hearted, mean bitch that could care less about him. But the grip she held on him spoke another story. It spoke the many nights she spent alone thinking about her child's well-being. Her embrace was filled with love. Her heart felt warm as the tears poured freely from her eyes.

CHAPTER 21

"So how is he doing?" Isaiah asked. Concern was written all over his face as the thought of his nephew's mental well-being was in question. Just a couple of hours ago, his nephew's life was put at stake because of a drug feud. Isaiah sat on the couch observing Leilani's demeanor; he searched for any sign of anger, knowing that the crisis could be fucking with her conscious. On the outside, she was secluded and quiet, not saying very much, but Isaiah knew better than to believe the façade she presented. Leilani's blood was boiling with animosity with the thought of vengeance fueling her.

"Well, the doctor checked him out and he's fine. There isn't anything wrong with him," Leilani replied.

"And his adopted mother?"

"I called Don and he insisted on having his doctors take care of her."

"Did you inform him on what happened?"

"I didn't go into great details and surprisingly he didn't ask many questions."

"Well, that's how he can be," Isaiah stated, knowing the truth as to why Don didn't question Leilani. He made the call to Don, informing him about the tragedy that had transpired. "So, La, tell me how do you feel about the chain of events?" Isaiah questioned.

"It was unexpected but there isn't anything that I can do about it," Leilani said. She focused her vision on the clothes before her. Folding Juelz's new clothing was the only way she would be able to disguise her true feelings from Isaiah. Neatly, she stacked all his clothing into a pile, not once looking into Isaiah's eyes.

"Bullshit La, you're fucking lying."

"What are you talking about now?"

"Don't you fucking know that I know you already?" he questioned. "You're avoiding eye contact with me, your attention is focused on folding some fucking clothes, and you replied to my question without a single fucking curse word in the response. So, La, I will ask you one more fucking time, how do you feel about everything?"

"I already told you Isaiah, I am fine."

Her words held no emotion in them: they were like a band-aid to cover the truth in her emotions. She wanted to break down and cry, but she wouldn't allow herself to do so. A woman of her stature was not allowed to have emotions. It was required that she be emotionless as this mental state was a sign of her strength. She held her composure, tuning Isaiah's voice out of her head. *I will be fine,* she thought, *hold it in.* Her thoughts whirled around her mind causing a catastrophe of emotions. It felt like she couldn't control herself as her chest tightened. Breathing became hard to do, resulting in her body perspiring. Folding the clothes seemed to be a never-ending task. *Why won't you fucking fold correctly,* she complained while refolding the same shirt for the dozen time. Her anxiety was beginning to get the best of her, as she could no longer control her breathing.

The memories of her past floated around her mind, messing with her fixation of folding the clothes. Her thoughts dragged her back to her first drug overdose that scared her straight. Her mouth grew excessively dry as the memory played vividly in her head.

******

Thump!

Thump!

Thump!

The sound of the headboard rhythmically smacking against the wall, filled the room. The air was thick with perspiration, making it hard for Rocky to breathe. Inserting his penis in and out of his thirteen-year-old lover's vagina held his attention. His surroundings didn't bother him nor did his motionless lover, who lay underneath him, higher than a kite. Thirty minutes prior to his sexual escapade, he entered her room prepared to have a quick session. She had recently lost their baby by the hands of her mother, but at that moment that didn't matter to him. He wanted her and he knew exactly how to get her: **get her high.** *That's exactly what he did; he injected her like he usually did, but used double the quantity to get her high, not caring for the results it would have on her body.*

His hot breath breathed in her ear, searching for the necessary reaction. He expected her to shutter at the sensation of his warm breath on her clammy skin, but she never budged. Instead, she glared up at the ceiling, hypnotized by the sight of the perfectly painted ceiling. Her thoughts were lost within the taunting white ceiling, ***pure and filled with***

innocence. It's perfect with no flaws. It's clean. It's … Not me. *The pain from the realization of her flaws caused her to shed a tear. Her innocence was ripped away from her without her consent. She was never given the chance to fight, and that was why she used drugs. It was the sole purpose of her turning to drugs looking for help with her reality. The drugs helped her cope with the pain she was currently dealing with, from losing her innocence to losing her child; it was beginning to take its toll on her mentally.*

"I love you girl," her stepfather whispered into her ear.

I hate you, you piece of shit*. She wanted to say it so bad but she was weak. Her eyes were burning for some rest, so she shut them. The euphoric feeling the drugs created rocked her into a sound sleep, taking her away from the world. Slowly, she fell deeper and deeper into the in between, as her body couldn't detoxify the drugs fast enough.*

Feeling her frail body go limp, Rocky stopped to stare down at the young girl underneath him. Calling her name, he became frantic with her not responding. ***Fuck****, he thought. Quickly, he jumped off the bed searching for the naloxone, a medication designed to rapidly reverse opioid overdose. Pulling open the dresser drawers, he ransacked it, searching for the life-saving medication.*

"Fuck, where is it?" he yelled out loud.

He continued searching through the drawers until his eyes spotted the black needle case. Quickly, he unzipped the case revealing the needle and the 0.4 mg of naloxone. Filling the needle with the necessary amount of naloxone, he walked over to Leilani and positioned her thigh at an angle that was best for him.

"Please God, let this shit work."

Injecting the needle into Leilani's thigh, he pushed down on the plunger, allowing the medication to enter her system. Instantly, he noticed the increase of her breathing as the color in her skin restored. Taking a deep breath, Rocky was relieved that she wasn't dead.

"Thank God," he said out loud.

Gaining consciousness, Leilani quickly turned over on the bed, releasing the little food she had eaten throughout the day. The sound of Leilani hurling filled the quiet apartment, making Rocky happy that she was still alive.

"You should have just left me to die."

"What?"

"You should have just left me."

******

"Leilani," Isaiah said, catching her attention. Finally, she looked up at him. Her face was contorted with stress. Trying to hide her emotions would cause her to have a mental breakdown at any given moment. Isaiah was familiar with this kind of Leilani. She would bottle up all her emotions until it was too late to save someone from her wrath. He walked over to her, grabbing ahold of her arms. "It's me Leilani, you don't have to cover up those old scars anymore." The words flowed out of his mouth like an open faucet. Leilani couldn't help the tears that fell from her eyes. The emotions took control over her as she wept into Isaiah's arms.

"I know this is a lot for you," he said, caressing her quivering body. He held onto her for dear life, afraid of losing her once again. The monkey habit she'd picked up from her childhood was a menace to her new life. She had been clean for over a decade, but the addiction still held a grip on her during her emotional state of mind. He wondered if the thought of the high still bombarded her mind. Isaiah had seen what drugs had done to her, and he never wanted her going back to it.

"Come La, let's go sit down," he instructed as he walked over to the couch with her still entangled in his embrace. "Everything will be ok," he comforted her. Gently, he caressed her clammy skin, comforting her from the pain.

"I am going to kill Sanchez," Leilani replied as she wiped the tears away from her face.

"That's an option, but for right now, I need you to calm down and think clearly. You just got your son back."

"I am thinking clearly. I am going to attack Sanchez."

"Well La, you're a boss now. You can have some of your workers carry out the hit."

"I did that before, but now this time it's personal; he came after my son."

Her mind became hazy with revenge as she put on her boots and jacket. The move Sanchez had made placed her in a difficult situation. Being the fireball she was, Leilani was not going to wait to make her move. Sanchez had attacked her son's home, so now it was time for Leilani to return the gesture.

"La, you don't even have a plan," Isaiah tried arguing.

"Does it look like I give a fuck about a plan?"

"I don't think any of your workers would be up to attacking this man."

"And that's ok, because I didn't plan on using them anyway." She left her apartment without a clue as to how she would carry out the hit. It didn't matter to her, but she was going to get shit done.

******

"Hurry the hell up," Lora yelled as she gazed up her arched staircase. Irritation ran through her body as she was now annoyed with her stepdaughter Melody. *I can't wait until she is sent back home to her fucking mother*, she thought as she placed her designer shades on the top of her head.

It was a bright and early Friday morning with Thanksgiving right around the corner. The holiday spirit was thick in the air as the ladies' morning plans consisted of the mother and stepdaughter duo spending time with each other. Shopping seemed like the perfect idea for a bond to be established between the two. But unfortunately, the hate between the two ran too deep for designer clothing to repair. Issues surfaced within the family once Carlos Sanchez took the hand of 18-year-old Lora Reznov in marriage three years ago. There were negative comments that went towards his new marriage, but Carlos never minded any of those negative opinions, even from his own daughter.

"I am coming, my fucking god," the eighteen-year-old complained. She descended the marble stairs, annoyed by the sound of Lora's Russian accent. Staring into the eyes of the woman that her father fell in love with, Melody could not feel anything but resentment. Her whole world was turned upside down by the pussy of a woman who was only three years older than her. The thought turned her stomach, as Lora could pass as her father's daughter.

"Let's go," Lora demanded.

Following behind the tanned Russian princess, Melody decided to keep all her rude remarks to herself. She had promised her father that she would at least try to form a bond with Lora. But the longer she stayed in the presence of her stepmother, the more annoyed she became. *Remember, try to be social with the puta,* she reasoned in her head. Together the duo entered their awaiting Mercedes with their minds wrapped around buying the latest merchandise. Silence fell upon them, increasing the tension. *This is going to be one long ass day,* Melody thought, turning up the volume to the radio. Tuning out Lora's stupid antics, she focused in on the road to their journey. It only took an hour for the duo to arrive at their destination. Before Lora could park the car Melody found herself hopping out of the moving vehicle.

"Really, you couldn't wait for me to park the car you little bitch," Lora exclaimed. She sat back, examining her stepdaughter stomp away, never once acknowledging her. Annoyed, Lora turned the car off before getting out. Briskly, she sat her designer shades on the top of her head as she entered her favorite clothing store, Gucci. She needed an immediate pain relief, and the Italian luxury brand was the only thing that could cure her anger.

The smell of the expensive leather infiltrated her nostrils, causing her taste buds to water. Adorning her body with name brand slaughtered cow skin enticed her. It fed the hunger for the lavish life that burned within her heart. Her childhood had been spent wishing upon a star for anything that would stop the hunger pains. Now 21 years old and married to a successful drug lord, the only pain she endured was from carrying the flamboyant blood diamond that rested on her ring finger. Life was good for Lora, as she proceeded through life without any worries. She ran through the clothing racks with only one thing on her mind, *how are these things going to fit in the Mercedes? I should have brought the truck.* For the next several hours, she ripped through high-end stores buying unnecessary items. None of the items she had purchased were needed, she wouldn't ever need anything if her last name remained Sanchez. It was the yearning for the lavish life that kept her sane; it diminished the truth about her past, and in a weird way it healed her.

The sun began to set as time inched closer to five in the afternoon. New York was colder than usual as a snowstorm threatened to hail down the streets. Lora walked out of her last store impressed with the hole she had placed on her husband's black American Express card. She clicked her winter boots over to her car where she spotted Melody waiting.

"It took you long enough. I have been waiting here forever," she complained.

"Well, I am sorry. I just had to bu—"

"I don't want to hear any of your fucking excuses. I've been standing here for damn near an hour."

"You should have tried calling me."

"I fucking did; you sent me straight to voicemail."

Unconcerned by the ranting teenager, Lora continued with unlocking the car. She couldn't care less about how Melody felt. *She's not the man that I have sex with every night,* she reasoned. They both got into the car without a word discussed between the two. Melody was highly annoyed with her stepmother, cursing her within the depths of her mind. The hour-long drive back home seemed to drag on. Once they arrived on their property, relief washed over them both.

"Can you grab some of the bags?" Lora asked.

"Get your own shit," Melody replied, exiting the car.

"Fucking bitch."

Lora shut off the purring engine and proceeded with entering her home. She would just send some of the workers out to retrieve her new belongings later. Entering the newly renovated mansion, Lora basked at the job the contractors had done on her home. The seven-million-dollar home glistened like a polished diamond, being the dream home for dozens of people.

"I am going to have a bubble bath," she said, turning around to shut the front door. Her eyes met the glare of a pair of eyes that were unfamiliar. She stood before her intruder stuck like a piece of bubble gum on the bottom of one's shoes. The sound of her increasing heartbeat vibrated within her body, notifying her that she was still alive. *Move, run, say something.* Her words remained hidden within her voice box. The intruder raised her hand high, bringing her weapon down, crashing it against Lora's skull.

Clonk!

******

"What the fuck?" Lora's voice cracked as she awakened to the bright lights that filled the dungeon-like basement. She glanced around familiarizing herself with the room. *This is Carlos's basement,* she concluded. It had been some time since she was last in the torture chamber, but she would never forget the eerie feeling of death that hovered over the space. *What the hell am I doing in Carlos's chambers?* she questioned. *Did he find out about the affair?* Confused, her head began to pound in pain. *The last thing I remember is being hit upon the head by some woman. I don't think Carlos has any woman enforcers.* Her mind began to roam in search of an answer for the unexpected turn of events. She felt confined to a tight space, moving her body around. Her bare skin rested against the cold metal causing goosebumps to form. Her hands were bound behind her back, with releasing herself being almost impossible. Wildly, Lora maneuvered her body trying to free herself from the restraints. The noise of her movements echoed within the cemented walls of the basement. She shook in the chair but to no avail; she remained detained.

"Ugh, what the fuck," she yelled into the damp air.

"All that moving you keep doing will not help you a single bit."

Looking up, Lora met the eyes of her assailant. She'd never met the woman a day in her life, but she recognized her features from a recent picture. She was one of Carlos's targets that he had paid to be attacked. Lora remembered walking into his office while the topic of their enemy was up for discussion. Walking out of the room was her first instinct, but her eyes were caught on the plastered picture of their biggest threat. Her name was thrown around the room leaving a bad taste in their mouth. All the men were well educated on their target as they had glared at some of her best work. Lora was intrigued with the brutality of the woman. She had never seen someone like her before. *Feminine yet held masculine strength.*

"You're that woman."

Confused, Leilani just stared at her in efforts of making sense of what she was saying. Leilani had hit her with the bat with some force, but she didn't think it could have caused any brain damage.

"What?"

"You're the girl that my husband wanted to kill."

"I am honestly flattered," Leilani replied as she turned facing the table. She eyed all the shinning blades that rested in front of her. For a person with a torture obsession, the table would have been perfect. But for Leilani, it wasn't about pleasing a sick obsession. She had a message to send and the tools were the perfect way for her to carve her message.

"Where is Melody?"

"She's dead," Leilani stated without any enthusiasm.

"What?"

"I killed her," she replied as she picked out her desired blade, glaring into her reflection that bounced off the knife. "You see, your husband made the wrong move by fucking with the Supremes' shipment. I returned the gesture by shutting his operation down. He counteracts my actions by digging up my closed adoption just to fuck with my son, putting my son's life in danger. So, Mrs. Lora Sanchez, it is my turn to retaliate."

Lora glared into the eyes of her reaper, seeking sympathy. She knew death was near but she wasn't ready to give up that easily. She had spent her childhood suffering from the hands of poverty, given up into the world of prostitution as means for her father to put dinner on the table for the week. Lora had witnessed the worst Russia had to offer. For the past three years, she indulged in the fabulous life, only for it to end in death.

"Please don't kill me," she begged.

"Oh, sweetie I won't kill you," Leilani smiled. "Well, at least not right about now."

Leilani walked over to Lora holding the knife firmly in her hand. Petrified, Lora shivered within the restraints of the chair. The scenery was comical for Leilani as she gripped her hand around the slim neck of the Russian Princess. Leilani had been watching her for a while, observing her daily routines. She saw how Lora treated her stepdaughter Melody and it was truly sad. There wasn't an ounce of love within the depths of Lora's heart.

"Please, I will scream and the guards will come in here," Lora stated.

"The chambers are sound proof." Leilani chuckled as she brought the blade down, swiping it against her vanilla, velvety skin. Screams escaped her thin, pink lips as blood gushed from the open incision. Unconcerned about Lora's painful cries, Leilani continued maneuvering the sharp blade, inscribing her message. Taking a step back, Leilani observed her masterpiece.

"And voila!" she said.

She glared at the message with a huge smile on her face. The message she etched into the huge organ was clear. There wasn't any uncertainty as to what her message pertained to.

"I am not to be fucked with," she read.

Placing the blade back onto the table, she stared at her other options. There were so many different knives that she didn't know what to choose. Her mind ran wild trying to find her next object while Lora continued to scream. The pain in her voice was evident, but Leilani hadn't done much to cause such pain. Confused, she picked up a hammer, turning around to face her hostage.

"I guess I should give you a reason to scream then," Leilani said.

"No, please, you don't have to do this."

"Actually Lora, I do have to do this."

Leilani fixated her eyes on the knees of Lora. They were tainted red as the blood from her thighs dripped down from her open wounds. Besides the blood covering them, Lora had pretty knee caps. Leilani thought it was weird as she had known knee caps to resemble ugly faces. But Lora's knee caps were far from that. They almost seemed perfect, without any scars or bruising. Quickly, she raised the hammer high, bringing it crashing down against her knee caps. The sound of bones crunching echoed through the thick air, syncing with Lora's loud cries. Tears escaped the corner of Lora's eyes, descending her red cheeks. The pain was unbearable but Leilani refused to stop. She continued to bash Lora's knees until her bone was very visible.

"Please no more," Lora breathed. She was barely conscious as the pain threatened to knock her out.

"No, honey, no sleeping," Leilani replied as she smacked Lora awake. "I am not finished yet."

For the next couple of hours, Leilani continued her attack on Lora. Sweat protruded from Leilani's open pores as she stood back, admiring the work she had done on her victim. The Russian princess was badly disfigured. There wasn't a plastic surgeon in the world that was good enough to make her look normal again. Wiping the sweat off her forehead, Leilani walked over to her tools table as she grabbed a napkin to clean her hands of the blood. The sound of a vibrating phone caught her attention. Glaring at Lora's phone screen, her lips spread into a smile. She swiped the screen placing the phone to her ear.

"Babe, I know you were looking for me earlier but I got caught up with some business. I just got home, where are you?" Carlos began to rant. Leilani listened intensively, patiently waiting for the man on the other line to stop talking.

"Well Mr. Sanchez, we both know the real reason as to why you were unavailable earlier."

"Who the fuck is this?"

"Oh, where are my manners; sorry, it's Leilani."

"You fucking bitch," he yelled. "Where the fuck is my wife?"

" You see Mr. Sanchez, you crossed the fucking line when you went after my family so I decided to send your wife into the belly of the beast. Your daughter on the other hand, it's too late for her," she responded, hanging up the phone. A sweat droplet descended her forehead as the thought of her actions replayed in her head. *Can I really do this?* she questioned herself. She'd provoked a war with a one-man army. The fellas didn't have a clue about her whereabouts as she wanted to do this all alone. But now, she began to second guess her decision. Waiting for the presence of her enemy, she stood patiently, facing the knives of terror. Her thoughts began to take control of her mind, reasoning her actions taken. The sound of the heavy basement door opening echoed throughout the room, putting life into a dying Lora.

"Please save me, help," she screamed. The torture she had endured was beyond bearable. Slowly, she was meeting her maker but not before yelling for help. "Help me please," she screamed.

"Shut the fuck up," Leilani responded, as she punched Lora in the jaw, knocking it out of place.

Carlos Sanchez slowly descended the cemented stairs with his gun drawn. He mentally prepared himself for the worst, as he didn't know what was going on. One minute he was escaping the wrath of his second girlfriend, ending up home where his wife was being held hostage. Once he made it down the last stairs, he wasn't prepared for the sight before him. His wife sat tied up to a metal chair, barely alive. Her jaw hung low while her face was practically destroyed. Blood discharged from every opening of her body.

"What the fuck did you do?" he questioned.

"I made my move, and the game is over," Leilani replied. Sweat seeped through her pores, descending her forehead. "You see Carlos, taking some of Don's shipment was one thing. But you took things too fucking far when you went after my fucking kid. For you to actually find Juelz would have to mean you went snooping."

"Well bitch, charge it to the game."

" Really, charge it to the game?" she chuckled. Pulling out her pistol, she positioned it to his chest, pulling the trigger. A loud shot rang through the moist air as Carlos's body tumbled to the floor. Slowly, Leilani walked over to his body, standing over him. She watched as he struggled to breathe. "Just charge it to the game," she responded as she pulled the trigger, sending a bullet ripping through his stomach. His blood poured out of his open wounds, seeping into the concrete floor. Leilani was sure that the way she shot him, would keep him alive for only a little while. His death would be long and slow until his blood drained from his corrupted body. The message she had sent was loud and clear for anyone who wanted to go after her. Her son was not to be fucked with.

CHAPTER 22

"How did you sleep last night?" Leilani asked.

"I slept good." Juelz replied as he shoved a pancake into his mouth. She stood before him, infatuated with his features. The child she had birthed was almost identical to her; she was amazed at how strong her DNA was. Juelz had inherited his mother's golden skin complexion along with her grey eyes. His thick, curly mane decorated his head like how Leilani used to keep her hair. Despite the similarities, Juelz had inherited some traits from his father. The way his lip curled while he indulged in his pancakes sent a chill down her spine. The memory she had of Rocky breathed right in front of her. His DNA lived on despite the fact Leilani had him buried six feet under the Earth's surface.

"What are the plans for my living arrangement?" he questioned.

"You will be staying with me. Once your adopted mother is better, I will have a talk with her about what should be done."

An awkward silence filled the space between the mother and son duo. Juelz began toying with a piece of pancake as his mind roamed into the pits of his thoughts. *Adopted mother?* he questioned. *I never thought of Ma as my adopted mother.*

"Now that you're in my life, what should I call you?"

"What do you mean?" Leilani questioned as she turned around, wiping her hands on the rag resting near the kitchen sink.

"Well, I've called my adopted mother Ma, it's something I'm used to doing. But now that you're in my life what should I call you?"

"What would you like to call me?"

"I want to call you Mommy, ya know because you actually pushed me out," he confessed. Despite being raised by a woman that wasn't his biological mother, Juelz held a level of respect for the woman who had birthed him.

"Then that's fine with me."

"Why did you give me up?" he blurted out.

"What?" like a deer caught in headlights, Leilani was taken off guard by his question. She knew it would come eventually, but she hadn't mentally prepared herself for this. For years, she debated in her head about telling her son the truth. But what could she tell him? That he was a product of rape. That his biological mother was a dope fiend that pumped her veins full of poison, or that his father was a drug dealer that had a fetish for young girls. Her truth was ugly, but it was the life that made her who she was today. The struggle she endured was her story to tell; she just didn't think she was ready to narrate the gruesome tale to her thirteen-year-old son. *Sugar coat it is*, she confirmed. "How about this, I will give you a basic summary and when you turn 18, I will give you the whole truth."

"Why 18?"

"Because Juelz, by then you should be mature enough to handle that vital information."

"I am mature enough now."

"No honey, you're not. I promise you I will give you the whole truth of why I gave you up. Right now, I will give you a sugar coated version."

"Fine."

"The reason I gave you up is because I couldn't take care of you at such a young age. I had to get my life together before I could bring myself back into your life."

"Do you have yourself together now?"

"Yes I do. You are my main priority."

She gazed into his pupils, meaning every word she said. If it wasn't for him, she would have still been strung out on the latest dope, or even six feet under. Having him was the greatest thing that could have ever happened to her. He gave her hope when she depended on a needle to keep her pumping. He gave her love when all she had was hate for the people who ruined her life. He meant everything to her, as she was willing to do anything to see the twinkle in his eye.

"I know that this is your first time meeting me, but believe me Juelz, I love you so much. You were my motivation at my darkest time. I know I've physically not been there for you, but I am now."

The pain in her voice was evident; she was sincere, meaning every word. Growing up, he always questioned his origin within his adopted family. His adopted mother never withheld the truth from Juelz, as he knew all along that he was adopted. He knew about his mother giving him up at such a young age, but the question that burned his soul was, *why did she give him up?* That was the question that no one had the answer to, except his biological mother Leilani.

Staring into his eyes, her mind went back to the night when she had given birth to him.

******

Fold the shirt in half with the arms together, now fold the arms back. Hmm, then fold the shirt horizontally. No, flatten the shirt to get the neat look. *Leilani's thoughts were focused on getting her shirts to be neatly folded. The strategic method was a procedure she was learning to perfect. Watching the local Chinese owner fold clothes at the laundromat, Leilani became intrigued with the way they could perfectly fold the clothes. It was a method they used, and Leilani took it upon herself to learn it. She needed something to keep herself busy and house chores were her answer. For the past couple of months, she'd managed to remain drug free. She hadn't had a needle penetrate her skin in months, and she felt great. Going cold turkey really messed her up for a month. For a month, she was bed riddled due to the spells of her withdrawal. Everything she endured during that month was worth it, because her child would be healthy and that was her main objective.* ***Keep this baby healthy.*** *That was all that mattered to her.*

"I am hungry," Leilani said to herself. Her stomach growled lightly in agreement at the thought of food. Not needing any more convincing, Leilani set aside the laundromat basket and walked over to the kitchen. Opening the fridge, she peeked in, hoping to see anything that would cure her hunger. Unfortunately, she didn't see anything appealing. ***Ugh, come on, there must be something that I could eat.*** *Determined to find something, her eyes scanned the refrigerator once more until finally her*

eyes landed on a package of cookies. "These will just have to do," she said.

Eight months into her pregnancy, Leilani was ready to give birth. Her small frame contained her pregnancy the best way it could. Her stomach wasn't noticeable as she wore baggy clothes to conceal her round abdomen. The plan she used to disguise her pregnancy worked well for her as no one knew about her pregnancy besides her mother and Rocky. Her neighbors found Leilani's baggy clothes to be weird, but they figured she was going through the pre-teen phase. Sitting down on the couch, Leilani opened the cookie package, indulging one by one into the sweet baked good. The sweetness of the chocolate chip cookie caused her tooth to instantly ache in pain.

"These are so good," she moaned. Painfully, she munched on the cookie despite her toothache. Indulging into the cookie, she was so focused on savoring the baked good that she didn't notice the door open until she heard her mother slam the door shut. Jiggling her keys vigorously, Roselyn had some trouble with taking the key out of the lock.

"Mierda," she spat angrily.

Leilani's eyes perked to the sound of her mother's voice. Roselyn hadn't been home in the past two days. She had left Friday morning with her return expected the following morning. But Saturday morning when Leilani woke up, Roselyn was nowhere in sight.

"Mom are you ok?" Leilani asked concerned.

Ignoring her daughter's question, Roselyn proceeded with making her way into the apartment. Her eyes remained low as she focused on getting into her bedroom safely. One foot at a time, she drunkenly made her way through the apartment.

"Mom, be careful." The warning escaped Leilani's lips but was fully ignored as her mother's foot collided against the laundry basket. Her whole body tumbled to the ground with a loud thud echoing throughout the apartment.

"Ma, are you ok?" Leilani asked as she ran to her mother's aid.

"Get the fuck off me," Roselyn yelled, pushing her daughter away from her. "I don't need your fucking help." Using her weight, Roselyn helped herself with getting off the floor. She was still heavily intoxicated, but she refused to show Leilani her drunk side. She didn't want her daughter to have anything over her.

"Mommy you don't look too good," Leilani mentioned. Her mother's once perfectly tanned skin tone was paler than usual. The excessive amounts of alcohol were beginning to catch up to her. Her tamed mane was placed into a messy bun to keep her throw up out of her face.

"Shut the fuck up," Roselyn barked. "If I look bad it's your fucking fault; you poisoned me."

"What?"

"You fucking heard me; you poisoned me."

"Why would I do that to you?"

"You want my man." The concept was bizarre as it was completely off from the truth. With the situation at hand, she had no choice. Leilani's innocence was forced away from her, but Roselyn refused to see it like that. In her mind, Leilani planned the whole chain of events. **She probably put that basket there in hopes of killing me.** *"You did all this shit on purpose."*

"What are you talking about?"

"You probably seduced my man into sleeping with you. You became pregnant on purpose. You did these things just to steal him away from me."

"I would neve—"

"Yes, you would," Roselyn argued. Her thin finger pointed in the direction of Leilani's face. With every word that escaped her mouth, her finger probed closer and closer to Leilani's face. "You're just like your fucking father. All you want to do is hurt me. But I won't let you do what he did to me. I'd kill you before you can do anything."

Confused, Leilani sat on the couch, unsure of what to say. She didn't understand where all the accusations were coming from. For years, her mother had animosity towards her but she never explained why. Roselyn would sometimes blame her anger towards Leilani's father and other times she would blame it on the fact that Leilani was born. Her mother hated her and Roselyn made it her business to make sure Leilani knew. She never sugar coated anything, making sure that Leilani understood that she was hated.

"Fucking bitch thinks she can take me out, she's got another fucking thing coming. I'll be damned if you take my man like that no good bitch, and then you gonna have the nerve to want me dead," Roselyn said as she went into the kitchen. "I got something for you," she replied.

Leilani listened on as she heard the metal utensils clank together in the drawer. Her mother walked out of the kitchen with a wild look in her eyes. The alcohol fueled the irrational thoughts that corrupted her mind. Raising the long kitchen knife in the air, all Roselyn could see was red.

Unable to contain her emotions, Roselyn charged towards her daughter. Swinging wildly, she aimed to cut her daughter's head off, but her hand-eye coordination was heavily impacted by the high levels of alcohol in her system.

"Come here you fucking bitch," she yelled. She lunged the knife forward, piercing the wall with the long blade. "Shit," she yelled, as she tried wiggling the knife out of the wall. Seeing this as her only chance, Leilani ran out of the apartment in search for safety. Escaping into the street, Leilani never turned back. She didn't care if her mother was still stuck in their apartment trying to take out a knife that was wedged into the wall. All Leilani knew was that she had to find a safe place to hide. Deeply inhaling the cold air, Leilani's lungs burned as she quickly inhaled and exhaled. Stopping to catch her breath, a sharp pain entered her abdomen, causing her to double over in pain.

"Shit," she exhaled. Her stomach tightened, making her uncomfortable in her bent over position. Standing up straight, she tried to make herself a little more comfortable. Fixing her posture only caused the pain in her uterus to become more painful. ***What the hell is going on?*** *she thought. Before she could try to analyze the source of her pain, the feeling went away as if nothing happened.* ***Could the hunger pains be coming back?*** *she asked naively.*

"It has to be; it's too early for me to give birth."

Gaining her composure, she continued her journey to nowhere. She had no clue as to where she was going. She just needed somewhere to hide. Somewhere to rest her mind. Somewhere safe. The abandoned laundromat, she thought. In her old projects, there was an abandoned laundromat that she would go to and hide, whenever she needed a quiet place to get high or just to be alone. Just as the thought of her sacred haven entered her mind, a bolt of pain invaded her uterus causing her to double over once more. Her breath became lost in her lungs as she was unable to breathe through the pain. Sweat dripped down her sideburns, agitating her even more. Clueless to the source of pain, she didn't care where it was coming from. All she needed was for the pain to stop and she had only one solution to her problem.

Dead leaves paraded around the projects covering all the broken needles, condoms, and pipes that laid scattered all over the ground. The streets were filled with little black kids that had nowhere to go. Dope fiends stayed trapped behind the walls that were sugar coated with Brooklyn's finest drugs. Leilani walked the streets of Brooklyn in a daze as the feeling of emptiness haunted her. Her mind ran blanks as her feet led her to a familiar place. She walked up to the door, lightly tapping on the wooden frame, feeling shocks of pain enter her wrist. Her body shivered as the sweet November wind crept through her clothes and up her spine. The door to the house flung open as one of Rocky's workers stood before her.

"What are you doing La?"

"I need a hit," she spoke softly. The worker stood before her confused on what she needed. He knew exactly who she was and knew that there was a certain rule pertaining to Leilani. Rocky had placed a ban on her; she was not allowed to be served by any of his workers. The worker remembered the words of his boss as he was adamant on not disobeying the very man that was feeding him.

"Sorry baby girl, but Rocky placed a ban on you. No one can serve

you."

"What?"

"Yes, so I can't do anything."

Staring into the beady eyes of the worker, Leilani grew annoyed. She needed something to ease her confused feelings. Heroin was the only thing that she believed could help her in her time of need. She needed the hit and was willing to do anything to get it.

"And here I am thinking that you're a boss," she said.

"Excuse me?"

"Nothing, I just thought you were a real nigga that followed his own rules."

"Listen shawty, the mind games won't—"

"Nah, I understand if you're scared of Rocky."

"What?"

"Yea, I mean what, he's only like 5'10 and you're like 6'3, so I see why you're intimidated by him. I hear shorter people can be quite violent," she said. Her words turned a wheel in the worker's head that he never thought was possible. She worked on his pride, knowing that as a man he had an image to maintain. She continued talking until she got what she wanted.

"Listen to me and listen good, I ain't scared of no other man besides God. So, here's your hit," he replied as he smashed the baggie into her hand. "Get lost."

"I definitely will."

She walked away from the house, making her way to an abandoned building that wasn't too far. The rain from the night before seeped through her shoes, soaking her feet. Mushy sounds escaped into the night air as she took a shortcut to her destination. Leilani entered the abandoned building from the back. The pitch darkness in the building swallowed her small frame. She was standing in the belly of the beast. The moist air caressed her face, causing her to shiver. A dull pain entered her back, paralyzing her for a few seconds. **Shit, the pain is coming back,** *she thought as she doubled over in pain.*

She walked deeper into the abandoned laundromat with the pain in her back intensifying. Vomit lingered at the back of her throat as she doubled over to release it. Nothing escaped; her body was beginning to play tricks on her. **All I need is this hit.** *It was a mind game that her body was playing on her. She didn't need the drugs to make the body pains to go away. It was all in her head. She sat down in a corner and began to prep for her first high in months. The smell of mold watered her taste buds as her eyes adjusted to the dark. Leilani opened her hand revealing her aluminum-foiled joy. She reached into her sweater pocket pulling out her Ziploc baggie containing all her tools.* **Thank God I didn't get rid of this.** *Without thinking, she wrapped the rubber rope around her arm in search for a vein. Preparing her work was a simple routine that she could do in her sleep. Once she had her liquid heated and in the needle, she took no time to inject it into her regenerating vein. She pushed down on the syringe, allowing her liquid joy to enter her bloodstream. Slowly, the feeling of emptiness escaped her pores as she ejected herself from the world of sin.*

Her mind entered a world where love wasn't being raped by your stepfather. In her drug-induced mind, love wasn't being punched in the *face because your mother couldn't stop her man from sleeping with you. Love in her drug world was anything she wanted it to be. Tonight, love would be great and destined. The love she wanted to endure would change her life forever. Her fear of living disappeared into the back of her mind as her body felt good. Every limb in her body went numb as her heart rate slowed down dramatically. She no longer felt the pain from her wounds nor her baby swimming in her uterus. What she felt was a high that lifted her into the sky where God kissed her scars away. He shredded all her pain, taking away the dark cloud over her head.*

"Lord, please make life better for me," she softly spoke as she stared into the only light coming from the small window.

Leilani's drug filled world came to a halt as the drugs couldn't uphold the next exchange of events. A shocking jolt of pain rushed through her uterus, paralyzing her. The pain wasn't like anything she had ever had in her life. Gripping her stomach, sweat formed at the base of her eyebrow. A warm gush of water released from within her as she felt pressure from her uterus. **Not here, not now; the baby isn't supposed to be here now. I'm not ready.** *Pulling down her sweat pants, she placed her hand on the opening of her vagina. She didn't feel anything, but she could feel the pressure increasing as the baby wanted to leave her womb. What the fuck am I supposed to do? she thought. Feeling the urge to push, she followed the pains of her body and pushed. Gripping her thighs, she pushed through the pain embedding her nails into her skin. Leilani's blood-curling cry replaced the moist air. She was alone and scared. She wept loudly as she attempted to bring life into the world. Her cries were filled with pure pain, reliving her years of abuse.*

"Get out of me," she screamed with tears pouring from her eyes.

She pushed one last time before she felt the huge load finally slide right out of her. Her painful cries were now replaced with the sound of life filling the abandoned building. Leilani stared down at her mini-me, amazed at what she created. The baby in her arms was her own child that she had birthed. She moved him into the moonlight that came from the window. She wanted to see all her baby's features. Instantly, she fell in love with him as he stared back up at her with such love. Finally, she could feel a love that wasn't filtered.

"I know you had a tough time in there but Mommy promises that she will never allow anything bad to happen to you," Leilani spoke softly, meaning every word she spoke.

Leilani grabbed some sheets that were lying around, wrapping her baby up to keep him warm. She then grabbed another sheet to wrap them together. As she lay there with her baby in her hands, she felt a slight wave of dizziness. She gripped her baby tightly as she fell into a deep sleep.

******

Juelz stood up to embrace his mother. He wrapped his teenage arms around her waist, inhaling her scent. This affectionate moment that they shared had been conceived throughout the years of absence. Surrounding her son with her unconditional love was finally coming true after investing many restless nights with the illusion of the moment before her.

"I am happy you came back."

"Me too," Leilani whispered into his ear as she placed light kisses all over his face. Despite Juelz being a teenager entering the gates of manhood, his heart turned into mush being nestled in his mother's bosom. "Now go get ready for school; you're going to be late," she said, releasing him from her embrace.

"Ugh, school," he complained, exhaling a huge sigh.

"I know it's shit, but the key to a successful life is knowledge," she spoke as she gave him a little push towards Emery's room that he was occupying. "Let that be one of the many lessons I teach you. If you wanna live comfortably, you need some form of education. Knowledge is key."

"I hear you Mama."

"You better with them big ole ears your father gave you," she said under her breath. The joke left her heart uneasy. Her mind had never thought of Rocky in that light before. He was always her mother's fiancé who brought a shit storm of misery into her life. Never had it dawned on her that he was the father of her child. Half of him created the biggest blessing in her life. That logic made her uncomfortable as it invaded her mind. *My greatest creation has the blood of my enemy running through it*, she thought, *ain't that some serious shit.*

Grabbing her car keys and cell phone, Leilani walked over to the front door waiting for her son. Today was going to be such a busy day as she had so many things to get done. Thanksgiving was right around the corner and the decision on how she planned on spending the holiday had not been made. Since she was no longer alone with Juelz in her custody, she had to participate in the family oriented holiday. He was still young, clueless about the true meaning behind some of the holidays he celebrated. Despite her beliefs, she would never force them onto her son, she'd rather him decide on what he wanted to put his faith into.

"Ok, I'm ready."

"Let's go baby," she said, as she led them onto their journey. Together, the two walked until they reached Leilani's 2014 Range Rover.

"Mom, what could I get as my first car?" Juelz asked randomly.

"Depends on how good your grades are."

"I already got that in the bag momma."

"Ok smarty pants, if you continue to get A's I promise once you get your license I will buy whatever car you want."

"You promise?"

" Yes I promise."

"Pinky?" he asked with his pinky sticking out. Leilani stared at him, wanting to crack a smile due to the seriousness in his face.

"I promise," she replied as she looped her pinky around his. "Now what car do you want anyways?"

"I was hoping for a Bugatti, but I know you don't got that type of money," he chuckled. "So, I will settle for a Nissan GTR."

"Boy, how you know I ain't got it?" she questioned.

"Because I know you're not that rich."

"Excuse me?"

"No offense Ma, but you ain't got it."

"Boy."

"Ok then Mom, what do you do for a living then?" he quizzed.

The question was so simple yet complicated. She stared into his eyes, confused as to what she should tell him. *Should I tell him the truth or lie? What the fuck do I tell him? Oh, son I knock the light bulb out of people's heads, I am the Grim Reaper of the streets. Oh honey, I put the bad people to sleep.* Her mind ran a bunch of responses that seemed appropriate enough for his age. Everything that she thought was PG-13, seemed to cover up the truth, and that's not what she wanted to do. She didn't want to lie to her son about anything in her life. The truth was necessary, but her truth was far from normal. Her whole life was rather far from normal. Just as she was going to reply, her phone began to vibrate, interrupting their conversation. *Thank you, God.*

"Hello?" she answered.

"La, its Carter."

"Oh hey."

"Hi, I was just wondering if you're busy now?"

"Well right about now I am driving my son to school; what's up?"

"You have a kid?"

"Yes, but that is not what you called for Carter, so what's up?"

"Oh sorry, I was calling to ask you if you could stop by Chaos and Ricky Bobby's studio session."

"Sure, is everything ok?"

"Yea, sorta kinda. I am just concerned that those two are wasting time and money in the studio."

"Why would you think that?"

"Well, for the simple fact that my producers are complaining about their professionalism."

"Don't worry about it Carter. I'll go over there to handle it."

"Thank you La, and please stress the importance of them working."

"I assure you I will handle it."

"Thank you."

"No problem," she replied before hanging up the phone. She didn't understand what the hell was going on, but she was going to deal with those two and straighten their asses out. Driving quietly, she focused all her attention onto the road as her mind battled a tough game of reasoning. She knew Juelz was waiting for an answer, but at the moment, formulating a response that was enough for them both couldn't happen. *I done shot people, took their lives away from them without a second thought about it, and here I am now in front of my son stuck on a simple reply.* Turning onto the block of his school, she pulled up in front of the rusted gates of the charter school he attended. *I wonder if this is where my money has gone over the years,* she questioned.

"What I do for a living is provide for you, I work my ass off in a dangerous lifestyle just to make sure that your adopted mother had enough money to produce the life that I could not give you. That is my occupation Juelz. I am a provider," she said grabbing ahold of his head, placing a kiss on his forehead.

"Ok Mom," he replied, confused as to how he should react to her confession. Instead of dwelling on the topic at hand, he placed a light kiss on his mother's cheek before he exited the car. Leilani sat back in the car observing Juelz making his way into the school building. *This is my only living child that is walking into a place to build his intelligence. I fucking missed all the other years of this shit.* She could feel her tears threatening to descend her golden cheek; lately, that is all she seemed to be doing, breaking down emotionally in public. It was like the torture of giving up her son remained on replay in her head; the feeling of uncertainty and the doubt of his safety was all too familiar to her. *Ugh God, why give us fucking emotions,* she complained. Lightly, she placed her foot on the gas pedal, pulling off into the morning rush.

"Don't worry, La, he is going to be fine." Her words were used to comfort her ill feelings; well that's what it was intended for. Silently, she drove to her next destination with her mind corrupted with scenarios of harm brought upon her son. When she had finally pulled the car up in front of the record label building, she had conjured up several scenarios where Juelz safety was put at risk. Sitting in the car wasn't an option, as she knew this would result in her mind building more horrific sketches of death. She was preparing to leave the car when she was side tracked by Luis the janitor.

"Hello Ms. Vasquez, how are we doing today?" Luis asked as he stood by the driver side of car.

"I am fine today Luis, what about you?"

"I've been trying to maintain, ya know, keep my head above the water."

"Just like everyone else," Leilani replied as she proceeded to exit from her car. Together, the two walked into the building making light conversation. Once Leilani reached her destination she said goodbye to Luis. He was such a nice guy, always smiling no matter what was going on his personal life. He was fighting a custody battle with his ex-wife for his five-year-old daughter and things were beginning to get ugly between the two. Being a very private man, he never disclosed this type of information to anyone until the lies he used to cover up his lateness no longer made sense. Leilani pulled the truth out of him, concerned about the well-being of her employee. Ever since then, Leilani wasn't so hard on Luis after learning about the problems in his life. He was able to clock in later and still be paid his full pay with no questions asked.

"Have a good day boss lady."

"You too, Luis. I will see you later," she replied. Turning her focus back to her reason for being there, she walked over to the door for studio one. The smell of marijuana seeped through the slit of the door, raising her suspicions. Placing her weight on the door, she pushed it open, absorbing the chaotic atmosphere. Laughter filled the drug-induced room as dozens of females roamed the studio, intoxicated on the finest hood drugs. Leilani could feel the anger within her boil over the deeper she walked into the studio. Music vibrated against her, replacing her heart rhythm. Looking around, she became disgusted at what was around her; there wasn't any form of decency as the girls performed sexual acts in pursuit of making it big in the world.

"I don't know what the fuck is going on, but this shit ends right fucking now," Leilani said as she walked over to the engineering sound board. Annoyed and agitated, she pulled out every chord in sight until the music that thumped through the studio ultimately stopped. All eyes were on her, as people wondered what the hell was going on.

"Yo, who cut off the fucking music—" Ricky Bobby strolled out from one of the backrooms annoyed at the chain of events. "Oh hey La," he said once he came eye to eye with her.

"Hey yourself, what the fuck is going on in here?" she questioned.

"What you mean what's going on in here?"

"I mean why you got all these hood bitches in here on the company's time, wasting fucking money?" The words flowed out of her mouth insulting the females that sat half-naked in the studio.

"Who this bitch thinks she fucking talking to?" one of the females asked. Leilani never turned to face her as she tried to keep her conversation focused on Ricky, knowing how bad her temper could be. "Pussy ass bitches come in here trying to shut shit down," the girl continued.

"Said the girl in the studio half-naked with a mouth full of cum juice," Leilani replied.

"Bitch," the girl's voice exclaimed with so much animosity. Noticing the disdain in her voice, Leilani turned around to face the person who was trying to test her. *Come on La, you ain't that well-known; these bitches don't know any better*, Leilani reasoned.

"Listen honey, I ain't gonna be too many bitches," Leilani said wagging her finger in the girl's face. Analyzing the physical features of the not so bright young girl, Leilani had to admit she was a very pretty girl; there was no doubt about it. The girl resembled a younger version of Regina Hall with her skin darkened into milk chocolate. Her eyes were big and bold as if they wished to make a statement. But all her cuteness went out of the window as she opened her mouth to insult Leilani.

"What the fuck you gonna do about it, bitch?"

Never the one to be told twice, Leilani drew her fist back then brought it against the girl's face. The sound of Leilani's fist connecting against the girl's cheekbone echoed throughout the silenced air.

"Don't let the name brand fool you honey; I am from the hood. I ain't all bark," Leilani said as she placed her attention back onto Ricky Bobby. "Playback the track."

The beat filled the air sending a sensational vibe that made the body unconsciously bob. *What the fuck is this nigga talking about the engineer beat is whack? This shit is too good,* she thought. Ricky Bobby's voice infiltrated the beat as his raspy voice blended well with the instrumental. Despite the chemistry, his rhyming was horrible. His lyrics had no punch line, he held no swagger, and his wordplay made absolutely no sense.

"Turn it off," Leilani demanded. Her face remained emotionless as Ricky Bobby tried guessing her feelings towards his track. He knew his wordplay was the best, only because the drugs he was on said so. *The song would have been better had the engineer done his job and made a bomb ass beat to play back in them streets*, Ricky reasoned.

"The engineer isn't whack. It is you sir; you are the whack one."

"Excuse me?"

"Nigga you heard me the first time; you sound high and off. Your punchlines are shit, your verse is shit, and your flow is shit. I am surprised Envy ain't take your fucking mic."

"Nah shawty, you are bugging."

"Nah, I'mma tell you who's bugging, and it's your dumb ass," Leilani said as she pointed her finger in his face.

"Get your finger out of my face."

"Or else what?" she interrupted with sarcasm gracing her voice. "What the fuck you think you gonna do? You think cuz you have two tear drops underneath your beady brown eyes that I am supposed to be afraid of your trigger pulling ass?"

"Jus—"

"Just shit, I am not the fucking one Ricky. If you think me punching homegirl was crazy, then you ain't seen shit yet. Now I'mma warn you fucking once because this is your first time working with me. If you don't get your shit to-fucking-gether and produce a fire ass radio playing track, I swear on my son's life I will bury your ass alive along with all my other demons. Do I make myself fucking clear or do I have to give you a fucking sample of my fist first for you to understand?" she questioned. Her voice never raised with anger but it poured with violence. She prayed that Ricky took heed to her warning because she really didn't want to kill him. He was a great rapper who had a future within the rap industry; all he had to do was remain focused. She got him out of the hood, but now he had to depend on himself to remain out of the hood. "You are an amazing rapper and I am not afraid to admit it. I will give you credit on it, but one thing is for sure, you keep up this rinky dink persona and I guarantee you, you will never see the real cash flow. Right now, you're out of the hood but you ain't make it big yet. Be that same grinding nigga I watched on YouTube flow about the streets of New York, not that 'can't rhyme for the life of him' nigga I just heard on that track that you played me."

"I hear you."

"Don't hear me, do that shit."

"Aight I got you."

"Good, now clear out this fucking studio. Get homegirl some medical attention because I might have broken her nose, and get behind the microphone and produce me a hit for the streets," Leilani responded as she walked over the girl who sat on the floor nursing her bleeding nose. "Where's Chaos?"

"He left for some privacy; he should be in the next studio over," Ricky replied.

She walked out of the studio completely drained from the events that occurred. Going into Chaos's studio, she entered the room consuming the music that was being produced. The hypnotic sound of his husky voice against the velvety hip-hop beat caused her to nod her head. He sounded so at peace behind the microphone as he scolded the industry girls for being too fast for him. Sitting down on the table, Leilani observed Chaos rap with his eyes closed. He was venting to the mic, impressing Leilani with his choice of words.

"*Said I ain't never need no trick bitch," he* rapped ending the song with the hook. He opened his eyes, surprised to see his boss observing him.

"You sound great," Leilani said.

"Thank you. How long were you sitting there?"

"Well I came when you began your second verse," she replied. "It sounds good. You leaving the other studio did work out, right."

"Hell yeah, I couldn't concentrate while they were making all that fucking noise."

"I know. Well I handled the situation so I don't expect Ricky to have any guests any time soon. One thing I need for you to do is make sure his ass remains focused on the goal."

"Which is?"

"Grind. There isn't any time for playing around."

"Gotcha boss."

"Good."

Leilani turned around, leaving Chaos alone to focus on his rap music. *Next thing to do is visit Miss Elena*, she thought as she exited the building. Getting into her car, she started her engine and pulled off into New York traffic. Leilani was clueless on what to expect from the meeting with Juelz's adopted mother. Not sure on what vibes Elena may be on, Leilani had to prepare herself for the possibility of dealing with a bitch. *She shouldn't be on anything crazy since Don put her up in a banging ass penthouse,* Leilani reasoned. After the incident with the Mexican cartel, Don felt horrible that a civilian was involved with their drug war. He decided on placing Elena in one of his penthouses with her own personal staff, along with the best medical team in America.

Pulling her car into a parking space, Leilani checked her rearview mirrors to confirm that her car was parked perfectly. *One time I need to waste time, is the time where I park perfect*, Leilani joked. Shutting her car off, she sat there behind the wheel contemplating her next choices.

"Do I really need to meet this woman?" she asked herself. "What if she's a bitch? What the fuck am I gonna do then? I won't be able to kill her; how the fuck am I gonna explain that to Juelz?" she rationalized out loud.

"I need to just get this shit over. If she gets crazy then I'll just have to trip her ass down a flight of stairs and break her hips," she reasoned. "She's old anyway."

Unbuckling her seatbelt, Leilani opened the car door proceeding to exit. Staring up at the 60-story tower that cut through the Manhattan skyline, Leilani was taken aback by the beautiful image. *Don really does have good taste,* she thought as she proceeded into the luxurious building. Maneuvering through the building, Leilani didn't have any trouble. Entering the elevator, she pressed the button labeled "PH." Fiddling with her fingers, she patiently waited for the metal doors to spring open revealing the immaculate million-dollar penthouse. *This nigga Don really knows how to spend his money well.*

"Welcome Ms. Vasquez," the butler greeted. "Can I be of assistance?"

"Hi Malcolm, I am here to see Elena."

"Certainly, she's in her room resting."

"Oh I can come back late—"

"No Ms. Vasquez, Ms. Elena is awake; you can see her now," Malcolm replied, turning around. Leilani felt as if he was almost telling her to go see the woman. A quick battle erupted within her head. *Should I leave or go see this woman?* Fuck it, she thought as she took Malcolm's lead through the extravagant home. The sun beamed through the floor-to-ceiling window panels illuminating the home. *This shit is too open,* Leilani thought as Malcolm stopped in front of a door. He knocked lightly, waiting for a response. Once he was granted access, Malcolm pushed the door open, leading Leilani into the room.

"Ms. Vasquez is here for you," Malcolm introduced.

The older woman looked up, focusing her eyes onto her unexpected guest. Taking the opportunity, Elena studied the young woman. Her long jet-black hair was neatly pulled back into a low ponytail, highlighting her beauty. *What a pretty girl,* Elena thought. Glaring into the eyes of her visitor, she recognized the bright glare; they were cold and metallic, resembling a glistening suit of armor. They resembled her ex's, whose eyes bore the same cold look. The longer she glared at her visitor the more she began to recognize her.

"You're Juelz's mother," Elena said.

"Yes I am," Leilani responded.

"Oh honey, come and give me a hug."

Elena opened her arms wide, anticipating the embrace of the mother of her adopted son. For the past 13 years, Elena anticipated this meeting. Granted, she never expected to meet the young mother in this predicament, but she was happy that she could finally meet her.

"I see where he gets his looks from," Elena said.

"You think he looks like me?"

"Of course."

Elena stared into the eyes of the woman who birthed the greatest thing to have ever entered her life besides her deceased daughter. Their conversation progressed as the two women discussed their son Juelz. Elena had her thoughts about Leilani before their meeting. Before, Elena criticized Leilani's decision to be hooked on drugs and be a mother at such a young age. She assumed that the young mother was just another woman who tried swindling the system for assistance. Sitting talking to Leilani, Elena watched as the woman's grey eyes melted every time she spoke about Juelz.

"He's your only child?" Elena asked.

"Yes, after I gave him up I focused on getting my life together," Leilani replied.

"You did a fine job."

Leilani stared at the woman; she thanked God that she decided to meet her. *Here I was being a little pussy,* she joked.

"Elena, I want to thank you for taking care of my son."

"It was a pleasure."

The two women continued their conversation, catching up on their lost times within each other's lives.

CHAPTER 23

Thanksgiving '12

The metal door sprang open, revealing the illuminated penthouse. Juelz's eyes lit up like the Fourth of July at the sight of the luxurious home. He didn't know anybody that lived in something so immaculate. Stepping foot off the elevator, Juelz's eyes diverted all over the home in search for his mother.

"Ma is up in this bomb place?" he questioned.

"Yea, she's staying up in this bomb ass place," Leilani corrected. Just like her last visit not too long ago, Malcolm greeted them with a smile on his face.

"Hello Malcolm," Leilani greeted.

"Ms. Vas—"

"No need for the Ms," she replied. "Just call me Leilani. This here is my son Juelz."

"Very nice to meet you," Malcolm replied, bowing before the guest. "You're here for Ms. Elena?"

"Yes."

“Right this way,” he said as he led the two through the penthouse and into the bedroom where Elena was. Before entering the room, Malcolm knocked lightly, waiting for permission to enter the privacy of Elena’s room.

“Come in,” Elena yelled through the thick door.

Opening the door, they entered the brightly lit master bedroom. Juelz couldn’t get over how beautiful the home was as he ran over to the floor-to-ceiling window panel that overlooked Brooklyn. Hues of pink and orange decorated the sky in preparation of the sun setting. Two suitcases rested on the bed as Elena stopped her packing to acknowledge her guest.

“Oh, honey,” she said, running with her arms open to embrace her son. “I’ve missed you so much.”

“I missed you too Ma. Where are you going?” Juelz asked while eyeing her luggage.

“Well Don has paid for me to go on a vacation, so I thought why the hell not. Spend the holidays on someone’s island.”

“Wait, Don did what?”

“Paid for my vacation. He called earlier to inform me that he basically paid for me to go away,” she said as she placed her attention back onto packing her suitcase. Leilani glared on, confused on Don’s generosity. *Why is he so friendly suddenly?* she asked herself. *He probably has a crush on her. I mean, she’s a very pretty woman.* Staring at the older woman, Leilani could see why he would be attracted to her. Elena stood 5’3, resembling the Hispanic actress Elizabeth Pena with her short haircut. *Hey, thugs need love too,* Leilani reasoned as she took a seat on the bed with Juelz following right behind her.

"So, Ma, where exactly are you going?" Juelz questioned.

"I am going out of town boy."

"Lady I am just asking; you know I like to keep tabs on you."

"Juelz, that is a grown woman," Leilani chuckled.

"That doesn't matter. I like to know what is going on with the women in my life."

"Oh, my gosh, I can already tell you're gonna be a lady's man," Elena replied, shaking her head. "Have them fast ass little girls running in and out of your momma's house."

"Not in my god damn house; maybe in yours Elena."

Leilani couldn't help herself from bursting into a fit of laughter. The sight of the woman who raised him and the woman who birthed him being happy, caused his lips to spread into a smile. Never in a million years had he thought that he would be able to spend special moments like this with them both. *I don't ever want this moment to end,* he thought.

******

"So, who are these people?" Juelz asked as he walked side by side with his mother. The holiday spirit oozed through his pores, as the concept of indulging in large amounts of food invaded his thoughts. *I need to have parts of that turkey and some macaroni. If they have lasagna, I might just get a plate of that too.*

"It's my boyfriend's family," Leilani answered. "I usually don't do this whole Thanksgiving crap, but because I have you now I want to follow tradition with you. This was the only open event I was invited to, so I decided why not come here instead of cooking at home in my smaller kitchen."

"Yea, since I will be staying with you more often, I think it's best that we get something bigger. I want to spend more time with you, but I don't want to fully leave Ma."

"Ok, so I'll start considering something bigger," Leilani said to hide the happiness in her voice.

"Yeah, don't pick anything like this," he replied, pointing his finger towards the massive mansion before them.

"Why not Juelz?"

"Because Momma, it looks gloomy." The grey stones that adorned the massive home gave it a depressed appearance, but Leilani knew better than to believe the exterior of the palace.

"Another key to success, never judge a book by its cover."

The mother and son duo walked through the circular driveway, weaving through the luxury cars that were parked. Leilani knew there would be a lot of people attending the dinner, but she wasn't expecting there to be this many people. Approaching the massive mansion door, Leilani pressed the illuminated button, notifying the people inside that there was another guest.

"I wonder how many people are in there?" Juelz questioned as he peeked through the stained-glass door. He couldn't see much, but he noticed a figure walking towards him. The door swung open with a tall dark man standing before the two. Juelz had never seen the man before but his face seemed familiar.

“I am glad you could make it baby,” Sincere said, exposing his shiny teeth. He wrapped his massive arms around Leilani, swallowing her small frame. It had been weeks since the two had seen each other. Sincere didn’t realize how much he missed his girl until he lay his eyes on her.

“I missed you too Sincere.” She placed a quick peck on his lips before breaking free from his grasp. “Sincere, I would like you to meet my son Juelz; Juelz this is Sincere,” she introduced.

“It’s nice to meet you man.” Sincere placed his hands into Juelz’s, shaking it firmly.

Juelz eyed the figure who was his mom’s boyfriend. He didn’t have a problem with his mom dating; she was a grown woman that could do whatever she pleased in her life. But for some reason, the facial features of her lover seemed familiar. It was as if he were staring into a mirror of his darker self. Instead of addressing his findings, he followed his mother into the mansion. The fancy architecture of the mansion amazed him; the exterior of the home could fool anyone as the interior was to die for. He had never been in a home like this one.

“This house is life bro.”

“You think so?” Sincere questioned.

“Yea, you got everything.”

“Yea I do. Don’t worry, when me and your mother move in together, you’ll be up in this bitch, probably with better stuff.”

Leilani didn’t bother replying as she didn’t care for the extravagant home. She was much simpler than this. The job that she did required strategic decision making. Being a person categorized as a minority today, it was unusual to see people of her color indulge in the lavish lifestyle. Purchasing an expensive item would bring unnecessary attention into her life. All she really cared for was a nice, decent place to call home.

"Princess, you've met Amiya before," he said as they came face to face with the mother of his child.

"Briefly."

"Nice to see you made it past the first round," Amiya stated, gripping her wine glass tightly.

"And it's nice to see you too." Leilani didn't bother to continue the back and forth between them as she walked past Amiya. She had no clue as to where she was heading, so she allowed Sincere to lead her into the kitchen. The fine smell of herbs and spices surrounded her as she walked into the cooking headquarters. The wise voice of the older generation filled the air of the kitchen.

"Mom," Sincere said interrupting the conversation.

"Boy, can't you see grown folks is having a damn conversation," an older woman retorted. "All them years I spent beating your butt and them manners still ain't settle into that thick ass skull of yours." Annoyed, Sincere's mother threw down her oven mittens, proceeding to wash her hands from the grease residue.

"I am sorry, but I want you to meet someone."

The older woman turned around, taking her attention off the task before her. Instantly, her eyes connected with Leilani, analyzing her features. Her dark onyx pupils had seen years of bullshit so she had become a pro at identifying a bullshitter. Keeping her poker face, she anticipated the introduction Sincere planned on making.

"And who is this?" she asked.

"Mom, this is my girlfriend Leilani Vasquez and her son Juelz. Princess, this is my mother Cassidy Anthony." Their eyes met as both women began to analyze one another. Cassidy stared into her eyes in search of any flaw that would harm her son. This was the only woman her son had introduced to her as his girlfriend; even the mother of his child was never formally introduced as the woman he was seeing. *This girl must be special if he brought her here to meet me,* Cassidy thought. A smile graced Cassidy's face as she held her arms out for an embrace. "It's nice to meet you."

Leilani walked into her embrace, wrapping her arms around Cassidy. The feeling of her warm body was different. Leilani had never encountered anything like this before; it was almost foreign. She was warm and inviting, securing her motherly arms around Leilani.

"And your son," Cassidy said while wrapping Juelz within her arms. "You are so handsome. Oh my gosh, how old are you my love?"

"I am thirteen."

"Believe me when I tell you Leilani, all the girls will be flocking to this young man. Be prepared to swat some away."

"Don't worry Mrs. Anthony, I sure will."

"Chile, don't call me by my married name. My husband died years ago; call me Mom or Cass."

Her warm smile was captivating; she reminded Leilani of Emmy Award winning actress Phylicia Rashad. She was truly beautiful with her skin bronzed without a hint of old age. Almost kicking 70 years of age, Cassidy was the epitome of black don't crack. Her youthful skin glowed a kind of wisdom that only a woman of her stature could obtain.

"I'm almost finished with dinner, so everything should be ready within thirty minutes."

"Ok Ma."

"Take your woman to socialize with our audience and I will keep my grandbaby with me in the kitchen."

Sincere stood, startled at his mother referencing Leilani's son as her own grandchild. He found it odd as his mother's persona was not the woman before him. *I'll address that shit later*, he told himself, taking a hold of Leilani's hand as they began their walk into the living room area where most of the guests were. Laughter echoed off the walls of the room as everyone tried enjoying their night. A game of dominos was being played, and the intensity of the game was only getting started.

"Wait, let me play real quick," Sincere said, dragging Leilani with him to the only open chair.

"Oh, nigga you tryna get your ass bussed?" Isaiah questioned as he handed Sincere his domino pieces.

"Nope, never that nigga." Placing Leilani on his lap, he positioned himself comfortably in the chair, preparing himself for his game. Together, the couple sat in their embrace, enjoying the comfort of one another. Being amongst family was something she wasn't used to, but the atmosphere was perfect. There wasn't any animosity, or any other ill feelings amongst them. It felt good being able to do this, even with the lifestyle they lived.

“Checkmate nigga,” Sincere yelled as he slammed a domino piece onto the marble table.

“Babe that is chess.”

“So?”

“You’re playing dominos.”

“Baby it’s the same shit,” he chuckled. Instead of debating the difference, Leilani focused her eyes on the room, observing the environment that was around her. A commotion was beginning to occur with two gentlemen that were far off. Their body language spoke of irritation as the men began going back and forth in an argument. Leilani recognized one of the guys as being one of their workers, but the next guy he was disagreeing with didn’t look familiar. *What the hell are these fools up to?* Jimmy, their worker, dipped his head onto the edge of the grand piano, inhaling the fairy dust.

“I know these muthafuckas ain’t getting high right in front of us, with our own product,” she said.

“What you said babe?” Sincere asked, only half paying attention to what was happening.

She didn’t respond as she placed all her focus onto the commotion that was transpiring before her. Their worker Jimmy and the other guy began to get physical, knocking each other to the ground. They began to bicker with one another, grabbing the attention of the guests that surrounded them.

“What the fuck are they arguing about?” Sincere asked with his eyes still focused on his domino pieces.

"I don't know, but they are starting to cause a scene."

She watched the scuffle unfold, paying close attention to their body language. Before she could blink her eyes, Jimmy pulled out his glock, pulling the trigger. A loud bang rang through the home, startling everyone. It was unexpected, giving most of the guests heart palpitations. Highly annoyed, Leilani stood up, proceeding over to where the commotion was, with Sincere following right behind her.

"Are you fucking stupid?" she asked, barely over a whisper. "There are dozens of people here and you decide to shoot someone with a whole bunch of fucking witnesses."

Her voice was calm, almost as soft as a feather, but that soft voice dripped with pure anger. It was embarrassing for her to watch her coked out employees make a fool of themselves, especially on such a family oriented holiday like Thanksgiving.

"I'm sorry boss, but Dean was trying to cheat me," Jimmy replied. His eyes were wild, laced with the finest dope in Brooklyn. His nose leaked with snot while his hair frizzed into a messy afro. His dark skin complexion was pale as he stood in Leilani's grasp, afraid of the repercussions of his actions.

"You better fucking hope this fool is alive or I fucking swear," she said.

"Don't worry about it Princess, take these two into the yard; we will deal with them shortly," Sincere ordered his workers.

These fucking people are insane, Leilani thought as she focused her attention back onto the onlooking people. Their eyes glared into hers, baffled at the chain of events that had just occurred. Some of the workers that had attended the dinner knew the life very well and weren't phased by the shooting, but there were others that stared into her eyes searching for answers.

"Don't worry people, the situation is going to be dealt with. Let's get back to partying," Sincere tried convincing. He wrapped his arm around Leilani, bringing her into a bear hug. Resting his lips at the opening of her ear, he began to whisper to her. "Princess, please do not do anything crazy."

"I can't promise you that Sincere."

"I know; let me handle it."

"No baby, I got this," she said, removing his arms from around her. She walked away, making her way to where they were placing Dean and Jimmy.

Sincere watched her walk away, confused on what to do. He didn't know if he should go after her or let her do what she did best. *If I try to interfere, Princess is going to fuck me up,* he reasoned. He walked away slowly, back over to the dominos table to resume his game.

"Where's wifey going?" Storm asked.

"To handle her business," Sincere answered nonchalantly.

"Does she always handle business alone?"

Confused on his line of questioning, Sincere stared into the eyes of his guest. He didn't understand why he was questioning Leilani, as everyone knew that the things done within their group were never to be questioned or repeated.

"Fuck you asking me all these questions for like you're a cop or something?"

"My fault bro, I was just curious."

"And curiosity will lead your dumb ass down the wrong road," he scolded. He resumed the game by slamming his domino piece onto the marbled table. The sound of the clay piece echoed throughout the home. The party went back to its original state, before the scuffle began.

"Boy!"

The sound of his mother's voice interrupted his concentration for the game. Sincere turned around to face the menacing glare of his mother.

"Yes Ma."

"Get yo' narrow behind over here," she demanded.

Quietly, he got up from the table and walked over to where his mother stood with a straight face.

"Yes Mama?"

"Is Leilani a part of the lifestyle?"

"What lifestyle?"

"Don't play dumb with me boy," his mother scolded. The look in her eye was tight, as if she already knew the truth, but needed him to confirm what was evident.

"Yes, Mama she is."

"That's all I wanted to know," she replied, dismissing his presence. Instead of questioning his mother, Sincere kept quiet, making his way to find his Princess.

Walking through the uplifting spirit of his guests, he made his way into the backyard where he knew his girlfriend would be. Silently, he maneuvered through the crowd until he reached his destination. The sound of light whimpers escaping into the cool air caught his attention.

"I am sorry, boss, I did—" *WHACK!* Jimmy's words were interrupted by the hand of his boss connecting to his face.

"I don't want to hear that ole' lame ole' fucking excuse about being fucking sorry," Leilani yelled. "There were civilians in that fucking dining room that could have gotten fucking hurt. You put those people's lives at risk just for your drug high," Leilani said. She continued her attack until Jimmy was on the ground, covered in blood.

"Princess, are you ok?" Sincere questioned.

"I am fine," she replied, while eyeing her swollen knuckles. "Such a great way to spend the holiday. Pour that shit on him," she stated. Jimmy's screams filled the air pleading for help. No one budged to save him from the torture that he was going to endure, as everyone knew how Leilani was. They were all afraid of how she would react. No one wanted to go against her orders. Like she demanded, her workers poured the gasoline onto one of their own.

"You see Jimmy, you were out of your fucking mind when you decided to start using our supplies for your drug habit. You fucked up big time when you decided to let your friend Dean into the circle," Leilani said calmly, as she pulled out the cigar that she had been holding on to for after the dinner. But now, she felt as if she needed it now. She placed the cigar on her lips as she placed the lighter at the tip. Lighting the cylinder of tobacco, she inhaled smoothly. "Not only did you let a fucking fresh face into the group without our approval, you let a fucking cop into our fucking family," she said, exhaling the tough smoke.

"What?" Sincere questioned.

"You heard me right baby; your worker Jimmy let a fucking undercover pig into our fucking circle. But it's ok, I will take care of it," she replied as she tossed the lighter on Jimmy's body, engulfing him into flames. Jimmy's body jumped up, dancing with the flames that were attached to the accelerant on his body. Everyone stared on, observing their fellow brother burn alive. The heat from his burning body threatened their safety. Scared, everyone moved out the way in efforts of avoiding getting burned.

"Show is over. Get y'all asses back into the house before my mother have a fit that y'all having barbecue instead of her cooking," Sincere demanded. He watched on as all their workers walked back into the house, leaving the body of their fellow comrade to burn. Once they were all gone, Sincere focused his attention onto his girlfriend, who was still puffing on a cigar. "Since when do you smoke cigars?" he asked.

"Five minutes ago," she replied while checking her watch.

"Ok Princess, since you're this big smoker, what are we going to do about this damn undercover cop?"

"It's already dealt with."

"What do you mean?"

"I dealt with the situation."

"What exactly did you do?"

"I got rid of the body," she replied as she smashed the cigar onto the brick that she sat on.

"What about the investigation that might have brought him onto us."

"I didn't find anything on him, but I'll be on the lookout for anything that interests the police."

Before he could reply to her, they were interrupted by the sound of the French doors opening. They both looked, anticipating the sight of the person who interrupted their conversation. Leilani immediately recognized the person before they could even speak.

"Mom, Momma Cass said for you and Sincere to bring your Apple, Sugar, Shake into the house," Juelz said snickering.

"What?" Leilani asked confused.

"She wants us to bring our asses into the house," Sincere chuckled. "Apple, Sugar, Shake stands for ass. Just like sugar honey ice tea stands for shit."

Finally catching onto the phrase, Leilani let out a light chuckle, finding the phrase to be hilarious.

"Now I know where you get your humor from."

"From?"

"Your mother; she sure is a clown."

Together, the couple walked into the house, hands wrapped around each other. The burning body of their now deceased worker had gone out, intriguing Juelz as to what had occurred. There was a burning body in Sincere's backyard, and Juelz wanted to know why. *Did he really set that body on fire?* he questioned. Rather than bombard his head with more questions, he walked into the house with his arm around his mother's shoulder.

"You're so damn tall," Leilani said.

"I know Momma, but I am only 5'8."

"Yea, well I'm 5'5," she chuckled as she hugged her only child.

"I am glad you guys finally decided to join us," Momma Cassidy said while eyeing the trio.

"Oh, don't worry Ma, I wouldn't miss this special dinner for anything."

"Yea, yea, yea; find a spot boy."

The trio joined the circle that was formed around the food. They all linked their hands together, bowing their heads. Momma Cass began the prayer thanking God for all that they were blessed with. Being the rebel, Leilani opted with keeping her eyes open, observing everyone silently, listening to the prayer recited by Sincere's mother. She analyzed their facial features as everyone took in the words of the prayer. It was as if Momma Cass was speaking the truth about what was going on within each individual's life.

"As your children, Lord we don't thank you enough for all you have given us. There were times where we questioned your decisions; forgive us Lord. We don't appreciate you enough and tonight we are surrendering as your children, thanking you for all that you have done for us," Momma Cass said. She finished the prayer, ending it in Amen, along with all the others reciting Amen. "Now you all can dig in," she responded as she handed the plates out to the anxious people.

Instead of taking out her food, Leilani sat back to watch everyone enjoy themselves. This was the first time in her life where she was surrounded by so many people that considered her to be family. She had seen her fair share of chaos, and tonight she was finally happy to be at ease. She had finally belonged to something, having some sort of value within the family. Her eyes met the glare of Isaiah and Essence as they were concerned for her.

"La, are you ok?" Essence questioned.

She stared into the eyes of her best friend, thankful for all the years that they had spent together. There had been some ups and downs within their relationship, but Leilani was just thankful that Essence had never switched up on her like dozens of other people had. It felt good having people that were dependable, as she had been through so much before. Her eyes glared back into the darkened pits of her adopted brother Isaiah. She thanked God every chance she had for placing Isaiah into her life. Her success was partly because of him. If he hadn't taken a chance on the young girl strung out on heroin, Leilani would not currently be in the lavish dining room today surrounded by people who cared for her. Tonight, she was grateful for everything God had placed in her life. These people held a place in her heart, which now made her touchable.

"Yes Essie, I am fine."

I now have everything to lose, she thought.

CHAPTER 24

5 years later

September 23, 2016

Papers lay scattered all over the mahogany table as Leilani sat searching for one paper. *Ugh, where the hell is this fucking receipt paper?* she questioned. She began lifting a countless amount of papers only to reveal more papers underneath. The pressure was on as she was becoming more and more agitated. A knock on the door interrupted her search.

"Come in," she yelled.

"La, everything is set up for the Music Ball," John said.

"Yes, everything is indeed set up except for one damn mistake; they delivered the wrong chandelier. I specifically asked for the crystal chandelier, not the punch bowl they delivered," she complained. "I need a fucking assistant because this is too much damn work."

"La, don't worry your pretty little head about the damn chandelier. I already have someone on it, and the company will be delivering the chandelier that you originally ordered."

"Thank God."

"Yes, you can thank God, but it's already four in the afternoon, and you are nowhere near ready for the ball, so go get dressed."

"I will."

"No La, I mean as in right now. You worked so hard to get here, and we were finally able to get the company off the ground," John boosted.

Within the course of five years, Carter's Dynasty had been resurrected from the dead. The label was on its last leg, but with the divided ownership and hot rappers, Leilani and John were able to place the record label within the top reigns of the music industry. Everyone wanted to be signed under their label or even be associated with it.

Tonight, was the Music Ball, a special event for the music industry to get together to witness the premiere of Carter's Dynasty's new artist and new music. It was going to be a star-studded event, but Leilani was nervous as hell. This was going to be her first time revealing her face as the co-owner of the record label. For the past five years, she had remained behind the limelight making executive decisions, while John would go into the public eye. She opted to stay home, but between Sincere and Juelz, there was no way in hell they were going to allow her to miss the most important event for her record label.

"So, what I'mma need you to do, is get your ass up, go home, and get ready for the ball," John said, as he began to lift her up off the chair. "I already sent the glam team to your home so they are waiting for you," he said.

"Ok, fine. I'll see you later at the ball."

"Yes, now go," he shooed.

She grabbed her items and made her way out of her office without a rebuttal. Her body was aching for her comfortable bed, but she wasn't even allowed into her bedroom, as Sincere knew that she would lock herself in there and sleep the night away. Walking towards her 2016 CLS 550 Mercedes, the sound of her phone ringing caught her attention. She dug inside her oversized purse until she pulled out her iPhone 6. The image of her son's aging face was plastered on the screen, causing her to smile.

"Yea babe," she answered.

"Ma, what time are you coming home?" her 17-year-old son questioned.

"I should be there soon, why?"

"Well, there are a bunch of people here for you waiting."

"Who is it?"

"I don't know."

"Boy, you let some unknown people into my goddamn house?"

"I am just joking; it's the glam squad."

"Ok, I am on my way now."

"Alright," he said hanging up.

Leilani placed the phone back into her purse, releasing a gush of warm air from her mouth. *I don't know what the hell I'mma do with that boy,* she thought. Time waited for no one as her little boy was becoming a man. In less than two months, Juelz was going to be turning 18 years old. It felt like just yesterday she had given birth to him in an abandoned building, high off heroin. Now her son was practically a man. *Time waits for no one.* Despite not being in her son's life for the first thirteen years, she had spent the last five years making sure her son was on the right path. Everything she had ever done was to ensure the safety of her son. She bought the record label because of him, and spent millions of dollars on stocks just to make sure that her son would never need for nothing. She became the biggest hit woman in all of America just to ensure that her son would always be financially ok. The love she had for Juelz grew more and more every day.

Getting into her car, she didn't waste any time pulling off into traffic. The office wasn't too far from the penthouse she now resided in. New York traffic was light as she pulled her car into her designated parking spot. She shut off the car before she got out, entering the brisk September air. Her eyes caught the wave of her neighbors who lived underneath her. The chirpy white people waved at her, happy to see her once again.

"Hi Ms. Vasquez."

"Hey Tim and Donna," she responded as she closed her car door.

"Hey, did Juelz tell you about our dinner get together we were having tonight?"

"Oh, he did. I forgot to tell you guys that I won't be able to make it; tonight is a big ball for the company."

"Oh ok, maybe next time."

"Yes, definitely next time. I'll see you around," Leilani said as she left the couple. Despite being so nice and naïve, Leilani felt like something was off with the two. They gave her a weird vibe that she could not shake off. *I need to do another background check on these people,* she thought to herself. Before moving into the building, Leilani had one of her workers conduct a background check on every person that resided in the building. Everyone came back cleared, but Leilani didn't trust it, as there were too many weird ass people in the world for her. Pushing everything to the back of her mind, she mentally prepared herself to be bombarded with people; she knew that John sent over the whole damn squad.

"Please Lord give me the strength to deal with these damn people," she said.

******

"Welcome ladies and gentlemen, to the first annual Dynasty Ball. I am your host Timothy Delafuego. Tonight's ball will be jam packed with musical performances from the artists of Carter's Dynasty, including a performance by Dynasty's top artists, Ricky Bobby and Chaos."

Leilani eyed the Philippine young man, praying that he wouldn't mess up his lines. She was against him hosting the show tonight as he didn't have any experience with hosting, but John insisted on giving him the spotlight. It was such a huge night with the ball containing A-list celebrities. Everyone was being watched under a microscope as the event was being streamed live on their music app Mozart. Millions of people were tuning into their ball observing what was going on.

"Ladies and gentlemen our first performer for the night is Carter's Dynasty's newest signed R&B artist Harmony. Round of applause for Harmony," Timothy announced as he walked off the stage. The pastel lights dimmed low as the artist walked onto the stage. She was gorgeous, catching the attention of many of the guests.

"Mom, how old is she?" Juelz asked while eyeing the beauty.

"19."

"You think she would want to get with a young fella like myself?" Juelz questioned seriously.

Leilani turned to eye her handsome son. The all-black Versace tuxedo fit his muscular frame perfectly. Over the years, Juelz had grown into his facial features, as he closely resembled P. Diddy's adopted son Quincy Combs. Feeling like he was coming of age, Juelz had decided to cut down his curly mane, taming it into a fade. Hands down, her son was a very handsome kid, and she knew soon there would be an issue with some little girl running in and out of her house.

"Boy, don't let me abuse you live on the music app," Leilani joked.

"Baby leave him alone; he's just becoming a man," Sincere chimed in, trying to save Juelz. Leilani placed her attention on him, almost ready to elbow him in his gut as he wrapped his arm around her shoulder, pulling her into his bear hug. The smell of his cologne was strong yet enticing. Between the smell of his cologne and his masculine grip, Leilani could feel herself becoming very wet. Since Sincere decided to keep a Caesar cut and grow out his beard, she had been finding him extra attractive lately.

"Would y'all get a damn room," Essence interjected.

"Oh, bitch shut up, acting like your ass ain't gonna get loved up as soon as we leave this damn ball," Leilani responded as she pointed her finger towards her and her date, Isaiah. The relationship between

Isaiah and Essence had progressed into a more serious committed relationship. Leilani was genuinely happy for the most important people in her life as they had finally found love.

"You damn right her ass gonna get loved up right after this damn ball," Isaiah responded while placing a light kiss on Essence's forehead.

The group chatted amongst themselves, enjoying the topic of the conversation. Over the years, their friendship had grown stronger than before as their loyalty remained the same. Everything was going well like Leilani had expected, until John walked over to her asking her to announce the next performer.

"I need you to announce Ricky Bobby and Chaos for their performance."

"What happened to the presenter you had scheduled?"

"The person won't make it out on time. You and Sincere could announce them."

"Hey, I don't mind doing it," Sincere said as he stood up, pulling on Leilani's hand. Leilani wanted to back down on the offer, but Sincere refused to let her go. "Princess come on, let's do it."

He held his grip around her hand while he followed John to the back of the stage. The music from the performance was loud and overbearing as John leaned forward giving the two their directions.

"Listen, it's pretty easy; just follow what is on the prompter."

"Ok, it better be."

The melodic tune of Harmony's music died down as the artist exited off the stage. The couple waited before they were cued to go on stage. Bright lights blinded them as they walked to the center of the stage. All eyes were on the young couple with people intrigued on their identity.

"Good night my fellow music listeners, my name is Leilani Vasquez; I am part owner of Carter's Dynasty. I hope everyone is enjoying tonight's ball as this is our first major event. Over the past couple of hours, you guys watched some of our new talent perform their debut singles. But right now, it is time for Carter's Dynasty's top artists Ricky Bobby and Chaos to perform," Leilani read.

"Tonight's performers have decided to debut a new song that describes the trap love that is so hard to find. When I first heard this song, I asked both Ricky and Chaos why they had decided to write such a lovey dovey song when they were strictly hip-hop. Do you want to know what they told me?" Sincere questioned. Leilani stared at Sincere, confused as to what he was doing. The teleprompter had been shut down by now but Sincere was still talking.

"They told me they were inspired by a couple with true love. They had been watching me and my lovely girlfriend interact with each other, and they knew that what we had for each other was real love. It wasn't something that had been formulated for the greed of money or the fast lifestyle. But instead, our love was built off mutual feelings. That is why Ms. Leilani Vasquez..." Sincere's words began to trail slowly as he took his hands out of his pocket, getting down to one knee. He held out the engagement box as he continued to speak. "I am asking you for your hand in marriage. We've been together five years strong, and I think it's time that I make you my wife. I've been through some dark roads, but you have always been the light at the end of the tunnel. I am willing to sacrifice my single life, just to spend the rest of my life waking up next to you. Now before my knee gives out on me, Ms. Vasquez, would you do me the honors and marry a brother?"

"Oh, my god, YES!" Leilani squealed with joy.

It was at this moment life for Leilani was complete. She'd seen everything there was to see in life. From the gutter, she built her way up to being one of the richest women in the world. Oprah Winfrey's bank account couldn't match her black-market money. Joy filled her body as she was lifted into the air by her fiancé. From the audience, to the excitement of being engaged, Leilani was in a daze.

"Are you serious about being engaged to me?" she questioned.

"Of course, Princess. What I should be asking is, are you ready to finally be tied down to me?"

"I can't wait."

******

His lips pressed against hers with such passion it caused her to shiver. The feeling of his hands roaming around her body sent a signal that it was time for Daddy to come home. Leilani had never felt this feeling before, despite her having been committed in previous relationships; this one before her was completely different. The love that they shared was so pure that it would be hard to imitate.

"Hold on, let me take out my keys," Leilani said as she tried pushing Sincere off her. Their night had quickly transitioned into the wee hours of the morning. After the ball had ended, Leilani had stayed back to help with the aftermath of the event. Knowing that she would be a while, Leilani had ushered Sincere and Juelz to go home; but being the devoted fiancé he was, Sincere had also stayed back just to ensure the safety of his Princess. Juelz had opted in going home as he was exhausted from all the hard work he had done earlier.

"Princess, you know damn well I won't be able to keep my hands off you," Sincere replied as he wrapped his arms around Leilani's frame.

"Boy, if you don—" She opened the door to her penthouse, engulfing herself into the chaos before them. Her breath remained stuck in her throat as she eyed her now trashed home. Glass lay splattered everywhere. Her furniture was destroyed as thick deep slashes were forever embedded into the expensive leather. The 75-inch flat screen television that once hung on the walls had been punched in, with the remaining shell of the TV resting on the floor. The sight of her now damaged home sent a shock of anger throughout her body. Then a light bulb clicked in her head. *Where's Juelz?* Leilani thought.

"Princess what th—"

"Juelz!" Leilani screamed, interrupting Sincere's sentence. The thought of her trashed apartment no longer bothered her as she ran through her home searching for her son. She entered her son's bedroom shocked to see what lay before her. The room resembled the aftermath of a hurricane as everything lay scattered on the ground. Blood decorated the once neat room, sending Leilani into a panic. "Sincere he's not here," Leilani yelled.

"I checked the rest of the house; I didn't find him either," Sincere replied. "I am going to call his phone."

"I'm going to check the security cameras," Leilani said as she ran out of the room straight to her office where the security system was. Quickly, she tapped the keys to the keyboard granting her access into her system. She pulled up the cameras, wasting no time searching for any evidence. After a couple of minutes of skimming through the videos, she found what she was looking for. Five assailants decorated her screen as she watched them break into her home, completely trashing it. She witnessed one person going into Juelz room and a couple of minutes later carrying out an unconscious Juelz. Confusion settled into her brain; sorting her emotions became harder to do as her reality began to set in.

"Did you find anything Princess?"

"Yes, call a meeting with everyone," she said.

Sincere stared at his fiancé, searching for her emotions. The fire he was accustomed to seeing no longer existed; her eyes held fear for the first time.

"Princess mayb—"

"Sincere call the meeting. I want everyone there."

2 hours later

Her eyes glared into the different pairs of eyes; she tried analyzing their glares. She wanted one of her workers to be the kidnapper as the nightmare would finally be over for her. Unfortunately, all her loyal workers stared back prepared to go to war for her missing offspring.

"I know that some of you are wondering why I called this emergency meeting. Well this morning when I came home, I walked into hell. My son Juelz had been beaten and kidnapped," her words trailed with the sight of her vandalized home torturing her mind. She met the glare of the dozens of eyes, sensing the love and admiration the people had for her. That wasn't what she craved. She didn't want the love from dozens of people, all she wanted was for her son to return home safe and sound. "I want my son back home. That's it you guys; do whatever you need to do to ensure that my son is home," she said.

Quietly, she walked away from her onlookers as she headed over to the section of the warehouse that she had designated as the computer room. Dozens of screens stood in front of her, each containing a different angle of her home during the time of the kidnapping. The IT guys she had hired kept analyzing the same footage, searching for anything out of the ordinary.

"Nothing new?" she questioned.

"Nope, nothing at all."

Viewing the video once more, she searched for anything irregular. *I am going to find something; the answer is there*. Those words repeated over and over in her head as they were the only thing pushing her right at that moment. Her son could be dead for all she knew, but she kept repeating that line, keeping hope alive. The LED screen plastered the image of her son's battered body being carried out of the apartment. She stared into the digital image of her son's once perfect face, heartbroken with the brutal behavior of the assailants.

"La." The sound of Essence's voice dragged Leilani out of her daze. She turned around to face her best friend who held out an iPhone. "The kidnappers are on the phone."

Quickly, Leilani ran over to the phone, snatching it from Essence's grasp. Placing the phone to her ear, Leilani listened to the heavy breathing of the person on the other line. She made a mental note of the person's stuffed nostrils, as this would be a key piece for finding her son.

"How much?" Leilani asked.

"How much what?"

"Money, how much fucking money do you want for my fucking son?"

"We don't want your money. This isn't about money Ms. Vasquez."

"Then what is it about?"

"This is about revenge. There isn't anything worse than a person hell bent on revenge."

"I swear to fucking God, if my kid is touched any more than he is, I swear I will turn this whole fucking city red until I get my son back."

"Ms. Vasquez, I don't think it is best that you threaten me. I am the one with the leverage. I have something that you want."

"Fuck you, I swear to God I will find out who you are and I will fucking torture the shit out of you and anyone associated with you."

"We will see about that Ms. Vasquez."

The line went dead with the dial tone echoing in Leilani's ear. Her heart skipped a beat as the worst began to corrupt her mind. All the attention was on her; everyone anticipated her reaction. They all expected her to throw and flip things out of pure frustration, but instead Leilani stood in her spot, frozen. Her mind ran a million times faster as she tried making sense of the situation. One minute she was in bliss, being a newly engaged woman, then the next minute the joyride came accelerating down, landing her straight into a nightmare. Her dream was completely over as the nightmare of her missing son had now taken over her life. Pain infiltrated the buttery feeling within her heart; life as she had known it was coming to an end.

"Ahhhhh," she screamed releasing the loud cry from within her body. The pain filled scream filled every crack in the warehouse. Everyone stared on, scared to react the wrong way to her outburst.

"Princess?" Sincere said.

"Sincere please just … Don't," she answered. Wiping the tears that threatened to descend her cheek, Leilani could feel the anger within beginning to grow. She didn't know how much destruction she could make, but she was going to find out.

CHAPTER 25

October 1, 2016

1 month since kidnapping

"Well Ms. Vasquez, all of your test results have come back normal, except for one."

"Ok, which one?" Leilani asked.

"Your pregnancy test came back positive."

She glared into the eyes of her doctor, puzzled with his choice of words. *He must have me confused with some other patient,* she thought. Thinking back onto the past couple of weeks, the thought of her missed period hadn't even bothered her. Lately it seemed as if stress had become fixated on her. Anxiety tormented her thinking process as the thoughts of Juelz in the possession of an enemy ran through her mind every day.

The doctor stared into the eyes of his patient, expecting her to be jumping for joy for her new bundle. Instead, the shell of his once vibrant patient sat in the chair before him with depression in her eyes. It was almost as if he had given her the worst news in the world.

"We can do the sonogram right now if you have the time."

"Yes, let's get this over with," she replied nonchalantly.

"Ok Ms. Vasquez, just give me a moment to set up the room."

Quickly, the doctor left her in the room by herself. She glared around the room lost in her own thoughts. *How the fuck am I pregnant?* she thought. Before the kidnapping of Juelz, she had been so preoccupied with getting the record label ball together that she and Sincere barely had any time to be intimate. Everything after the ball had gone downhill since then. A nurse entered the room, directing her to the sonogram room where her doctor sat waiting for her.

"Ms. Vasquez let's lay down and get you gelled up" the doctor said. Leilani followed his instructions as the lights went low and the screen for the sonogram was turned on. A little pressure could be felt where her uterus was, as the image of her unborn child was plastered on the screen.

"This is your baby, which seems to be very healthy. Based off your last period and the growth of the baby, you are 20 weeks."

His words were muted as Leilani stared into the screen that contained the pixeled image of the fetus that grew in her uterus. She wanted to be happy, Lord knows she wanted to be, but she just could not bring herself to feel any form of joy.

"Would you like for me to print pictures?"

"Yes please."

The doctor pressed quickly on the pad before handing over several pictures of her fetus. Leilani took the pictures into her hand analyzing the features she saw within the image. This was her third pregnancy, but her first normal pregnancy. She had been so doped up during her first pregnancy that she was oblivious to any of her symptoms. She didn't know any of the procedures into maintaining a healthy pregnancy.

"I looked at your charts, and your stress level seems to be kind of high. I would suggest that you find some form of peace within your life or else the health of the baby will be at risk," the doctor said as he began to wipe off the cold gel on her stomach.

"I'll try Doctor."

Despite not being completely overjoyed with the new pregnancy, Leilani would never do anything to harm any of her children. She would do whatever it took to make sure her child would be born healthy and drug free. Concerned, Leilani stayed back to discuss some healthy choices for her and the baby. Once she had all the information she needed, Leilani wasted no time heading over to the warehouse where her operation of "Find Juelz" was underway.

Entering the darkened premises, Leilani gave her greetings but with her head focused on going to one area, her office. Her timbs tapped lightly against the concrete floor as she made her way into her office. Turning on the light, she illuminated her suspect board, resuming where she had left off before her doctor's appointment. Her bulletin board held photos from the night of the ball, including months prior to the kidnapping.

Taking off her coat, Leilani revealed her all-black Nike Tech suit that held onto her body frame. Her reflection bounced off the blackened Mac computer. Staring into the screen, she analyzed herself. *I don't even look that pregnant,* she thought. She had noticed her slight weight gain, chalking it up to the stress, not suspecting anything else.

"I would never do anything to harm you my little bug, but right now Mommy has to focus on bringing your brother back home safe," Leilani said speaking to her abdomen.

Focusing her attention back onto her private investigation, Leilani began to analyze what was before her. A huge bulletin board covered in hundreds of photos of the crime scene stood before her. She had seen these photos a dozen times and nothing new seemed to be coming from the images. *Let's start from the beginning again*, she thought as she stared into the picture of the assailants that entered her home.

"While they were in the home, they had a getaway car with a chauffeur?" she questioned herself. Picking up another picture, she focused her attention onto the getaway car that had sat outside her building. "No license plates, but a full image of the driver." Intrigued with the possibility of a lead, she turned on the computer and began to type away. Placing the driver's face through a facial recognition database, that she paid to be hacked, she sat waiting for the results. A light buzzing rang through the air, catching her attention. Peeking over to her vibrating iPhone, the word 'Hubby' flashed against the screen along with a picture of her and Sincere. Letting out a gush of air, she prepared herself mentally for an argument. That's all that the couple had been doing for the past month.

"Hello," she answered.

"Did you come home last night?" his deep baritone voice boasted through the tiny speakers of her phone.

"Yes, I did; why do you ask?"

"Well, I am asking because I woke up this morning to an empty bed."

"Ok."

"Ok, it would have been nice to wake up next to my fiancé and then treat her to breakfast."

"Sorry, I had things to do."

"Like?"

"Things, Sincere." Hearing the agitation in her voice, Sincere needed to calm himself down because they both were on the edge. Knowing his temper, he didn't want to cause an argument. Inhaling the thick air, he exhaled, getting rid of his bad vibes.

"Princess, I understand that the shit you're going through is rough, but you are neglecting us and that will only make us grow apart." His words were pleading with her heart for her to do better. She had been neglecting her relationship with Sincere. All her time and energy had been focused onto getting her son back. She couldn't bring herself to do anything else. Prepared to answer him back, her words were lost within her mind as the computer screen lit up with the information that Leilani so desperately needed. No longer paying him any attention, Leilani diverted her attention back onto the screen that displayed the information of the getaway driver, *Mario Marino 4904 Avenue M*, she read. Gathering up her jacket, Leilani prepared herself to leave.

"Are you even listening to me?" Sincere asked.

"Yes babe, I am."

"Really?" he questioned. "Then what did I say?"

"You're talking about having dinner tonight."

"Ok, so I am expecting you tonight."

"Alright I will be there."

"Don't play with me Princess. If I have to, I will drag your ass by your fucking ponytail."

"Ok bye, I will see you later." Before Sincere could reply, Leilani had hung up the phone with her destination locked into her brain. Her feet moved to a rhythm that she could only match. Exiting the warehouse, Isaiah watched her every move. Tempted to stop her, he decided against it, as he knew it would not lead into anything good. The pent up anger that she desperately tried to hide was leaking out in a greater amount the longer Juelz remained missing. He silently said a prayer hoping that she would not do anything crazy that would risk her life.

The cool October air caught her off guard as she began to put on her jacket. Getting into her car, she set up her GPS, while she allowed the car to warm up. *Please God, I am asking you to protect me on this journey of bringing my son back home*. Starting the car, she pulled off with her destination set on her mind. No plan in mind, Leilani began to create one quickly.

"How should I go about this?" she asked herself. The more she thought about what she could do the harder it was for her to come up with a plan. "Fuck it," she finally said once she realized that wouldn't be able to come up with something.

The New York traffic was smooth for a Saturday night; she hadn't expected to reach her destination in such a short time. Parking a block away from the home, Leilani cut the engine off sitting in utter silence. Things in her head was chaotic and she needed to get herself together before she did anything. Closing her eyes, she remained silent in the vehicle allowing the quiet night to soothe her. Her anxiety was beginning to fuck with her causing her fingers to fidget.

"Come on La, get them trigger fingers straight," she said to herself. Getting her nerves under control, she exited the car with her mind on right. The night wind blew lightly against her hair away from her face. Walking, her timbs lightly tapped the pavement floor as she entered the front yard of her target. Her fist knocked lightly on the door as she quickly analyzed her surroundings. The door yanked open and the person she had been looking for stood before her with a scrawl on his face.

"Who you are looking for?" he asked with an attitude.

"You must be Mario Marino."

"Yea, why?"

Pulling out her gun, she pistol-whipped the 6'4 tall man. His tall frame fell backwards granting Leilani the access into the home that she needed. Closing the door behind her, she locked the both out from the world. Staring down at the man cradling his open wound Leilani took a hold of her target by his collar causing him to sit up to face her.

"Now, I am simply here for some information on a kidnapping

that you were involved with. Either you can cooperate or I can get more physical than a simple pistol-whipping."

Staring into the eyes of his assailant, Mario didn't think much of the pint-sized beauty. His voice broke into a fit of laughter only upsetting an already agitated Leilani. Stomping him out with her size 8 timberlands, she pounded until the white carpet turned maroon. She was very careful as she didn't want to kill him, but she wanted him to feel as if he were going to die.

"I'mma ask again, you were involved with a kidnapping a month ago. You were the driver for the getaway car. Now all I want to know is who was behind the kidnapping. Who hired you?"

"Fuck you, I am not going to tell you shit," he yelled.

"Fuck me?"

"Yes bitch, fuck you and your bastard of a fucking son."

His words triggered something in Leilani that she had never fel before. Her motives were no longer fueled by the concept of gettin information on the kidnapping of her child. At that very moment, he blood boiled with pure rage from the disrespect. His words insulte her in the worst possible way. Positioning the pistol in his stomach Leilani pulled the trigger allowing the bullet to rip through his organs Yelling out in pain, her target tried to throw her off him but a quick ja to the bleeding gunshot wound caused him to back down.

"I asked you before about my fucking kid, you can either answe my fucking question or I will make the pain worse."

"Fine, please just stop no more," he cried out.

“Tell me what the fuck I want to know. Who was behind the kidnapping of my fucking son?”

“ I don’t know I was hired by my uncle to handle the job.”

His answer did not answer the question she had asked. Digging her fist into his open wound, she listened to him yell out in pain.

“I swear to you, I don’t know their names all I know is that it was both a man and woman.”

“Give me more Mario or I will dig my fucking finger into this hole that’s in your side.”

“Please no, I swear to you all I know is that the female has a flower tattooed on her finger.”

“Her finger?”

“Yes, like a red flower could be a rose I don’t know it was a pretty bad tattoo.”

“What about the kidnappers?” she asked. “What you know about them?”

“Four guys,” he said breathing heavy. “Four guys, I know they go by Tazz, Hendrix, Gutter, and Wolf.”

“You did good Mario, now I won’t kill you,” she replied as she stood up. Tucking her pistol into the small of her back, she turned around prepared to leave. She had come in search for some information. Granted she didn’t get exactly what she came for at least she was leaving with some info about who the four men were.

“Wait where are you going?” Mario yelled behind her. “Aren’t you going to get me some help?”

"Hell no, I said I won't kill you. Doesn't mean I will let you live."

CHAPTER 26:

November 5, 2016

2 months since kidnapping

"So, gentlemen let me hear what's new with the kidnapping?" Don asked as he took his seat at the head of the wooden conference table. Two months had passed since Juelz was taken, and no useful information had been discovered. The kidnappers knew that Leilani didn't have any leads on them so they used this to taunt her. Don found it so depressing to watch the once vibrant young woman deteriorating right before him. Having the urge to do something, Don decided to call a meeting with all the police officers that were on his payroll, which included the Chief of Police, Captains, and Lieutenants. Scanning his eyes around the room, he quietly waited for an answer from the people in the room.

"Well Don, there hasn't been any trail left behind by the kidnappers," Captain Krueger said breaking the ice.

"What the fuck do you mean the kidnappers didn't leave a fucking trail?"

"They made a clean kidnapping, precisely not leaving behind any evidence."

"Really?" Don questioned finding their reasoning to be intriguing. "So, you mean to fucking tell me that the highest-ranking officers of New York fucking City cannot get a lead on the kidnapping of a kid?"

Staring around the room, Don could not believe the bullshit that he was hearing. Every man that sat comfortably around the conference table was enjoying their prosperous life for one reason. Don kept each one of them on his payroll. Every month Don would cut a hefty check off to the men with the expectation that they would work together to get the job done of fulfilling his demands.

"Don it's just not that sim—"

"Listen to me, I pay each one of you fuckers a hefty pay check," Don interrupted. "When I ask for something simple like find who the fuck kidnapped a kid I want fucking answers."

Aggravated, Don pulled out his cigarette packet in search for some relief. The past two months were beginning to take its toll on him. Since Juelz's been missing, it caused a butterfly effect on his life. Slowly he was losing the tight grip he once had on his world. Leilani was losing her mind as she had now been corrupted with the thoughts of getting her son back by any means necessary. She was running around Brooklyn taking the title of the Grim Reaper, as she was killing people left and right without a care for the repercussions. Not caring about whose life she was taking placed Don in some bad blood with the mafia. Placing the loosely wrapped cigarette at the base of his lips, he lit the other end anticipating the addictive nicotine. Inhaling the cancerous blend, he held his breath, allowing his lungs to be saturated with the perfectly infused tobacco. Releasing the smoke, he could feel his nerves beginning to calm down. Taking another puff, he held it before releasing a cloud of smoke into the air.

"I am going to say this one time and one time only," he said calmly. "Find the fucking piece of shits that kidnapped Juelz, or else I will destroy the once happy lives you all have grown to love."

Outing the cancer stick onto the wooden conference table, Don stood up to leave. He had finally had it with everyone. *Once this nightmare is over, I am going to go on a fucking vacation. All these motherfuckers are raising my fucking blood pressure,* he thought.

******

A white sheet of snow lay beneath her feet. She hadn't seen anything more beautiful than the unbothered fresh snow. ***Crunch, crunch, crunch,*** *the snow crunched underneath her feet as she aimlessly walked the winter mix. Her body shivered from the feeling of the brisk, cold winter air. Goosebumps formed on her naked skin in effort to generate body heat. Wrapping her arms around herself, she continued her walk. Her body was on fire as blood leaked from all her open wounds. In a daze, she placed one foot in front of the other in search for her haven. The once perfect sheet of snow that lay beneath her feet turned a dark hue of maroon as her blood slowly saturated the ice crystals. She was dying. This was it. Her life was finally coming to an end. Every muscle in her body knotted up in the realization that she would never make it out of the winter mix.* ***The fight to live was pointless as she looked forward; there isn't anywhere else to go,*** *she thought. Her weight could no longer be held up by her frame. A small gush of air escaped her mouth as she* *dropped down to her knees. It wasn't long before her upper body followed suit, dropping onto the thin sheet of snow.*

"So, this is how it ends?" she breathed. Glaring up, her eyes met the faint glow of the sunrise. ***What a beautiful way to die,*** *she thought. Her blood-riddled body rested peacefully, awaiting the Grim Reaper's arrival.*

Darkness surrounded her with the thoughts of death bombarding her thinking process. Every day, she had conjured up numerous scenarios on how her final moments on Earth would be. *The amount of bloodshed I've done, I doubt God would give me such a peaceful death,* she thought. The sound of the door opening and shutting caught her attention as she wondered who had entered her office.

"Hey honey." The peachy voice filled the quiet room as Essence made her way inside.

"Hello Essence."

Looking around the room, Essence quickly took in the two months of work Leilani had done. Dozens of pictures were pinned on the wall with circled faces. Essence had some ideas as to who the face were but she wasn't really sure.

"So, how's everything going?" she asked, deeply concerned.

"No new news, but I am trying."

The monotonic tone within Leilani's voice spoke volumes. Leilan was spiraling quickly into depression and no one knew what to do, a she wouldn't allow anyone into this dark time of her life. Leilani wa riddled with guilt, believing that her son's kidnapping was her faul She tormented herself everyday with the question, *how do I get Jue back?* For the past two months, she worked searching for the answe to that question. Quickly approaching her breaking point, she no longer could fathom living another day in this form of depression. No number of tears could fix the pain she felt from losing her child. She worked so hard in trying to put fear in the City of New York for some answers, but all she got back was bloodshed on her hands. She wasn't getting anywhere in her investigation and that feeling of falling wasn't subsiding. It felt as if her feet were traveling forward down a dark well. The expected thump of the end of the well never comes, and she's still falling deeper into the well.

"La, you know I can help," Essence said. "The two of us together, we are a force to be reckoned with. We can be that dynamic duo to bring home Juelz, but you must let me in. You need to let me help you so we can bring your son home."

Leilani stared into the eyes of her best friend of over 10 years. The eagerness radiated off Essence as she wanted to help; she wanted things to be how they once were before the kidnapping. Essence was willing to do anything to bring happiness into their darkened world.

"Essence, I'm good," Leilani replied nonchalantly.

"But Leila—"

"I said I am good," Leilani said sternly.

Taken aback by Leilani's response, Essence stood there baffled. She couldn't understand why Leilani was acting the way she was. All Essence wanted to do was bring Juelz safely home; she was willing to do whatever she could.

"La, I kn—"

"Leave," Leilani interrupted.

"But—"

"Just go."

Glaring at her best friend of years, Essence could see the toll the kidnapping was putting on her. Her eyes were distant and dead, beaming with depression. The glow Leilani once possessed was dimmed, accommodating her dull eyes. Essence wanted to fight for her best friend's sanity, but knowing Leilani, her mind was already set and there wasn't any changing her mind.

"Ok La, if you need me though I'll be right outside," Essence replied before leaving.

"Ok."

Exiting the room, Essence immersed herself back into the rush hour within the warehouse. Staring down at the workers in the warehouse, Essence searched the crowd for a familiar pair of eyes. After some time, her eyes landed on the onyx colored pupils. *There he is,* she thought as she descended the metal stairs in pursuit of her person of interest.

"I need to talk to you," she said interrupting the conversation he was having.

"Hold on let me finish up—"

"This is about your fiancé so I need you right now," Essence replied sternly. Hearing the urgency in her voice, he ended the conversation he was having with the worker informing them that they would pick up on the topic later.

"What's up?" he asked.

"I am concerned about Leilani."

"Me too."

"No Sincere, you don't understand; she is not doing so good."

"Essence, what do you want me to do?"

"The only thing you can do is be there for her. She's going through a dark time and she is prone to insanity."

"I've tried Essence, I really have tried to be there for her but every time I try she pushes me away."

"She's stubborn as hell but you have to be strong. She's going to mentally break down soon if Juelz isn't found, and I'd rather someone be there to console her than her losing her life for doing something irrational."

The door to Leilani's office opened and Leilani came out putting on her jacket. Confused, Essence wondered as to where she was going. *I hate being out of the fucking loop,* she thought as she took her phone out and began to text her boyfriend.

"I'm texting Isaiah right now to see if she called him to go anywhere."

"Aight."

Essence watched as the message box bubbled, anticipating Isaiah's message. A blue box dropped in the message window, and quickly Essence read the message:

Yes, I am going to meet up with her now. She said she found a lead with the niggas involved, the text read.

"Ok he's going with her."

"At least she has Isaiah."

"I know, but still you need to be there for her. I don't fucking need my best friend dying ok," Essence said. "She made it through some tough shit and she's gonna make it through this."

******

"Who are we after?" Isaiah asked as he sat in his car staring off into the buildings.

"The four guys that were involved with the kidnapping."

"How did you find them?"

"I have my ways," Leilani replied not wanting to waste time. "Now I found the first two, Tazz and Hendrix."

"The other two, no location on them?"

"No, but it's ok. I am hoping to get everything I need from those two."

"Aight La, say no more," Isaiah replied as he cocked back his favorite piece. "No holds bar?"

"None."

The anxiety within Leilani was at an all-time high as it had been two months since Juelz had been home. Things weren't looking up for Leilani; she no longer could face her family and friends with the thoughts of her failed parenthood tormenting her. She wanted this nightmare to already be over and she needed it to end now. Grabbing her desired tubular weapon, Leilani exited her car tucking the cold steel into the small of her back.

A weird feeling washed over Leilani, instantly she cupped her swollen abdomen. She didn't know how to describe the feeling as the uncontrollable motion happened in her uterus. The baby that grew within her was wide awake as it moved within the organ.

"You ok?" Isaiah asked as he noticed the weird facial expression.

"I am—"

"You're nervous?" he questioned.

"Umm, yea," Leilani agreed, continuing their journey into the building complex. Leilani was six months pregnant with her fiancé's second child. No one had a clue that she was pregnant as she hid it from everyone around her. She reasoned her decision, thinking that it would be best for everyone to focus on getting Juelz back rather than focusing on her pregnancy. *Once I get my son back, I'll throw a big fucking party.*

Together both Isaiah and Leilani took the flight of stairs to the fourth floor; it would have been easier if they took the elevator but they both knew there were cameras in the elevators. They wanted to go undetected so their best option was the flight of stairs. Once they got to the fourth floor, Isaiah opened the door for his sister and watched as she walked by, with his eyes focused on her stomach. For the past month, he noticed her weight gain; she was a little bit thicker but he couldn't really tell because she always wore baggy clothing. She no longer wore anything that was form fitting. He changed his mind and decided that he would ask her at another time.

"What apartment?" he asked.

"4H"

"How we are doing this?"

"I have the key to the apartment."

"What the fuck, how?"

"The super for this building owed me a favor because I handled a problem that he had a while back," Leilani responded as she placed the key into the lock, slowly she turned it, and opened the door, granting her access into the home.

The lights were turned down low as loud thumping erupted through the two-bedroom apartment. Moans escaped through the thin walls as both Leilani and Isaiah strained their ear to hear where it was coming from. *Oh, someone's getting fucked,* Leilani thought as she pulled out her weapon with Isaiah following suit.

"Two bedrooms, so we do it for both?" Isaiah whispered.

"Yea."

They both agreed on the plan, separating to their designated room. Leilani counted to three before she busted through the room door, scaring the occupants that were engaged in an intimate session.

"What the fuck?" Hendrix yelled out loud, surprised to see the woman before him.

"Put some clothes on and get out the bed," Leilani responded. "Me and you got a lot to talk about playboy."

"Bitc—"

"Listen, I ain't gonna be too many names before I let my hammer rip. Get fucking dressed and come into the fucking living room," she said.

Hearing the calmness in her voice, Hendrix and his one night stand followed their intruder's instructions as they both threw on their clothes. Once they were finished, Leilani waved the gun in the direction of the living room.

"Go," she mouthed. They slowly filed out of the bedroom, finding a spot on the living room couch. It wasn't long before they were met by Isaiah and his two people.

"Now," Leilani began, "ladies I am going to let you go, as I do not need you for anything."

Before Leilani could say anything else, the two girls got up running out of the room, leaving the guys alone with the intruders. Tonight was supposed to be a fun one night stand, not an escapade that would result in their death.

"Ok, we are finally alone fellas, so let's get down to business," Leilani said as she fixated her attention on the guys. "Two months ago, you guys and two other gentlemen were involved in a kidnapping. You guys entered the apartment and took some items, along with a teenager. The teenager that you took was my son. Now I don't care about the items that you took, you can keep those. None of those items are valuable compared to the life of my son. All I want to know is where have you taken my kid?"

Both men stared at her with their emotionless glares. They knew exactly what she was talking about but opted to keep quiet. A staring match initiated as Leilani waited on the suspects to answer her question.

"Are we opting to remain silent?" she questioned, turning to Isaiah for reassurance.

"I guess they are," Isaiah responded, staring at Leilani. The eagerness emitted from her pores as the theory of her getting closer to her son influenced her mind. Isaiah wanted to see his baby sister happy. For the past couple of months he missed her. The loss of her son had turned her into an anti-social person who became fixated on video recordings and maps. He wanted to get her back into that happy space where she wanted to wake up and enjoy the rest of her life. He wanted her back to her old self, and the only way he could help bring her back to that state is by getting her son back.

Leilani pulled her weapon out, smashing the butt of the gun against Hendrix's skull. A loud crack echoed off the walls as Hendrix cradled the open wound on his head. Blood poured from the wound altering the suede couch's color to a dark maroon.

"Now I asked you a fucking question," she said. "Where is my son?"

"I don't know shit," Hendrix spat.

"Really?"

"No, we did the job and that was it."

"Ok, someone had to hire you so who the fuck is your boss?"

" Fuck you I ain't telling you shit," Hendrix yelled.

"Tazz, do you wanna take over and let us know something?" Isaiah questioned, noticing that they weren't getting anywhere with the questioning. They needed to place fear into the hearts of the two men and pistol-whipping them wasn't doing that. Isaiah prepared to say something but was side tracked as Leilani left the living room in pursuit of something. All three men stared at each other, confused on what the hell was going on. *Where the fuck is she going?* Isaiah questioned himself. His question was answered as Leilani walked back into the living room with a look in her eyes. Completely in a daze, Leilani walked over to them with a red gasoline tank in her hand.

"Since you guys don't want to tell me, I guess you won't be telling anyone anything," she replied as she tilted the gasoline tank forward, splashing the flammable gas all over the two guys. "Now I'mma ask y'all one more time, where the fuck is my kid?"

Staring into the eyes of both men, Isaiah could see the fear within them. *Shit I'd be scared too if this girl did some shit like that to me,* he thought. He stood behind Leilani, watching the chain of events unfold.

"We were hired by some Italian guy named Antonio Ricci and his girl," Tazz admitted.

"What's the girl's name?"

"I don't know; she was never introduced to us. Only thing Ricci told us was that she was his girl."

"Ok, give me some more info on her."

Tazz stared up at the woman who held his fate in her hand. He hadn't expected any of this to happen. If he would have known that the kid he kidnapped belonged to the psychotic woman before him, he would have contemplated his involvement in the kidnapping.

"The woman had a bad flower tattoo," Tazz said.

"What do you mean?"

"On her hand, she has a flower that looks like it wasn't done right."

"That's it?"

"Listen La, it's better than nothing," Isaiah interjected.

For the next hour, both Hendrix and Tazz sat in their seats being questioned about the people that hired them to do their job. Their answers never changed, but Leilani still asked them the same questions just to ensure they weren't lying. Sitting in their seat, their bodies soaked in the flammable fluid causing Tazz to be nauseous.

"Listen Miss, we told you everything we know; now please can you let us go?"

"Oh sure, just give me one minute," Leilani replied as she sat down the gasoline tank. Taking out the switchblade from within in her pocket, she cut the tape that Isaiah had bound them with. "I appreciate you guys actually helping me. Sorry Hendrix about the pistol whip, but I just needed more information on my son."

"Nah I understand."

"Yea."

Isaiah stood there confused on the actions of his little sister. *Why the hell is she releasing them?* he questioned. *We came here to do something and now you letting these niggas go.* A million questions ran through his head as he grew concerned about the decision Leilani was making.

"It's just that today is my son's birthday; he turned 18," Leilani said pulling out a small box. Both men were oblivious as to what was happening, as they kept their focus on removing the tape off them. "My only child, ripped from the safety of his home. The home that I spent years grinding in the streets for. The home that I've killed hundreds of men for. The same home that I guaranteed as safe. The same fucking home that you guys broke into and kidnapped my only fucking son.

The same home that remains trashed till this day. All because of you fuckers."

Swiftly, Leilani ran the red tip of the wooden stick against the coarse striking surface. The wooden tip glowed the perfect hue of orange as Leilani tossed the lit match onto the couch. In no time, both men became engulfed in flames. Their bodies danced alongside the orange flames trying to put them out, but the more their bodies gyrated the angrier the flames became. The wrath and fury of the flames explained Leilani's anger as it ate the souls of Juelz's kidnappers.

"Call 911; tell them about the fire on the floor. I don't want the whole building to burn down and these people lose a home over these fuck boys," Leilani told Isaiah as she turned around to exit the apartment.

CHAPTER 27

December 25, 2016

3 months since kidnapping

2:30 a.m.

Am I happy?

The question rang throughout her mind as she searched for an appropriate answer. Glaring up at the ceiling of the master bedroom that she shared with Sincere, Leilani racked her brain for an answer. Was she happy? The answer was fuck no. She hadn't been happy in months, and everyone knew it; it wasn't a secret. She was sinking deeper into a depression as time progressed. The change was evident; the people who were around her noticed the difference within her. She no longer smiled the same nor did she have the same sense of humor. She had become more distant, isolating herself from general population.

Can I ever be happy again?

The answer to that was so obvious. She knew deep down in her heart that the only way she would ever be happy again would be if she got Juelz back. That was the only way; it was the only solution to her problem. Believing in the theory that violence would end her nightmare, she had become a plague to New Yorkers. Her murder scenes made headlines on every top magazine in America. The people of New York read these papers every morning, intrigued by the mystery of the countless murders. Everyone had their opinion on the reason behind the killings. Many believed it was part of another drug war, or there was just another crazed serial killer wrapped in their thoughts about their victims being evil. No one conjured up the theory that the murders were based off a mother searching for her missing child. Becoming New York's crazed serial killer not only placed fear in the community, it also placed Don in a bad position. Bodies were dropping from some of the biggest drug organizations that Don was affiliated with. Wanting to save her from the consequences of her actions, Don placed himself in the center of her rivalries. He became the mediator between her and all her new rivals, which was ruining his reputation. The Supremes' business ventures were beginning to also feel the effects of Leilani's murder spree as dozens of their partnerships were backing out of doing business with them. The team needed things to turn around fast before their empire came crashing down.

Laying down in bed, Leilani's eyes focused onto the bland paint that covered the ceiling. She needed a miracle to happen as she was beginning to lose herself within the thoughts of revenge. Shifting on her side of the bed, she became uncomfortable.

"Shit," she exclaimed as she cupped the lower portion of her abdomen. A tightening sensation invaded her uterus as she lay there. "I know baby. I didn't forget about you."

Leilani was in her third trimester and no one knew about her pregnancy. She hid her pregnancy well, often wearing extra baggy clothing. Sincere was clueless; he hadn't seen her bare skin in three months. When she had first heard the news about her pregnancy, she decided that she would tell everyone once she got her chaotic life under control. Sadly, she never could, and now she lay in bed next to her sleeping fiancé who had no clue about her child-bearing status. Rubbing her protruding abdomen, she began to soothe her baby who could sense her high stress levels. Despite being so hell bent on finding her only son, Leilani made sure she was taking care of herself physically for the sake of her unborn child. She never missed a doctor's appointment, she took her prenatal vitamins regularly, and she made sure she ate and remained active. The only thing she was at fault for was being overly stressed. Her doctor warned her about the repercussions for her high stress levels.

"Princess, why are you up?" Sincere mumbled, almost not audible.

"Can't sleep," she admitted.

Sincere placed his massive hand on her round stomach. Slowly he rubbed her abdomen, unconsciously soothing the overwhelmed fetus that grew within her uterus. Frozen in place, Leilani lay there nervous about what to do. Before she could do anything, Sincere pulled her closer towards him as he rested his head on her stomach. *He's going to fucking kill me*, Leilani thought, *why the fuck did I wait so long to tell him about the pregnancy?* A million concepts ran through her mind as she tried to think of answers for the billion questions he would be asking. A muffled sound escaped his lips as Leilani quieted her thoughts to hear it better. Light snores filled the room as Sincere fell back asleep. A gush of air escaped her lips as she breathed in relief. Feeling comfortable under the grasp of Sincere, Leilani lay underneath him, enjoying the sensational feeling. She missed this kind of attention. She was tired of people always asking her if she was ok, or if she needed anything. She was simply tired of people talking to her. She wanted things back to how they were. People looked at her with pity and sympathy as if she were some weak, helpless woman. She hated that form of pity with a passion.

Placing her hand on Sincere's head, she gently caressed him, playing with his hair. Slowly, her mind began to wonder to the thoughts of their unborn child. *I hope my baby doesn't have this big ass head of yours*, she chuckled.

"Lord knows, I don't think I could push out a watermelon," she said to herself. Up and down, her hand stroked her fiancé's Caesar cut as she admired his handsome facial features.

Between the couple, there were some great features that they both possessed. Leilani hoped like hell that their unborn child was the perfect mixture of them. Lost in the trance of love, the faint vibration of her phone almost went unnoticed. Glancing at the illuminated iPhone screen, Leilani was confused on the unknown number that flashed across her screen. Tempted to ignore the call, she decided to answer.

"Hello?"

"It's been so long," the caller responded.

"Who's this?"

"Doesn't matter who I am, what matters the most is how desperate are you to get your son back?" the caller asked.

"What?"

"You heard me, how desperate are you?"

"What do you want?"

"I will give you back your son, but I want something in return."

"What is it?"

"I want you."

"Excuse me?"

"In exchange for your son, I want you." The deep baritone of the caller's voice creeped Leilani out. "You said you would do anything for the safe return of your son, so there you go. I want you to give yourself up in exchange for your son."

"I will do it," she replied without any hesitation.

"Good."

Leilani didn't have to second guess her decision as she slowly moved Sincere away from her. The kidnapper rattled off the information Leilani needed and told her the rules to getting back her son.

"Come alone; if someone follows you or even intervenes with the exchange, your son will be killed."

"I got it."

"After you have successfully given yourself in, your son will be available in three hours at your front door."

"I understand."

"See you soon," the creepy voice replied in a mocking tone. The sound of the dial tone rang in her ear as she looked up to the ceiling, releasing a gush of air from her mouth. She had just made a deal with the devil himself and she didn't care. Her only concern was making sure that she would get her son home safe and sound. She had spent the past three months torturing herself about the endless possibilities on what could have been going on with Juelz; hundreds of scenarios corrupted her mind. All she needed was for her son to get home safe and she'd be ok. *I don't even give a fuck about what these niggas think they can do. I'll make it out alive,* she convinced herself.

11:30 a.m.

The soft rapping on the door filled the massive master bedroom causing Sincere to stir in his slumber. Entangled within the folds of the satin sheets, his eyes fluttered open. The soft knocks on the door continued as his son Cason tried to get his attention. Confusion filled his mind as he slowly sat up, taking in the bright light that illuminated his bedroom.

"Come in," his raspy voice yelled. The door slowly opened as his 15-year-old son walked into the room smacking on his morning cereal. "You can't open your gifts until Princess gets up."

"Pops, what are you talking about?" Cason asked confused. "Leilani isn't even here. I came to tell you that there is a package downstairs waiting for you."

"Ok, I'll be down in a minute."

"Hurry, cuz that package was heavy as shit when I had to carry it into the house."

"Boy if you don't fuckin—"

"My fault, I'm just saying it was heavy as hell," Cason responded as he left his father's room.

What the hell am I gonna do with that fucking boy? Sincere questioned himself as he tossed the covers over to the other side of the bed. Picking up his phone, he sent Leilani a quick text telling her to come home as soon as possible. Quickly, he got in the shower to rinse off the sleepiness that still lingered. Once he was done, he threw on some clean clothes and headed downstairs to see what all the fuss was about. Descending the staircase, his eyes caught the large package that sat waiting patiently for someone to open it up.

"Cason come down so you can open your gift," Sincere yelled out loud as he grabbed the letter opener that rested on the table. He glared at the package inspecting the tags that stated the origin of the package. *Queens, New York. Save U- storage.* He'd never heard of the company nor did he remember ordering from any company affiliated with the storage company. Using the letterhead knife, he split open the tape revealing the contents within the box. Sincere pushed aside the small white cushions in search of the merchandise.

"What the fuck is in here?" he questioned, pushing more of the foam to the side. Strands of thick curly hair began to appear. Confused, Sincere began to dig some more, now intrigued by the merchandise. *Nah it can't be,* he thought to himself, *this fucking can't be true.* "Juelz?"

CHAPTER 28

"Juelz?" Sincere called out.

"Please help."

Staring into the eyes of his stepson, Sincere grew the urge to throw up the contents within his stomach. The sight of Juelz's malnourished body caused his stomach to turn. The once pretty boy who focused solely on his looks no longer looked the same. His face was swollen beyond recognition due to the beatings that he received on the regular. The golden hue that was envied by men diminished into a gloomy death look. Gently, Sincere picked up Juelz's long, malnourished frame. His once 175lb body was replaced by the famished 120lb body frame that Sincere cradled in his arms. Loud thuds rained down the stairs as Cason came running down preparing to unwrap his Christmas gifts.

"What the fuck?" Cason exclaimed at the sight of Juelz.

"Help me bring Juelz upstairs into the bedroom," Sincere instructed.

Following the directions that were given to him, Cason ran over to aid his father during this time of need. Together, both father and son carried Juelz up the stairs until they approached the spare bedroom. Walking into the room, they placed Juelz's body on the mattress as

Sincere began to pull out his cell phone. Quickly, he dialed the number to their private doctor that they kept on their payroll. Staring down at the teenager that he helped raise for five years, Sincere could feel his heart getting heavy with emotions. Juelz's body was adorned with dozens of open cuts. His body endured so much pain that it was going numb.

"I should have been there to help," Sincere cried. "I should have never stopped looking."

1 hour later

Warmth wrapped around the grand living room as the lit fireplace contained dancing flames. The Christmas joy that filled the room went unaccepted by the leaders of the Supremes. They were unmoved by the allure of the gigantic evergreen Christmas tree that was perfectly decorated to match the white ambiance of the living room. No one cared for the perfectly wrapped Christmas gifts that remained under the tree, nor did anyone care for the white Christmas socks that were pinned against the fireplace. Their attention was primarily focused on the purpose of Sincere calling the emergency meeting.

"Are you going to say anything or will you continue to pace the freaking living room like a maniac?" Isaiah asked, watching Sincere's uneasy movement.

"I found him."

"What?" they asked confused.

"I found Juelz."

"Thank fucking God."

A sigh of relief escaped both Isaiah and Essence's lips as the thought of Juelz being safely returned invaded their thoughts. The past couple of months had been hell for everyone and they were glad that it had finally come to an end.

"He's in really bad shape."

"What do you mean?" Don asked.

"When I took him out of the box, he did not look too good. Right now, the doctor is upstairs checking him out."

"How's Leilani taking it?"

"That's the thing; she's not here," Sincere answered.

"What do you mean she's not here?" Isaiah asked.

"She left a note saying that she turned herself over to the kidnappers in exchange for Juelz."

"Wait, what?"

Handing over the perfectly written letter, Sincere allowed both men to read what their loved one had left behind. Baffled by what was written, Don questioned the decision Leilani made.

"You have to understand Don, Leilani would do whatever it takes to ensure that her son is safely home."

"How the fuck are we gonna find her?" Don questioned.

"I don't know and I don't care how, but we will find her no matter what it takes."

"Yes, we definitely will because she's pregnant with my child,"

Sincere revealed.

"What the fuck are you talking about now Sincere?"

Sincere pulled out the rectangular black and white picture, showing it to both Don and Isaiah. Confused on how to feel, Sincere watched both men as they were startled by the pregnancy news.

"I found it hidden in the night stand."

"But why would sh—"

"Right now, I don't care about that. We just need to find Leilani quick and fast," Sincere stated.

******

The stale smell of cigarettes lingered around the darkened room Humidity attacked her as the light sheen of her perspiration glistenec against the limited light that entered the room. *Where the hell am I* Leilani questioned. Her memory was restricted by the recent event tha occurred. *Come on La, what the hell happened before I ended up here* Her mind slowly began to replay the exchange of events. *I remembe driving downtown Brooklyn and then shutting the car off once I got t the Brooklyn bridge. Then I waited under the bridge when a black ba went over my head.*

"Fuck, I was thrown into the back of van," she remembered. Fuck

She moved around on the metal chair to break herself free fror the restraints. Using all her weight, Leilani began to move the chai scraping the metal against the concrete floor. *Concrete floor... I mu be in a basement,* she analyzed. Her eyes diverted around the darkene room as she tried to become familiar with her surroundings. N *windows, shit; might be soundproof.* Her chances of escaping the room were very low. She had no clue how she would escape. The door to the basement opened, allowing the light to partially illuminate the dim room. A broad figure descended the cemented staircase.

"I am glad that you are awake." The thick Spanish accent of the kidnapper sounded familiar.

"Is my son safe?"

"I gave you my word that your niño Juelz would be returned to your home, but I do not know about him being safe." His deep chuckle twined with humor left a weird feeling with Leilani. It was creepy, reminding her of a villain in a movie that had succeeded with an evil plan.

"How about you show your bitch ass face," Leilani said.

"Oh honey, this isn't a face you haven't seen before," he said as he flicked on the lights revealing his identity.

"You fucking bitch," Leilani yelled as she recognized the man before her. "You're fucking supposed to be family."

"I am not your fucking family. Just because my brother has accepted you with open arms, does not mean I have to," Don Cheadle admitted.

"So, this whole time when I was searching for my fucking son you had him the whole entire fucking time?" Leilani yelled out in anger.

"Yup."

"You knew the plans the whole time; that's why I could never seem to get closer."

"You are indeed one smart girl," Don Cheadle chuckled.

"Why do you have a problem with me?" Leilani questioned. "I have done nothing to you and I barely communicate with you. What could make you hate me so much that you would kidnap my fucking son?"

"Do you know how long you have been working for the Supremes before you were given your position?"

"I don't know Cheadle, tell me."

"You didn't even work for it. You were given the position that was supposed to go to me," he yelled. "I fucking worked hard for that position and all you had to fucking do was waltz into our fucking circle and ruin any chance of me ever getting that position."

"Really Cheadle, that's why you did all of this?" Leilani asked puzzled. "You hated me that much?"

"You see, that's where you're wrong." Cheadle stated. "I don't hate you that much, but I know someone who hates you more than I do."

Their attention diverted to the opening of the metal door as a female figure descended the staircase. Slowly, the hourglass physique revealed her identity, causing Leilani to choke on anticipation. *Oh, hell fucking no, this must be a fucking joke.* Despite several plastic surgeries done to her face, Leilani immediately recognized the woman who was the mastermind of nightmare episode that invaded Leilani's life. Those soulless eyes beamed a familiar glare that tormented Leilani; it hadn't changed over the years not once. They still contained the same resentment even after seventeen years.

"Roselyn."

Her mother stood before her resembling a brand new porcelain doll. Her new looks closely resembled Puerto Rican actress Roselyn Sanchez. Leilani had to admit her mother did look gorgeous with her new face.

“Thank God those plastic surgeons were able to fix you up,” Leilani admitted.

“I know right, let’s hope they’ll be able to do the same for you once I am done with you.”

CHAPTER 29

"People I need y'all to be fucking focused. Leilani gave herself up at this fucking location. We lose full surveillance once she gets closer to the Brooklyn bridge. A white van is shown leaving this area twenty minutes later. I want the license plate searched; use those fucking plates to get a fucking lead. Come on people. Let's get this shit done; my fucking pregnant wife has been missing for 24 hours. I need her home, so let's get fucking to it," Sincere yelled out to his workers.

Hurriedly, all his employees ran at the bass of his voice. Since Leilani had gone missing things had not been looking good for anyone. Tempers were high as the tension between everyone was beginning to increase. The holidays were meant for families to spend time together basking on what they were grateful for. None of the workers were even allowed the chance to bask in the aftermath of Christmas as they all received the alert to come back to work.

"So, what's the plan?" Isaiah asked.

"What do you mean?"

"How are we gonna get back my sister?"

"I don't know. I just need to find her location first, then I'll be able to work off that."

Isaiah stared into the eyes of the man he claimed as his brother for years. He really liked Sincere, never finding a reason to label him as disloyal or anything of that nature, and that's exactly how Isaiah wanted to keep it. He wanted to remain in the family that he built with Sincere and Don but if he had to, he wouldn't think twice about killing either man if he suspected any of them were involved with the chaotic events that were torturing their lives.

"Listen bro, just find my fucking sister y," Isaiah demanded.

"What the fuck you think I am doing?" Sincere questioned.

"I don't know, but 24 hours have passed and we still don't have her."

"Well nigga how about you actually do something rather than just standing there."

"What the fuck you think I'm doing?"

The tempers between the two began flaring as both of their egos played a huge factor in their bickering. Sincere wanted to remain calm as they were both under a great deal of stress, but he had no problem with calling Isaiah out on his shit.

"Listen man, I am trying to find her, but if you're just gonna be standing there like a fucking eagle watching over everyone, how do you expect to find Princess?" Sincere questioned.

"I'm doing what I know best."

"And I am too."

"We all are," the thick Spanish accent interrupted. Both men turned in the direction of where the voice was coming from. Their eyes fell upon Don Cheadle who stood there with grief written all over his face. “It’s sad that this is happening.”

“Nigga what?” Sincere asked confused. “You always had a fucking problem with La, why now you’re all sad and shit? How I know you ain’t fucking take her?” Sincere questioned.

“Because no matter how much we bicker and fight, I would never want to hurt a woman,” he replied calmly.

“I doubt Cheadle would do some shit like that,” Isaiah interjected. “Leilani was family.”

“Don’t matter; everyone is a suspect until my Princess comes home.”

“It’s ok Sai, I understand where he’s coming from, but I assure you I had nothing to do with this. I am just as surprised as you are.”

******

Perspiration leaked off her lean body as she inhaled and exhaled rapidly. Staring down at her masterpiece, Roselyn was satisfied with the work she had done on her victim. Over the past hour, Roselyn had used her chain-wrapped fist to deliver blow after blow to Leilani’s face. The beauty queen that she resented for years sat with her head hung low. Her life was seeping onto the cemented floor, pooling at the base of her feet.

“That was fun,” Roselyn said while unwrapping the chains from her fist.

“For … who?” Leilani asked barely over a whisper. Pain invaded her jaw that threatened to snap out of place. She couldn't control the amount of blood that escaped her mouth due to her loose jaw.

"For me of course," Roselyn admitted. "I haven't had that much fun in forever."

Sweat glistened off her physique as she began to wipe all the blood that splattered on her. She had spent a lifetime waiting for this opportunity, and she finally had the chance to show her daughter all the pain and hatred that she had harvested over the years.

"Why do you dislike me so much?" Leilani asked as she spat out a wad of blood that creeped out of her mouth.

"Dislike?" Roselyn repeated with a chuckle at the end of the question. "Dislike, honey I do not dislike you. I actually hate you."

"Why? I've done nothing to you. Why do you hate me so much?"

"Listen, my resentment for you wasn't something that I conjured up one blue morning. You were doomed the day you were born as you are a product of love."

"What?"

"You were the product of a couple who loved each other unconditionally," Roselyn spoke. "I came to this country in hopes of having a better life. Things in Colombia were horrible due to the crazy drug enterprise that was on the rise. You couldn't walk in the streets without bypassing a shooting; it was too dangerous for my family to live any longer. My father was murdered by the drug cartel and at that moment, my mom realized we couldn't be there anymore. The first chance that we had, me, my sister, and my mother ran away, finding our way to the States. We were happy that we could escape that lifestyle but it was all pointless as we had now entered another hell. We came to America expecting to find jobs and to live comfortably, but that wasn't the case. We were broke, we had no food, no clothes, nothing. The only thing that we had were our pussies. Being the hustler that I was, I used it to my advantage. I learned English fast and learned the language of money. In less than two years, me and my mother used our beauty and pussies to secure us a lifestyle. My mother sacrificed my little sister because at the time she was a teenager. She was only 15 years old when we first came to this country; she was still a little girl. We believed that it was best that she remained in school; she needed to have an education and we didn't want the streets to ruin her. So, me and my mother slept with all these men, giving them the illusion that they were special to us. They were all the same to me. I didn't look for a relationship with any of them. They were simply another pay day for me. All of them except one. He was a big shot that ran a huge drug cartel in Miami at the time. I didn't care that he was using me as a drug mule. Whatever he wanted, I was willing to give him. The one thing I couldn't give him, he decided to go to the next bitch for." Fidgeting with the silver, thick chain that wrapped around her fist, Roselyn could feel the tears threating to descend her face. The pain from the heartbreak that occurred over thirty years ago still held an effect on her. The scars were old but still felt fresh. "He fucked the next best bitch getting what he wanted out of her. I watched those two for years while I sat in the background like a piece of trash. He loved her. I saw the look he would give her, so I knew it was real. Not long after they were together they had a little baby girl. She was so beautiful. She was perfect; the perfect combination of her parents. I tried so hard to hide the envy within my heart; I really did. I tried to be happy but I just couldn't. One night, the couple wanted to go out and enjoy some quality time. So, I offered to babysit their daughter. That night, the couple went out and enjoyed their time together. When they came home, their million-dollar mansion had been burned to the ground with their daughter in it."

"That's very sad that you would go to extreme lengths to ruin the life of a couple. But what the fuck does all this have to do with me?"

"Well princess, you see, their daughter never died that night in the fire. I burned the house down that night and took their daughter with me to New York where I raised her under her new name: Leilani Elena Vasquez."

"What?"

"Yes sweetheart, I am not your real mother," Roselyn answered. "You are the offspring of Don and my baby sister Elena Vasquez."

Roselyn wrapped the thick silver chain around her fist, proceeding behind a tied up Leilani. A creepy smile paraded on her face; Leilani recognized the sinister grin. The smell of her peach apricot and sandalwood cedar amber tickled the tip of Leilani's nose. *I fucking hate that scent,* Leilani thought as she mentally prepared herself for what was going to happen next. Swiftly, Roselyn wrapped the silver chain around Leilani's neck pulling as tight as she could, cutting off all the circulation to her head. The links on the chain dug deeper and deeper into her neck as Leilani struggled to breathe. The sound of Leilani gasping for air filled the soundproof basement.

"I fucking took you in to prove that I could be that motherly figure Don needed for his kids. I took you in and you just ruined relationship after relationship," her words began to get distant as Leilani began to slowly slip unconscious. The fetus within her uterus panicked, sensing its mother's stress. Her tiny restrained frame wiggled in the chair in hopes of breaking free. But it was pointless as the oxygen in her brain began to deplete. *This is how it all ends?* Leilani questioned.

"Yes, this is how it all ends," Roselyn said, answering the question that bothered her thinking process. In one swift move, Roselyn punched Leilani, knocking her unconscious.

CHAPTER 30

Beep

Beep

Beep

The sound of the EKG machine echoed through the room as Sincere stood at the doorframe watching Juelz sleep. *He looks so peaceful,* he thought as he walked deeper into the room. The swelling in Juelz's face had gone down slightly, but still his stepson was unrecognizable. His cheek was the size of a grapefruit, accompanying his busted lip. The gash on his forehead was cleaned daily as new skin began to form. Juelz looked nothing like himself.

"Hey," Sincere said to the unconscious teenager as he grabbed the only chair in the room turned hospital room, pushing closer to the bed. Several tubes and wires protruded from his body as Juelz depended on a machine to do his breathing. "I hope you're comfortable in this room. I didn't feel comfortable with having you up in some fucking hospital with everyone seeing you in this state. Shit sounds kind of selfish, but I don't mean it like that."

The sound of the EKG machine beeping rang in his ears as he tried getting his thoughts together. The stress that he had been enduring for the past couple of months made it hard for him. Sincere wanted desperately to talk to someone about his problems but didn't have anyone he felt comfortable enough to talk to. Staring at his unconscious stepson, Sincere just felt the need to let everything out. The tears poured freely from his eyes, as he was no longer able to keep his emotions in.

"I don't know what the fuck to do Juelz; your mother is missing and she's pregnant with your little brother or sister," Sincere cried into his palms. "What the fuck am I supposed to do?"

With no leads on Leilani's location, Sincere felt helpless. Having such a high status with so many connections, Sincere felt helpless, as there wasn't a thing that he could do. Any lead he found ended up cold leading into a dead end.

"I refuse to lose your mother Juelz; I can't lose her so soon. I don't even remember the last time I was so fucked up over someone, probably when my father was murdered," Sincere said as he wiped his face dry. "Don't worry though Juelz, I'mma bring your mother home and your little brother or sister."

Meaning every word that he said, Sincere had plans on bringing his fiancé home no matter what it took. He didn't care if he had to sacrifice his soul just to make sure that those two returned home. Whatever it took, he was willing to do it.

The door to the altered room creaked open as an unexpected guest walked through the door. Sincere kept his eyes fixated on her as he was confused on her presence. She stood at the frame of the door, nervous about how to approach Sincere. The silence between them grew, making it awkward between the two.

"How can I help you Amiya?" Sincere asked hastily.

"I just wanted to check up on you; heard you weren't doing too okay."

"I am doing fine."

Sincere stared into her big, brown eyes, searching for a reason as to why he was once so in love with her. He wondered how could he have been so blind to her conniving ways when her pores oozed with wickedness.

"That's good," she replied as she decided to walk closer towards him.

"Yea, is that all you came for?"

"What?" she asked innocently. "I can't come over to see how my baby daddy is doing during such a traumatic event?"

"Whatever."

"I mean come on Sin, we've been broken up for years now but I will never stop caring about you."

"Ok Amiya, it's nice to know."

"I am serious Sincere. I have done nothing but care for you."

Sincere watched her as she walked closer to him. He had no clue as to what she was up to, but Sincere refused to entertain her foolishness. Placing his chin into his hands, Sincere placed his focus back onto Juelz, who lay in the bed hooked to several machines. Leaning forward, Amiya made sure her face was directly in front of Sincere, blocking his view of his stepson.

"You know I still love you right?" she asked. Puckering up her lips, she leaned forward in pursuit of kissing Sincere. Quickly, Sincere turned his head and lightly pushed her face away from his.

"Are you fucking crazy?" Sincere asked.

"What?"

"I am engaged."

"So what?"

"That means I am not doing this shit."

"Fuck is you being so loyal to this bitch?"

"Because Amiya, that's what you do when you want to be with someone. You respect them and remain loyal, something you ain't too fucking familiar with."

"See, you sticking up for a bitch and you don't even fucking know her back story," Amiya replied shaking her head. "So busy running away from me, not even realizing that you ended up falling in love with a bitch that is much worse than me."

"Oh please."

"You don't believe me?"

"No one is worse than you."

"Really?" she asked puzzled. "Not even the bitch who killed your father?"

Sincere's ears perked up at the sound of his father's murderer being mentioned. It had been over 18 years since his father was found murdered in an apartment by a junkie. No one could find the person who placed his father six feet under. Since he was a little boy, Sincere had vowed that he would find the person who killed his father.

"What the fuck are you talking about?"

"I know who killed your father."

"Who?" he asked.

"It's the same bitch that you speak so highly of."

"What?"

"Yes, that bitch Leilani that you praise, is the same junkie bitch that murdered your father in cold blood." Amiya chuckled with a look of satisfaction written all over her face. "And you thought I was wicked."

******

Twisting her wrist, Leilani tried her best to adjust her hands to the tight restraints. Her body ached in every possible way as it prepared itself to deliver the baby within her uterus. A tight sensation invaded her uterus, slowly transitioning into sharp pains. *No, not now,* Leilani thought. The cramps began getting intense as she tried not to cringe with both Roselyn and Don Cheadle watching her. Both her legs and arms were restrained to a medical table. As her body was sprawled out, there was no way for her to hide. Leilani was clueless as to what both the psychopaths had planned.

"Leilani, why's your stomach so pudgy?" Don Cheadle asked as his eyes never left her naked body.

"Been eating good," she mustered.

"Stop lying, are you pregnant?"

"Are you?" Leilani questioned.

"I see you like to play games," Roselyn responded with a smile.

"Nothing has changed huh?"

"Nothing ain't ever changed," Leilani responded.

Roselyn slowly walked away, leaving Leilani alone with Don Cheadle glaring down at her. The look in his eyes would have made anyone shit their pants as he fantasized about torturing Leilani. He'd spent the past couple of years envisioning the reality before him. *There certainly is a God,* he thought as he grinned at Leilani. Roselyn reentered the room with a silver bucket and a barbecue lighter.

"Now, let's see how far you're willing to go before you tell the truth," Roselyn said as walked over to the two of them.

"What the fuck do you think you're going to do?" Leilani questioned.

"We are gonna have some fun."

Roselyn dug her hand into the silver bucket, slowly pulling out a rat. Leilani's eyes bugged out at the size of the rodent. The black rodent wiggled its large body as Roselyn held its tail between her fingers. *Oh, fuck no,* Leilani thought as she tried wiggling her body free.

"Now I am going to ask you this one more time, are you pregnant?"

"Fuck you," Leilani spat. A contraction ripped through Leilani's uterus causing a thin layer of sweat to form on her skin. Leilani wanted to scream out in pure agony, but she turned her face to the wall, gripping the Velcro restraints.

"Ok."

Roselyn place the squirming rodent onto Leilani's stomach, covering it with the silver bucket. Using the barbecue lighter, Roselyn lit the lighter placing the flame onto the silver bucket. The tiny paws of the rat walked all over Leilani's stomach as the rodent grew agitated from the heat that accumulated within the steel bucket.

"This may seem pointless, but my dear daughter the rat is beginning to grow agitated within the hot bucket. The more agitated he becomes, the more moving he's going to do until finally he's going to begin chewing his way to safety," Roselyn explained. The furry rodent's mind began to get clouded as the heat irritated him. His paws began to dig into Leilani's stomach, and his teeth chewed on her skin causing Leilani to moan in pain.

"I am going to ask you again are you with child?" Roselyn asked.

"Fuck you!"

Roselyn chuckled at Leilani's toughness, knowing that soon she would have to give up. *I don't know why you're still fighting it,* Roselyn thought as she stared down at the little girl that she had raised as her own. Dozens of open wounds adorned her naked body from the hours of torture that she endured. Roselyn knew Leilani was strong physically and mentally, but she wanted to break her down. Roselyn was jealous of the strong woman Leilani could make herself into after those years of abuse. *The fucking girl was a dope fiend and had a fucking kid. How was she fucking able to get her fucking life together?* Roselyn questioned herself.

"Are you pregnant?"

Leilani turned her head once more as a contraction began. Holding all the air in her lungs, a single tear escaped her eye now that reality began to settle in. *I don't think I can do it.* Leilani believed this whole time that she would be able to escape from the kidnappers and get back home to her son. The thought slowly escaped her mind as she lay on the medical table going through labor, being tortured with an aggravated rat. Her chances of making it out alive diminished as she lay restrained on the medical table.

"Are you pregnant?" Roselyn questioned. The steel bucket began to change color due to the flame that rested on the surface. The rat that was restrained behind the steel walls clawed and chewed its way through Leilani's skin as he searched for a haven.

"Yes, I am fucking pregnant," Leilani said unable to deal with the pain anymore.

"Good, now was that so hard?" Roselyn asked as she removed the bucket from Leilani's stomach. A red ring had eaten into her flesh as the rat tried scurrying off Leilani. Quickly, Roselyn picked up the rodent by his tail, dropping him into the steel bucket. "One more question, is Sincere the father?"

"Roselyn, go fuck yourself."

"I will after you answer my question."

"Fuck you."

"By the way you're reacting, I think he is the father," Roselyn said as she handed the bucket over for Don Cheadle to hold. "And if he is, then that's one fucked up family story."

"What the fuck are you talking about now you crazy bitch?"

Roselyn placed her hands on her thighs as she inched down to get closer to Leilani's face. Staring into Leilani's bright eyes, Roselyn wanted so desperately for the glow within her pupils to be put out. *This bitch always walks around like her shit don't stink, like everything within her life is perfect. But little does she know....*

"The father of your unborn child is the son of Rocco "Rocky" Legrand."

"What?" Leilani asked confused.

"Yes honey, that man that you're madly in love with is the offspring of the very man that ruined your childhood," Roselyn chuckled. "Rocky always went after what he wanted, even in his grave he's still a persistent bastard."

Leilani stared up at the ceiling lost within her thoughts. The news of Sincere's paternity left her dazed. Her last memory of Rocky was of the fateful night where she took the life of the man that had brought great agony into her life.

******

The loud cry of her newborn infant woke her up out of her sleep. Confused and in a daze, Leilani looked around the abandoned laundromat familiarizing herself with her environment. She knew exactly where she was, but was unaware as to why she was in the abandoned laundromat. The wailing sound of the child caught her attention as she glared down to the source of noise. ***What the fuck happened?*** *she asked herself. Lightly rocking the crying baby, she racked her brain to remember the events that occurred prior.*

"I remember doing laundry and then Mommy came home. After things got crazy, I left and then..." Her mind ran a blank. She couldn't remember anything no matter how hard she tried. The bright November

sun beamed into the darkened laundry room illuminating what could not be seen in the dark. Leilani's eyes fell upon the empty syringe that rested on the floor.

"Shit," she called out. "Fuck, I went back."

She couldn't believe what was right before her. She was completely disappointed in herself as she stared down on the used syringe. For a couple of months, she had been doing good remaining clean for the sake of her child, but last night she broke that promise she'd made to her child. Slowly she rocked her son back and forth in her arms comforting him. Tears slowly descended her face with the thought of her actions tormenting her brain. **What if I permanently damaged my baby? How could I do that to him?** *Sobbing uncontrollably into the stale towel, Leilani was unable to control herself.*

"How am I supposed to raise you?" she questioned herself. "You could have some sort of problem and it's all because of my selfish needs. All because I couldn't stay the fuck away from that needle."

Holding onto the baby, she seemed to calm down as her child was sound asleep. The sound of his peaceful snores echoed into her ear causing her heart to melt. Nothing seemed wrong with him and she prayed it remained like that. At this moment, something clicked in her head like a light switch. **I must give him up,** *she concluded,* **I can't risk his health and safety.** *Her mind was made up as she stood up with her child in her arms. A wave of dizziness washed over her as she closed her eyes, placing her hand on the wooden table for support. Once the dizzy spell subsided, she made sure her appearance was appropriate before she walked out of the darkened laundromat.*

The sun beamed down blinding her. Despite the bright sun, it was still cold for a November morning. The wind crept up Leilani's open sweater causing her to shudder. She pulled her son closer to her chest enclosing him within her sweater. I hope you can't feel the cold air, she thought. Despite wrapping the baby up in several old towels and keeping him close to her chest, Leilani was still very paranoid. Let me get you safely somewhere. Quickly, she moved her feet making her way over to the nearest hospital, Woodhull. In less than five minutes she entered the hospital walking straight to an information desk.

"Hi," she smiled.

"How can I help you," the clerk asked nonchalantly.

"Um, can I have a piece of paper and pen?"

"Here."

Taking the paper and pen, Leilani walked over to a quiet area that wasn't occupied with any waiting patients. Taking the pen, she began to scribble her message onto the paper. The dried blood on her hands smeared over the paper as she tried writing. Clutching her son in her arms, she lightly rocked him back and forth hoping not to wake him up. Finishing her letter, she stood there confused on the decision she was making.

"This decision is the best decision. I can't give you a normal childhood," she said trying to convince herself. "It's already bad enough that your mother is a 13-year-old drug addict who was raped by her stepfather. Crazy ass way to enter the world," she chuckled. "I already started off bad and I don't want you to end up like your father or like me. I want you to be greater than this. You won't even remember this moment

nor would you remember me. That's ok; just know that your mother gave you up because she loves you and not because you were hated."

"Honey, do you need some help?"

Turning to face the person talking to her, Leilani faced the nurse. Scared shitless of being in trouble she slowly backed away prepared to run. The nurse placed her hands out defensively as she was concerned for the girl.

"Listen honey you're not in trouble. I just came over here concerned because I noticed the blood on your bottom."

"Shit I thought I cleaned it up," Leilani said.

"It's ok, I just want to help," the nurse answered with pleading eyes.

"Just to help?"

"Yes love, all I want to do is help."

"Ok fine, I need your help but you have to promise me one thing."

"Ok."

"Promise me that you will do whatever to make sure that he's ok."

"Yes."

Leilani rocked slowly, looking down at her peaceful son. The tears seeped through her eyes as she became emotional once more. She didn't know if what she was doing was the right thing.

"I ...Ugh, gave birth to this little guy last night in an abandoned building. I just want to give him what I never had so that's why I am here. Please make sure he gets a good family," Leilani asked teary eyed.

"Yes baby," the nurse answered as she held her hand out ready to

receive the baby. Looking down at her son, Leilani fell in love for the first time ever. Her heart felt heavy with grief as she rained kisses down on his pink cheek. Just do it. She handed over her son to the nurse.

"Here's this note; please just make sure he's ok," Leilani asked.

"I promise."

The nurse stared down at the infant lost within his beauty. His little face was a spitting image of the girl. Looking up, the nurse expected the little girl to be still standing there but she was gone.

******

"Where have you been?"

"Holy shit you fucking scared me," Leilani said as she gripped her chest.

"Where the fuck you been?" he asked once more.

"Don't worry about it."

Focusing back on packing her clothing, Leilani didn't give Rocky any attention. She needed to hurry up and pack her clothes so she could get the hell out of the apartment. After leaving her son at the hospital, Leilani had devised a plan to get back onto her feet. She didn't know if it would work but she didn't care. All she needed to do was to get the hell out of her mother's apartment with her belongings.

"Don't you hear me talking to you?"

"Yes."

"Why you ain't replying?"

"Because Rocky, there isn't anything to say. Things got heated over here so I left," she replied.

"Really?" he questioned as he took in her appearance. Something was different about her, but he just couldn't put his finger on it. Looking around the room, his eyes stopped on the blue jeans that she had on the night before. The maroon hue that was on the crotch area caught his attention. "What is that on your jeans?"

"Nothing just sat on some ketchup."

Walking over to the jeans, he picked them up analyzing the blood residue. He had his suspicions about what it could be but didn't want to believe it. The wheel in his head began to turn as several scenarios played in his head.

"Lei, did you have the baby?"

"Roc—"

"Answer my question."

"Roc—"

"You fucking bitch," he yelled as he threw her pants to the ground. Charging towards her, he grabbed her by the neck. "Where the fuck is my child?"

Rage set in his head as he closed his massive hands tighter around her neck. He had no clue on what could have happened with the baby and the possibilities were endless. His mind conjured up several scenarios with none of them ending good. ***My child could be at the bottom of the Hudson River or underneath several boxes waiting for the arrival of the garbage men who were scheduled for that area to take out the trash.***

"Tell me what the fuck happened with my kid."

"I can't —"

Releasing her neck, Rocky allowed her body to drop on the ground. Her breathing was shallow and short as she tried regulating her oxygen intake. Staring down at her, Rocky grew impatient.

"I am waiting."

"I had the baby and he is safe," she replied, still struggling to breathe.

"Ok, where the fuck is he so I can bring him home."

"I brought him to the hospital."

"Ok good which hospital?"

"Woodhull."

"Let's go; we are going there now," he replied as he yanked her up off the ground. Dragging her through the apartment, he was prepared to take her back to the hospital to rescue his son. He had no clue what she did, but he didn't care as he was going to get his son back no matter what it took.

"Let go of me. It doesn't make sense; it's too late," Leilani replied, as she tried yanking her hand from his grasp, failing miserably as he was much too strong.

"What do you fucking mean it's too late?"

"It's too late."

"What the fuck did you do to my kid?"

"I gave him a chance."

Releasing her from his grasp, he stared into the grey eyes that he once loved. Confusion erupted through his mind as he couldn't comprehend what Leilani was trying to say. ***What the fuck does she mean she gave him a chance?***

"What do you mean you gave him a chance?"

"Exactly how it sounds. I gave my son up so he can have a chance at being something."

"You did what?" he yelled. The rage within him threatened to burst, revealing his true colors. He couldn't believe what he was hearing. Unable to control himself, he leaned forward reaching for Leilani's neck. Quick on her feet, Leilani stood, running away from her attacker. Rocky followed closely behind her as he desired to choke her until she was lifeless.

"You fucking bitch; you gave my fucking son up?" he yelled as he followed her into the kitchen. Grabbing a fist full of her hair, he yanked her head back causing her to look at him. "You gave my son to them crackers so he could grow up in the broken system."

"No, I gave my son up for him to have the chance of being great. The chance that I had ripped away from me when you decided to turn me into a woman," she yelled back. Taking hold of the knife that rested on the counter, Leilani jabbed the sharp edge of the blade into Rocky's abdomen. Shock was written all over his face as he couldn't believe the chain of events. Releasing her hair, his hands landed on his abdomen caressing his open wound. Yanking the blade out, Leilani stared into his eyes. The same eyes that held so much love for her pleaded with her.

"I'm giving our son the opportunity to not end up like his father. Our son will have a chance to learn something besides the streets. The child that you ejaculated into me will not grow up to prey on a little girl. He will not force drugs into her system just so he can enjoy her. My son, the one that I pushed into this world in an abandoned laundromat all alone, will not be a product of the streets. He will grow up to be greater

than all of this. My son, is exactly that, my fucking son; because after today he no longer has a father." Plunging the knife deep into Rocky's chest, Leilani watched as the man who caused her years of heartache dropped to his knees. Life seeped out of his open wounds decorating the white kitchen tiles red.

"Goodbye Rocky."

******

A tight sensation penetrated her uterus slowly transitioning into sharp pains. *No, not now,* Leilani thought. The cramps began to get intense causing her to moan out loud. *I need to untie myself.* She wiggled her wrists in every angle in hopes of freeing herself from the restraints.

"Please God, help me," she cried. "I don't want to bring my child into this world restrained to a table."

In the past six hours, she had been tortured by a rat and then left to die in the cemented basement. The tears poured freely from her eyes as her nightmare became her reality. She was going to give birth to yet another child all alone. *Please, God just help me,* she thought. Gripping the Velcro restraints, Leilani yanked her wrist back and forth in an effort to loosen the holds. Using all her strength, she tried her best with breaking the restraints.

"Get the fuck off me!" she yelled. A loud tear erupted through the air as she was finally able to free herself from the holds around her wrists. Quickly, she sat up to tear off the holds that were around her ankles. A pain shot through her uterus, causing her to crouch over in pain. The contractions were getting closer as her child wanted to enter the world. Freeing her ankles, she got off the medical table using it to brace her weak body. A warm liquid trickled down her leg forming a pool around her bare feet.

"Not again, not like this," she cried. Tears streamed down her swollen cheeks as reality sunk in. It was as if history was repeating itself. She had gone through the same painful process all alone and by herself.

Her nails dug deeper into the metal table as she could feel her second child preparing to make its entrance into the world. Sharp pains invaded her lower area.

"Oh my god, I can't do this again." Her words disappeared into the moist air. Bending her legs, she squatted, relieving the pressure she was feeling. Another shock of pain erupted in her uterus causing her to release a blood-curling shriek from her dried, bloody lips. Straining her muscles, she pushed with all the energy she could muster up. Blood poured from every inch of her body, mingling with her perspiration.

"Come on," she cried. Using her muscles, she pushed again. Placing her hands at the opening of her vagina, her hands glided against the bulge that protruded out. *The baby is almost out.* Quickly, she pushed once more bringing the infant's shoulders down. She placed her hands once more at the opening of her vagina, and she pushed again, allowing her newborn to enter the world. The loud cries of her baby filled the moist air.

"Aren't you a beauty?" Leilani asked as she gazed at her wailing infant. Grabbing a towel that rested on the table, Leilani wrapped her infant up, cuddling it to her chest. Tears poured profusely down her face as she couldn't believe what had just occurred. *Holy shit I just fucking gave birth again.* Sitting in a pool of her own blood, she cradled her child. Humming lightly, a wave washed over her as she began to feel light-headed. Her body had taken a beating and she needed some rest, but instead of granting herself the time to recuperate, she sat on the floor soothing the infant.

"I didn't see any little pig tail, so I am guessing you are a little girl."

Nothing could have prepared Leilani for this moment. It was as if she were falling in love all over again as her daughter stared back up at her with her big grey eyes. Softly, Leilani caressed the top of her head intrigued by her unique beauty.

"I'll never leave you sweet pea. You can always count on me to be there no matter what."

The sound of the dungeon-like door sprung open and shut; the vibration ricocheted off the concrete walls. Leilani wanted to hide her daughter from her kidnappers but there wasn't anywhere for her to put the child. *Shit, come on La think fast.* Feverishly, her mind searched around the basement but to no avail; she couldn't find anything that she would be able to use. The footsteps of her kidnapper descended the staircase until finally the designer shoes landed on the concrete floor.

"What the fuck?" Don Cheadle asked.

"What, you've never seen a baby before?"

The two kidnappers stood before Leilani, surprised at the chain of events. Confusion was written all over their faces as the plan incorporated them killing Leilani before she gave birth to the child. They both stood their brainstorming on how they could accommodate the infant into their plans.

"Take the baby," Roselyn demanded.

"Are you sure?"

"Yes, I am. I have a plan." Following the orders of his partner, Don Cheadle walked over to Leilani prepared to take the child away from her.

"Don't you fucking touch my baby," Leilani yelled. Like a mother cub trying to protect her offspring, she attacked. Her fist flew fiercely as she began to pounce on Don Cheadle.

"I need some assistance here," he called out. Roselyn walked over and tried her best to restrain Leilani just enough for Cheadle to get the infant.

"No, get the fuck off me." Forcefully, Don Cheadle yanked the child from out of arms. Fearing what was going on, the baby loudly wailed at the top of her lungs for her mother. Gathering up enough energy, Leilani continued to fight. It didn't matter that her body was sore from the abuse she had received earlier. Not caring about the damage she was doing to herself, her focus was getting her daughter back. Her fist connected to Roselyn's face as she sent another jab to Roselyn's side. Leilani was in for the fight of her life.

"You'll never see your daughter again," Roselyn chuckled.

"Bitch, you wish."

Leilani pounded on her enemy's chest. Every punch Leilani threw, Roselyn matched her with the same one. Tackling her weak opponent, Roselyn got on top of Leilani beginning her attack. The pain from her years of heartbreak poured through her fist. Yanking her fist back and forth she pounded it against Leilani. Her face burned with a familiar kind of feel and fresh scratches adorned her face. Leilani was attempting to gouge Roselyn's eye out.

"You really think you can kill me and this will all be over?" Leilani asked.

"Yes, I know I can." The fight between the two continued as Leilani tried her best with pushing Roselyn off her. Her muscles were sore from the previous abuse. Contractions erupted within her uterus as her body forcefully pushed out her placenta. Blood pooled around her bottom. She was tired of fighting and just wanted everything to be over. Leilani didn't want to do this anymore. Her mind was made up as she began to reason with Roselyn.

"This anger in you, you have to let it go. I don't care about revenge or the stupid, petty shit. I just want to go back to my daughter. That's all I want to do." Staring into the pits of Roselyn's hues she hoped like hell Roselyn would reason with her. The years long beef between the two was pointless. Leilani learned how to cope with what happened during her childhood. All she wanted to do was provide a better life that she never was given a chance to have. The more she reasoned with Roselyn the more it began to make sense to her. The fight within the woman who raised her began to go down as Roselyn lowered the knife. Taking a deep breath, Leilani let her guard down. *It's over,* she thought. Roselyn glared into the eyes of the little girl that she had raised as her own. All the years of her pent up aggression simmered underneath the closed lid.

"I can't," Roselyn softly said, still on top of Leilani.

"What?"

"I can't let this shit go," Roselyn said as she took Leilani's head, smashing it on the concrete floor. "You will not win bitch; not this time."

Leilani's body went numb as she could no longer feel the pain. The last image she saw was the sight of her mother with a crazed look. It was the look of pure satisfaction. Roselyn had finally won the game that she was playing in her head. It was all over.

CHAPTER 31

The cemented wall was grey with splatters of red blood decorating it. Officially it had been a week since Leilani had given herself up in exchange for her son's safe return. At this point in time, Leilani was clueless as to how she made it this far. Her body emitted blood from every wound that decorated her body. She'd gone through days full of endless torture, and at that moment she was on the brink of death. Chained to the ceiling, Leilani's naked body was on full display. The masterpiece that Roselyn had carved into her skin was the perfect portrayal of all the years of her pent up anger.

"Give me back my baby," Leilani mumbled as her head swayed back and forth. "All I want is my baby."

She was growing lethargic and needed to get out of the basement before she lost the game that she played with her mother. Leilani couldn't afford to lose as she now had a lot to live for. Her new life after her childhood had taken years to create, but Leilani spent 18 years building a life that would overcome her past. Transitioning from a 13-year-old troubled teen to a music mogul that ran part of the world's elite drug organization, Leilani had done amazing for herself. *I can't lose all the hard work I've done over the years to this hating ass bitch,* Leilani thought, *I need to make it out.* She didn't know how she was going to free herself from the steel chains that hung from the ceiling, but she was going to figure something out. Her eyes scanned around the room in search for anything that would help free her. There wasn't anything available within her reach.

"Fuck," she thought as she looked up at the ceiling. *Help me God, please,* she begged. Her eyes glared up at the structure of the chain used to restrain her. *How the fuck is the chain being held by a screw?*

"What the fuck?" she said out loud as she began pulling on the chain. Loose particles fell from the ceiling dropping onto her face, but it didn't faze her as she continued pulling on the chain. Come on, she begged, watching the screw unhinge from the ceiling. Her eyes never departed from the ceiling as her life depended on this screw. *Once this screw gets loose, I swear on the soul of my kids, I am going to light this bitch up*, she thought as she continued pulling on the chain. The silver links came crashing down on her face as her goal of becoming free was accomplished.

"Oh, now it's over for you bitches," she said out loud. Still chained to the silver links, she was still restrained, but there was a lot of damage she planned on doing with the chains. Quickly, she walked up the cemented stairs, stopping at the steel door. Taking a deep breath, she needed to prepare herself for the war that she was going to start. *Please Lord guide me during this time of destruction,* she silently prayed, *you got me this far, please get me out of this hell hole*. Pushing the heavy door open, Leilani walked out into the open. Her eyes quickly scanned the hallway, searching for anyone. Two guards stood posted in front of the bathroom in a deep conversation. The hallway was dark as she creeped her way over to them, hoping to not get caught. Swiftly, she leaped forward, wrapping the chain links around the first guard catching him by surprise. She tightened the links around his neck while wrapping her legs around the next guard. Holding on for dear life, she choked both men until they fell unconscious onto the ground. Releasing them, Leilani grabbed the key ring full of keys, along with the pistol that rested in one of the guard's holster.

"Thank you," she said as she walked into the first available room. Switching the light on, she squatted on the ground with the keys. Her fingers fidgeted as she searched for the key that would unlock her chain. Placing the fourth key into the lock, she turned the key unchaining herself. *Oh, now it's on bitches,* she thought as she pulled the cuffs off her. Looking around the room, Leilani searched for any available clothes. Her eyes landed on a pair of sweats. Quickly she ran over and threw on the clothes, ignoring the pain that shot through her body.

"Now, just to find these fuckers and my baby," she said as she cocked the pistol, preparing for the war that laid ahead of her.

Slowly pushing the door open, Leilani walked back out with her pistol drawn. She noticed three men who stood at their post engaged into a deep conversation. Without any hesitation, Leilani shot off three rounds, killing each of them. Hurriedly, she entered the room they guarded.

"What the fuck are we going to do about this?" Don Cheadle asked as he stared at Roselyn, searching for an answer.

"This is part of the plan," Roselyn replied.

"Yea, but she wasn't supposed to die so soon. She was supposed to sign over the rights of the company over to us."

"Don't worry about that, I have a plan," Roselyn reassured him.

"It wouldn't matter because the both of you won't be doing shit anytime soon," Leilani said.

Both Roselyn and Don Cheadle engaged in their conversation, unaware of Leilani's presence. Growing agitated, Leilani raised the pistol to the ceiling.

BANG!

The loud bang ricocheted off the walls, demanding attention. Leilani stood at the door frame with her smoking Beretta M9. She anticipated her suspects turning towards her, but unfortunately both Don Cheadle and Roselyn remained engaged in their conversation. What the fuck, Leilani thought. Growing agitated, Leilani walked over to the two, demanding their attention.

"Y'all don't fucking hear me ta—" Leilani began to tear them a new asshole when her thinking process was interrupted by the sight of the unresponsive body on the ground.

"What do you think could have been the cause of her death?" Don Cheadle questioned.

"I don't know, maybe when I slammed her head on the ground?"

"Yea, she didn't really wake up after that."

Leilani stared at the unresponsive body that lay on the ground. *Why the fuck am I on the ground?* she questioned. Her face was barely recognizable as it had swelled to twice it's normal size. Blood dripped from every open wound that decorated her abused body. She was naked and cold as her life slowly leaked onto the cemented floor.

"So, what should we do with the body?"

"Have the building cleared out; torch the place with the body," Roselyn responded.

"What? No you fucking bitch, I'm still alive," Leilani yelled as she looked between Roselyn and Don Cheadle. There wasn't anything she could do; her fate had been decided for her without an ounce of consideration. "I am not dead. I am right here."

Roselyn glared down at the woman that she had raised as her own. The battle was finally over. She could now live without being in competition with the deceased beauty. Roselyn squatted down, getting closer to the lifeless body.

"I win bitch," Roselyn smiled. "I finally beat you."

EPILOGUE

"Breaking News: Reporting live from East Flatbush, a woman was found dead after firefighters extinguished a blaze inside a Brooklyn home. The fire occurred earlier today and it took firefighters approximately an hour to tame the flames. The body discovered in the flames has not been identified yet, but evidence left behind indicates that the victim is Leilani Vasquez, part owner of the music label Carter's Dynasty."

The television blared the breaking news but went unnoticed. Sincere sat back in his couch as he tilted the bottle of Hennessey backwards. The warm, golden cognac warmed his insides, intensifying the effects of the popular alcohol. His mind evolved into a realm that only the Hennessey could control. Lost within the battle that erupted in his mind, Sincere brought the nozzle of the bottle to his lips, preparing to take a swig, but he was interrupted by the sound of the female whose face was planted in his lap, choking on the length of his penis deep within her throat.

"Yo, stop that shit," he barked as he proceeded with taking the bottle to the head. The liquor burned a familiar sensation that silenced the voices in his head. He desperately wanted them to shut up, and alcohol seemed to be the only thing that would quiet those voices.

"Mhmm." The woman between his lap relaxed her throat allowing his long member deeper within her moist esophagus. A light vibration rang in the air catching his attention. Picking up his smartphone, Sincere concentrated his attention onto the name that was plastered on his screen. Not wanting to answer, Sincere decided against it as he brought the 5.5-inch screen to his face.

"Yo."

"They just confirmed it," Don said into the phone.

"What are you talking about?"

"The body they found in the fire is Leilani's."

"Ok."

"Yea they didn't find any other remains, so they believe that she had the baby. I put out an Amber Alert for it."

"Aight."

"Aight?" Don asked irritated. "That's all you fucking have to say?"

"Yea nigga, what the fuck you want me to say?"

"Your fucking fiancé has been confirmed as dead and the only fucking thing you can say is aight?"

"Don, I'mma be honest with you playa. I really don't give a fuck about that lying, conniving bitch. As far as I am concerned, that fucking bitch could rot in fucking hell," Sincere yelled as he hung up the phone.

His body temperature increased significantly as the concept of his fiancé being dead began to settle. Taking another swig from his bottle, he wanted to forget about her. The pain that his love for her conceived was unbearable for him. Throughout the years of his relationship, Sincere studied the art of love, altering himself to be right for her. He'd given her everything he possibly could and the one thing he desired, she wasn't able to give. He desired the truth behind the death of his father, and she was the only one who knew what occurred that faithful day. She was the only one who could tell the *Tale of a Dopefiend.*

THE END

Looking for a publishing home?

Royalty Publishing House, Where the Royals reside, is accepting submissions for writers in the urban fiction genre. If you're interested, submit the first 3-4 chapters with your synopsis to submissions@royaltypublishinghouse.com.

Check out our website for more information: www.royaltypublishinghouse.com.

Text ROYALTY to 42828 to join our mailing list!

To submit a manuscript for our review, email us at submissions@royaltypublishinghouse.com

Text RPHCHRISTIAN to 22828 for our CHRISTIAN ROMANCE novels!

Text RPHROMANCE to 22828 for our INTERRACIAL ROMANCE novels!

CPSIA information can be obtained
at www.ICGtesting.com
Printed in the USA
LVHW05s1545020518
575706LV00015B/947/P

9 781981 2117

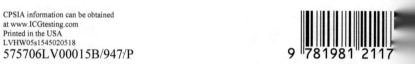